I0594586

THE STARS THAT BECKON

BOOK 1 IN THE STARPATH SERIES

KEVIN J SIMINGTON

Copyright © 2019 by Kevin J Simington

All rights reserved.

No part of this book may be reproduced in any form or by any electronic or mechanical means, including information storage and retrieval systems, without written permission from the author, except for the use of brief quotations in a book review.

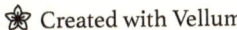 Created with Vellum

1

Zac's last day on Earth began with the same mundane routine that characterised almost any other day. As he reluctantly struggled to the surface of consciousness, cocooned within the snugness of his cosy bed, he had no idea of the brewing storm of events that was gathering on his horizon - a maelstrom that was about to pluck him out of his ordinary life and sweep him up into a tsunami of cosmic proportions.

"Okay! Okay! I'm awake!" he complained, opening one eye and peering dubiously into the gloom, as if he was still deciding whether to join the rest of the world.

The gentle pinging, which had been gradually rising in intensity, ceased.

"Windows clear," he mumbled.

The side wall of his bedroom became transparent, and the dull grey light of the new day seeped grudgingly into his room. He swung his legs over the side of the bed and sat looking through the one-way transparency at the grimy exterior wall of the neighbouring apartment block. He stretched and yawned, rubbing sleep from his eyes as he waited for the sluggish synapses in his brain to start doing their thing.

"Play messages," he said.

"Sorry, Zac, there are no new messages this morning."

"Really? Nothing?"

"Zip."

He was starting to get a little worried. *That's two nights in a row that she hasn't called.* In their three years of marriage, he could only remember a couple of occasions when Annisa had missed their evening phone call, and only then because she had pulled a late-nighter at her lab. But even on those occasions, there had been a recorded voicemail on his comm-net the next morning. She'd never missed two nights in a row.

Of course, he knew roughly where she was, within a few million kilometres; either in geosynchronous orbit on Kepler Station, or on the Moon, in the Armstrong Research Facility attached to Luna City.

She's probably fine. I'm worrying about nothing. She'll probably call tonight and offer a perfectly logical explanation.

Even so, it was frustrating not being able to call her. Civilians, even spouses, could not initiate calls to the DANSA comm-net.

He shuffled into the living room and did a few stretches.

"Hey Angie," he said.

"Hey Zac," answered the disembodied voice.

"What's happening?"

"Not much. You look like crap."

"Gee, thanks. Very helpful of you to point that out."

"My pleasure. The truth will set you free, bro."

"In that case, living with you must make me the most liberated guy on the planet."

"My personality factor is currently set at 80 percent. Would you like me to dial it down?"

Zac considered the possibility. "As tempting as that is, I think I prefer you the way you are."

"Fine. In that case, what would you like for breakfast, O Great Master?"

"Two fried eggs, bacon, sausages, fried tomato, toast and some freshly squeezed orange juice."

"Very funny. Which radioactive continent would you like all that sourced from? And maybe afterwards, you could go for a walk outside without your breather-mask, just to top it off."

"They say that sarcasm is the lowest form of wit," Zac replied, walking toward the treadmill in the corner of the lounge room.

"I always pitch my conversation to match the intellectual level of the recipient."

"Ha, ha. You're hilarious."

"I like to think so."

Zac slipped on his joggers and stretched his right calf muscle, which had been a bit tight lately.

"I guess I'll just have some of that delicious yeast porridge in about 40 minutes. Run treadmill Program 8: Bondi Beach scene."

* * *

A little over an hour later, exercised, fed, showered, shaved and dressed in his most comfortable jeans and his favourite retro-Hawaiian shirt, Zac walked into his adjoining office and sat at his desk.

"Rainforest scene please, Angie. No sound."

"Certainly, Dr. Perryman," she responded. The demarcation between office and the rest of the apartment was very clear: Angie always maintained a strictly professional persona when Zac was in his office. The four walls of the room instantly transformed, and Zac was immersed in the tranquil scenery of a pristine, pre-holocaust rainforest. There were very few places left on earth where such a scene now existed. To this day, the entire northern hemisphere remained largely uninhabitable; a smouldering nuclear wasteland bearing mute testimony to the violent conflict of the late 21st century.

"Diary?" Zac enquired.

"You're free all morning. You have a lecture at 13:30: 'The Antecedents of the Democratic Alliance of Nations Counter-Offensive.' The only other item for today is a faculty meeting at 15:00, at which you've been asked to give a progress report on your research."

"Fine. We'll stream my previously recorded lecture. Just ping me if there are questions or comments from any students. Apart from the faculty meeting and the outbreak of a fourth world war, I don't want to be disturbed."

He sat at his desk trying to summon the motivation to start work but he couldn't shake the disquieting sense of worry regarding his wife. He glanced at the photo that sat on the corner of his desk. It had been taken at Sydney University, after the ceremony where he had received his Ph.D. There, standing beside him, also in doctoral gown and cap, was his future wife, Annisa, the proud recipient of a doctorate in biology. Slim, dark-haired, olive skinned. Not even the shapeless gown and ridiculous academic cap could hide her stunning Balinese beauty. One week after that photo had been taken, they had married. Two weeks later, they had moved to this apartment in Macapá, Brazil, the capital city of the Democratic Alliance of Nations and the headquarters of DANSA, the Democratic Alliance of Nations Space Agency.

It had been a difficult move for Zac. Macapá wasn't anything like Sydney, Australia, where he had lived all his life. Macapá was grey and sullen, with dirty skies and worrying radioactive levels, requiring breather masks and rad-suits when venturing outside. Until he had moved here, he hadn't appreci-ated how fortunate he had been to grow up on the only continent to have avoided nuclear bombardment. But moving to Macapá had been essential for Annisa's new job.

DANSA had head hunted Annisa for her doctoral work, *"Reprogramming Molecular Nanobots for Use in Artificial Blood for Long Term Cryogenic Stasis."* Zac was tenured to the history department of Sydney University and he could work from anywhere, but Annisa needed to be at Macapá, where the Equatorial Tether Lift was located, because she spent 20 days off-world each month.

Seeing the photo of Annisa reinforced Zac's concern. *Where is she? Why hasn't she called?*

As he sat there worrying, he heard the front door chime, and Angie interrupted him.

"Dr Perryman, there are three gentlemen at the door."

"Who are they?"

"I don't know. I can't access their biochips."

"What do you mean?"

"Their chips have military-grade encryption."

The hairs on the back of Zac's neck rose, and he felt a stab of anxiety.

"Open the comm line and give me a video feed."

The rainforest scene disappeared from the wall in front of him and was replaced by the image of three men, one heavyset and balding, and two younger men, slightly to the rear. All three were dressed in dark pants and zipped battle jackets with DANSA insignia.

"Yes? Can I help you?" asked Zac.

The balding man in front held a DANSA identity card out towards the door and said, "Dr Perryman, I'm George Leonidis, head of security for DANSA. I just need a few minutes of your time."

Zac saw Leonidis turn and whisper something to the two younger men standing behind him, and as he did so, the bottom of a blaster holster could be seen protruding under-neath his jacket.

"OK. Just a moment," said Zac.

He disabled the comm and sat for a moment, thinking. What was going on? Could this be related to Annisa's lack of contact? He walked into the kitchen and grabbed his personal network device, slipping it over his wrist.

"Angie, I don't know what's happening here. But just to be safe, I want you to make sure all my files are uploaded to my secure cache in the cloud. And I want you to upload a copy of yourself there as well."

"OK, Zac."

Zac walked to the front door and said, "Open." The door slid back, and George Leonidis stood smiling at him.

"Hello, Dr Perryman. Sorry for this inconvenience. I just need you to come with me."

As he spoke, the two men with him pushed past Zac into the apartment and began opening drawers and cupboards.

"Hey, what's going on?" Zac asked. "What are they looking for? I haven't given them permission to enter my property!"

"Nothing to worry about, Dr Perryman. Standard security procedure. They're just doing their job. Now if you will just accompany me, please."

"Is this about my wife? Where is she? Is she OK?"

"I am not at liberty to say anything at this point, but if you will just come with me, everything will be explained."

"Where are we going? You said you just wanted a few minutes of my time."

"As I said, I am not at liberty to say. And I apologise for the slight deception. Unfortunately, we require considerably more than just a few minutes of your time."

"I'm not going anywhere until you tell me what's going on!"

"Dr Perryman, we can do this the easy way, or the hard way. It's really up to you. I have the authority to arrest you if you refuse to cooperate, but I'd much rather you come of your own volition. I dislike having to use force - it aggravates my heartburn."

Zac thought furiously. He knew he hadn't done anything wrong, and maybe this way he would find out where his wife was. He nodded his head and admitted defeat.

"OK. Let me get my breather mask."

"No need for that where we are going, Dr Perryman. This way, if you please."

As Zac stepped out into the hall, Leonidis called through the doorway, "I want a thorough search, gentlemen. Every square centimetre. Report back when you're finished."

As Leonidis guided him towards the elevator, Zac assumed that he was being taken to DANSA headquarters, a few kilometres East, in the high-rise central business district overlooking the Amazon River.

He was wrong.

They took him to the moon.

I f it wasn't for the fact that he was worried about his wife and that his home was being ransacked by two strange men, Zac would have thoroughly enjoyed the trip. As it was, despite his worry, he couldn't help but be awed. After all, historians didn't usually get to go into space.

The journey was initially mundane. The apartment elevator took them down to the subway station directly underneath the building. The convenient access to the subway was one of the reasons he and Annisa had chosen this apartment. A maglev pod arrived soon after they reached the platform and George Leonidis bundled Zac on board. As the pod smoothly accelerated out of the station, Zac looked enquiringly at Leonidis, seated beside him.

"We're heading away from the city. Do you mind telling me where we're going?"

Leonidis merely shook his head and remained mute.

"Great! Terrific!" said Zac. "It's so nice to live in a society of trust and open communication."

Leonidis continued to ignore Zac, taking a small data pad out of his jacket pocket and tapping away on it. Zac shook his head in disgust and sighed in exasperation. With no one to talk to and nothing but the dimly-lit tunnel walls to look at through the window, Zac decided he may as well get some work done as well.

He activated the data pad he had brought with him and opened the file of his soon-to-be-published book, *The Fractured Planet*, which was the novelised version of his doctoral thesis: "*Pre-War Political Tensions of the 21st Century and Contemporary Correlations.*" His publisher had sent him a proof copy, asking him to check it thoroughly. He scrolled to the inside back jacket cover, where his publisher had insisted that they print a full-length photo of him wearing holed jeans and one of his many beloved retro-Hawaiian shirts. *Although only 29 years old, Dr. Zachary Perryman is widely regarded as a leading historical expert on the antecedents of the Faith Wars of the late 21st century. Known as the 'Hippy Professor,' his easy-going, laconic Aussie nature and his unconventional approach to academia make him extremely popular with his students and with conferences wherever he speaks.*

Zac still wasn't entirely comfortable with focusing on his Australian background as a selling point for his book. He wanted to be recognised solely for the merit of his research, rather than for his blonde-haired surfer looks.

He made a mental note: *I might get them to ditch the 'Hippy Professor' thing.*

He scrolled to the front inside jacket cover. "*From our vantage point of the 24th century, the Faith Wars of the 21st century and the nuclear winter that followed are a grim but vague memory. The events that led to that conflict are even more vague. However, it is said that those who do not learn from history are destined to repeat its mistakes. Dr. Perryman is convinced that the same factors that precipitated the last conflict are in play once more. The Fractured Planet analyses the disturbing similarities between the tensions of the 21st century pre-war world and today's escalating rhetoric between the Democratic Alliance of Nations and the One World Caliphate.*

Zac was reasonably happy with that description, although he might ask if it could also include a brief reference to the current alarming rise in UFOs, the colloquially termed Undercover Faith Operatives — a growing number of citizens within the Democratic Alliance of Nations who were being recruited and radicalised by the Caliphate.

He scrolled to the chapter entitled *"The Silent Tide."* This was the chapter his publisher had suggested needed a rewrite, and Zac agreed. Somehow, he needed to convey a stronger sense of foreboding. He needed to strengthen his argument that the rising tide of Caliphate UFOs now being uncovered by DANIS, the Democratic Alliance of Nations Intelligence Service, signified a prelude to another major world conflict— perhaps worse than anything yet experienced.

He had barely made a start on the revised chapter, however, when Leonidis gruffly announced that they were getting off at the next stop. Zac glanced up at the live sim-map and saw that they were about to arrive at the ETL, 12 kilometres due West of the city.

"The Tether Lift?" Zac asked, surprise evident in both his face and voice.

Leonidis gave the slightest nod, but remained stubbornly mute.

"Is there something wrong with your vocal chords?" enquired Zac, hoping in vain to elicit some kind of verbal response.

The pod burst into a brightly-lit subterranean terminal and slowed to a smooth stop. A few moments later, as they ascended the travelator to the concourse above, a holographic image of a smiling flight attendant hovered in mid-air, issuing instructions.

"Welcome to Equatorial Tether Lift Terminal. Entry to the terminal requires appropriate authorisation. Please ensure that your biochip has today's DANSA clearance code. Biochip updaters are located at the top of the travelator. Please update your biochip, if necessary, prior to reaching the scanning gates."

George Leonidis pulled out a small biochip editor from his jacket pocket.

"Here, give me your hand," he said to Zac.

Zac reached out his left hand and Leonidis held the portable editor against the back of his wrist until it issued a satisfied ping.

"There. You're authorised."

"You're so kind and generous," Zac responded, facetiously.

Once through the scanning gates, Zac found himself inside a massive enclosed terminal concourse, circular in shape, approximately 200 metres in diameter, with a domed transparent ceiling at least 50 metres high. At the centre of the concourse was a massive black cylindrical wall, extending as a column from floor to ceiling, about 100 metres in diameter. Leonidis steered Zac across the broad concourse to a large sliding door at the base of the column, attended by a smiling female flight attendant and two grim-looking security guards. Leonidis and Zac had their wrists scanned.

"Welcome Mr. Leonidis," said the flight attendant. "We've been holding the pod for you and your guest. It's ready for departure as soon as you are both on board. Please use these disposable breather nodules during your walk across the open concourse."

She handed them both what appeared to be two small, button-like filters joined by a thin, flexible piece of plastic. Zac copied Leonidis, who had inserted the filters into his nostrils, leaving the plastic joiner dangling between them.

"Please remember to only breathe through your nose while you are in the open air," said the flight attendant.

The door at the base of the column slid open and they entered the hollow, roofless interior of the central column.

They walked across the circular concourse towards the Tether Lift at its centre. Zac had never seen the tether cable in real life before, and it was truly impressive. At least 15 metres in diameter, the cable extended up from the floor of the concourse and disappeared into the sky beyond. At the base of the cable, on the side closest to them, was one of the two pods, a semi-circular conveyance with transparent walls, floor and ceiling, almost as large as Zac's one-bedroom apartment. Their wrists were scanned one last time as they entered the pod, and then they discarded the breather nodules, placing them in a bin just inside the door. As they entered, Leonidis turned to Zac.

"Do you get vertigo?"

"I don't know. Why?"

"The attendant can issue you with contact lenses so that the walls will appear to be translucent; you won't be able to see out. Some people don't like heights."

"I think I'll be OK."

"Suit yourself. Just don't throw up on me."

"Thanks for the vote of confidence! Besides, it's still a free world; I'll throw up on whoever I like."

The majority of the interior was filled with about 40 comfortable-looking padded chairs, attached seamlessly to the transparent floor and facing towards the outer transparent walls. There were about 20 people already seated and strapped in.

"The best seats are at the front," Leonidis said, strapping himself into one. Zac took the chair next to him and, as he did so, the door slid closed and Zac heard a faint hiss as the pod was pressurised for ascent.

"Welcome aboard Equatorial Tether Lift Pod 1," said a pleasant female voice, seemingly emanating from the walls around them.

"Please fasten your lap belt and remain seated with your belt fastened during the initial acceleration phase. Acceleration of 0.25 G will last for approximately 1 minute, at which time we will have reached our maximum ascent speed of 500 kilometres per hour. A green light on your armrest will indicate the end of the acceleration phase. At that point, you will have approximately five minutes where you may unfasten your belt and move around the pod. After this you will be instructed to resume your seat and refasten your lap belt, due to the gradual loss of gravity. We will dock with Kepler Station, at a height of 120 kilometres, in approximately 17 minutes. If you feel nauseous at any time, please use the sick bags located in the side pocket of your chair. Ear pods are located in your armrest. Channel 1 provides a brief commentary on the technical aspects of the Tether Lift's design and operation. Channels 2 through 10 offer a range of music. Enjoy the ascent."

Zac already knew most of the technical aspects of the Tether Lift, through conversations with Annisa. The tether itself was constructed of a high-tensile composite of boron nitride nanotubes and maranium, a metal mined on Mars. The tether cable extended not just to Kepler Station, but hundreds of kilometres beyond it, anchored to a massive asteroid in higher orbit which stabilised both the tether and Kepler Station by its own higher geostationary orbit.

As Zac reflected on these technical details, he felt a mild vibration through the soles of his shoes, and immediately the pod lifted off the ground to begin its smooth, noiseless ascent. As the pod rose above the cylindrical walls of the base station, the sprawling infrastructure of the terminal came into view, rapidly diminishing as the pod accelerated upward. The city of Macapá to the east and the mountains to the west, however, were obscured by the murky, polluted air of the post-apocalyptic world. After only a few moments, the pod was enveloped in thick brown-grey clouds, and all view of the ground below was lost. Swirling mists raced past them at ever increasing speed, and condensation streamed down the windows as they punched a hole through the clouds. Several minutes later, they burst through into bright sunlight just as a green light chimed into existence on the armrests of each chair. Some people unbuckled and moved to the viewing area at the front, but Zac stayed comfortably where he was, looking through the clear floor just in front of his feet. The clouds receded rapidly and over the next few minutes the Earth's curvature slowly became apparent. Turning to Leonidis beside him, he saw that the security chief had his eyes closed.

"So, dude, now that you've got me trapped in this bubble, do you want to tell me what's going on?"

Without opening his eyes, Leonidis replied, "I'm not at liberty to say."

"What about my wife? The least you could do is tell me if she's OK. Has something happened? Where is she? Should I be worried? I mean, where's your human decency, man?"

"Sorry, I've been instructed to say nothing."

Zac shook his head and looked away in frustration. Several minutes later, the green light turned to red on his armrest, and a disembodied voice instructed people to return to their seats and buckle up. Zac began to notice a growing sensation of lightness.

"Why don't they have artificial gravity on these things?" he asked Leonidis.

"Because gravity generators weigh a ton, and you would only need it for the last five minutes of the ascent. Once we dock with Kepler Station, we'll come under the influence of their grav-gen."

Zac began to experience true weightlessness, and for the next five minutes the sky around him darkened and the Earth became a dirty brown globe below his feet, almost completely covered in clouds. His arms and legs were floating freely and the only thing holding him to his seat was the belt around his waist. Eventually, the disembodied female voice announced,

"Deceleration will commence in 30 seconds. Please tighten your lap belt and ensure that you have secured all loose items."

Shortly afterwards, Zac felt the strain against his belt as his body was decelerated towards the roof of the pod. About a minute later, the pod came to rest inside a docking bay on the underside of the space station. The view of the Earth below disappeared as the retractable floor of the docking bay slid across below the pod, clamping around the tether cable and closing the pod in. For several seconds, a loud hissing sound could be heard as the docking bay was pressurised, after which a retractable platform extended itself towards the pod, making contact with the base of the pod with its spongy silica edge. As it made contact, gravity was suddenly restored to the pod, and Zac plopped down into his chair.

The disembodied female voice informed them, "Welcome to Kepler Station. We hope you enjoyed your ascent. Have a nice day!"

After disembarking from the pod, Zac found it difficult to believe that he was 120 kilometres above the Earth. Not that he had much time to enjoy looking around, as Leonidis rushed him through a series of corridors until they reached a doorway marked 'FTLS Bay'. That's when it dawned on Zac where they were going.

"Fast Transit Luna Shuttle?" he said. "You're taking me to the moon?"

"Yes," said Leonidis.

"And that's where Annisa is?"

"It's not up to me to say."

"Oh, for goodness sakes!"

"Listen, Dr Perryman, just be patient for a little longer and everything will be explained. It will be a three-hour trip: 90 minutes constant acceleration at 3G until we reach the turn-around point, and then 90 minutes deceleration. It's not partic-ularly comfortable, but it's fast. Are you OK with that? We could take the slow transit shuttle, which accelerates at 1G, but it takes a hell of a lot longer."

"Let's just get there as quickly as we can," said Zac. "I want to get this over and done with."

About an hour later, he wished he hadn't said that.

3

Kitchener Tyler strapped herself into the left seat of the shuttle cockpit and turned to her co-pilot, who was already going through pre-flight checks.

"I haven't flown with you before," she said, reaching out her hand. "Name's Kit."

"Bane Kalawaia," he said, taking her hand.

"Islander?" she asked, noting his olive complexion and curly black hair.

"Yeh. Grandparents were from Hawaii. But I grew up in Santiago, Chile. Family wanted to get as far away as possible from the dirty air."

"I don't blame them," Kit replied. "I'm from Christchurch, New Zealand. Same reason. Clean air, most of the time. Real food, nice people. Wish I was back there right now, instead of stuck inside these tin cans eating yeast steaks and drinking recycled urine."

"I try not to think about whose urine I'm drinking," Bane said, smiling.

"You been doing the Luna shuttles long?" Kit asked.

"Couple of weeks," Bane replied. "Just had two years doing

the Titan run. I'm glad to be out of it. Those moon miners are seriously space wacky!"

"You're not wrong. Well, welcome to the Luna ferry service. It's a doddle compared to the long-haul flights you've been doing."

They finished their pre-flight routine and Kit asked her co-pilot, "Who've we got on board today?"

Bane checked his passenger list. "The usual assortment of researchers coming on shift, plus two love-struck honeymoon-ers, a serious-looking security guy and a hippy in a Hawaiian shirt."

Kit shook her head. "It takes all kinds I guess." She punched her comms button. "Kepler control, this is FTL-1. We're ready to roll."

"Roger FTL-1. Umbilical is retracted and docking tube is depressurised. You're cleared for hard-dock release."

There was a whirring sound followed by a clunk, as Bane initiated undocking, and then faint intermittent hissing as he used maneuvering thrusters to get them into clear space.

Kit punched the comms again. "Kepler control. This is FTL-1. Baby bird has left the nest."

"Roger FTL-1. Have a good one, Kit."

"Thanks, Terry. See you tomorrow."

Ninety minutes later, as the shuttle neared turn-around, travelling at a respectable velocity of just over 269,000 km per hour, Bane said, "This is the part I've been looking forward to."

"What do you mean?" asked Kit.

"You have quite a reputation. I'm told you do the slickest flips in the service."

"Well, to be honest, there's not much competition," said Kit. "Just about everyone else uses the automated maneuvering thruster system, which is as slow as a wet week. Even a trained monkey can push that button. I like to be hands-on. It's faster and it keeps me sharp."

"So how do you do it? What's your secret?"

"I assign both nose pitch thrusters to my left joystick, the two rear pitch thrusters to the right stick, the front yaw thrusters to my left foot pedal and the tail yaws to my right foot. Then I just keep one eye glued to the front window for visual feedback, one eye on the yaw and pitch readouts and another eye on the gravitational alignment display."

"Umm. But that's ..."

"Then, when our alignment's within spitting distance of the moon's gravity alignment, I punch in the auto system for a final tweak, and we're set. It saves about two minutes of fluffing around, and it's a lot more fun for the passengers."

"I'm sure it is."

"Just watch and learn, my Jedi apprentice!" said Kit.

She punched on cabin comms and announced, "Ladies and gents, my name is Kit Tyler, and I'm your captain for today's flight. We've reached our turn-around point. In a few moments I'm going to cut the main drive, flip this can on its end and then kick the drive back on. Please make sure your lap belts are securely fastened. We'll be flying backwards from this point on, but don't worry, I polished the rear-view mirrors before we left."

A few moments later, Kit said to Bane, "OK. Here we go. Time me." With that, she flicked the fusion drive off, and both of them lurched forward as acceleration was immediately cancelled. Without waiting a moment, Kit started operating the thrusters with rapid-fire bursts. The stars in the front window revolved crazily and the alignment readouts cycled through readings almost too quickly to see.

Bane asked, "Do you need me to ...?"

"Shut up."

A few more quick movements of hands and feet, and the universe stopped spinning. One or two more quick thruster adjustments, and Kit punched on the auto thruster system.

With a few tiny thruster bursts the computer brought the spacecraft into perfect linear alignment with the moon. A green light came on and Kit punched in the fusion drive, pushing them both deeply back into their seats again.

"How'd I do?" she asked.

"32 seconds."

"Damn! You put me off! Next time, don't say anything."

A little over 95 minutes later, the shuttle was on the tarmac at Luna City Terminal, Bane having executed a perfect vertical three-point landing onto its fuselage wheels, using its altitude thrusters.

"That wasn't too shabby," Kit told Bane.

"Thanks," he replied, acknowledging her typically understated Kiwi compliment. "I've landed a few of these things in my time."

A tow vehicle, known colloquially as a Bug Tug because of its bug-like appearance, swiftly maneuvered the FTL alongside the terminal nexus, and an extendable docking tube attached itself to their exit port. A few minutes later, crew and passengers were crammed into a large lift as it descended into the cavernous underground labyrinth of Luna City. Kit glanced at the guy in the Hawaiian shirt, who looked distinctly uneasy. She hoped he hadn't puked all over her nice clean shuttle.

4

Zac was relieved to get off the shuttle and back into artificial gravity. He'd been feeling queasy ever since the pilot of that damn shuttle had spun them around like a top. He glanced to his right. *That must be her over there.* She and the other pilot next to her were wearing grey jumpsuits with blue DANSA insignia. She looked tomboyish. Slim build, medium height, with short, dark hair. Dark nail polish and stunning hazel eyes, with a mischievous glint to them. She had the hint of a smile at the corners of her mouth, as if she found everything and everyone around her mildly amusing. Zac found himself intrigued, despite wanting to be cross with her.

In an attempt to take his mind off his queasy stomach after the mid-transit flip, Zac had listened to an info-stream through his earphones, which had explained some of the technical aspects of Luna City:

Luna City utilises naturally occurring hollow lava tubes and lava chambers, about 30 metres underground. These are sealed and lined with bioplastacon, a composite of locally mined anorthite and silica, infused with bioluminescent bacteria that provide diffused lighting throughout the base. Artificial gravity is transmitted via an aluminium-based sub-floor structure.

The voice had droned on, helping to distract him from his motion sickness:

The moon is a rich resource for mining, containing large deposits of silica (SiO_2), alumina (AlO_3), lime (CaO), iron oxide (Fe_2O_3), magnesia (MgO), and titanium dioxide (TiO_2). This means that the most abundant element on the moon is oxygen, locked in these oxygen-bonded minerals and metals. Because of this, ample breathable oxygen is produced as a natural by-product of the manufacturing of various metals and plastics. The base is powered by nuclear fusion, using the helium-3 isotope that is also in abundance on the moon.

Now, as he entered Luna City, he was able to appreciate the impressive technological achievement that the colony represented. The lift opened onto a large, roughly circular chamber, about 20 metres in diameter, with corridors leading off in various directions. Signage indicated the destinations of the corridors: Habitation and Cafeteria, Starlight Casino, Galileo Observatory, and Armstrong Research Facility. The lift buttons had indicated that mining, water harvesting, food production and power generation were located at a lower level.

The occupants of the lift split up, heading down separate corridors. Leonidis guided Zac into the corridor for the research facility, and after 50 metres they came to a bulkhead with an airlock door. A sign on the bulkhead read, 'Democratic Alliance of Nations Space Agency: Armstrong Research Facility'. Leonidas held his wrist against a biochip reader and the airlock door slid open. They entered the airlock and cycled through it. Exiting the airlock, Zac found himself in a long, wide, central corridor with glass-walled laboratories opening off to each side. People in white lab coats were bustling about, and the labs appeared to contain an impressive array of equipment that was mostly unrecognisable to a history-trained professor.

"Where are we going?" Zac asked.

"The boss wants a word with you," Leonidis replied.

A moment later they came to a T-intersection in the corridor and turned right. There were no labs in this section, just offices. Finally, they came to an open door with the signage 'Dr Simon Wisecroft, CEO, Armstrong Research Facility'. As they entered the spacious office, Dr Wisecroft was finishing a com-call on his terminal.

"Double the security team at the reactor site. And I want two security personnel stationed at the Genesis airlock at all times."

"Yes sir," said the disembodied voice from the comm.

Wisecroft leaned back in his chair and exhaled loudly. Noticing them, he said, "Ah, George. And Dr Perryman. You made good time. Please sit down." He didn't stand or offer his hand, and Zac sensed an undercurrent of hostility. As Zac sat in the chair opposite the desk, he noted how much older Wisecroft looked since they had met at a DANSA social function more than two years ago. Even so, he retained his sophisticated good looks. In his early 50s, he was tall and athletic, with a thick head of black hair with distinguished streaks of grey. But Zac also noticed how tired and strained he looked.

"Dr Perryman, we have a bit of a situation here, and I think you can help us."

"OK ..." said Zac, with a puzzled expression on his face.

"I'll be blunt," said Wisecroft, "because things are moving rather quickly." His eyes drilled into Zac, and he leaned forward in his chair. "Where is your wife?"

Zac blinked several times in astonishment and experienced a wave of anxiety. "What do you mean?" he asked.

"I think my meaning is pretty clear," said Wisecroft. "I'd like you to tell me where Annisa is and, more to the point, what the hell she might be doing right now."

Zac's head was spinning. "I don't understand. How am I supposed to know where she is? She's been up here with you for the last two weeks. Are you telling me you've lost my wife?"

Wisecroft leant back in his chair and stared at Zac. He glanced briefly at Leonidis, who had positioned himself in a standing position directly behind Zac's chair.

"OK," Wisecroft said. "If that's how you want to play it." His eyes drilled into Zac. "Perhaps if I tell you what we already know, it might loosen your tongue a little." He paused and gathered his thoughts. "This morning we became aware that six people had dropped off the grid: an engineer based at the reactor, another at the water extraction plant, a third based at the gravity generator, and two of our research scientists. They didn't show up for their shifts this morning, and a search of the bio-monitoring system shows that their biochips have all been deactivated sometime through the night."

"And Annisa is one of them?" Zac asked, his emotions reeling.

"Yes," said Wisecroft. "And I think you know exactly what is going on."

Zac felt his anger rising. "What? How the hell should I know?!"

Ignoring Zac's outburst, Wisecroft continued. "I've had a technical team examining the comm logs of each of the missing people. In the case of three of them—a maintenance officer, the reactor engineer, and your wife—they have sent and received regular encrypted messages going back several months. The incoming messages originated from a geosynchronous comm satellite over Nairobi, Kenya."

Zac spluttered, "You can't possibly be implying ..."

"Oh, but I am, Dr Perryman," interrupted Wisecroft. "That is precisely what I'm implying. It's a Caliphate satellite. Your wife has been sending and receiving encrypted messages with the Caliphate. Furthermore, we have discovered additional encrypted messages originating from the comm station in your apartment, coinciding with your wife's periodic presence there."

"You think my wife is a UFO?" asked Zac, incredulously. "Some kind of Undercover Faith Operative for the Caliphate?"

"That is exactly what I think."

Zac suddenly felt sick. Anger was replaced by shock and bewilderment. "It doesn't make sense," he said. "She can't be ... I know my wife ... It's not possible." Zac's mind was working furiously. "Besides, I would know ..."

"Precisely," replied Wisecroft. "Considering your own interest in that field, you would, indeed, know. Which brings us to you." Wisecroft typed something into his console, and the wall behind him displayed an enlarged excerpt from a document. "I am sure you will recognise this, Dr Perryman. Your doctoral thesis. Let me draw your attention to some interesting statements. '*The escalating hostilities of the 2040s and '50s owed more to Western reactionism and racism than to any real threat from Caliphate leaders.*'"

"Yes, but that was just ..."

"And then there is this: '*Increasingly, the harsh restrictions and sanctions imposed by the Western democratic nations backed the emerging Caliphate nations into a corner from which their understandable response was aggression*'."

"You're taking my words out of context," said Zac. "You can't possibly think that I'm ..."

"On the contrary, that is precisely what we do think." Wisecroft punched a button on his console, and a picture appeared on the wall behind him. "This is a photo of you with Imam Aabad Bukhari, taken at a mosque in Nairobi, Kenya, in 2349. As you would be aware, Imam Bukhari is known for his extremist views. I also note that you are wearing traditional

Caliphate clothing, and you appear to be getting on very well with the Imam."

Zac felt the colour rising in his face as his anger returned. "This is getting ridiculous! That was my research trip for my doctorate! Wearing traditional clothing was just a means of showing my respect. I met with a number of clerics while I was there, and every meeting was cleared with the DAN consulate."

"I'm sure it was," replied Wisecroft. "It is said that the most effective way of operating under cover is to be out in the open."

Zac started to object again, but Wisecroft held up his hand. "Enough! We don't have time for word games. Events are escalating." He activated his comm. "Send Dr. Leibman in, please."

Wisecroft punched another button on his console, and a map of the world appeared on the wall behind him. The continent of Africa was covered in red dots. "Approximately 30 minutes ago, the Caliphate activated all their ground-based missile silos, as well as their missile-capable orbital satellites." The picture on the wall changed to a 3D image of the Earth surrounded by at least 40 orbital red dots. "The Democratic Alliance of Nations has responded in kind." The image of the earth changed again to a globe surrounded by as many blue dots as red ones. On the ground below, the South American continent was a mass of blue dots. "All DANSA bases and facilities are now in lockdown."

As he spoke, a side door to the office opened and a middle-aged, nondescript man in a white lab coat entered, carrying a small black case.

Ignoring the newcomer, Wisecroft continued to address Zac. "Dr Perryman, we are on the brink of war; the precipice of mutual annihilation. At such a time we can no longer afford the luxury of humanitarian niceties. I believe you may have some information that can help us track down your wife and her co-conspirators, and perhaps circumvent a planned act of terrorism on this base. I cannot control what may be about to unfold on Earth, but I will do whatever it takes to protect the lives of the 900 people who are currently on this base."

Wisecroft nodded to his assistants. Leonidis stepped forward and grasped Zac's head firmly in his hands as Dr Leibman removed an atomiser syringe from his black bag.

"What are you doing to me?" exclaimed Zac. "I've done nothing wrong!"

"If that is so," said Wisecroft, "then you have nothing to fear. You will not be harmed in any way. We are not animals, I assure you. This is a perfectly safe but very effective psychoactive drug that suppresses your inhibition centres and stimulates serotonin and endorphin secretion. A truth serum, if you like. I'm told it is a very pleasurable experience."

Before Zac could respond, Leibman quickly inserted the atomiser into Zac's nose and pressed the electronic activator. A soft hiss could be heard, and almost instantly Zac's brain seemed to explode in a burst of bright light. A warm pink glow descended upon his consciousness as he slumped in the chair. That was the last thing he remembered for several hours.

When he finally came to his senses, he was no longer on the moon.

5

Elizabeth Canning stood at the head of the large oval table and looked at the worried faces of her colleagues. The fifteen men and women in front of her had been talking and debating vociferously a moment ago but had fallen silent and stood as she entered the conference room.

"Thank you, ladies and gentlemen. Please be seated."

She had just come from a troubling conversation with her daughter. "Mommy, I'm scared. Is there going to be a war?" Melody was 11 years old and a natural worrier, although until now her worries had centred around what she would wear to her friends' birthday parties and, more recently, whether any boys in her class liked her.

"No, sweetheart, of course not," Elizabeth had assured her. "No one wants another war, not even the people doing silly things at the moment. Everything is going to be all right. There's nothing to worry about." Elizabeth had stroked her daughter's unruly head of red hair and held her close.

"If there isn't going to be a war, why are we here? And why couldn't Daddy come, too?" Melody had asked. She had still not accepted her parents' separation and couldn't understand why they couldn't still be a family.

"I just needed to meet with some people, and this was the best place to do it. Daddy will be fine. He's very busy, but you can see him again as soon as we get back home." Elizabeth had given her daughter a kiss on the cheek and said, "Now I want you to do your schoolwork, please. Rowena will look after you, and I will be on the next level up, in a meeting. I'll be back down to tuck you into bed tonight."

They were deep underground, in a strategic command bunker a few kilometres west of Wellington, New Zealand, having flown there from Macapá, Brazil, overnight. The Wellington command bunker had been set up decades ago for just this sort of crisis, and the Caliphate was believed to be unaware of its existence. It was probably the safest place in the world right now, but Elizabeth knew that if they couldn't stop this madness, there would be nowhere safe on the face of the Earth.

Seated in the conference room now, Elizabeth glanced towards the lean, grey-haired general immediately to her left. "General Armitage, what's the status?"

The general activated the wall screen at the far end of the room, and a map of the world appeared. "Madam President, Africa is lit up like a damn Christmas tree. Every one of their silos is now fully armed and on a hair trigger. Their satellites too. We've responded in kind. The whole world looks like it's covered in fairy lights."

Elizabeth looked at the map of the world. The blue lights indicated that their own thermonuclear weapons outnumbered the red lights, but not by much. "If the worst happened, how effective would our sentry satellites be in neutralising their rockets?"

Armitage leant forward. "Our lasers have to hit the rockets in the first half of a rocket's flight, before it deploys its warheads. Each rocket has up to a dozen nuclear warheads, of about 1 megaton each. Once deployed, the warheads scatter over hundreds of square kilometres, and they would be just two damn small and there would be too many of them for our sentries to target."

Elizabeth persisted, "So, would we be able to neutralise all their rockets before the warheads deploy?"

Armitage looked uncomfortable. "Not all of them, Madam President. Best-case scenario, maybe 75 percent."

"What's the worst case?"

"Worst case, we might only be able to get a third of them."

There was a moment's silence around the table as everyone digested that news.

Elizabeth looked towards her Head of Intelligence. "Eli, what have you got for us?"

Eli Goldstein leaned forward in his seat and spoke with his usual clipped precision. "Madam President, as you know, yesterday's coup lies at the heart of current developments. The assassination of the moderate caliph, Hasib Farooq, has brought the extremist Aabad Bukhari to power. To put it bluntly, the guy is a lunatic. We've been tracking him for years. He is a committed jihadist and believes that he has been raised up to finish what they started three centuries ago. I have an excerpt from a speech he gave three months ago." Goldstein pointed a remote control towards the wall screen and Bukhari appeared, speaking at some kind of outdoor rally.

"For too long we have tolerated the wickedness and unbelief of infidels. We have slept with snakes. We have made deals with scorpions. But no more! The Great Prophet calls us to rid the world of the pestilence of unbelief. We will cleanse the world with fire! We will visit the vengeance of Allah upon all who deny him, to the praise of his name!"

Goldstein froze the recording. Bukhari was depicted with spittle flying from his lips and the light of fanaticism burning fiercely in his eyes. The room was silent for a moment as they all stared at his face.

The president broke the silence. "So, this madman has his finger on the button. Is he just posturing? Has he made any ultimatums?"

Ramona Ortega, Secretary of State, spoke up. "Over the last 24 hours, the Caliphate have shut down all diplomatic channels. They have not responded to any of our requests for dialogue. We simply don't know what they want. We are continuing to send your message of peace and goodwill, Madam President, but at this stage we have no idea if Bukhari is even listening. Furthermore, an alarming number of UFOs—Undercover Faith Operatives within the democratic nations—have gone off-grid. Many of them have been under surveillance for some time, but within the last 24 hours their biochips have either been deactivated or removed, and they have completely disappeared."

"What is it they actually want?"

"World domination," responded Ortega. "I know it sounds clichéd, but there is no other word for it. The jihadist teachings proclaim that it is Allah's will that all infidels—that's us— must either convert or die. For centuries mainstream Muslims have simply overlooked or interpreted those portions of their scripture differently, but Bukhari and his followers seem determined to carry out those instructions literally. Mankind's expansion into space in recent centuries has added further fuel to the fire of their religious zeal. They believe that Allah created mankind for this planet only, and that by leaving it we are showing our disrespect for the home he gave us. They believe that the devil is inspiring us to leave the Earth."

Elizabeth Canning stared down the length of the table, the wheels of her mind spinning. She stood to her feet, and everyone at the table began to stand as well. "No, no. Please sit. I just need to move. I think better on my feet." The president began pacing up and down the room, with every eye following her. "What would happen if Bukhari was removed from the equation?" she asked.

Ortega spoke up again. "With Bukhari neutralised, the most likely candidates to replace him are all moderates, and none of them want war. The most likely scenario is that Bukhari's removal would result in immediate de-escalation."

The president continued pacing for a moment and then stopped opposite John Duggan, Director of Regional Security. "What's our ability to mount an op, John?"

"Madam President, we have a long gun already in place in the capital. He's a long-term deep-cover operative who could be activated immediately. Bukhari's over-confidence is making him a soft target. He is moving freely around the capital, including public appearances at prayer services several times each day. If we have a green light from you, the situation could be resolved within the next few hours."

Elizabeth looked around the table. "Comments? Does anyone have a better suggestion?" No one spoke, all eyes glued to the president. She moved back to the head of the table, where she stood in deep thought for a moment. "John, you have a green light. General Armitage, we will remain at Level 5 alert, but I don't want anything done to further aggravate the situation and force Bukhari's hand. No asset movements. No drone launches. We need to sit tight and hope Bukhari is listening to our communications." She took a deep breath and said, "That's all for the moment. We will reconvene in one hour. By then I want ..."

The sound of an alarm interrupted her, and footsteps could be heard running in the corridor beyond the door. The president pressed a button on her desk, and the wall to her left became transparent, revealing the sunken operations centre below them. Dozens of people seated at monitors were all speaking urgently into their headsets, while others were running and yelling. The enormous live status screen on the far wall showed what they all feared. Dozens of curved yellow lines had begun to rise from the red dots covering the African continent and from other red dots in orbit. At the top of the screen, the three words they had hoped never to see, flashed ominously in red: 'Multiple Launches Detected'. As President Canning ran from the conference room, someone behind her muttered, "God help us all!"

6

E ven centuries after its invention, the thermonuclear fission-fusion bomb was still the most efficient means of killing the maximum number of people in the minimum amount of time.

In the sky above Rio de Janeiro, a one-megaton thermonuclear warhead travelling at 21,000 kilometres per hour registered that it had reached the optimal height of one kilometre above the city. An initial tiny explosion took place within the warhead. One millionth of a second later, a single neutron collided with the nucleus of a Uranium 235 atom, splitting the nucleus into two and emitting 200 million times the energy of the neutron that had impacted it. The reaction also released three more rogue neutrons, which then impacted other U235 nuclei, splitting them and instigating an exponentially accelerating chain reaction. Within one ten-thousandth of a second, the fireball created by the growing fission explosion was 200 metres in diameter and had a temperature of 100 million degrees Celsius, six times hotter than the sun. After five seconds the fireball was nearly two kilometres in diameter, engulfing the central part of the central business district below.

The many thousands of people in the heart of the city were simply vaporised. Buildings were obliterated, steel was melted. Nothing was left.

The intense heat from the explosion continued to radiate outwards in the form of a thermal pulse, accompanied by X-ray and gamma radiation. Travelling at nearly the speed of light, the thermal pulse killed everyone within a four-kilometre radius, instantly incinerating them. Anything flammable was immediately consumed. As the pulse continued to expand outwards, it cooled to only a few hundred degrees and was no longer able to kill instantly. Instead, it inflicted third-degree burns up to seven kilometres away, leaving many victims to face a slow, painful death from those burns over the next days and weeks.

Following a few seconds behind the thermal pulse came the shock wave. This high-pressure body of air produced fatal internal injuries up to seven kilometres away and flattened everything in its path. Even though it was only a wave of highly compressed air, for anyone caught in the open, it was like being hit by a train. Internal organs were liquefied. Eyes were blown out of people's sockets. Eardrums burst. Brains were jellified.

And, of course, the radiation fallout from the blast would continue to kill people and poison the Earth for thousands of years.

Josepha Castillo was a conscientious schoolteacher, who loved children and worked hard to make her lessons engaging. She had been teaching first grade at Saint Catherine's Primary School, on the outskirts of Santiago, Chile, for 23 years, and was dearly loved by the school community. Today she was reading her students the story of Saint Francis of Assisi and making her students laugh as she mimicked the sounds of the various animals who came to the godly man for his care. The sound of a siren interrupted her story. It was coming from the business district three kilometres away. *What is that? A fire alarm? Some kind of emergency service alert?*

Suddenly there was a bright flash of light, brighter than anything Josepha had ever seen. She put her hands up in front of her face and instinctively closed her eyes. Even so, she found that she could see through her closed eyelids and was amazed that she could see all the bones inside her hands and arms, as if she was having them X-rayed. She opened her mouth to warn the children to get down on the ground, but before she had time to speak, she and all the students in her class simply ceased to exist, instantly reduced to their component atoms.

Demetrius Konstantinidis cooked the best fish and chips in Sydney. At least, he liked to think so. He had owned and operated his shop in Chatswood for only 12 years, but it had become renowned for its fresh seafood and its delicious, crunchy golden chips. The secret was his cooking oil. He used only the finest blend of oil, and he changed the oil every single day. People came from all over the North Shore for his fish and chips. 'Demi's Is Best' announced his street sign, and many people in Sydney agreed. Tonight was a slow night. Demi was taking a break out the back, leaving his daughter and niece in charge of the shop for a few minutes. They were good workers, but Eugenia tended to overcook the chips sometimes. He looked across the hills to the skyscrapers of the city and breathed in the sweet-scented night air, feeling a deep satisfaction with the life that he had built for himself and his family. The sudden burst of light instantly blinded him, completely burning away his retina. Demi felt no pain, just a brief moment of bewilderment before the searing heat of the thermal pulse charred him to the bone.

Alarms were sounding all over Kepler Station, attached to the tether cable high above the Earth. Jen Mason, duty officer in the control room, yelled above the noise, "Somebody turn those damn alarms off! I can't think with all that racket! Now, someone tell me what the hell is going on!"

As silence descended upon the space station again, Tony Kirchener, second officer, pointed to his radar and thermal imaging screens and said, "We're tracking multiple ICBM launches. Originally at least 40 hostiles, and even more of ours. Defensive systems on both sides have taken out about half, but we are looking at MAD right now." Mutually Assured Destruction. An icy silence greeted that announcement as the full import sunk in. Kirchener continued, "Warheads are being deployed as the ICBMs reach their targets. There are detonations all over the southern hemisphere. Too many to count."

Another alarm started up, this one more strident than those previously. "Now what?" asked Mason.

Chez Rainger, the comms officer, answered, "We've just lost the tether. The ground terminal at Macapá has been destroyed and the cable has been severed at the base. We've got about five minutes before that shock wave travels up the cable and shakes us to pieces!"

"Get everyone out of the docking bay and blow the cable!" said Mason.

Rainger replied, "There's a pod on its way up, Ma'am. It's due to dock in two minutes."

Mason swore under her breath. "Patch me through to the docking bay." She paused for a moment to gather her thoughts. "This is Duty Officer Jen Mason. Who's in charge down there tonight?"

The voice over the comm replied, "It's John Padgett, ma'am."

"John, all hell's breaking loose down below. The tether cable has been severed and we need to blow it, but we've got a pod still on its way up. Do you think you can evacuate the pod and clear the dock within 90 seconds of its arrival?"

"It'll be tight. But if I don't wait for full pressurisation before starting evacuation, I think I can manage it."

"OK. Let me know the second the last passenger is safely through the airlock."

Rainger interrupted, "Ma'am, we've got two unauthorised shuttle launches!" She activated the shuttle comm and said, "FTL-3 and FTL-4, please advise why you have undocked." There was no response. "FTLs 3 and 4, who is on board and why have you undocked?" Still no response.

Kirchener announced, "Radar indicates both shuttles are accelerating. Based on current trajectories, the best guess is they're heading for the moon."

Mason swore softly and said, "Keep trying to contact them, Chez. John, how are you doing down in the docking bay?"

"The pod has docked, and the passengers are disembarking now. Thirty more seconds and we can blow the tether."

"Good. Count me down as the airlock cycles." Turning to Kirchener, Mason said, "Tony, blow the cable on my go." To Myra Kerslake, her orbital navigator, she said, "Myra, I want full lateral maneuvering thrusters on my go, plus three. Get us as far away as you can from that cable, as quickly as you can." Activating the station-wide comm, she announced, "This is the command centre. We are about to execute an emergence evasive maneuver. Please secure yourself as best you can."

The crew in the control room waited expectantly, and a few moments later John's voice came over the comm, "Cycling the airlock now. 5, 4, 3, 2, 1, Go!"

"Blow the tether!" yelled Mason. The space station shuddered as the tether bolts blew, and a moment later, everyone was thrown sideways as the maneuvering thrusters began accelerating them clear. Thirty seconds later, Mason said, "Cut the thrusters, we're well clear now."

Except they weren't.

A refraction wave of kinetic energy had travelled up the

tether cable at close to the speed of sound. The cable was now acting like a whip, anchored to the asteroid in a higher, faster orbit. By sheer chance, the cable whipped across the 300 metres of space that separated it from the space station and, in the blink of an eye, neatly sliced the station in two. The sudden decompression sent a sparkling explosion of debris radiating outwards like a beautiful, incandescent space-borne flower. The crew never knew what hit them.

7

Zac Perryman had never felt better, floating in a warm glow of drug-induced contentment. He had moved from his chair and was sitting on Simon Wisecroft's desk, with his legs dangling over the edge. He began swinging his legs in a circular fashion while staring at them in fascination. "Hey guys, this is awesome! You should try this. It feels amazing!" he said.

Dr. Wisecroft nodded to George Leonidis and said, "He's completely harmless. He knows nothing. At least now we know that he isn't involved. On the downside, we've just wasted two hours chasing up a blind alley, and we're no closer to finding our missing staff or uncovering whatever it is they're planning."

"Come on, guys!" said Zac, continuing to swing his legs. "Why aren't you doing it? It's the most amazing thing! Come and sit next to me, Georgy Porgy!"

"What do you want me to do with him?" asked Leonidis.

"He's as high as a kite," said Wisecroft, "and I don't think he's going to sleep for a while. You're just going to have to babysit him."

"Great. Thanks very much. That sounds fun."

"It's one of the perks of your job, George."

"I perked up once," said Zac. "All over the dinner table. Ruined the lasagne. You ever perked up, Georgy? You look like a perky kind of guy."

"Dr Perryman," said Wisecroft, speaking slowly and clearly, "George is going to take you to the staff lunchroom. I'm sure you would appreciate something to eat by now."

"Cool," said Zac, jumping off the desk. "Come on, Georgy Porgy."

George just rolled his eyes as he guided Zac out the door and down the corridor. As they disappeared, a comm channel beeped at Wisecroft, with an ID tag telling him it was the control centre. He accepted the feed and his Head of Communications, Michael Gates, appeared on his screen. "Dr. Wisecroft, we have a major situation. I just received a transmission from a Titan cargo vessel, the Herschel. It's just achieved Earth orbit, inbound from Titan. It's in geosynchronous orbit at the tether point, except there's no tether and no Kepler Station."

"What do you mean?"

"Kepler has been blown to bits, sir. There's debris everywhere, and the tether is detached from the base station. It's now degrading the orbit of the anchor asteroid, which, if the calculations of the Titan crew are correct, will impact Earth within the next 12 hours. We're talking about a major impact. But that's not the worst of it. All hell has broken loose on the surface. There appears to have been a major nuclear exchange. The Herschel comm officer says there are mushroom clouds over just about every major city in the southern hemisphere. EMT pulses seem to have wiped out all ground-based comm channels and circuitry. Right now, we're looking at a silent, radioactive globe that has just been taken back to the stone age."

"God help us," said Wisecroft. "What about the other manned satellites? Has the Herschel been able to make contact with anyone?"

"They've located debris where there should have been satellites in mid-Earth orbit. Most of them appear to have been destroyed by missiles. Because of the EMT pulse, we have no way of knowing for sure whether there are any survivors in orbit." Gates paused for a moment, looking at another screen. "Just a moment, I'm getting a video feed from Herschel. I'll patch it through to you."

Wisecroft's screen suddenly depicted a view of Earth from 200 kilometres altitude. Shining, spinning debris could be seen in the foreground, creating tinsel-like glitter covering an ominous-looking world. Huge mushroom clouds obliterated large sections of Africa, which was currently passing below. The enormity of the catastrophe overwhelmed Wisecroft as he sat staring at the screen.

"Sir, the captain of the Herschel wants a word. I'm patching him through now."

An olive-skinned face appeared on the screen. "Dr. Wisecroft, I am Captain Jason Hunziker of the Herschel. As you can see, we've got one hell of a mess here."

"I can see that, Captain. Is there anything we can do from here? What's your own situation?"

"Well, we're getting low on supplies, having just pulled a long haul from Titan. At this stage I don't think we should even consider trying to get down to the surface. For starters, we can't be certain hostilities have ended, and we have no way of communicating with any survivors. I think we're going to have to make our way to you and wait it out."

"Of course, Captain. We can accommodate you and your crew. We'll be ready to ..."

An alarm sounded from the bridge of the Herschel and a voice could be heard off-screen saying, "Captain, radar and infra-red sensors are picking up two missiles, 120 clicks out and closing fast."

Captain Hunziker spoke off-camera for a few moments.

Urgent commands were issued, and panicked replies could be heard in the background. Hunziker came back into view. He calmly looked into his comm screen and said, "I'm terribly sorry, Dr Wisecroft, I'm going to have to decline your very generous invitation. It looks as though we are not going to make it for dinner after all. Please express my ..." The screen went blank.

Gates' face appeared again. "Sir, we've lost all comms with the Herschel. They're gone."

Wisecroft ran his hands through his hair. *The whole world has gone mad*, he thought.

"Sir, I'm picking up something else here," said Gates.

"Is it good news, Michael? We could use some right now."

"I'm not sure, Dr Wisecroft. There are two shuttles inbound from Earth. They aren't on any schedule I've got, and they aren't answering our hails. Their electronic signatures ID them as FTL-3 and FTL-4, which aren't due until tomorrow."

"How far out are they?"

"They must have flipped about an hour ago. They're about 30 minutes out."

"OK. I'm assuming they're survivors from Kepler. Thank goodness someone made it out alive. Keep monitoring their progress and keep me posted. Let me know if you establish contact." Wisecroft shut down the channel and sat staring at the blank screen, trying to come to terms with all that had happened. The Earth was a disaster zone. Millions or possibly billions of lives lost. The Tether Lift gone. Kepler Station gone. Humanity sent spiralling back into the dark ages. Would the world ever recover? Would mankind even be able to survive on a planet that must now be facing thousands of years of deadly radioactivity?

He stood up and had taken only two steps towards the door when the floor beneath his feet shook so violently that he fell to his hands and knees. An alarm sounded somewhere, and confused shouting could be heard from various parts of the research facility. He got to his feet and made it a few metres down the corridor when a second explosion knocked him to the floor once more.

Wisecroft had thought the situation could not get any worse.

But he was wrong.

Very wrong.

8

K it Tyler enjoyed her layovers on the moon. Today she would only be here for a few hours before her scheduled afternoon departure, but that still allowed some time to unwind. Her first stop was always the gym at the Casino, which was light years ahead of the tiny gym on Kepler Station: treadmills, bikes and rowers with 3D Immersive Sensory Virtual Reality (ISVR). The millionaires who stayed at the Casino wanted the very best, and she got to enjoy it all for free as a member of the flight crew. Today she spent a total of an hour and a half, rowing through glacial fiords, running through rainforests and riding through the Swiss Alps. Then she hit the spa in the adjacent room - a large, heated hot tub with an adjoining cold-water lap pool. The water was conveniently sourced from the huge ice deposit 400 metres directly under the city, estimated to be over 80,000 cubic kilometres in volume.

Feeling energised and refreshed, and now very hungry, Kit then visited her second favourite place on the base, the cafeteria. Because of the abundance of fresh water and the unlimited power supply from the fusion reactor, the aquaponic farm on Sub-Level 2 produced the best range of fresh fruit and vegetables in the solar system. And, once again, it was all hers to enjoy for free.

It was in the cafeteria that she met up again with Bane, who was having a coffee. "What've you been up to, Islander-boy?" she said as she tucked into her yeast steak with salad and fries.

"Nothing much," he said, giving her a furtive glance.

"Finding your way around here OK?" she asked.

"It's a bit of a maze, I must admit. I got lost a couple of times. I still haven't quite worked it out," he said.

Kit took out her foldable network tablet and opened up a drawing page. "Here, let me show you," she said, starting to draw on the tablet with her finger. "Sub-Level 1, which is where we are now, consists of a central lava cave, surrounded by four much larger caves." She drew a circle in the middle of the page, surrounded by four larger circles. "The central cave is just a small chamber housing the main lift, linked to the Terminal on the surface, where we docked. The lift services Sub-Levels 1 and 2. On Level 1, there are four corridors branching out from the central chamber, leading to each of the much larger caves: Armstrong Research Centre, Galileo Observatory, Starlight Casino, and the largest cave of all, Habitation and Cafeteria, where we are now." As she spoke, she drew the relevant details on her rough map. "Each of these four large caves, or zones, as they are commonly called, is also linked by a series of further connecting tunnels extending around the perimeter of the base. Each zone also has its own smaller lift to access the surface and Sub-Level 2 below."

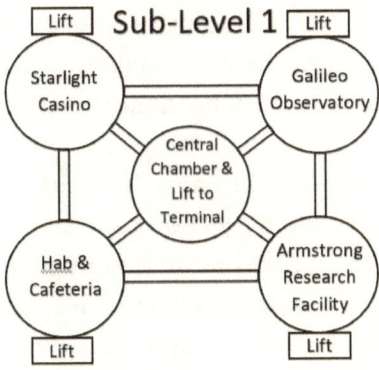

"Sub-Level 2 is about 50 metres below us and consists of another four lava caves surrounding a central chamber, in a similar layout to Level 1. Down there, we have the aquaponics farm, water harvesting plant, fusion reactor, life support with the artificial gravity generator, and engineering department. And all of those have a similar system of linking tunnels."

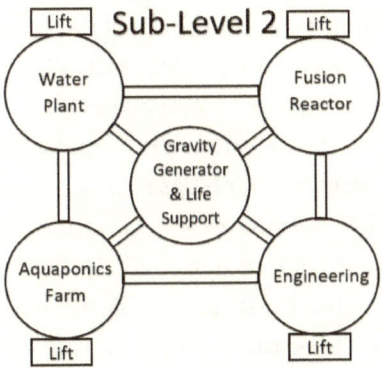

Kit kept up her narration as she continued to scoff down her steak and salad. "Most of the caves and some of the tunnels were pre-existing, from ancient lava flows. Needless to say, a lot of extra excavation had to be done initially to get it to its current layout."

"Pretty impressive," said Bane. "I've had a bit of a wander around, although I couldn't get down to Level 2."

"No. Pretty tight security around here. They don't want any wayward billionaires wandering into the fusion reactor and pressing the wrong button. Guests are limited to the observatory, casino, and hab zone. Did you check out the observatory?"

"No."

"It's pretty cool. Obviously, it's underground, so you don't see the stars directly. The observatory has 30 private 3D viewing booths linked to a series of multi-array telescopes, about one click north of here on the surface. It's a big attraction for the mega-rich. I'm good friends with Sue Skuthorpe, the observatory supervisor. If things are quiet, she slips me in for free and gives me a booth."

"Has the base ever had any accidents? Decompression? That sort of thing?"

"Not since completion. In the early days, while it was being constructed, there were some accidents. But today the base is pretty safe. There are airlocks everywhere, at each end of every connecting tunnel. Any sudden decompression will automatically close every airlock on the base."

Kit pushed her empty plate away and gave a satisfying belch as she leaned back in her chair. "Ah, you gotta love fresh food!" she said. She noticed that Bane had been glancing frequently at the clock on the nearby wall during their chat. "Are you waiting for someone?" she asked.

"No," he replied, looking once more at the clock. "But I think I'll go for another wander. We're due to fly out in an hour and I need to stretch my legs." He stood up and gave her a curiously sad look. "Thanks for the chat. It's been nice getting to know you." With that, he turned and walked away.

Nice getting to know me? she thought. *He's a bit intense. Maybe he's just a loner; someone who's not all that crash-hot at relationships.* She shook her head and ordered a coffee, or what passed for coffee on the moon: a pleasant-tasting hot drink with a mild artificial stimulant. A few minutes later a female waitperson arrived, tipped the coffee all over Kit's head and sat on her lap.

It wasn't intentional.

She was simply knocked off her feet by the explosion.

9

D r. Simon Wisecroft pushed himself to his feet and found that he had launched himself into the air. He hit his head on the ceiling and then drifted back down to land lightly on his feet. The artificial gravity was gone. That must have been the second explosion. What was the first? He had to find out what was going on. He started to run down the corridor towards the control centre and fell forward again, landing gently on the ground. *Damn! I'm going to have to learn how to run in one-sixth gravity!* He adjusted his gait, lengthened his stride and attempted to adjust his balance as he went. He didn't fall again, but he was sure he didn't look particularly graceful. All around him he could hear concerned voices. As he ran down the corridor, he kept yelling, "Stay where you are until we know what is happening!"

In the centre of the research facility was the control centre for the whole of Luna City. There were dozens of monitors showing video feeds from key areas of the base, along with comms and specialised monitoring stations for life-support systems. Wisecroft made an undignified entrance into the command centre, sliding across the threshold and crashing into the back of a staff member at a monitoring station.

"Sorry," he said.

He saw his Chief of Security, George Leonidis, with a bemused Zac in tow, enter the command centre from a door on the opposite side of the room. Zac was literally bouncing off the ceiling, jumping up and touching the ceiling with his hands and landing back on his feet.

"Hey guys, you should try this!" he said, with a goofy grin on his face.

Leonidis asked, "What the hell just happened?"

Lance Catrell, the Control Centre Coordinator, was seated at a console, wearing his ever-present '2001: A Space Odyssey' baseball cap. "There have been two explosions. One of them, as you can guess, knocked out our gravity generator and life support. As far as I can tell, life support systems for producing oxygen and filtering the air have been completely destroyed."

"How long can we survive without life support operating?" asked Wisecroft.

"About eight hours before carbon dioxide poisoning sets in. But that's not the worst of our problems."

"It's not?"

"No. The first explosion is more serious. It was in the fusion reactor control room."

"What damage was done?" asked Wisecroft.

"Not sure yet, but it can't be good. We haven't been able to contact the reactor staff. I've got security teams on their way down there now."

"Do you have the video log of the explosion?" asked Wisecroft.

"I'm just bringing it up now, sir."

An image of the interior of the fusion reactor control room appeared on an adjacent monitor, with a rolling time indicator in the bottom right corner. "This is a few minutes before the explosion," said Lance. Everything appeared normal. Three staff in white lab coats were on duty. Two were sitting at the long control desk facing the thick window that looked out onto the reactor, and the supervisor was standing behind them with a data tablet in his hand. Nothing happened for another minute, and then, suddenly, there was a spray of blood and gore from the back of the supervisor's head, and he fell to the floor. The two who were seated turned towards the door with a shocked expression and, almost simultaneously, both of their chests erupted in a spray of blood. A moment later, two people walked into view, both wielding what appeared to be some kind of primitive gun made of plastic. One of them removed what appeared to be an explosive device from a backpack. He placed it on the control panel desk and spent several moments activating it. Both people then turned around and looked directly into the camera, knowing they were being videoed.

"It's Dr Perryman!" exclaimed Lance.

Zac was looking at the screen, too. "Hey! It's Annisa! I told you she wasn't lost, Georgy Porgy." He started waving at the screen. "Hi, Anni! You'll never guess where I am."

Wisecroft said nothing, but felt an intense heaviness in his heart as he looked at the face of Annisa. He didn't recognise the other person but assumed it must be one of the other missing base staff. As he watched, Annisa and her collaborator placed an arm around each other and smiled, raising their fists triumphantly into the air.

A moment later, there was a blinding flash and the screen went black. There was stunned silence among the observers as they considered what they had just witnessed, although Zac was now sitting in a swivel chair, twirling himself around.

"How did they gain access to the control room?" asked someone standing beside Wisecroft.

He answered, "Annisa is a senior research team leader. She

has clearance for full access to the entire base. She must have momentarily reactivated her biochip."

"But why ...?" began the other person.

""Why" is not important right now," Wisecroft said bluntly. "We need to know what damage has been done and what we can do about it."

A comm channel opened up and a female voice on the other end said, "Control Centre, we can't get to the reactor! The tunnels have completely collapsed in this section. It looks like the explosion also took out the Observatory on Level 1. I sent a team to check out the grav-gen and they can't reach that section either. The Level 2 tunnels have collapsed there as well. The central chamber and main lift directly above, on Level 1, are still intact, so the second explosion can't have been as big."

Leonidis leaned forward and spoke into the comm. "This is George Leonidis, Chief of Security. Is that you, Martinez?"

"Yep." Natasha Martinez was Leonidis's deputy; a fiery Colombian, tough as nails and extremely efficient.

"Good. I want all security personnel to be on full alert. Guard the entrance to every section, and I want a double detail stationed at the entrance to the research facility. Shut down all movement through the tunnels until we get a handle on what's going on."

"Roger. On our way."

Wisecroft looked at his Control Centre Coordinator. "Lance, bring up the reactor readings. We need to know what we're dealing with."

Catrell brought up a new screen, full of graphical interfaces and readouts. "Does anyone know how to interpret this data?" asked Wisecroft.

"Let me look," said a new voice at Wisecroft's side. Dr. Arno Manchester, the head of nuclear physics, had just entered the control room, only slightly more gracefully than Wisecroft had. He slid into the chair alongside Lance and began typing instructions. He was silent for a full minute, then sat back and whispered softly, "My God ..."

"What? How bad is it?" asked Wisecroft.

Manchester's face had turned pale. "The containment field generator has been damaged. The fusion reaction is accelerating out of control."

"Can you shut it down?" asked Wisecroft.

"No. Without the containment field, there is nothing we can do." Turning in his chair, Manchester looked up at Wisecroft and calmly said, "We have a cascading reaction that is completely beyond control. When it goes critical, it's going to blow a hole in the moon at least two kilometres wide and almost as deep. There will be nothing left of this base."

There was complete silence in the room.

"How long have we got?" asked Wisecroft.

Manchester swivelled his chair to examine the monitor again. He called up a calculator and crunched some numbers. "Assuming the reaction continues at its current rate, and also assuming we can maintain the flow of water to the core, we have about eight hours."

His words were still hanging in the air when another major explosion rocked the base, knocking Wisecroft and several others to the ground. Control room lights dimmed momentarily and then regained their luminosity.

"Where was that?" asked Wisecroft, picking himself up off the floor.

"Just a moment," said Lance. He scrolled through various screens and readouts, and then swore loudly. "The water harvesting plant is offline. I'm getting nothing from the water plant control room, and water pressure in the feed lines has dropped to zero." He turned to Manchester and said, "We just lost the water for the reactor."

Wisecroft swore. "Can this get any worse?!" No one said

anything. He turned to Manchester. "How does that impact our timeframe?"

"It's not good. Not good at all," replied Manchester. "I can't say for certain yet. I'll have to watch the reaction rate and make some calculations. The lack of coolant will at least halve how much time we have. We may even have as little as two hours. I'll let you know as soon as I can." He began crunching more numbers and making notes on his data pad.

Lance interjected, "I've just scanned the video logs for the gravity generator and water plant control rooms. The same sequence of events took place there as in the fusion reactor. Two terrorists enter, shoot the control room staff and then detonate a bomb while smiling at the camera."

Wisecroft looked at Leonidis. "At least that accounts for all six of our missing personnel."

"Yes, but I don't think we should assume it's over, sir," said Leonidis. "There may be others who are still lying low, maintaining their normal routine and waiting for a chance to act. Even if there are no others, these six could have planted other devices around the base on delayed timers."

Wisecroft addressed Gates, his comm officer. "Michael, give me an open channel to address the research facility, plus engineering and aquaponics."

Gates punched a button and gave Wisecroft a nod. Wisecroft gathered his thoughts for a moment and took a deep breath.

"Attention, please. This is Simon Wisecroft. We have a grave situation on our hands. We are currently under terrorist attack. We have accounted for six known terrorists, who are now deceased, and we are unsure whether there are any others. The water extraction plant, the gravity generator and the containment field generator for the fusion reactor have all been destroyed. I won't try to soft-sell this to you. We have lost control of the fusion reactor. It is undergoing a cascading fusion reaction that will culminate in a catastrophic explosion within the next few hours. Consequently, we are abandoning the base."

He paused to gather his thoughts and to let the information sink in. "We will use Genesis to evacuate all research staff and as much equipment as we can salvage. Some civilians and non-research staff will initially be evacuated using shuttles, which are closer to that part of the base. I am aware that Genesis wasn't scheduled for launch for another week, but we don't have a choice. We may only have two hours to evacuate, so we need to work quickly and efficiently. All engineering staff make your way immediately to Genesis and, once there, bring life-support systems online. Also, see if there is any way we can channel whatever remaining water we have on the base to top up the tanks on board Genesis. Most importantly, the main propulsion drive needs to be operational within two hours. Aquaponics staff, strip the farm completely clean. Transfer everything we've got, including all seed stores, to the aquaponics module on board Genesis. Use the access tunnel on Level 2, via engineering. Research Centre staff, I want everything of value stripped from here and taken on board. It's now 12:20. At precisely 14:20 we are leaving the moon. Work fast, people. That is all."

Wisecroft felt a tap on his shoulder and turned around. Zac was moving his arms in jerky motions and asked, "Hey doc, can you do the robot?"

10

W isecroft turned to Lance Catrell, the Control Centre Coordinator, and said, "We need to evacuate everyone. How many civilians do we currently have on base?"

Lance scratched his head through his Space Odyssey baseball cap and gave Wisecroft a worried look. "A lot less than we did half an hour ago."

"What do you mean?"

"While you were on comms, I was assessing the damage. The explosion that took out the water plant on Level 2 also destroyed the Casino above it. Martinez just reported that the whole cave system there has completely collapsed. Biochip readouts indicate there were nearly 300 people in the Casino at the time of the explosion, but I'm not getting life signs from any of them now. There were also over 120 civilians and staff in the observatory and its precincts when the blast from the fusion reactor control room took it out. No sign of life there now, either."

Wisecroft was visibly shaken. "We need to assemble all surviving civilians and non-research staff in the cafeteria so we can do a head count. We should be able to evacuate the survivors on the shuttle currently docked at the terminal and the two that are on their way. How soon until they arrive, Michael?"

"They're about 10 minutes out, sir."

"How many can each shuttle carry, Lance?"

"About 50 safely."

"OK. Open a channel to Martinez." Gates punched a button on the console and nodded. "Martinez, this is Simon Wisecroft, do you read me?"

"Yep."

"What tunnels are still intact?"

"The whole of Level 2 has collapsed except for aquaponics and engineering and the tunnel that links them. On Level 1 the central chamber is still undamaged, so we have access to the lift and the shuttle terminal, but the casino and observatory and their linking tunnels are all gone."

"OK. Take your team to the hab. We'll assemble everyone in the cafeteria. Once you've done a head count, I want you to lead everyone to the central chamber. We'll be evacuating them via shuttles."

"Roger. On my way."

Wisecroft turned to Gates. "Open a channel to the hab. I need to address the civilians now." Gates nodded. Wisecroft took a breath and started speaking. "Ladies and gentlemen, can I have your attention please? This is Dr Simon Wisecroft, director of this facility. As you are no doubt aware by now, we have some serious problems. There have been several instances of sabotage on the base, resulting in some serious damage; so serious, in fact, that we will have to evacuate the base as soon as possible. I need everyone to assemble in the cafeteria area immediately. My deputy security chief, Natasha Martinez, will meet you there and will lead you to the main terminal chamber, where you will be boarding shuttles. The shuttles will take you to lunar orbit, where we will arrange transfer to another vessel. Please go straight to the cafeteria. Do not deviate to retrieve possessions and do not attempt to access any other areas on the base. There are collapsed tunnels which may be in danger of further collapse. If you have friends or loved ones in other areas, please leave them for us to find. I ask that you remain as calm as possible. Thank you."

Wisecroft, sat back in his chair, running his hands through his hair and breathing out a big sigh. "Have I forgotten anything, Lance? Anything I've missed?"

"There might be one thing."

"What?"

"Genesis." Lance paused and gathered his thoughts. "The terrorists knew of its existence. In fact, the two renegade scientists, Drs Perryman and Klausman, have been part of the team that has been working on getting it ready for two years. They have had full access to the ship for the whole time. They must have predicted that we would plan to use it to evacuate. I can't believe they would have left it untouched."

"You're right," admitted Wisecroft. "We have to assume that they've either disabled an essential system or else they've planted some kind of explosive device on board. Unfortunately, we don't have a choice. We either stay here and die, or we take our chances on board Genesis." He turned towards Leonidis. "George, securing Genesis has got to be your priority now. Take a team and scour every inch of the ship, inside and out. You've got about 90 minutes to find whatever they've done to it."

"What about him?" asked Leonidis, indicating Zac, who was currently lying on the floor in a corner of the room, sound asleep.

"Leave him here; we'll keep an eye on him. Gather your team and get going."

"Will do."

Zac started snoring gently.

11

K it ran from the cafeteria, down a corridor beside the kitchen marked 'Staff Only'. She entered the flight crew ready room, quickly ditched her civvies and donned her flight suit. There was no sign of Bane, so hopefully he was already on his way to the shuttle. She figured that their pre-flight check would have to be quick. As she ran back through the cafeteria area, she noted the prevailing atmosphere of general panic. People were falling over, struggling with the low gravity, shouting instructions, calling out to friends and loved ones. She noticed a very overweight but well-dressed man with an old-fashioned Texas drawl abusing the female waiter who had previously spilled coffee on Kit. The Texan was yelling, "This is a disgrace! I only just got here yesterday! What sort of security do you guys have that you can't even keep a small base like this safe? I want to speak to someone in charge!"

Kit skidded to a halt beside the pair. She grabbed the Texan by his collar and spun him around in the low gravity, throwing him off-balance so that he ended up sitting on his largely proportioned backside on the ground. "Listen, cowboy," she said. "Your money bought you a ticket to the moon, but it didn't buy you the right to be an arsehole! This waitress is just doing her job, and she doesn't need an arrogant bonehead like you abusing her! I'm the captain of the shuttle that's supposed to fly your sorry arse out of here. I'm not sure how we're gonna fit everyone on, and right now I'm putting you at the back of the queue!"

She winked at the waitress, who mouthed a silent *thank you*. Kit spun around and continued running towards the tunnel leading to the main terminal chamber. As she did, the worry that had been nibbling away at the edge of her consciousness burst to the surface. *How are we going to fit everyone on the shuttle?* As far as she knew, her shuttle, FTL-1, was the only one on the base. Perhaps other shuttles were on their way from Kepler station, but even with all four, they could only extricate 200 people. As far as she knew, there were nearly 1,200 people on the base. How were they all going to be evacuated?

However, she didn't have time to worry about the problem any further, because as she came to the airlock for the terminal tunnel, half a dozen DANSA personnel came through the doorway and immediately blocked her path. "Whoa! Where do you think you're going?" asked a no-nonsense-looking female who was clearly in charge. This must be Natasha Martinez, Kit thought. She had a small nose ring, several ear piercings and jet-black hair in a short back and sides style, with a floppy fringe half covering one eye. Kit, who knew she exuded a tomboy aura herself, felt positively feminine and dainty standing next to Martinez.

"I'm Kit Tyler, the shuttle pilot. Just on my way to ready it for launch."

Martinez looked her up and down, took hold of her left wrist and scanned her biochip. "OK, you're good to go. I'll be bringing a load of passengers down the tunnel in about ten."

Kit started to move through the still-open airlock, then

turned and asked, "How are we gonna evacuate everyone? There's only one shuttle here."

"Control tells me there are two more about to land," answered Martinez, already starting to move off.

"Yeh, but there are 1,200 people to evacuate," said Kit.

"Not anymore, there aren't," answered Martinez as she walked away.

Kit's heart sank as the import of those words sank in. "How many ...?" she started to say, but Martinez was gone. She turned and ran through the airlock, which had both doors wide open as a result of the emergency evacuation code one of the security team had entered into the keypad. *At least we won't have to waste time cycling small numbers of people through the airlock one group at a time*, she thought to herself. She ran down the tunnel using long loping strides best suited for low gravity and came to the central cavern. She punched the button for the lift and a minute later exited the lift into the small terminal above ground. She was already running through her pre-flight check-list in her mind and was so preoccupied with her thoughts that she didn't immediately register what she was seeing through the viewing portal. Or rather, what she *wasn't* seeing.

The shuttle was gone.

12

Comm officer Michael Gates frowned as he looked at the screen in front of him. "Dr Wisecroft, my radar screen is showing that the shuttle has just lifted off."

Lance leaned over his shoulder, punched a comm button and said, "Martinez, this is control, do you read?"

"Loud and clear."

"Have you already loaded passengers onto a shuttle?"

"Not even close. We're still mustering. There's a lot of panic going on here. It's like herding cats."

Lance turned to Wisecroft, who was standing beside him. "What the hell?" As he spoke, the comm came to life and an unfamiliar voice addressed them.

"Hello Control, can anyone hear me?"

Lance leaned forward. "You're speaking to Lance Catrell, in the Control Centre. Who's this?"

"This is Kit Tyler in the terminal building. I'm the pilot of the shuttle, at least I'm meant to be, but right now I'm looking out at an empty tarmac. Do you mind telling me what you've done with my shuttle?"

Lance responded, "Our radar shows it accelerating away from the surface. Do you know who is flying it?"

"I guess that would be my co-pilot, Bane Kalawaia. Are you saying you didn't give him clearance to take off?"

"That's correct."

There was a pause in the conversation as both parties processed the information.

Wisecroft spoke up. "We have to assume hostile intent. Lance, what's the most likely scenario here?"

Catrell considered for a moment. "The shuttle has no weapons, so I can't see how ..."

"The shuttle IS a weapon," interrupted Kit over the comm. "It's a high-velocity projectile with substantial mass."

"She's right," said Wisecroft to Lance. "Where is the most likely target?"

"The most vulnerable place is where Kit is right now, the terminal building. The cavern underneath is the closest part of the base to the surface; only 10 metres or so. If the shuttle impacted there, it would penetrate the central chamber below, resulting in explosive decompression of what remains of the tunnel system." He looked again at his radar screen and swore.

"The shuttle has reversed its ascent! It is accelerating back towards the base!"

"Kit! Get out of there now!" yelled Wisecroft.

Kit didn't need a written invitation. The lift was already open, and she dived in and pressed the button for Sub-Level 1. The door closed agonisingly slowly, and the lift descended with equal deliberateness. "Come on, come on, come on," she muttered. An eternity later the door opened, and Kit shot out of it. As she sprinted down the tunnel back towards the habitation zone, she saw the first passengers starting to file through the open airlock. As she neared the airlock she started screaming, "Get back! Get back! Decompression! Get back! Close the airlock!" The passengers froze, with puzzled expressions on their faces. Natasha Martinez, however, was trained to react quickly. She was standing in the doorway in the hab-side of the airlock, and grabbed the nearest passenger and hurled him backwards into the hab. Kit noticed that the fat Texan had somehow managed to worm his way to the front of the queue and was the first passenger through the doorway, standing just inside the tunnel. Kit didn't slow down. With a certain degree of satisfaction, she dropped her shoulder and charged into the big man. He let out a loud "Oomf" as he flew backwards in the low gravity, knocking over two people behind him in the process and landing on top of one of them. The irate Texan opened his mouth to protest, but whatever he said was drowned out by the sound of a loud explosion in the central chamber, followed immediately by a tremendous wind howling through the airlock towards the now fractured chamber.

Kit was not a heavyweight. At 55 kilos and 162 cm, she'd often been referred to by friends as a pocket rocket. Now, for the first time in her life, she looked like she was about to achieve lift-off. The gale-force wind held her horizontal to the ground as she clung grimly to the outer lip of the airlock. The wind shrieked and howled around her, and debris hurtled past at frightening speed. Inside the cafeteria area, people were sliding towards the airlock. Anything not tied down became airborne, battering those inside the airlock before being sucked down the tunnel and ejected into the vacuum of space through the gaping hole in the top of the central cavern.

Kit's fingers began to slip, and she knew she only had seconds left. As her grip was about to fail, a hand with a swirling tattoo attached itself to her wrist and started pulling her in. Kit looked up into the steely green eyes of Natasha Martinez and saw the veins pop out in her neck as she strained against the wind's vicious pull. Another security officer grabbed her other wrist, and together they hauled Kit into the airlock as the door was closed.

The silence after the shrieking gale was eerie, except for the occasional cries and whimpers of those who were either in shock or injured. Kit looked at Martinez and said, "Thanks for that. Thought I was in a bit of trouble there."

"No problem. There's not much of you. On the other hand, if it had been Tubby over here," she said, indicating the overweight Texan still lying on his back behind them, "I would have let him go. He could have plugged the hole for us."

They both shared a smile, and then Martinez cocked her head to the side and said, "You'd better get that sewn up."

"What?" said Kit. She put her hand to her face, and it came away wet. She looked down and saw that the left side of her flight suit was soaked in blood.

"Your cheek is sliced wide open," said Martinez. "You've got yourself a second mouth on the side of your face."

Martinez stood to her feet and stepped out of the airlock into the cafeteria. There were people lying everywhere. It looked like a war zone, which, in reality, it was. "OK, people, listen up," she yelled. Her words had no effect. People were crying out and whimpering. She sensed a rising level of hysteria and knew she had to get on top of it quickly. "I said, quiet!!!" she yelled. This time, she got the desired effect. "If you can hear me, it means you're alive, so be thankful and stop panicking; you're not helping anyone, and it only uses up valuable energy. We're safe now, and I promise you we are going to get you out of here. For the moment, let's deal with the immediate issues. Is anyone injured? Please raise your hand." Several hands went up. "Anything life-threatening that can't wait for five minutes?" No one responded. "OK, good." She looked around the room. "At the risk of using a cliché, is there a doctor in the house?" She paused, and no one responded. "Do we have a doctor here?" Again, there was no response. "OK, anyone with medical training at all?" A tentative hand went up. It was the waitress who had tipped coffee all over Kit.

"Yes. I'm training to be a doctor. But I'm only halfway through my third year. I'm on student vacation at the moment."

"Congratulations," said Martinez. "You just graduated. Grab a med kit from the kitchen and set yourself up on those tables over there." She looked back over her shoulder towards Kit. "Supergirl, you're up first."

Kit plonked herself down at a table as the waitress came back from the kitchen with a substantial-looking med kit. "We seem destined to bump into each other," said Kit.

"Yeh. Thanks for what you did earlier. I'm not always as assertive as I should be."

"No problem. I'm Kit, by the way."

"Jasmine, but my friends call me Jaz."

Kit looked closely at her for the first time. Maybe 168 cm tall, shoulder-length red hair, with a smattering of freckles across a dainty nose. She had the kind of natural good looks that didn't need cosmetics to turn heads. "So, you're a med student? You look a bit older than the typical student."

"I'm a late bloomer," she said with a smile. "I spent five years working with an aid organisation in Santa Cruz, Bolivia. I reached the point where I wanted to do more. I was volunteering at the local hospital, because they were short of nurses. In the end I enrolled in medicine at DANSA Academy, in Macapá."

"Wow! The Academy? I heard they only took geniuses."

"I managed to pass the entrance exam," Jaz said modestly.

"That explains how you managed to land this cushy vacation job."

"Yes. Academy students get placed at DANSA facilities during vacation breaks. It's good money and we get to see some interesting facilities."

Jaz had been cleaning Kit's wound and now began suturing the nasty gash.

"Have you done this before?" asked Kit.

"Plenty of times in Bolivia. Don't worry, I know what I'm doing. You'll have a bit of a scar for a while, until you get some skin rejuve done."

"I'm not worried," said Kit. "The boys aren't exactly lining up to ask me out. I think I intimidate them."

"After watching you deal with that man earlier, I can understand why," responded Jaz. She worked silently for a few more moments. As she tied the sutures off, Jaz looked at Kit and asked, "Tell me honestly. Are we going to get out of here?"

Kit looked up at Jaz's calm, intelligent face and answered truthfully, "I really don't know."

13

"What's the damage?" Wisecroft asked Lance.

"Sensors indicate that the central chamber is completely compromised. But the perimeter tunnel between us and the hab is still open."

Wisecroft turned to his head of nuclear physics, Francis Leibman, who was continuing to monitor the escalating fusion reaction. "How long until it blows, Frank?" he asked.

"It's accelerating faster than I expected. At this rate, we've got about 70 minutes until it goes critical."

Wisecroft leaned over Gates' desk and punched a comm button. "Martinez, do you read me?"

"Yep."

"How many people have you got there?"

"We've got 158 survivors here in the caff."

"Is that all? Are you sure?"

"Yep. Counted them twice. There were a lot of civvies in the casino and in the observatory when the bombs went off. I gotta tell you, there are some very frightened people in front of me right now."

"We can't do anything about their feelings right now; we've got to focus on getting them all safely out of there. I need you to bring them all through to the research facility, as fast as you can. We're going to use Genesis to evacuate everyone now. The tunnel through to here is intact and the airlock doors to the facility are open. We'll have personnel on this side take everyone through to Genesis. Make it fast, Martinez. We don't have much time."

"Roger."

Wisecroft said to Gates, "Michael, patch me through to George." A moment later he had his security chief on the line. "George, how's the search on board Genesis going?"

"Nothing yet. But we're looking for a needle in a haystack here. Genesis is 700 metres long and 150 metres wide, and I've only got a handful of people searching. We're checking all the obvious places, using EM and radiation detectors. Engineering are checking life support and drive systems, but nothing has shown up yet."

"OK. Keep looking."

Wisecroft ran his hand through his hair and turned to Lance, his control room coordinator. "It doesn't make sense. I can't believe they would sabotage the base but leave Genesis untouched."

"Maybe it's just the base they wanted to destroy," answered Lance.

"No," said Wisecroft. "I don't believe that. Genesis represents everything the Caliphate stands against. They believe that Earth is humanity's only home and that it is an affront to Allah to try to leave it. A starship capable of travelling to another solar system and colonising another planet is anathema to them. They would do everything in their power to neutralise Genesis."

Michael Gates spoke up, "Um ... guys, I think I might know how they're going to try to do that."

"How?" asked Lance.

"I'm tracking the trajectory of the two inbound shuttles. They should be slowing their descent by now, but instead they are both accelerating towards the base. The computer projects that the point of impact will be directly over the Genesis chamber."

"How long till impact?" asked Wisecroft.

"Less than a minute."

"Warn everyone in the chamber to take cover - get inside Genesis if they can!" said Wisecroft.

As Gates communicated the warning to those in the chamber, Wisecroft spoke to Lance.

"Will the shuttles be able to penetrate?"

"Depends where they hit. The cavern is over a kilometre long. At this end it is 300 metres below ground level, but where it exits in the side of the crater, the cavern roof is only 150 metres thick. My guess is that even at that point, the roof could take a single hit and remain intact. But two shuttles impacting the exact same spot, one after the other, could bring the roof down and block the exit."

"That must be their plan," said Wisecroft.

Gates had barely finished issuing the warning before they heard and felt the first impact, followed about ten seconds later by the second. The ground shook beneath their feet and a few items fell off desks and consoles, but the explosions were not as severe as the previous detonations the base had experienced.

"That's two less terrorists using up our oxygen," muttered Gates.

A moment later the comm channel came to life. "Hey! Does someone wanna tell me what the hell that was!"

Gates turned to the others and said, "It's Grizzle, the chamber supervisor. I guess that means the chamber's still intact." Gus Grizole, who had always made a point of emphasising the pronunciation, Griz-o-ley, was, at 68, the oldest person on the base. He had no formal qualifications and had the sunny disposition of a piece of sandpaper, but he had been on the base for 50 years and had earned the respect of everyone.

"Hey! Are any of you eggheads even listening up there? Or are you all on your latté break?"

"Hi, Grizzle. Nice to hear your cheerful voice," said Lance.

"Don't soft-soap me, boy. I just had a rock the size of a dinner plate miss me by a cat's whisker. Wanna tell me what just happened, or is that above my pay grade?"

"Caliphate terrorists just tried to crash two shuttles through to the chamber."

"Oh, is that all?" said Grizzle facetiously. "I thought it might have been something serious."

"Gus, this is Simon Wisecroft. Is there any damage down there?"

"Nothing serious, boss. A few rocks peeled off the ceiling. One of the crew has a bruised shin and won't be doing any more work today. But the lazy bugger wouldn't know a hard day's work if it leapt up and bit him on the bum anyway."

"Gus, we're going to start evacuating the civilians and all remaining staff onto Genesis," said Wisecroft. "I need you to get them on board as quickly as possible. We have less than an hour to get clear of the base before it blows."

"Righto. I'll get it done." Grizzle obviously forgot to mute his comm connection, because as he walked away, he could be heard muttering, "Great! Just what I need - a ship-load of spoilt tourists!"

Wisecroft turned to his comm chief. "Michael, contact aquaponics and engineering and update them on our time-frame. Hurry them along. Tell them their areas need to be completely evacuated in 40 minutes. Lance, make the same public announcement over the comm in this facility." Turning around, his eyes roved around the control room and a frown appeared on his forehead. "Where is Dr Perryman?"

The others turned around and looked.

Zac was gone.

14

K it and one of the security personnel were leading a procession of civilians through the tunnel towards the research facility. Martinez's previous reference to herding cats wasn't far off the mark. The tunnel was only 500 metres, but the combination of low gravity, lack of fitness and generalised panic was turning the evacuation into a shambolic mess. There were two security personnel somewhere in the middle of the exodus and two more at the rear. Martinez and one other security team member were doing a final sweep of the hab zone to make sure no one had been left behind. Kit had introduced herself to the beefy security guy walking with her, but he had merely grunted at her, refusing to be drawn into conversation, so she had decided to call him Grunter.

Kit had heard from Martinez what had happened to the shuttle, and she was struggling to process the information. Bane had seemed a well-balanced, if somewhat introspective person. Certainly not your stereotypical terrorist. *How had he and the others managed to maintain a façade for so long? Some of them must have lived false lives for years, gaining degrees, getting married, building careers they knew they would one day throw away. What sort of person does that? What sort of person is willing to throw away everything they have lived for, everyone they have befriended and loved, even their very lives? And what about all the people they have left behind? Colleagues, family, lovers and partners - all of whom have been betrayed and used.*

"Hi!"

Kit had been daydreaming as she walked along and had not noticed him until she almost bumped into him. The guy in the Hawaiian shirt was standing in front of her with a goofy grin and a glazed look in his eyes.

"Hey, I know you!" he said. "You're the pilot who almost made me puke," he said. with an even more idiotic smile. He leant forward and whispered, "But I didn't. I swallowed it back down." He seemed to think that this was something to be immensely proud of. *Either this guy's on something or he's a couple of sandwiches short of a picnic,* Kit thought to herself.

Grunter said, "You're going the wrong way, buddy. You need to turn around and come with us."

"No thanks. I'm going for a swim."

Just then, Grunter's personal comm, attached to his lapel, came to life. "Attention, all security teams. This is Dr Simon Wisecroft. We have a missing person, Dr Zac Perryman. He's wearing jeans and a Hawaiian shirt. He can't have gone far. If anyone locates him, please escort him back to the control room. He is medicated and may be acting strangely."

Zac leant forward and yelled into Grunter's lapel, "Hi Simon! It's me! Zac! I'm going for a swim!"

Grunter said, "Got him, Dr Wisecroft. He's with the civvies. We're just about to enter the research facility now."

"Good. In that case, please take the good doctor straight through with the other civilians and get him on board Genesis. I'll send Dr Leibman down to the cavern to give him a sedative. I think that might be best for all concerned."

"I'm not concerned," said Zac, smiling at no one in particular. He reached out and squeezed Grunter's enormous bicep. "Hey, dude! Those are some serious weapons you've got there!" To Kit, he whispered, "I bet he eats like a horse."

Grunter gently swung him around and propelled him forward. "Let's all go for a swim together, Dr Perryman. Just come along with us."

As they walked into the research facility, Kit turned to Grunter and asked, "What's Genesis? Some kind of shuttle?"

Grunter raised his eyebrows and said, "It's a tad bigger than that. You'll see."

They walked through the long central corridor of the research facility, noticing the frenzied activity as white lab-coated scientists and technicians stripped the labs of essential equipment and bustled down the hallway ahead of them with arms fully laden. They turned left at a T-junction and then right into another corridor that ended with an enormous airlock door, which stood wide open. Crossing the threshold, they found themselves in a large vestibule, with two lifts on the left and a large descending set of stairs on the right. Grunter turned and addressed the line of people behind him. "OK, folks, this is where we go down. The lifts are being used by the research staff to evacuate important equipment, so unless you are physically compromised in some way, we're taking the stairs. We're going down about 100 metres, so there are a lot of steps. Please be careful, but don't dawdle. We are in a bit of a hurry."

"Is this the way to the pool?" Zac asked Kit as they started to descend.

"Yes, I think so," she answered, suppressing a smile.

Kit wasn't sure what she was expecting, but whatever it was, she was not prepared for the sight that met her eyes when she emerged at the bottom of the stairs. She found herself on a smooth, concrete-like concourse inside an enormous cavern.

"Wow!" exclaimed Kit.

"Where's the pool?" asked Zac.

The cavern was a naturally formed ancient lava chamber, roughly cylindrical in shape, except for a perfectly flat, man-made floor. Kit found it hard to accurately gauge the dimensions but guessed it must be about 300 metres in diameter and about a kilometre in length. While the cavern was impressive, Genesis was enigmatic. Lying along the middle of the cavern was a huge, black, shiny brick. At least, that is what it looked like to Kit. It appeared to be longer than a football field and at least six stories high. No wings. No portholes. No radar dishes or antennae. Just a massive, black, squat brick, with four huge engine nozzles protruding from the rear. The rest of the brick looked featureless except for a series of loading bays that were open along the side, at its base. The doors to the bays, each about 30 metres wide and 5 metres high, had swung down to form ramps. Alongside each of the loading bay doors was a closed shuttle bay door, about 20 metres wide. Dozens of people were scurrying in and out of the spacecraft via the loading bay ramps, carrying boxes and equipment. Robo-loaders were transporting the larger items into the bays, and they raced backwards and forwards across the tarmac at dangerously high speeds.

A man in blue DANSA overalls addressed the growing file of people exiting the stairwell. "Keep moving folks. Follow Daniel here," he said, indicating another staff member. "You're heading towards the furthest loading bay. Please be careful going up the ramp. Once you are inside the bay, make your way to the lifts about 80 metres in, on your right. You will be going up to the lounge deck, on Level 5."

Some people began moving in the direction indicated, but some remained where they were, overawed by the immensity of the cavern. Kit stared at the spacecraft, trying to make sense of it.

"Don't stand there gawking!" said a gruff voice off to the side. "Keep moving! This isn't a damn Sunday School picnic!"

Kit turned and saw the origin of the voice, a wiry, grey-haired old man with a stubbled beard and a scowl on his face. He was wearing official DANSA overalls and had a lapel comm. Kit read his name tag: Gus Grizole.

"We're not going to the picnic, thanks," said Zac. "We're just looking for the swimming pool."

"The what?" answered Grizzle, with a bemused expression.

"The swimming pool," repeated Zac, smiling contentedly. "But I haven't brought a towel. Will I be able to borrow one?"

"Pickle my grandmother!" muttered Grizzle, shaking his head.

Kit leaned over and whispered, "He's on medication, apparently."

At that moment, Francis Leibman arrived and gently took hold of Zac's arm. "Hello, Dr Perryman. Do you remember me from earlier? I'm Dr Leibman. We have your cabin ready for you, if you will allow me to show you."

"Is it near the swimming pool?" asked Zac.

"Yes, of course," answered Leibman, as he led Zac towards the spacecraft.

Still shaking his head, Grizzle asked Kit, "Is he your boyfriend, miss?"

"Goodness, no!" she exclaimed. "I barely know him."

"Well that's something to be thankful for. That boy's so high, he's in orbit."

"Is there anything I can do to help, Mr Grisole?" Kit asked.

"Call me Grizzle, miss, everyone else does." He seemed to notice her flight suit and name badge for the first time. "You a pilot?"

"Yeh. But I can drive a forklift, and I can remote a robo-loader if you need help."

At that moment the ground shook, and a deep rumbling was heard for several seconds. Some of the civilians looked around in panic, but a nearby DANSA employee calmed the crowd, saying, "Nothing to worry about, folks. Just a tremor. Keep moving please."

Kit, however, wasn't convinced that all was well. As the exodus of people filed past her, she said to Grizzle, "That didn't sound good."

15

As the control room shook, Wisecroft said, "Now what?!"

Arno Manchester, who was continuing to monitor the fusion reactor meltdown, said, "It's not the reactor."

"It didn't sound like a detonation," said Lance. "More like some kind of tremor."

As they continued to check various sensors, the comm came to life. "Control, this is Dupont on the security team. Do you copy?"

"Yes, Dupont," answered Lance. "Go ahead."

"The tunnel from the hab has just collapsed. I am at the tail end of the evacuee line and we were just entering the research facility when we heard the collapse. I went back to investigate. The tunnel has completely collapsed about 50 metres back."

"Are any of the evacuees injured?"

"No, not from the collapse. We were well past that point when it happened. But Martinez and Boyd are still back in the hab. They were doing a final sweep."

"Copy that," answered Lance. "They'll have to go down a level to aquaponics and use the tunnel through to engineering.

We'll handle it from here. You just get the evacuees onto Genesis as quickly as you can."

Lance turned to Michael Gates, "Patch me through to Martinez." He paused until he got the thumbs-up. "Martinez, this is Lance in control. Do you copy?"

There was a pause, and then Martinez's voice came online, shaky and breathless, "Yeh. Gotcha."

"Martinez, the tunnel through to ..."

"Yeh, yeh. We know. We were just about to come through. A few seconds later and we would have been flattened. We've gone down a level and we're running through aquaponics as we speak. The place is deserted. You did a good job evacuating here. Hold on a sec, we're just entering the tunnel through to engineering." There was silence for a few seconds and then, "Um. Lance? We've got a bit of a problem."

"What?"

"The tunnel has collapsed here, too."

"Is there any possible way through?"

"Yeh, no problem," said Martinez. "We can dig it out with our fingernails. It will only take a month or so."

"Hang on a moment," said Lance. "We'll work the problem from this end. I'll get back to you shortly." He muted the channel and swore loudly.

Arno Manchester, head of nuclear physics was looking at his terminal screen. "I'm checking the sensor readouts for the central chamber where the shuttle crashed. The whole roof structure collapsed in that last tremor. There must have been a natural fault running through to the Level 1 tunnel, which caused it to collapse in sympathy. The Level 2 tunnel was probably already weakened by the explosions on that level, and this was probably the last straw."

Wisecroft spoke up. "So, just to clarify, the entire tunnel system is gone on both levels?"

"Yep," answered Lance in a whisper.

"And there's no other way out of there?"

"That's right."

"Arno, how long until the reactor blows?"

"It's escalating linearly now, so I can predict fairly accurately. We have about 25 minutes left until the core goes critical."

"In that case," said Wisecroft, "we need to be out of here in 10 minutes. We can't do anything for Martinez and Boyd now." He spoke to Gates. "Give me a base-wide open comm." He took a breath. "Attention all personnel. This is Simon Wisecroft. We have 25 minutes until the reactor goes critical. In exactly 10 minutes from now, we are sealing the doors on Genesis and launching. If you are not on board by then, you will be left behind. Do not attempt to access any other parts of the base, as the tunnel system on both levels has now completely collapsed. Please make your way to Genesis now, with all urgency. That is all."

There was silence in the control room. Gates spoke up. "Martinez and Boyd would have heard that."

"Yes. I know," said Wisecroft. "They also know that there is nothing we can do for them now." He turned to the others in the control room. "Gentlemen, it's time we evacuated. There's nothing left for us to do here."

As he spoke, a comm channel came to life. "Hello? Control? Any of you eggheads still up there?"

"Go ahead, Grizzle," said Wisecroft.

"Dupont just came through with the last of the evacuees. He said that Martinez and Boyd are trapped in the hab. Is that right?"

"Yes. There's nothing we can do."

"Well, there's a young girly down here who disagrees. She's driving a bug tug into the main airlock lift as we speak. Once she gets to the surface, she's going to drive around to the airlock lift for the hab and meet them there."

"Gus," said Lance, interrupting, "when she gets there, the bug tug won't fit in the hab airlock lift. That lift is only designed for a few people. And Martinez and Boyd don't have spacesuits. How can they get from the airlock into the bug tug?"

"Kit said you'd say that. But she's figured out a way. The bug tugs all have two emergency vacuum suits. She's taken one on board for herself as well. She'll take the two spare suits with her into the hab lift for the others."

"It might just work," said Lance to Wisecroft.

"Maybe. But we are launching in exactly nine minutes, and I'm not waiting for anyone. I can't risk the safety of hundreds of people for the sake of three."

"OK, Gus," said Lance. "We'll inform Martinez."

He punched a comm button. "Martinez? Do you copy?"

"Yeh. We heard Dr. Wisecroft's announcement. We're just discussing how we'll spend the last 25 minutes of our lives. It's either ice cream or sex. And I'm looking at Boyd right now, and, I gotta tell you, the ice cream option is looking very appealing."

"You might have to put those plans on hold. We need you to get to the hab airlock lift as soon as you can. I mean right now! Run! I'll explain as you go."

16

K it floored the pedal on the bug tug as the outer door of the lift opened, and it leapt forward onto the lunar surface. She turned sharply to the right, sending up a fine spray of regolith from her wheels. She had the accelerator pressed to the floor and was already at the vehicle's top speed. With almost a kilometre to the hab lift, Kit knew it would be close as to whether they made it back in time for the launch. Every ounce of her being was willing the vehicle forward, and she found that she was leaning forward in her seat as if to urge it on. As she drove, she stuffed the two spare folded emergency vacuum suits down inside the front of her own suit and zipped her front zipper up to her neck. The timing was going to be tight. She ran the numbers again in her head. Nearly two minutes to pressurise the hab lift and descend. One minute for Martinez and Boyd to zip themselves into the suits. Another two minutes for the lift to ascend and depressurise. Five minutes total, and the countdown timer on the cabin clock indicated seven minutes left until lift-off.

As she drew near to the square surface lift structure, she pulled the clear head piece up over her head from behind her and finished zipping up the one-piece clear suit. She punched the depressurisation button when she was still 100 metres out from the lift so that the cabin would be completely depressurised when she got there. As she arrived at the lift, she swung the wheel hard and braked, executing a finely judged sliding stop, spraying regolith high into the air. She cracked the cabin door and leapt out onto the lunar soil, running as fast as she could to the airlock door, hampered by the tightly extended clear suit that had blown up like a balloon around her. There was enough air trapped in the suit for several minutes, but she wouldn't need that long.

The airlock was already depressurised, and the door was already open. The last person to use it had obviously exited rather than entered the hab. She initiated pressurisation, and as soon as the green light blinked on, she hit the descend button and unzipped herself, removing the two spare suits from inside the trouser legs in her suit where they had fallen when her suit had expanded.

The lift stopped descending and the door opened, revealing Martinez and Boyd standing there. "What took you so long, Supergirl? You had me worried. I thought I was going to have to settle for having sex with Boyd."

"Here," Kit said, throwing the emergency suits to them. "Get in and zip these up as we ascend." She punched the button as they got in, and the doors closed. As the lift ascended, she said, "There are only two seats in the vehicle, so Martinez, you're going to have to sit on Boyd's lap."

Martinez turned to Boyd. "Listen to me very carefully, soldier," she said, fixing him with her steely dark eyes. "I'm not an officer, so I don't want anything standing to attention, if you get my meaning!"

"Yes, ma'am!" he said with mock severity. "I wouldn't dream of it."

"Actually, I think you *do* dream of it, Boyd, that's the problem. Let me be clear, if I feel any movement at all among the lower ranks you'll be marching with a limp for a week!"

The lift stopped as they finished zipping their suits closed, and Kit punched the decompression button. The air was pumped from the lift with painful slowness, but finally the light on the outer door turned from red to green, and Kit unlocked the door and thrust it open. The bug tug was parked only three metres away, but even so it was a slow three metres. The low gravity was awkward, and their suits had expanded so that movement was limited. Breathing was also difficult in the very low pressure that existed within the fully expanded suits. Boyd clambered into the passenger seat fairly easily, but Martinez was having difficulty squeezing through on top of him.

"Damn it!" she exclaimed, after a second failed attempt. "With these suits fully expanded, I can't fit in." Unfortunately, Kit couldn't hear her, because she didn't have a lapel comm, but she could see Martinez's problem. Precious seconds were ticking by, and Kit, who was by now sitting in the driver's seat with her own door closed, realised they would have to come up with a solution fast. She leaned over to Boyd and touched the head of her suit to Boyd's, so that he could hear her. She shouted, "You're gonna have to let some air out of your suit. You'll need to take a breath, but not too deep, or your lungs will burst with the decompression. Then crack the seal on your suit for a split-second and seal it straight up again. You and Martinez have lapel comms. Tell her what you're going to do. When she sees you crack the seal, she needs to dive head-first across your lap. I'll pull her across to me, so that she is lying face-down across both our laps. As soon as she's in, I'll close your door remotely from my controls. Got it?"

Boyd pulled away from her and nodded. He chinned his comm and Kit could see his lips moving as he communicated with Martinez, who then nodded. Martinez backed up a step and readied herself for the dive. A moment later, Boyd cracked the seal on his suit and resealed it almost instantly. His suit almost completely deflated in a decompressive explosion and Kit worried that he had let too much air out. There was no time to think about that, however, as Martinez came sliding across Boyd's lap. Kit grabbed her outstretched arms and pulled her all the way across and quickly hit the door-close button. She punched the button to re-pressurise the cabin but didn't wait for full pressurisation before reaching across to Boyd. He was out cold, and there was a small trail of blood trickling out of his ears. Kit unzipped his suit head and then unzipped her own. Martinez was also unzipping, and Kit said, "You need to help Boyd. He lost too much pressure. There's an oxygen mask in the emergency kit behind him. I need to drive."

Kit fired up the vehicle and spun the wheels as she took off at top speed. She glanced at the countdown clock on the console. Ninety seconds to go. They weren't going to make it. She activated an open channel on the comm. "This is Kit Tyler, to Genesis. Can you hear me."

"We hear you, Kit. This is Lance Catrell, on Genesis bridge. How are you going?"

"I've got them! We're on our way back now. Wait for us! I think we're going to be a little late."

"How late?"

"Two minutes to drive this snail back to the airlock, a minute to pressurise the lift, about 30 seconds to descend and about 45 seconds to drive across the tarmac and up the ramp into a Genesis loading bay."

"That should be OK ..." began Lance, but he was cut off by another voice.

"Ms Tyler, this is Dr Wisecroft. I'm sorry, but I am not prepared to compromise the safety of the entire ship and hundreds of lives. The launch time is non-negotiable, and we can't afford to wait beyond it. In exactly one minute we will be closing the last loading bay door and launching. If you can't make it back, I suggest you turn your vehicle now and head for the depression that lies five clicks north. You may be able to shelter from the worst of the blast there."

Martinez looked at Kit and said, "Boyd is in a bad way. He needs medical treatment or he's not gonna make it."

Kit said to her, "OK. We're going to have to call their bluff." She activated the comm again. "Hello Genesis? Does anyone read me? Your transmission just cut out. I think the receiver was damaged in one of the explosions. If you can hear me, I've got Boyd and Martinez, and we're heading back now. Boyd is injured and needs urgent medical treatment. We will be about three minutes late."

Wisecroft came on the air again. "This is Dr Wisecroft on board Genesis. Turn your vehicle and head for the hills immediately. Get to safety. We cannot wait for you. Repeat. We will not wait for you. We will begin launch sequence in 30 seconds."

"He's a callous bastard!" said Martinez.

"Yes," said Kit. "But I'm broadcasting on an open channel and he knows that everyone is listening in. If he launches without us, he's gonna lose a lot of love. All I can do is keep calling his bluff." She opened the channel again. "Kit Tyler calling Genesis. I'm still not receiving any transmission from you. If you can hear me, please wait for us. I am on my way back with Martinez and Boyd, and we need to get Boyd to the infirmary ASAP. I can see the Genesis airlock, and we should be driving into the lift in about 40 seconds."

The countdown clock on the dashboard ticked over to zero, and as it did, Wisecroft's voice came over the comm again. "Time's up, Ms Tyler. I believe you can hear me. We are closing the loading bay door now. I'm sorry. Please head towards safety now. We may be able to pick you up later, depending on our orbit. Good luck. Over and out."

"Hell!" said Martinez. "I don't think he's bluffing. Maybe we should head north?"

"No, that's not an option," said Kit. "The O_2 level is indicating one hour of breathable air remaining. There is no way a shuttle will be able to get back to us in that time. If we head north, we will die of asphyxiation. I'd rather take my chances and get blown to bits. Besides, Boyd isn't going to last another hour, anyway."

She keyed the comm channel open again. "This is Kit Tyler again. Still not receiving any transmission from you, Genesis. We are running out of oxygen and have an injured person on board. Please wait for us. I repeat, please wait for us."

She had rolled the dice. Now all she could do was hope and pray.

17

On the bridge, Simon Wisecroft turned to Lance and said, "Instruct the loading bay staff to close the last door." Turning to the flight deck, he said, "Captain Christensen, you have the ship now. Initiate the launch sequence."

Lance looked shocked and said, "But Dr Wisecroft, they're only three minutes away."

"Damn it, Catrell!" said Wisecroft. He strode over to the comm desk and punched a button. "Bridge to loading bay. Grizzle, do you copy?"

"Yes, boss."

"Good. Close the loading bay door immediately."

"OK, boss."

Wisecroft turned to Lars Christensen, a classic blonde-bearded Swede, complete with Captain's cap and white shirt with epaulettes. "Take her out, Captain."

Christensen replied, "Aye. Just as soon as that door is closed."

They all sat waiting for the one remaining red light on the console to turn green. And they waited. And still they waited.

"Grizzle! What's the delay getting that door closed?"

"I'm just closing it now, boss."

They waited. And waited some more. The light stayed red.

"Grizzle!! What the hell is going on down there? Why isn't that door closed?"

"Boss, I'm pushing the button, but it ain't closing. I think there might be a faulty switch on the console here."

"Damn it!" yelled Wisecroft. Turning to Christensen he said, "Can you override it from up here, Captain?"

"Yes, I can. If you're sure that's what you really want," Christensen replied, with a raised eyebrow.

"Of course I'm sure!!" exploded Wisecroft, beginning to turn apoplectic. "Close it now and get us out of here!"

The captain flicked a switch and a red light began flashing, accompanied by a soft buzzing alarm. "It seems we have a problem, Dr Wisecroft. The sensors indicate that there is something on the threshold of the doorway. The door has a built-in safety system. The door mechanism won't operate until the doorway is completely clear."

Wisecroft was now turning slightly purple with rage. He punched the comm button violently. "Grizzle!!!"

"Yes boss," came the lazy reply.

"There's something blocking the doorway. It won't close. Can you see anything?"

"Let me see. I'm looking ... I'm looking ... No. All clear, boss."

"Grizzle! I swear, if you are playing games here, I'll ... I'll ..."

"Yes, boss?"

"Aaagh!" Wisecroft let out a roar of frustration and thumped his fist on the edge of the console.

"Lance!" he yelled. "Get down there immediately and fix the problem! And I mean immediately!"

Lance jumped up from his chair and ran into the lift. Thirty seconds later, he emerged four floors down and ran to the open loading bay door. There was a box placed precisely across the threshold of the loading bay door, and Grizzle was sitting contentedly on top of it, with one leg crossed over the other, smoking a pipe.

"Grizzle! What the hell are you doing?!"

"The right thing," he answered, taking a puff from a pipe.

"Move that box now! That's an order!"

"Or what?" Grizzle pointed to some of the other loading bay workers, who were standing around watching the scene unfold. "Are you gonna beat up an old man in front of these people?"

"You're gonna get us all killed, Grizzle!"

"Stop wetting your pants and show some backbone, boy," replied Grizzle. "We'll still have a good six or seven minutes to get clear, and Wisecroft knows it. He's just worried about one thing - saving his own skin. Me? I'd rather die as a humanitarian than live as a coward." He looked steadily at Lance. "What about you?"

The comm burst to life. "Lance? What's happening?"

Lance and Grizzle stared at each other in silence.

"Lance? Do you copy? Answer, damn it!"

Lance stared at Grizzle for a moment longer and then activated his lapel comm. "Dr. Wisecroft, there appears to be a fault with the sensors and the console. I've got one of the tech guys looking at it as we speak. He's found the problem, and he says it will only take him a minute or so to fix it."

There was no response from Wisecroft, but Lance could imagine him throwing something across the bridge and screaming. Lance walked across to the box and sat next to Grizzle. "Do you smoke?" asked Grizzle, offering him the pipe.

"If Wisecroft saw you smoking that, you'd get the sack," said Lance.

Grizzle merely shrugged.

"Besides, it's a disgusting habit," said Lance, taking it and having a puff. He handed it back to Grizzle.

"It's good, isn't it?" asked Grizzle.

"The pipe?"

"No. Doing the right thing."

"Yes, it is," answered Lance. "Here, give me another puff."

A mild alarm sounded in the distance, and a yellow light could be seen flashing at the far side of the concourse about 400 metres away, near the rear of the spacecraft. "Here they come," said Grizzle. "You can tell your boss he can get ready to launch, once he's finished changing his diaper."

The large lift door on the far side of the cavern opened and the bug tug came roaring out of it, still shedding regolith dust from the surface. Lance was talking to Wisecroft, telling him that the technicians had repaired the faulty console and were about to close the door. Grizzle moved the box to the side and stood straddling the threshold, waving his arms in the air to beckon Kit towards the ramp. The bug tug roared up the concourse, turning at the last moment, and came flying up the ramp. Lance activated the door-closing mechanism as the vehicle screeched to a stop inside the huge loading bay. Kit and Martinez jumped out of the vehicle simultaneously and Martinez said, "We need help here! Get a medic!"

Two medics came forward; one of them was Jaz, from the cafeteria, the other a young medical officer attached to the Genesis crew. "That was quick," said Kit, as several strong hands lifted Boyd down from the cabin.

"We've been waiting for about three minutes," answered Jaz. "Grizzle called us down here as soon as you started transmitting."

Kit looked at Grizzle, who was standing over Boyd. "Thanks, Grizzle. We owe you one."

"You owe him more than one," said another loading bay worker. "We would have launched minutes ago if Grizzle hadn't defied orders and refused to close the door."

"How is the lad?" asked Grizzle, clearly uncomfortable with being the centre of attention.

"He's unconscious but stable," replied the white-coated

doctor. His name tag read, 'Dr Ben Miller', and he didn't look to be all that long out of med school. "Let's get him on the gurney and get him to sick bay." As they lifted Boyd onto the gurney and wheeled him away, Martinez started to follow, but Ben said, "Just leave him with us, if you don't mind. Things are a bit chaotic at the moment. I'll send for you when he can have visitors."

Kit looked around at the loading bay. It was rectangular in shape, approximately 50 metres deep and 30 metres wide. The left 50-metre-long wall had a bank of lifts and a series of small office-like cubicles built into it. The right wall bore the words 'Shuttle Bay 1' printed in large letters and had an airlock door leading into the adjoining shuttle bay. At the rear of the loading bay was what appeared to be a maintenance and storage area. She guessed that there would be an identical loading bay and shuttle bay on the opposite side of the ship. And there were a further four of these back down the length of the ship on either side. It was all very impressive.

"Hey, why aren't we moving?" she asked.

Lance Catrell was walking past, on his way to the lifts, and stopped to answer her question. "We are. In fact, by now, we will have launched. This ship has state-of-the-art artificial gravity and inertial dampening systems. It's designed so that as soon as that door closes, the cavern's emergency air evacuation valves explosively depressurise the cavern. The massive airlock doors at the cavern entrance open and the mag-lev system built into the floor of the cavern is activated, lifting us off the ground. At the same time our main propulsion drive fires up, accelerating us towards the entrance at approximately 8Gs. What that means is, about 30 seconds after we closed this loading bay door, we shot out of the cavern at an angle of 22 degrees, travelling at a velocity of 80 metres per second. Am I boring you yet?"

"No! Please go on."

"The cavern entrance is located halfway down the cliff,

inside a crater nearly two kilometres deep. As we shot out of the exit, the ship's maneuvering thrusters began adjusting our angle of ascent, swinging us around until our main drive nozzles were pointing straight down. This flying brick is currently standing on its end, accelerating away from the moon. You and I are now standing on the side of the ship, at 90 degrees to our direction of flight and to the surface of the moon."

"Very cool!" said Kit.

Martinez, however, wasn't listening. She was looking towards the bank of lifts where Boyd had been taken, with a deeply worried expression on her face.

18

Zac woke up with a splitting headache. He swung his feet over the edge of the bed and sat up.

"Windows clear," he said, staring at the blank wall. Nothing happened. "Windows clear," he repeated. Still nothing. "Angie?" he said. No answer.

He blinked the bleariness from his eyes and looked around the room, noticing the unfamiliar surroundings for the first time. *Where am I?* It was a much smaller room than his bedroom. In fact, it was just a cubicle, barely big enough to contain the single bed he was sitting on. He sifted through his sleep-fogged memory and began to piece together snippets of memory. He recalled being whisked off to the moon by a bald-headed security dude. George. Yes! That was his name. He remembered being in Simon Wisecroft's office and being quizzed about his wife's disappearance. His wife was missing! Simon was accusing her of being some sort of terrorist. *And he thinks I am a terrorist too!* Fresh indignation welled up within him. He would go and give Wisecroft a piece of his mind!

He looked around his cubicle again. *Where am I, and how did*

I get here? The last thing he remembered was being in Wise-croft's office. *I must be somewhere on the base,* he thought.

The door opened, and a middle-aged man in a white lab coat walked in, holding some kind of electronic tablet. "Ah, Dr Perryman. Our monitors indicated that you had woken up. How are you feeling?"

"I've got a headache and I'm thirsty. If I didn't know any better, I'd say I had a hangover. Where am I?"

"First things first," he replied. "Let's get you optimal, and then we can answer your questions." He looked at the screen on his tablet. "Your biochip readings indicate that you are mildly dehydrated, but apart from that you seem in good shape. Blood pressure, heart rate and O_2 saturation are all nominal. In fact, they are better than nominal. You seem to be in very good shape."

"I keep fit. Where am I? And who are you?"

"I am Dr Francis Leibman. Do you remember me?"

"No. Should I?"

"No. I didn't expect that you would. Here, drink this," said Leibman, taking a small, clear plastic bottle from his lab-coat pocket and handing it to Zac. "It is an ultra-fast rehydration formula with a mild pain suppressor. You will feel better almost instantly."

Zac didn't need convincing. He unscrewed the top and downed the fluid in a series of thirsty gulps. Licking his lips, he said, "You still haven't answered my question. What is this place? And how did I get here?"

"As to the first question, you are on board Genesis, a DANSA starship, currently in orbit around the moon. You were brought on board less than two hours ago and were given a fast-acting sedative with an extremely short half-life. There should be no residual sedative left in your system by now. As to how you got here, the answer is a little compli-cated. Dr Wisecroft has requested that he speak with you as soon as you feel up to it. I think he can best answer your questions."

"A starship? Why? What are we doing here? And why did I need to be given a sedative?"

"As I say," replied Leibman, "I think Dr Wisecroft is best able to answer those questions. Are you happy to meet with him now?"

"Sure. Let's go. Wisecroft has got some explaining to do!" Zac got to his feet and stretched, feeling considerably better already.

Leibman glanced furtively at Zac and said, "Would you like us to provide you with some more suitable clothing, Dr Perryman? Perhaps a jumpsuit, or at least some more practical trousers and shirt?"

Zac glanced down at his holed jeans and Hawaiian shirt. "Why? What's wrong with what I'm wearing? Dude, these retro-threads cost me a small fortune!"

"As you wish," replied Leibman, with arched eyebrows. "I'm sure they are the height of fashion somewhere. Please follow me."

Walking out of the cubicle, Zac found himself in a well-equipped medical unit: a long, wide corridor that had treatment cubicles to the left and various medical stations to the right, in a similar generic layout to most hospitals worldwide. Leibman and Zac turned right into a short corridor, ending in a series of lifts, one of which was already open. As they entered, Leibman held his wrist under the biochip scanner and said, "Bridge." The doors closed, and a few moments later, with no sensation of movement, they opened again onto a completely different scene.

A short corridor from the lift opened onto an expansive bridge that extended 50 metres to left and right. The front wall comprised a large central screen with a series of smaller screens to each side. Some showed external views, while others displayed visual readouts of various systems. The central screen displayed a stunning view facing forward of the ship, with a partial view of the moon to the right of the screen and the star-speckled blackness of space to the left.

"Ah, Dr Perryman," said Wisecroft. "It's good to see you up and about. As you can see, we are in stable orbit around the moon at the moment. It's quite a view, isn't it?" Wisecroft was sitting at a console in a long line of consoles, staffed by crew in official-looking uniforms. "You're feeling better, I hope?"

Zac stared ahead, taking in the view and trying to process his surroundings. "Considering I have no memory of how I got here, I guess I'm doing OK," he replied.

"As to that," said Wisecroft, "it may be better if we adjourn to the conference room."

He led Zac to a room opening off the back of the bridge, furnished with a rectangular table and twelve chairs. "Please, take a seat," said Wisecroft, indicating a chair to his left as he seated himself at the head of the table.

"No, I'd rather stand, thank you," replied Zac. "The last thing I remember is you interrogating me, accusing my wife and I of being terrorists. Where is Annisa? Have you found her?"

"Dr Perryman, quite a lot has happened in the last few hours. The base was attacked by terrorists. Three bombs were detonated, and three shuttles were hijacked and used as missiles to create further destruction."

"What? Why don't I remember this? Where was I?"

"I apologise, Dr Perryman. We thought you might have been involved, and we needed information urgently. We gave you a harmless but very effective drug - a truth serum. The drug is also a powerful amnesiac, which explains why you have no memory of the events immediately before and afterwards."

"You drugged me?!"

"We were in the midst of a crisis and we were short of time. We quickly discovered that you knew nothing."

"Of course I didn't! I remember telling you so!"

"Yes. I apologise, but we had to be sure. We were desperate to find the missing staff."

"So, where is Annisa? You can't surely still believe she's a terrorist?"

"Dr Perryman, I need to show you a video. I think it would be best if you sat down for a moment."

"What video?" Zac asked, remaining on his feet.

"I'm sorry," said Wisecroft. "There is no easy way to do this." He leaned back in his chair. "Play video," he said.

A video started playing on the far wall, with no sound. Zac watched in growing horror as he witnessed the slaying of staff in some kind of control room. As the terrorists turned towards the camera, smiling triumphantly, Zac took a step towards the screen. "Annisa!" He watched incredulously as she and her colleague stood arm in arm, fists raised in defiance, until a blinding flash brought the footage to an end. He collapsed into a chair and continued staring at the blank wall. "No ... no ... it can't be ... she would ... she would never ... she's not ..."

"I'm very sorry, Dr Perryman. Your wife apparently fooled us all. As did the others."

"She's dead?" Zac asked, tears beginning to roll down his cheeks.

"I'm sorry. Yes. As are her fellow conspirators."

Zac sat down and placed his head in his hands. Everything he thought he knew about his world, his life, now seemed uncertain. Had Annisa just used him to gain credibility? Was he just her cover? Did she ever truly love him, or was their marriage just a convenient sham? His mind was reeling. A sob escaped his lips.

"I'm sorry for your loss, Dr Perryman."

Zac was dumbfounded, unable to speak.

"The base was completely destroyed," continued Wisecroft. "The fusion reactor went critical. Hundreds of lives were lost. We barely managed to escape in time."

Zac shook his head in disbelief, as if trying to shake himself awake from a bad dream. "I think I need to be alone for a while."

"I'm sure you do," said Wisecroft. "But, firstly, you need to be aware of the full extent of what has happened."

"There's more?"

"Unfortunately, yes. The result of which, you and everyone on board are going to need to make a choice."

"What kind of choice?"

"The kind that will determine the rest of your life."

19

Z ac's mind was reeling. He had been given a temporary cabin in the crew quarters, two levels down, and for the past hour he had sat on the edge of the bed, trying to process everything that had happened. Despite the devastating, world-shattering events that Wisecroft had described to him, Zac couldn't move past his overwhelming sense of betrayal by the woman he loved and who he thought had loved him. He was overcome with a strange mixture of grief and anger. *How dare she use me like that!* He kept thinking back to their first meeting in the university student bar one Saturday night. Annisa had seemed such a vibrant, flirtatious girl, and Zac could not clearly remember who had chased whom. He just remembered feeling as though he had won the lottery when she had let him kiss her. Six months later, they were married. Several friends had commented on the speed of their whirlwind romance, but Zac had waved their concerns aside, caught up, as he was, in the euphoria of their new romance. *Was it all a sham? Did she ever truly love me? At what point was she recruited by the Caliphate?*

He scanned back through his memory, trying to find clues that would make sense of it all. His mother had never really warmed to Annisa and had even tried to talk him out of their hasty engagement. When Zac reacted angrily, his mother answered in her usual forthright manner: "I won't pretend to like her, Zac. There's something insincere about her that troubles me. Something that doesn't ring true, but I can't put my finger on it. Can't you at least put the wedding plans back another six months to give yourselves time to get to know each other?" But Zac had refused to listen, and his relationship with his mother had been strained ever since.

He continued to dredge through his memories. Were there any hints of Annisa's secret loyalties? Any signs in their brief life together that she had been keeping things from him? The only incident he could point to was about six months ago, when he walked into her office at home and she immediately shut down her comm link, terminating whatever discussion she had been having. He remembered her guilty expression, which she had quickly tried to cover with her usual vivacious teasing and joking.

"Who was that?" he had asked.

"Just one of my many old boyfriends trying to seduce me again, but I told him I wasn't interested since my husband is such a red-hot lover." Her passionate kisses soon led them to the bedroom, where whatever half-formed questions he may have had were soon forgotten.

Was I that easy to fool? he wondered. *Was she already radicalised when we met at university?* Probably. But he would never know now.

A beep sounded over the cabin comm, followed by Dr Wisecroft's smooth voice. "Ladies and gentlemen, the information meeting will take place in ten minutes. Please ensure that you are comfortably seated and can easily see a viewing screen." Wisecroft had announced, nearly an hour ago, that there would be a meeting to update everyone on their situation.

Zac was already aware of much of the information that was about to be presented, and it only added to his consternation.

In consideration of the grief that Zac was experiencing, Wisecroft had given him the option of remaining apart from the other passengers, who were all congregating in the dining and lounge decks, in Zone II. Being fully cognisant of all the facts now, Zac anticipated that there would be a lot of grief and shock among the passengers following Wisecroft's imminent broadcast, and he hadn't thought he could cope with that on top of his own personal pain. But as he sat on the bed, he suddenly felt the overwhelming need to be with others. He needed to feel connected; that he wasn't alone. He walked out of his cabin and along the corridor to the bank of lifts. Entering an open lift, he held his wrist to the scanner and said, "Dining." Wisecroft had given him clearance for a number of areas on board the ship.

A moment later the doors opened, revealing a huge open space, about 100 metres by nearly 200 metres. The space was interspersed with dozens of floor-to-ceiling columns, each housing several food and drink dispensers. Hundreds of people were seated at tables and chairs, some with bandages and various cuts and bruises. Zac found the noise overwhelming after the solitude of his cabin, and he was suddenly unsure of himself. He stood looking at the sea of people, all talking and gesticulating, and felt lonelier than he had ever felt. *I've made a mistake*, he thought. *I don't want to be here.* As he turned to re-enter the lift, he heard a voice say, "How was the pool, Doc?"

He turned around, searching for the owner of the voice. Sitting at a nearby table, against the back wall, was a young lady looking at him with a mischievous grin on her face. He scanned his memory and recognised her as the shuttle pilot who had brought him to the moon.

"The what?" he replied, perplexed.

"The pool," she said. "You were going for a swim in the pool."

"What pool?"

"Exactly."

"Um ..." he articulated, with a stunning display of vocabulary. "Er ..." he added, just in case anyone should doubt his verbal prowess.

"You look like you could use a coffee and a seat," she said. She kicked the spare seat next to her out from the table. "Come and join us. You seem like you're mostly harmless now."

"What was I before?" he asked, taking the offered seat.

"You were off the charts. You were quite amusing, actually. They could put you on the stage as a comedy act."

"Oh no," Zac said, wincing. "Please tell me I didn't do anything too embarrassing."

"Nothing X-rated, if that's what you mean. What were you on, if you don't mind me asking?"

"I don't know," he admitted. "It was something they gave me, against my will."

"They?"

"Dr Wisecroft."

"Bastard!" Kit said. "He almost killed me and two security staff. Martinez was one of them," she said, indicating the dark-haired girl with multiple facial piercings sitting beside her.

"Bastard," Martinez echoed, giving Zac her steely glare.

"Well, it seems as though we have a unanimous verdict on that issue, at least," said Zac.

"What's with the Hawaiian shirt, Doc?" asked Martinez, with a smirk. "Did you catch the wrong shuttle or something?"

"What's with the nose ring?" countered Zac. "Is that to hang your front door key on?"

Martinez turned to Kit and said, "I think I liked him better when he was high."

Kit looked at Zac and cocked her head sideways. "Nah, I like him better this way. He was a complete dork when he was high."

Zac cracked his first smile in hours, and said, "You do know that I can hear you, don't you?"

Kit said, "Did you hear anything just then, Martinez?"

"Nope. Unless you're referring to that mildly annoying buzzing."

Just then, four large screens around the perimeter of the room came to life and Wisecroft's face stared out at them.

"Here we go," said Kit. "This should be interesting. Did anyone bring popcorn?"

20

"L adies and gentlemen, thank you for your patience. I am Dr Simon Wisecroft, head of DANSA research and, at this point in time, the commanding officer of this vessel. The purpose of this communication is to provide you with a detailed, frank assessment of our current situation." He paused for a moment, as if to gather his thoughts.

"We have just undergone a significant terrorist attack. Three bombs were exploded on our moon base, and three hijacked shuttles were crashed into our facility. One of the bombs precipitated an uncontainable meltdown in our fusion reactor, which necessitated our evacuation of the base. Twenty minutes after our launch, the reactor went critical, resulting in an explosion that destroyed the entire base, creating a new crater over two kilometres wide on the surface of the moon."

Kit turned to Martinez and said, "Twenty minutes! There was plenty of time for them to wait for us!"

"Bastard," said Martinez.

"Bastard," agreed Kit.

Wisecroft adopted what he hoped was an empathetic facial expression and continued. "We have experienced significant loss of life. Many of you have lost friends, colleagues and loved ones. There were nearly 900 people living, working and visiting at Luna City. Only 328 people were successfully evacuated on board this vessel." He paused to let that information sink in.

"While we are right to grieve our loss, we are also facing issues that require our immediate attention. We are currently safe, in a stable orbit around the moon, but approximately 30 minutes after launch, security teams who were completing a search of this vessel located a large explosive device hidden near the antimatter drive. It was on a delayed timer, set to explode one hour after activation of the drive. We were unable to safely disarm the bomb, and so it was jettisoned into space, where it exploded at a safe distance from us. As far as we have been able to ascertain, there are no further threats to our safety. The terrorists responsible are all dead, and no other explosive devices have been located. We are safe—for the moment." He let those last three words hang in the air, foreshadowing what he was about to say next.

"Unfortunately, the terrorist attacks we experienced on the moon were only the tip of the iceberg. Significantly worse events have taken place on Earth. The event we have feared for centuries has come to pass. A major nuclear exchange has taken place between the Democratic Alliance of Nations and the Caliphate, with devastating results." There were gasps and shocked murmurs throughout the dining room.

Wisecroft pressed on. "Over the last few hours, we have pieced together a picture of what took place. Nearly 200 thermonuclear missiles were launched, many of them carrying up to a dozen individual warheads which separated during flight and targeted different locations or facilities. Some would have been destroyed by our laser satellite defence system, but it appears that many warheads, hundreds in fact, slipped through. Hundreds of cities and towns world-wide have been levelled." Groans and cries could be heard all over the dining room, but Wisecroft, safely ensconced on the bridge, simply ploughed on.

"All the manned space stations and most of the satellites have been destroyed. Kepler Station is gone. The Equatorial Tether Lift from Macapá has been destroyed, as has the city itself. The Earth is now covered by many hundreds of nuclear mushroom clouds. We have been able to establish a link to a minor weather satellite that remains intact, which has provided us with an image of our planet as it now appears." A view of Earth appeared on the screen: a murky ball of grey-brown cloud. Circling the Earth were hundreds of thousands of shimmering pieces of wreckage, the remains of space stations and satellites that had been destroyed. The volume of shocked, heart-broken groans and cries intensified, and Wisecroft, anticipating this from his elevated distance, allowed some time for people to absorb the terrible image on the screen.

Wisecroft's face reappeared on the screen. "Electromagnetic pulses from the explosions have wiped out communications worldwide, so we have been unable to make contact with anyone on Earth. There will certainly be survivors, but they face a bleak future. In fact, an event even worse than everything I have just described is about to unfold. The orbit of the Kepler anchor asteroid, to which the tether cable is still attached, is now deteriorating rapidly. The maneuvering thrusters attached to the asteroid are unable to halt its orbital decay. In approximately eight hours from now, it will impact the Earth. The asteroid is approximately 18 kilometres in diameter. Most of this will still be intact when it strikes the Earth, travelling at nearly 30,000 kilometres per hour. The tether cable, stretching nearly 200 kilometres in length, will also impact the Earth along with the asteroid, travelling at the same velocity. To give you some idea of the catastrophic nature of this unfolding disaster, it is believed that the asteroid that wiped out the dinosaurs was only about half the size of this asteroid." Wisecroft paused and took a dramatic breath. "To put it bluntly, mankind is facing an extinction-level event."

Now there was stunned silence in the dining room. No one spoke. They just stared at the image of Wisecroft's face, unable or unwilling to process what they had just heard.

"The initial impact will create a fireball that will extend for millions of square kilometres, and the shockwave will travel around the Earth at a speed of tens of thousands of kilometres per hour. The earth will be plunged into a dark winter that will last for centuries. The lethal radiation from the nuclear exchange that has just occurred will last even longer. The Earth will be unliveable, and it is difficult to perceive how anyone left alive after the final impact of the asteroid and its cable will be able to survive. We simply cannot return to the Earth. We have to accept that the home we once knew is gone."

Now people became vocal once more. Shock, grief, outrage and fear all welled up and overflowed. People cried out, and a sense of panic swept through the room. Zac, who had already heard all this from Wisecroft, was moved to sorrow afresh, as he witnessed the reaction of people around him.

"Bugger!" said Kit, in her usual succinct manner. Martinez simply sat there with an expressionless face, calmly looking around the room as if she were an observer and not a fellow-participant in this crisis. Zac found himself wondering what made her tick and whether anything could penetrate her gruff exterior.

As Wisecroft continued, the noise quickly died down. "Over the last two hours, we have been assessing our options. It appears that a similar terrorist attack has taken place on Mars. Mars City is not responding to our attempts at communication, and we have just received imagery from an orbital satellite showing an immense crater where the settlement used to be. However, there are three smaller off-world settlements that remain untouched: The mining base on Titan was untouched, as was the secondary Mars base - a mining facility in the northern hemisphere - and the Aldrin Research Facility, on the far side of the moon. We have been in contact with these three facilities. They remain unharmed and fully operational. Although each of those bases is small compared to Luna City, between them they could accommodate all of us who are now on-board Genesis. They have viable food production and life support. It would be a squeeze, and it would not be very comfortable initially, but we would survive."

"But there is another option." He paused for dramatic effect.

"Genesis was not built to simply travel around our solar system. It is a starship, designed to take humanity to a new home in a different solar system. When the terrorist attack occurred, we were only days away from launching. The ship is almost fully stocked and equipped, and we were undertaking final testing of its systems. A skeleton crew was already in place who would have flown the ship to Kepler Station, where, over a period of about a week, the full complement of crew and passengers would have come on board. Over the previous 18 months, 900 people had been selected and trained to take part in this mission. This was not common knowledge, and it was kept from the public's gaze for a reason."

Wisecroft's steely gaze stared out from the screen. "The Earth was dying, even before today's terrible events. As you know, the Earth's ecosystems have never fully recovered from the damage inflicted by the Faith Wars of the late 21st century. Despite the technologies we have developed since our great-great-grandparents managed to survive the nuclear winter, the damage to our planet has proven to be irreversible. Our leading scientists concluded long ago that mankind's greatest hope for long-term survival lay in finding a new home. And so, the Genesis project was born.

"For the last 200 years, the world's greatest minds have

poured themselves into this project. Astronomers searched the galaxy looking for habitable exoplanets. Scientists created new technologies. Engineers designed new systems. New metals were created, new propulsion drives were built and tested, new methods of producing food and water and life support were tested. Almost every technological advancement that has bene-fited mankind over the last two centuries is a by-product of the Genesis Project. Construction of this starship commenced 80 years ago, before any of us were born. We are safe today on board this vessel because of the dedication of thousands of people who dreamed of the impossible and who were committed to something bigger than themselves."

"Most of the passengers and crew who trained for this mission will not be part of it now. They are either already dead or they will perish in the disaster that is about to impact the Earth. But you are here. Although smaller in number, we have enough people on board this vessel to make a fresh start on a new planet; to create a viable colony on a world unspoilt by the violence and greed of mankind's past.

"I am now going to hand over to DANSA's senior astronomer, Dr Carla Zangetti, who will share some exciting news with you. Because we have found a new home."

21

C arla Zangetti's face appeared on the screens in the dining and lounge decks of Genesis. She appeared to be in her late 40s or early 50s, with piercing blue eyes and blonde hair tied up in a bun. She spoke with crisp authority, with just the hint of an Italian accent.

"As you know, mankind has been searching the cosmos for habitable exoplanets for nearly 400 years. To date, we have catalogued nearly 600,000. But the factors necessary to sustain human life are many: the right star, the right distance from a star, the right atmosphere, the right sized planet, the right chemical composition, liquid water, active tectonic plates, a molten core, a magnetosphere, a moon for tidal stimulation of the ecosystem, just to name a few. The list is extensive, and the longer we searched, the more apparent it became that Earth-like planets are extremely rare. About 150 years ago, we began launching probes to investigate the most likely candidates. Over the ensuing years, 12 probes were launched. These probes travelled at speeds up to half the speed of light and were programmed to send back images and data when they reached their target planets. To date, we have received images back from ten of the probes. Nine showed rocky, barren planets, without atmospheres. The tenth revealed this."

An image appeared on the screen, and there were gasps of surprise all across the dining room. A stunning blue-green world with white clouds floated in the blackness of space. Glimpses of an unfamiliar continent revealed that it was definitely not Earth.

Carla Zangetti smiled as she continued her presentation. "Data sent back by the probe indicates that its atmosphere is very close in composition to the original atmosphere of Earth, before we ruined it. The planet is 78 percent ocean, has a mass 6 percent greater than Earth, and is within the habitable zone of its star, which is a G type, main sequence star, like our sun. The planet does not have an axial tilt as does Earth, but its elliptical orbit around its star, of 380 days, provides the variation of seasons. It will be slightly more temperate than Earth, with both hemispheres of the planet experiencing the same season simultaneously."

Carla smiled again. "Think of Hawaii, as it used to be before we ruined it." She paused and then became more serious.

"That is the good news. Unfortunately, it is not the closest star system to Earth. The planet orbits the star Icarus R-421, which is a rogue hyper-velocity star, meaning that instead of rotating around the galactic core with the rest of the stars in our Milky Way galaxy, it is moving outwards from the elliptic plane of the galaxy at a considerable rate. Thus, its distance from Earth is changing all the time. When our probe arrived in its system over 80 years ago, it was 12.8 light years from Earth. Today, it is 14.3 light years distant." The image of the planet flashed back up on the screen, with the tag: "14.3 Light Years."

Kit was watching the screen, mesmerised, as she considered the unblemished planet that was being presented to them. She turned to Martinez and Zac, saying "OK, I get what she's saying. I hope you guys really like sleeping."

"Boring!" moaned Martinez.

Zangetti continued. "If this starship was capable of travelling safely at the speed of light, with instantaneous acceleration and deceleration at each end of the journey, it would take us 14.3 years to reach the planet, plus however much further the star and its planet would have travelled during those years. However, Genesis is only designed to reach a cruising speed of about half the speed of light. Factoring in the time spent accelerating and decelerating at each end of the journey, plus the additional distance the star will have travelled by the time we reach it, the total journey will take approximately 40 years."

There were gasps of shock and disappointment, and conversations broke out all over the dining room. "Told you," said Kit.

"40 years?" said Zac. "But that means I will be in my late 60s by the time we ..."

"Just wait, my young Jedi apprentice," interjected Kit. "Things not yet known to you there are."

"Very cool, Yoda," said Martinez.

Zangetti, who was no doubt receiving auditory feedback from the dining and lounge decks, waited until the comments had died down.

"To make such a long journey feasible, we have developed a form of cryogenic stasis, whereby you will sleep for the entire duration of the trip. Your metabolic processes will be slowed to a tiny percentage of their current values. Your blood will be augmented with synthetic blood, containing trillions of nanobots that will take over the metabolic processes of your entire body at the cellular level, without the need for your organs to work at all. During your sleep you will age at one-twentieth of the rate that you age now. When we arrive at our destination, you will have slept for 40 years, but your body will only have aged two years. And when you awaken, it will seem as though you have only just closed your eyes for a moment."

More conversation broke out among the audience as people considered the ramifications of what they had just learned.

Wisecroft's face appeared again on the screen. "Ladies and gentlemen," he began, "we have the chance to start afresh. To build a new life on a new, unblemished world. To walk freely on the surface of a planet without needing masks or protective suits. To breathe fresh air and feel the warmth of the sun. To grow crops and build homes and create a safe world for our children and for the many generations that are to come."

"There is a place on board Genesis for everyone who wants to join us on this expedition. But no one will force you to come. If you choose to stay, you have two options. We can either transfer you to the Aldrin Research Facility on the far side of the moon before we leave Luna orbit, or we can transfer you to the mining facility on Mars. Before leaving our solar system, we will be spending several days in orbit around Mars, picking up some supplies and some additional crew and volunteers from that base who wish to join us. Due to the acceleration capabilities of this vessel, it will take us only seven days to reach Mars, and we will remain in orbit for several days while the necessary transfers take place. So, you have some time to decide."

The camera zoomed in on Wisecroft's face, as he adopted what he hoped was a wise and compassionate expression. "I know we are all experiencing shock and grief at the moment, but we must look to the future. I urge you to join us. We will need as many people as possible if we are to have a viable population on the new world. We cannot save our friends and loved ones now, but we can, and must, save ourselves, for the sake of humanity's future. That is all for the moment."

The image of the new world appeared on the screen as Wisecroft's message ended. Kit sat frowning as conversation broke out all around them.

"You're looking sceptical, Supergirl. What's up?" asked Martinez.

"He's wrong!" said Kit.

"What do you mean?" asked Zac.

"He said we can't save them," she replied. "But we can! This ship has the capability to stop the asteroid from impacting Earth! It has more than enough power to stop the decay of the asteroid's orbit and move it away from the Earth. Why aren't we doing that?"

Martinez raised her eyebrows and said, "I think I know why. Because he's too worried about saving his own skin. Did you notice he said, 'We must save ourselves'? He's doing to Earth what he tried to do to us."

Kit stood to her feet. "I need to talk to him! This disaster doesn't have to happen!" She looked at Martinez. "How can I get to the bridge? You're on the security team; have you got access?"

"Not yet. I only just got here with you, remember?"

"I have," said Zac.

"You have what?" asked Kit.

"Access to the bridge. Wisecroft cleared my biochip."

"Wow! What are you, an astrophysicist or something?"

"No. A history professor."

Kit shook her head and blinked her eyes in bewilderment. "Of course you are. That makes perfect sense. Every starship needs a history professor." She looked at Martinez. "Are you coming with us?"

"Of course I am. I'm looking forward to catching up with the guy who tried to leave us for dead."

22

"How certain are you that there are no more explosive devices on board, George?"

"Pretty certain, sir," answered Leonidis. "We've scanned every section of the ship, visually and electronically. There's no trace of anything else that shouldn't be here."

"OK. But let's remain vigilant." Wisecroft looked at the white-bearded Lars Christensen, seated at the other side of the conference table. "How are we placed for crew, Captain?"

Christensen scratched the side of his beard. "A skeleton crew is the best description. We have one of everything—pilot, co-pilot, navigation, comms and scanning, reactor engineer, main drive engineer—just enough to get us from the moon to Earth in a single shift. But no replacements. No second- or third-shift teams. Plus, we have ten shuttles housed in Genesis's shuttle bays, but only two shuttle pilots. We were going to pick up the full crew at Kepler Station."

"I see," said Wisecroft. "Of course, we will be picking up some additional personnel from Aldrin Research Facility and from the Mars mining base, and some of those may be suitable for some of those roles. Apart from that, we will need to select some suitable passengers to undergo emergency retraining to fill some of the gaps.

"Lance," he said, turning to Catrell, "I want you to examine the personal details in the biochip scans of our passengers. Come up with a shortlist of 20 you think could be suitable for some intensive training."

The door to the conference room opened and Kit burst in, followed closely by Zac and Martinez. "Hi, Simon," said Zac, with a mock apologetic look on his face. "I hope you don't mind; I brought some friends with me."

Christensen's executive officer stuck his head through the doorway. "Sorry, Captain. I tried to stop them."

"Dr Wisecroft," said Kit. "You're making a mistake. We can stop this disaster from happening!"

"Sadly, the disaster you are referring to is inevitable, Ms Tyler. There is nothing we can do."

"Yes, there is! If the antimatter drive on this ship is as powerful as I think it is, we could maneuver Genesis against the asteroid and use it to arrest the asteroid's decaying orbit! I spoke with an engineer in the loading bay and he said Genesis has a push field generator, which would protect our hull from damage."

"Yes, I agree. Our main drive does have the necessary power to push the asteroid out of its impact trajectory. But you are forgetting one thing: the Caliphate. Just a few short hours ago, a Titan cargo vessel arrived in Earth orbit and was blown to pieces by a Caliphate missile. We have to assume that they are still capable of doing that to us. Our push field generator will not protect us from a direct missile attack."

"But you don't know that!" spluttered Kit. "The attack is over. For all we know, there are no missiles left. And surely even the Caliphate can't be that stupid that they couldn't work out that we're trying to save them!"

"On the contrary, Ms Tyler, they have already proven themselves to be profoundly 'stupid', to use your word. Otherwise they would never have started a conflict that was destined to result in mutually assured destruction."

Kit's face was becoming suffused with indignation. "So that's it? We just turn our back on humanity and leave billions of people to die? All because there is a slight chance that there is a missile left in a silo somewhere and that someone still feels inclined to use it? I don't believe this!"

"Ms Tyler. I am not a monster. I assure you; I feel a deep sadness at our inability to assist. But I cannot risk this ship and the lives of everyone on board. This mission is the result of centuries of blood, sweat and toil. It is mankind's crowning achievement. It will carry humanity to the stars and open a new epoch for the expansion of the human race. I will not, I *must* not, throw all that away on the kind of risky venture that you propose."

"Coward," muttered Martinez.

"I beg your pardon?" said Wisecroft, indignantly.

"You heard me. You were willing to leave three of us behind on the moon, to save your own skin, and now you're doing the same to millions of people!"

"You're way out of line, Martinez!" shouted Wisecroft, standing to his feet and pushing his chair violently backwards. "I won't stand for that kind of insubordination!"

"Then sit back down," said Martinez.

Kit interjected before things escalated any further. "So is that it? Is the decision final? We're not going back to help? We're not even going to try?" She looked around the table. "Does no one else have a problem with this?"

There was silence, although a few people seemed uneasy and could not look Kit in the eye. She shook her head in disgust and turned to go. "Let's get out of here! I don't want to even breathe the same oxygen as these people!"

"Wait," said Zac. Everyone turned to look at him. They had

forgotten he was even there. "How many shuttles have we got?" No one spoke for a moment.

"Ten," answered Captain Christensen, finally. "But we only have two shuttle pilots."

"Three including me," said Kit, turning back around.

"Plus the pilot and co-pilot of Genesis would be capable of flying a shuttle," added Martinez.

"I've been scanning the biochip data of our passengers," said Lance Catrell, indicating the data tablet in his hand. "Two of the engineers who were attached to Armstrong Research Facility have shuttle pilot qualifications."

"That's seven," said Martinez.

"Wait!" said Wisecroft. "What's this about? What are you suggesting?"

Zac looked at the command team seated at the table. "If we can't save everyone, we can at least save some. The shuttles could get in and out before the asteroid strikes. Seven shuttles equates to 350 people we could rescue. That's 350 more people that we could take with us."

There was silence as people considered this.

"No," said Wisecroft. "I won't allow it. The same issue is at play. You risk having our shuttles destroyed by missile strikes."

"Not all our shuttles," said Christensen, with a meaningful look at Wisecroft. "And if we don't send our pilot and co-pilot, we would only be risking five shuttles. Even if the worst happened, and we lost all five, we would still have five shuttles and two pilots."

Lance, who had been furiously working some calculations on his tablet, spoke up. "The asteroid's orbit is decaying faster than expected. It must be because of the tether cable. It's going to impact in a little over three hours."

"What acceleration are your shuttles capable of?" asked Kit.

"Five Gs," said Christensen, "and they are equipped with inertial dampening."

Kit took out her pocket tablet and crunched some numbers. "At five Gs, with a midpoint flip, plus time for re-entry, we could be landing ..." she paused while she did a further calculation, "in two hours, 10 minutes."

Christensen said, "Genni, please confirm Ms Tyler's calculations."

A pleasant female voice responded immediately, seeming to emanate from the ceiling and walls. "Ms Tyler's calculations are incorrect. It would take a minimum of two hours *eleven* minutes, provided the desired landing site was at the optimal point in the Earth's rotation."

"Yeh, but you haven't seen me flip!" said Kit defensively, looking up at the ceiling.

"What about a landing site?" asked Lance, scratching his head through his Space Odyssey baseball cap. We would need to find an area free of radiation, with a landing strip still intact."

Christensen answered, "From the satellite images that we've seen, New Zealand, Tasmania and some of the Pacific Islands look unscathed."

"This discussion is completely moot," said Wisecroft. "I won't authorise the use of our shuttles for such a risky operation."

"But I will," said Christensen, staring down Wisecroft. "I'm the Captain of this vessel, and I will not stand by and do nothing when it is within our power to help."

"I am the Commander of this mission!" said Wisecroft, the beginnings of a belligerent whine creeping into his voice.

"Are you?" said Christensen. "You were never intended to be the Commander. You were slated as the science advisor for this mission. Commander Lazenby would have been in charge, had he not perished on Kepler Station. I think that leaves the issue of ultimate command wide open, don't you?"

"This could be construed as mutiny, Captain Christensen!"

"No, Dr Wisecroft. It can only be mutiny if there is a clear chain of command, which there currently isn't, and we certainly don't have time to resolve the issue now. If this rescue mission is going to happen, we need a quick decision." Turning to Kit, he said. "You have a go."

"What about reverting to Plan A?" she asked hopefully. "Using Genesis to move the asteroid?"

Christensen responded, "Sadly, I have to agree with Dr Wisecroft on that issue, but for different reasons. Our push field generator is only designed to withstand high-velocity particle bombardment while travelling at a significant percentage of the speed of light. It would offer no real protection from something as massive as an asteroid. Your shuttle mission is our only real option."

Christensen stood up. "We'll need to hurry. I will send down the two shuttle pilots from our crew. Mr Catrell, please mobilise the two engineers with shuttle training from your team. I'll have my comm chief advise the shuttle bays to have the vehicles ready to launch ASAP. We'll sort out landing destinations while the shuttles are én route. Let's go, people! We haven't got a minute to lose!"

Everyone ran out of the room, except Simon Wisecroft and George Leonidis, both of whom remained sitting. Wisecroft was a vision of smouldering rage. He looked at his chief of security and said, "We're going to have to do something about them, George."

"Yes sir," replied Leonidis.

23

The shuttles had flipped 30 minutes earlier and were now approaching Earth under extreme deceleration. If it wasn't for the inbuilt inertial dampening systems, the crews would be experiencing extreme discomfort. Landing sites had been allocated: three sites in New Zealand—Auckland, Wellington and Christchurch—as well as Hobart in Tasmania, and Noumea in New Caledonia. Those towns and cities had not received nuclear strikes, and prevailing weather patterns had not yet blown fallout their way. Each of the five shuttles had a pilot and a volunteer trainee co-pilot, the latter being the result of a last-minute decision, recognising the need to train more shuttle pilots. Kit turned to her co-pilot and said, "Do you think you've got a handle on the basics now?"

"I think so," Zac answered.

"Just remember, let the computer do all the hard work for you."

"Sure."

Zac had volunteered, partly because he couldn't sit back and allow others to go into danger when it had been his idea. And there was no doubt that this was a dangerous mission. As the shuttles hurtled earthwards, Zac was intensely aware that this could end very badly. He glanced at Kit beside him and wondered how she managed to look so calm; he was sure his heart rate was through the roof. *I wonder if this is how all "heroes" feel?* he wondered. *Maybe all the heroic deeds throughout history were simply carried out by people who were equally terrified but refused to give in to the fear? Is this how Pliny the Elder felt as he and his men sailed towards the shores of Pompeii to rescue the citizens from Vesuvius's deadly eruption? Was his heart pounding like mine?* Zac reflected that Pliny never made it out alive. Hundreds of people were rescued by the lifeboats that day, but Pliny was overcome by poisonous fumes and died on the beach. He glanced back over his shoulder at their space-age lifeboat and sent up a silent prayer that they would all make it back to Genesis safely.

He glanced again at Kit and was acutely aware that, as a history professor, he had no real skills to contribute to the mission. At least by training as a shuttle pilot, he might prove useful at some point. He also hoped that doing something like this would take his mind off the tide of grief and hurt that threatened to overwhelm him. He felt a terrible numbness deep in his soul. *How could I have been so naive to believe that someone as vivacious as Annisa could love someone as boring as me? I was a fool! I was naïve! She must have been laughing behind my back the whole time!*

Kit looked at him, sensing some kind of inner turmoil. "You haven't told me how you ended up wandering around the moon in a drugged stupor."

"I told you. They drugged me."

"Yeh, but why?"

Zac wondered how much he should share. *Oh well, it's going to come out sooner or later,* he thought. He took a deep breath and let out a long sigh. "My wife was one of the terrorists. She blew up the fusion reactor. She murdered hundreds of people." He stared straight at Kit, gauging her reaction, waiting for her to register disgust and loathing. There was a long pause while Kit digested the information, the wheels of her mind spinning.

"And they thought you were involved?"

"Yes. She and some other staff went missing on the base. Wisecroft thought I would know something."

"But you didn't."

"No. I am a naïve idiot. She fooled me for three years."

"Don't beat yourself up. It sounds like she fooled everyone." Kit glanced at him again. "Did you love her?"

"Yes. At least I loved the idea of her; the 'her' that she presented to me. But it wasn't the real 'her', was it? It was a pretence. A false persona. I fell in love with a fraud. What does that say about me?"

"I think it says that you're normal. Better than normal, actually. It says that you have a heart that's ready and willing to trust, and to love, and to give yourself to someone. And that's a good thing. Don't lose that."

Zac looked at her with raised eyebrows. "When did you become a counsellor?"

"You haven't seen my bill yet," she said with a smile.

The comm pinged, and Lance Catrell's voice impinged on their counselling session. "Kit, do you copy?"

"Yeh. Go ahead, Lance."

"What's your timing on landing?"

"Two more minutes' deceleration and then we commence re-entry. Given that we will be well below orbital velocity by then, we should be landing in about 12 minutes from now."

"Copy that." He paused. "Kit, the situation is changing rapidly. Satellite images indicate that the tether cable has broken up. There are three sections, each at least 50 kilometres long, that are falling separately now. They are going to impact the Earth prior to the asteroid."

"When and where?"

"Our computer modelling indicates four separate impacts. American Samoa in 22 minutes. The Solomon Islands in 24 minutes, and Papua New Guinea in 25 minutes from now. The asteroid will impact somewhere near Singapore a few minutes later."

Kit swore. "That hardly gives us any time on the ground!"

"That's correct," said Lance. "The shock waves from the tether cable impacts will be travelling at 30,000 kph. They will reach your landing sites within two minutes after each impact. That means that each of you has a maximum of only seven minutes on the ground before you need to launch. I've patched the other shuttles into this transmission. Shuttle Four, you're landing at Noumea. You will only have five minutes on the ground. Do you all copy?"

One by one, each of the shuttles acknowledged the message. Lance continued. "Good. This means you will have to grab whatever civilians are closest, on the tarmac and in the nearest terminal buildings. Bundle them into your shuttle and then get the hell out of there. Do *not* wait for anyone! Do you understand?"

The shuttle pilots all acknowledged, and Lance signed off, wishing them all good luck.

"We're gonna need it," Kit said to Zac. "Tighten your seatbelt, Doc. I hope you didn't have too much to eat for lunch, because I don't think even the inertial dampeners are going to cope with the maneuver I'm about to pull off."

24

E lizabeth Canning was normally a patient woman, but her patience had finally run out. She looked at the faces around the conference table and said, "I'm giving the order to leave the shelter. It's been five hours since the EMP knocked out our electronics, and we have no idea how long until communications will be restored. It might be days, weeks or even months. In the meantime, we are blind and deaf down here, and we are not doing anyone any good."

"But Madam President," said General Armitage, "the surface could be radioactive. We have no way of knowing if it's safe."

"We have no way of knowing anything down here, General," responded Elizabeth. "I will not hide in a hole in the ground. Besides, at no point have we felt tremors indicating detonations near us. I suspect New Zealand has been spared, and, if that is the case, I will not go down in history as the president who stayed in hiding when the world above needed her."

She looked around the table. "We will leave the technical staff down here to continue attempting to restore communications, but it's time for us to leave. Let's open the rabbit hole and see what has become of our world."

Five minutes later, surrounded by her security team and her war cabinet, she stepped out of the lift in a concrete bunker built into the side of a hill. They emerged into a grey, overcast afternoon. At first, they could perceive no difference from any other typical New Zealand late afternoon. But as they stood looking around them, two differences gradually became apparent. First, there were no engine noises of any kind. No planes overhead, no cars on the nearby country roads, no compressors or man-made noises. Just an eerie silence. The electromagnetic pulses from nuclear detonations all over the world had completely fried even the simplest of electrical circuits. The second difference was the clouds. Far above the scattering of low cloud, there was an ugly, dark-brown cloud layer that covered the entire sky, seething and roiling, in constant motion. Looking at her watch, Elizabeth realised it was only a little after 2 in the afternoon, yet the darkness made it look like early evening. She turned to her entourage. "Does anyone have any suggestions about how we can get into town? I don't suppose any of these vehicles with modern computerised engines are going to be working," she said, indicating the adjacent hangar full of government cars.

One of the base staff spoke up. "Ma'am, we have a restored 20th century vintage bus behind the hangar. It's EMP-proof— no electronic circuitry of any kind, just a very basic combustion engine. It's been maintained in pristine condition for such an emergency."

"Good. Bring it around." Turning to one of her security team, she said, "Bring my daughter up. I'm not going anywhere without her."

Fifteen minutes later, the president of the Democratic Alliance of Nations arrived in Wellington in a 1965 Dodge bus, along with her war cabinet and security team. As they drove through the city streets, there was an eerie silence. No vehicles were moving. No machinery could be heard. The sound of their engine echoed off the walls of the buildings. People were milling about on the sidewalks and standing in the streets, looking around them in puzzlement.

"Where to, ma'am?" asked the driver.

"Take me to the city council buildings," said Elizabeth. "I want to speak to whoever is in charge."

Five minutes later, they pulled up outside the council building in Wakefield Street and disembarked. Puzzled shopkeepers and office workers were standing around on the sidewalk. Computers were down. Electricity was blacked out. Nothing was working. The city had ground to a halt. Walking into the reception area with her entourage, Elizabeth asked directions to the mayor's chambers. A large Maori man who had been standing at the window, looking out into the street, turned and said, "No need. I'm the mayor. Lionel Tuatini."

"Elizabeth Canning," she said, holding out her hand.

"I know who you are," he said, shaking her hand. "What's happened?"

"The Caliphate launched a full-scale attack. There has been a major nuclear exchange."

"Why weren't we warned?" he asked.

"I'm sorry. There was no warning for anyone."

"How bad is it?"

"I honestly don't know," Elizabeth admitted. "But it can't be good. At the point when we lost comms there were literally hundreds of missiles in flight. Even if only a quarter of those made it through to detonation, we are all in for a pretty grim time."

As she spoke, they became aware of a growing roar. An aircraft of some kind flew directly overhead, rattling the windows. They ran out onto the street and saw an impressive-looking space shuttle banking towards the south-east, lowering its landing gear.

"How can that shuttle still be flying?" Elizabeth asked.

"No idea, ma'am," answered General Armitage. "But that might just be our ticket out of here."

"Let's get to the airport," she said. "Are you coming, mayor?"

"No. I need to stay and coordinate essential services. But please keep me informed if you can, Madam President."

Lionel watched the ancient bus as it roared down the street. He had no idea that he only had minutes left to live.

25

The shuttle came screaming in across the city, low and fast. Kit spotted the airport to the south-east and banked hard left to line up the runway. She struggled with the controls, saying, "These things are a dream in space, but they fly like a brick in an atmosphere." The Genesis shuttles were capable of making a vertical landing, using landing thrusters located on the underbelly, but that kind of maneuvering took far too much time - time Kit did not have. They would have to make a high-velocity touchdown. As they made their landing approach, she suddenly swore.

"There's a stalled plane on the main runway!"

Thinking fast, she jerked the controls quickly to the left and then back to the right a few moments later.

"Hold on, Doc! We don't have time for another approach. We're going off-road! I hope that grass isn't too boggy."

The shuttle touched down heavily on the runway, bounced once and then stuck. Still travelling way too fast, Kit steered it off the runway onto the grass, narrowly missing the stalled passenger airliner. As the speed bled off, she aimed straight for the terminal building, cutting straight across the various taxiways and connecting tarmacs. At the last moment, she swung the shuttle around to face out towards the runways again, then throttled back the main engine to idle. They were a mere 10 metres from a set of stairs leading up to the terminal building above. Opening the cabin door, they both jumped to the ground, a distance of a little over a metre.

Yelling above the noise of their idling engine, Kit said, "You grab people from the tarmac, and I'll head inside the terminal. It's 14:20 now. We launch in exactly seven minutes! Go!"

There were people standing nearby on the tarmac, airport staff of various kinds. Zac ran over to the nearest group and yelled, "You need to get on board the shuttle now! An asteroid is about to impact Earth! The shockwave will be heading this way in a few minutes!" As he said it, he realised how insane he must sound. He also didn't exactly look authoritative. He was wearing faded jeans with holes and a Hawaiian shirt, and probably looked like he'd been smoking too much wacky weed. The people on the tarmac just looked at him with bemused expressions.

"Please! I'm not joking! Either get on board the shuttle and live, or stay here and die, your choice! We're leaving in five minutes!" Zac looked around and saw some other staff nearer the terminal. He ran towards them, shouting a similar message. As some of the airport staff began to respond and move towards the shuttle, Zac saw a line of civilians hurrying down the stairs from the terminal building. Kit appeared to have had more success than he.

She briefly appeared at the top of the stairs and yelled, "Move your arses, people. We leave in four minutes! Zac, help them on board!" She turned and disappeared into the terminal building again.

"Quickly! This way!" said Zac.

The first civilians began arriving at the shuttle. Zac started helping people on board, lifting children into the arms of parents and shoving the less athletic from behind. Airport staff who had previously dismissed Zac as a lunatic had now joined the line and were climbing on board. The minutes ticked by too quickly, and the shuttle was filling. The last passengers clambered on board as Kit ran up.

"That's it," she said. "We're out of time. We launch in one minute. How full are we?"

Zac had clambered aboard the shuttle and gazed down the length of the cabin. "All the seats are taken and there are six people sitting on the floor."

"That's not good," said Kit. "This bird has a maximum take-off capacity of 50 passengers." She thought about it for a moment. "OK. I'm not kicking anyone off. But don't let any more on." She jumped on board and turned left towards the cockpit. "Secure the door and I'll get us moving!"

Zac was just starting to swing the door closed when an ancient yellow bus screeched to a stop metres from him. People jumped out and a woman who looked vaguely familiar ran towards him. "Where are you going?" she asked.

"There's an asteroid about to impact," said Zac. "I'm sorry, we can't fit anyone else. You need to take whatever cover you can."

"Where are you going?" she asked.

"Genesis," he answered, not sure whether she would understand.

Somehow, she seemed to know what he meant. She turned around and yelled, "Bring Melody! Now!!"

A man came forward holding the hand of a young girl. "Mummy!" said the girl, running to the woman. "What's happening? I'm scared."

"You're going for a ride on this plane, and I'll catch up with you later."

"No! Mummy! No! I don't want to leave you!" The girl

wrapped her arms around her mother's waist. The woman looked up at Zac and pleaded, "Please. Take her."

"I'm sorry," said Zac. "We're full. We can't fit anyone else."

Kit stuck her head out of the cockpit door and screamed, "Zac! Close that damn door now! We're out of time! And don't let anyone else on!"

The engines rose to a crescendo and Zac started to close the door. The woman untangled her daughter's arms from around her waist, picked her up and threw her through the half-closed doors. The girl landed on her hands and knees and screamed, "Mummy! Don't leave me!" The shuttle started rolling forward, and the woman yelled back, "I'll always love you, remember that!"

The girl scrambled to her feet and tried to jump out of the door, but Zac held her back as the shuttle quickly picked up speed. Kit's voice yelled from the open cockpit, "Zac! Close that damn door!!" A woman in a nearby seat came and took the screaming girl from his arms, and Zac closed and bolted the door. He scrambled through to the cockpit and strapped himself into his seat.

"Glad you could make it," Kit said, sarcastically. "Hope I didn't inconvenience you at all."

The shuttle was tearing across the grass between tarmacs.

"We're way too heavy for a vertical take-off," said Kit. "We'll have to do this the same way we landed—the old-fashioned way."

As they came to the runway, Kit violently wrenched the shuttle around, lining it up on the remaining runway with the stalled passenger jet now behind them. The shuttle was accelerating explosively, but there was very little runway left. "It feels sluggish," Kit said. "We're way too heavy. This is gonna be very close!"

The end of the runway loomed in front of them. A low-lying fence barred their way, and beyond that was the ocean. "Come on, come on, come on," muttered Kit, leaning forward in her chair, willing the shuttle to get airborne. At the last possible moment she pulled back on her controls, urging the shuttle up. Grudgingly, the wheels left the tarmac and the shuttle gained a few metres of altitude. As they passed over the barrier there was a thud and a shudder. "I think we just lost a wheel," said Kit. She retracted the undercarriage and the shuttle started to respond more gracefully. It roared skywards as Kit increased the incline as much as she dared, scrounging every centimetre of altitude she could get.

"We were two minutes late taking off," she said. "We've got about two and a half minutes to get above the shockwave. Normally we'd make it, but we're overweight. I think we're about to get a nasty kick in the arse. You'd better tell the passengers to hang on tight, because the inertial dampeners probably won't cope."

Zac switched on the cabin comm. "Folks, we might be in for a bit of a rough ride in a moment. If you're in a seat, strap yourself in as tightly as you can. If you don't have a seat, find somewhere to wedge yourself and hang on tight." He switched off the comm and they sat in silence, listening to the engine screaming as it hurled them skyward. Time slowed, and Zac felt himself perspiring. He was gripping the arms of his seat tightly and found that he was leaning forward, willing the shuttle upwards.

The sky began to darken, and Kit said, "We're out of time, and we're still a thousand metres too low. We're about to get slammed, but the air's pretty thin up here, so we might just make it. Hold on!"

Nothing happened for a few moments, and then, suddenly, they were slammed back into their seats as they were hit from behind. A burst of blinding light poured through the front screen, and they were shaken violently from side to side. There were screams from the passengers behind, and there was the sound of random items being shaken loose around the cabin. And then, just as suddenly, it was over. Kit stabilised their ascent, and the shuttle emerged into the blackness of space. The stars shone like diamonds, and the side viewing ports in the cockpit framed the curved horizon of the Earth as it steadily shrank behind them.

Zac gazed out of his side window and saw another huge explosion light up the clouds with a yellow and red glow. A rolling shockwave spread outwards across the surface of the planet with terrifying speed, and a glowing mushroom cloud rose up through the atmosphere, seeming to punch a hole through to the very edge of space itself. A tear rolled down his face as he realised that he would never set foot on Earth again. *God help them,* he thought. *God help us all.*

26

Things were chaotic after the shuttles returned to Genesis. There were 260 newcomers who were traumatised and grief-stricken. Their lives had been spared, but they now had to come to terms with the fact that a few minutes after they had boarded their shuttles, everyone they knew and loved had almost certainly perished. Many people were overcome with survivor guilt. Most were numb with shock and disbelief.

In the midst of the chaos in Shuttle Bay 1, an 11-year-old girl was sobbing inconsolably. A middle-aged woman was trying to comfort her, asking what her name was, but the girl remained unresponsive to her questions.

Zac was doing his best to help wherever he could and noticed the girl who had been thrown onto the shuttle at the last moment by her mother. He could not even begin to imagine the mix of desperate emotions that the mother must have felt, knowing that she would probably never see her daughter again. Zac wished he could do something to ease the girl's grief, and he knelt down in front of her. He had two nieces of similar ages whom he loved dearly and who loved him in return, and as he looked at the girl, he realised he would never see them again, either. Deep sorrow welled up within him, and tears overflowed his eyes. The girl saw his tears and for some reason reached out to him. She wrapped her arms around his neck and buried her face against him and sobbed, saying over and over, "I want my mummy. I want my mummy."

Zac said, "I know you do, sweetie. She's gone. I'm sorry. I'm so sorry."

As he said this, something broke within him and he began to sob. At first, he tried to hold it in, but his sorrow rose up like a tide and swept him away. He cried for love lost, for the billions of innocent lives blotted out in an instant, and for the senseless evil that had caused it all. For minutes, the grown man on his knees and the little girl hugged each other and cried, sharing a bond of grief, and, somehow, drawing comfort from each other. Finally, Zac's tears stopped flowing, and the tide of sorrow receded, leaving him feeling cleansed and whole. He used the hem of his Hawaiian shirt to dry the girl's eyes, as her sobs gradually subsided.

"I suppose we should introduce ourselves," Zac said, attempting a smile. "My name is Zac Perryman. What's yours?"

"Melody."

"What's your last name, Melody?"

"Canning."

A light bulb lit up in Zac's brain. He suddenly knew why he had recognised Melody's mother.

"Your mother is Elizabeth?" he asked.

"Yes," she answered in a subdued voice.

"The president?"

She nodded.

"OK," he said, his mind reeling. "We're going to look after you now." He stood up. *What do I do now?* he thought to himself, looking around for help. The woman who had attempted to comfort Melody had disappeared. As he stood looking around, he felt Melody slip her hand into his. He looked down at her and saw that she was looking up at him, to see if it was OK. He smiled at her and gave her hand a squeeze. *Come on, think! What do I do with an 11-year-old orphan?*

"Are you two OK?" asked a friendly voice.

Zac turned towards the voice and saw a young woman in a white lab coat with a med kit in her hand.

"I'm Jaz. I work in the med bay. Are either of you injured in any way?"

Zac found himself staring into her bright green eyes. "Um ... er ... no ..." he said vaguely. Then he snapped out of his stupor. "But Melody, here, could use another friend. She's by herself." He raised his eyebrows in what he hoped Jaz would recognise as a plea for help, rather than a strange leer.

Jaz knelt down beside Melody. "Is that right? Well, I am in need of a friend as well, because I'm all alone, too. I was just about to head up to the dining room to get something to eat. Do you want to come?"

Melody shook her head. "I want to stay with Zac," she said, squeezing his hand harder and stepping closer to him.

"Well he could come, too. What do you say, Zac?"

"Sure. Let's all go together."

A few moments later, they stepped out of the lift into the expansive dining room. They made their way to a dispenser and selected some kind of sweet biscuits. Zac and Jaz grabbed a cup of tea and Melody got a flavoured soy drink. They made their way to a large, unoccupied table at the back of the room. Jaz was chatting to Melody continually, and the girl had thawed remarkably quickly. She and Jaz were already laughing at silly jokes and sharing stories. Zac breathed a sigh of relief. He looked around the dining room as it began to fill up. A meeting had been scheduled shortly to induct the newcomers and sort out living arrangements.

"Hey Doc, what's happening?" said Kit, as she and Martinez

plonked themselves into empty chairs next to him. Martinez had co-piloted one of the other shuttles.

"Not much," said Zac.

"Who's the little chickadee?" asked Martinez, indicating the girl.

Zac leaned closer and whispered, "Melody Canning. The president's daughter."

"Where's the president?" asked Martinez.

"She didn't make it," responded Zac. "Melody is alone here."

"That's a rough deal for the kid," said Martinez.

"Looks like she's found a friend," said Kit, indicating Jaz, who was currently having a secret whispered into her ear.

Just then a mountain on two legs loomed up beside Zac and slapped him on the back.

"Hey bro! How ya doin'?"

Zac craned his neck around and looked up into a beaming, dark brown face. The guy was at least 190 cm tall and built like a tank—not fat, just solid muscle.

"Um ..." he said with his usual alacrity. "I'm sorry. Do I know you?"

"You do now!" beamed the Islander. "We're from the same home, bro!" he said, indicating Zac's Hawaiian shirt.

"Oh, my shirt? Actually, no, I'm not Hawaiian. I'm from Sydney, Australia. I just like Hawaiian shirts."

"Australia, eh? OK, that's almost as good. Tell me, my friend, do you surf?"

"Yeh. Or I used to."

"Long board or short?"

"Long. Nine foot."

"Good, bro! Good! You are respecting the ocean. Short boards dishonour her. They cut and carve. On a long board you are in tune with the rhythm of the ocean. I think we're going to be good friends! What is your name, bro?"

"Zac."

The big man reached out his hand. "My name is Keolaku-paianaha Ka'aukai," he said, shaking Zac's hand. Zac found his hand engulfed in a hand the size of a dinner plate.

"You wanna run that name past us again, dude?" said Martinez.

"Keolakupaianaha Ka'aukai," he repeated. "Keolakupa-ianaha is a traditional Islander name, meaning 'an extraordinary, wonderful life', and Ka'aukai means 'the traveller'."

"Well, that second meaning is about to come true for you in bucket loads," said Kit. "Let's hope the first one does as well."

"Amen, sister. Amen!" said the big Hawaiian. "Do you mind if I sit alongside my brother?" he asked, indicating Zac.

"No. Please be our ..." She never got a chance to say 'guest' because he reached down and lifted her and her chair up and over Martinez and placed her gently down on the other side.

"Thank you, little sister," he said, dragging a chair from nearby and sitting in the newly vacated space.

"So, Keola ... kup ... er ... Keolakupa ... um ..." Zac mumbled. "How do you say it again?"

"Don't worry, bro. My friends call me Keo."

"OK. Keo. Where are you from exactly?"

"My people are from Waimanalo Bay, Oahu, originally. But we have lived in Ahipara, on the North Island of New Zealand, for three generations. The surf is good there, man!"

"So how did you come to be on board Genesis?" Kit asked.

"I came to Wellington for a rugby match. I was about to fly home when the world went crazy. I came here on Zac's shuttle," he said, patting Zac on the back again. "When I saw his shirt, I knew it was a sign."

"You were on board my shuttle?" said Kit. "No wonder we had trouble taking off!"

"My soul is light," he replied. "It is the soul that matters, not the body." He looked around the table. "A soul that is filled with faith and love is light. A soul that is filled with hate and bitterness is heavy."

"Speak of the devil," said Martinez, as Wisecroft's face appeared on the screens. "Here's Doctor Evil himself."

27

The first part of Wisecroft's latest address was primarily directed to the newcomers who had been rescued by the shuttles, summarising all that had happened and introducing them to the Genesis mission. In the process, he confirmed the catastrophic disaster that had befallen Earth. The final impact of the asteroid had been even worse than expected. A wave of destruction had swept around the globe at over 40,000 kilometres per hour, devouring everything in its path. The Earth had been laid bare, and it was difficult to imagine any living organism bigger than a microbe surviving. The planet was now a barren, radioactive wasteland, facing a life-prohibiting winter that might last for centuries. They simply could not consider going back there. Despite the enormity of loss that everyone on board was experiencing, there was little in the way of compassion or empathy in Wisecroft's manner; just cold, hard facts.

As Wisecroft neared the end of his doomsday speech, Keo said, "That man has a heavy soul."

"You got that right, dude," said Martinez.

"Heavy as lead," agreed Kit.

"Like a black hole," added Zac.

Wisecroft concluded his presentation by urging everyone on board to join the Genesis mission, saying, "There is nothing here for us anymore. Our destiny lies on another world; a fresh, new world where we can start again. A place where we can build a safe future for our children, and their children. I hope you will join us. I will now hand over to Captain Lars Christensen, who will explain some of the practicalities of life on board Genesis."

Christensen's white-bearded Nordic face appeared on the screen. "Ladies and gentlemen, I trust you are not in too much distress. This is a very difficult time for all of us."

"He has a light soul," said Keo to the group.

"Yes, he's a good man," answered Zac.

Christensen continued, "I want to explain the basic layout of Genesis and the living arrangements from this point onwards."

A basic schematic appeared on the screen.

GENESIS

Command	Living		Life Support	Hibernation	Power
AI	Recreation		Air & Water	Hibernation	
Bridge	Lounge		Gravity Gen	Hibernation	
Comscan	Dining		Food Production	Hibernation	
Crew Q	Sleeping		Food Production	Hibernation	
Medical	Sleeping		Engineering	Storage	
Shields	L	S	L	S	L	S	L	S	Shields

(Right side: Fusion Reactor / Anti-matter Drive)

"As you can see, Genesis is shaped like a brick." This elicited laughs and comments from a number of people around the dining room. "You are, no doubt, familiar with the fanciful science-fiction depictions of spaceships, with wings and streamlined aerodynamic shapes. A starship, however, does not need these things, because it is not designed to fly through an atmosphere. It travels through the vacuum of space, and so it can be any shape at all. For our purposes, building Genesis in this shape was the most practical and cost-efficient. The only time Genesis will ever engage with the atmosphere of a planet will be at our destination, when it will make a vertical landing, tail first, balancing on its propulsion drive.

"Our vessel has five distinct modules: command, living, life support, hibernation and power. Each module, as you can see, has different levels. Banks of lifts are situated between the modules, providing access to the different levels as well as access from one module to the next. Unless you have authorisation, you will only have access to the living module and the medical level in the command module."

"Genni, the most sophisticated, self-aware artificial intelligence that humankind has ever created, takes up the whole of the top level of the command level—although she takes exception to the term 'artificial intelligence', preferring to refer to herself as an 'augmented intelligence'. Genni will be in charge of Genesis for 40 years while we all sleep." There was an outbreak of chatter at that point, and Christensen let it subside before continuing.

"I won't go into detail about every level in every module, but I will pick out a few. The very bottom level of Genesis has a series of loading bays and shuttle bays, five of each on both sides. Most of the loading bays contain a large array of farming and industrial equipment that will be essential for establishing life on a new world. Fore and aft of the shuttle and loading bays are the push field generators, or shields. These are crucial for our journey to the stars. As we accelerate to a significant fraction of light speed, these shields will envelop our vessel in a push field that will protect Genesis from being damaged by high-velocity collision with the particles of dust and debris that permeate the universe."

"The power module at the rear contains the fusion reactor, which provides internal power for the entire vessel. It also contains our main propulsion drive, a newly developed antimatter drive. This drive will accelerate us at eight gravities for 35 days, until we reach our cruising speed of approximately half the speed of light. It will then switch off, and we will coast at that speed for nearly 40 years, until we undergo 35 days of deceleration at the other end. The antimatter drive is the most efficient drive ever built, utilising 99 percent of the liberated energy as pure thrust. It can also operate indefinitely, as it creates antimatter from the constant bombardment of dust particles on our vessel's shields. You will not feel any accelera- tion or deceleration, due to our very efficient inertial damp- eners and artificial gravity generator." Captain Christensen paused briefly and smiled. "I won't bore you with any further technical details."

"The hibernation zone is where you will sleep in cryogenic stasis for the duration of the journey. Dr. Zangetti has already explained some of that process to you. There are 900 cryogenic pods on the various levels of this zone, as this was the antici- pated number of people that we planned to take on the mission."

"The life support zone includes our yeast farm and aquaponic farm, which are completely automated and tended by basic robots. While we are awake, these farms will produce all the fresh food that we will need. Genni will deactivate the farms once we are all asleep and will reactivate them one month prior to waking us."

"The mission plan is that once all personnel have been transferred to the new world via the shuttles, Genni will execute a vertical landing using the propulsion drive. At the last moment, she will activate thrusters and land Genesis on its side. Genesis will then become our initial city, while we build more appropriate dwellings."

"That brings me to the living zone. While we are awake, I encourage you to utilise the recreation deck as much as possi- ble. There is a large amount of gym equipment and a variety of playing courts: tennis, squash, micro-soccer, basketball. It is important that we maintain our fitness and health while on the voyage to our new home. The lounge deck, as well as containing the obvious lounge areas, also includes two cinemas, each of which can seat 200 people. There are thousands of movies in our database. You can schedule a movie using the data screen at the door to each cinema, or also from the data screens in your cabins."

"The food dispenser consoles in the dining room are active 24 hours a day, but to encourage interaction and bonding we will ring a meal chime throughout the upper levels at 0700, 1300 and 1800 each day. There are 588 people on board and there are 450 seats in the dining room, so a large percentage of our population can eat at the same time."

"The sleeping cabins, on the bottom two levels, each have two beds, but as there are 450 of them, many of you will be able to have a cabin to yourself. To select a cabin, simply scan your biochip twice at the internal scanner and press 'confirm' both times. Only you, and your room-mate, if you decide to share, will then be able to access your cabin, ensuring privacy."

"Obviously, many of you have arrived on board with only the clothes that you are wearing. There are dry-cleaning laundries and communal bathrooms interspersed throughout the corridors. There are also storerooms next to each laundry, stocked with plain jumpsuits in various sizes. Please only take one suit to begin with."

"We will have one more day in lunar orbit, making some transfers to Aldrin Research Facility, then a seven-day journey to Mars. We will be in Mars orbit for approximately three days while we transfer people and supplies to and from the Mars base. In twelve days' time we will begin our journey to our new home."

"There are more detailed explanations of our vessel and our mission plan on the data screens in your cabin. Please also take note of the daily communications that will be posted there. Genni is also available to answer any questions you may have. You can communicate with her directly, simply by addressing her, anywhere on the vessel. She has the ability to converse with everyone on board simultaneously, and once you have scanned your biochip and spoken to her the first time, she will identify your voice each time."

Christensen paused for a moment and then concluded by saying, "This is the greatest undertaking ever attempted by humanity. It is also the most important. Each one of you will have a vital role to play. I hope you will stay and be a part of it. Thank you."

The screen changed to a view of the pristine blue-green world that would be their new home, and conversation immediately erupted all across the dining room.

Melody looked across the table. "Are you going, Zac?"

"You bet! I wouldn't miss it for the world," he said, winking at her.

"I wish my mum and dad could be here with me," she said, her eyes welling up with tears.

"I know," said Jaz, putting her arm around Melody and stroking her head. "I wish they could be here, too. But they would be very happy to know that you are safe, and that there are people who are going to look after you."

"Are you going to the new planet, Jaz?" she asked, looking up at her new friend.

"Of course!"

"In that case, I'm going too," she announced, bravely.

"I hope there's surf," said Keo.

28

Ten days later, life on board Genesis had settled into a daily routine. Mornings and early afternoons were spent in training sessions, learning skills that would be essential for their survival and development. Each person was expected to learn two skills. The entire morning, divided into two sessions separated by morning tea, was spent learning and practising their primary skill. The early afternoon was spent on their secondary or "elective" skill. Skills ranged from the practical to the highly theoretical: Farming, hunting, animal husbandry, engineering, carpentry, electrical, cooking, sewing, mechanics, mathematics, physics, biology, chemistry, astronomy, genetics, medicine, navigation, geology, pilot training, computer coding, and much more. Genni conducted the majority of theoretical classes and even some of the practical ones, due to the shortage of fully qualified people amongst the makeshift crew.

The ship was alive with classes and workshops occupying every nook and cranny. It was a race against time. The initial mission team of 900 people had been selected because of their considerable skills in at least one of these areas, and they had trained for 18 months in preparation for the mission. Had they come on board at Kepler Station as they were scheduled to, they would have already been fully trained and prepared for the challenges of the new world. The conglomeration of souls currently on-board Genesis represented, on the whole, a much lower average skill level. According to the long-established mission protocol, they had only a couple of weeks available to train before the long hibernation began, and once awake again, they would immediately be thrust into the challenges of having to build a new world on a virgin planet. The science team was currently considering the possibility of delaying hibernation for an additional two weeks, to allow a longer period for training, but this would be the absolute maximum they would allow. Well-documented research had determined that when untrained civilians were confined in a space vessel for more than a month, without the ability to see the distant horizon and sky, a small percentage developed disturbing psychological symptoms, including a form of psychosis colloquially known as 'space wobbles'.

Zac had selected pilot training as his primary skill and medicine as his secondary. Martinez had chosen pilot training and hunting. In fact, she was an instructor for the afternoon hunting class. Some of the key instructors spent all three daily sessions teaching their skill, the two morning sessions teaching those who had selected it as their primary skill, and the afternoon session instructing those for whom it would be their secondary skill. The only skill that wasn't run in the afternoons as a secondary skill was pilot training, as the morning session had more than enough participants for their requirements.

Some of the scientists aboard Genesis were now having to wear more than one hat. One of the glaring gaps in expertise among the science team was in the area of agriculture, which was to have been headed up by Dr. Rudolf Stein, a professor of biology and agriculture at the University of Otago. He had been training a team of agriculturalists and farmers in New Zealand for the past 18 months, and they had been scheduled to join Genesis at Kepler Station immediately prior to Earth departure. Of course, they never made it. The closest person Genesis now had to an agricultural expert was Regina Boyle.

"But my degree is in biology, with a doctorate in cryogenics!" she had responded when approached by Wisecroft. "I haven't studied botany since I was in high school!"

"Yes, I know," he replied, "but you're the closest thing we've got to a botanist and agriculturalist. There are a few colonists with some basic experience in farming, but no one with the requisite knowledge to oversee the establishment of agriculture on a new world. We need someone in charge who can analyse the basic chemistry and biology of new plant species and food crops and ensure that we don't poison ourselves or die of malnutrition."

Consequently, Regina found herself furiously devouring literature from Genesis's extensive electronic library as she attempted to prepare herself and her team of budding farmers for the vital role they would play in the new colony. She also spent many hours in discussion with several colonists who had lived or grown up on farms, and together they examined some of the state-of-the-art farming equipment in the storage holds, to familiarise themselves with the technology.

There were only 38 children on board, all of whom had arrived via the emergency shuttle evacuations. Those of school age spent the two morning sessions in 'school,' in a corner of the lounge area, with Genni as their teacher and a couple of adults with teaching experience helping with supervision. Each child had a tablet and headphones, and Genni tailored their individual lessons according to their abilities. The first morning's lessons had identified Melody as a mathematical prodigy. Her mother had deliberately kept it quiet, wanting to keep her out of the limelight, but Melody had been receiving private tuition since the age of 4, to foster the incredible gift that she had been born with. She devoured books on mathematics and was already studying advanced formulae at doctoral level.

Melody had found a soulmate in Jaz, who had taken her under her wing, and was her cabin mate. The young girl still occasionally cried at night for the mother and father she had lost, but Jaz had made it her mission to love this little girl and, as much as possible, to fill her days with joy and laughter. In the afternoons, Melody and Jaz were inseparable. Melody became Jaz's unofficial "assistant" in the medical bay, and very quickly became known as 'the little angel'. She especially looked forward to each afternoon, because she also got to spend time with Zac, who came down to the med bay for training each day.

Zac, himself, had undergone a transformation. The deep hurt of his loss and the sense of betrayal that had threatened to overwhelm him had gone. Somehow the cathartic expression of grief that he had shared with Melody had purged the grief from his soul and had allowed him to move forward. Maybe Keo was right; maybe a soul could be light or heavy, depending on what it was you chose to hold onto. Zac still experienced sadness at his loss, but it no longer dominated or defined him. The challenges of each day, and of the mission itself, gave him a purpose to live for, and the joy and laughter of new friendships sustained him.

Moreover, he found himself thinking of Jaz often. His afternoons in the med bay were the highlight of his day, and he couldn't deny that she was the main reason he had chosen that elective. He found Jaz utterly enchanting; her classic red-haired beauty, her warm, caring heart and her fun-loving nature all combined to overwhelm his defences. And he could tell that the chemistry was mutual. Several times in recent days they had held each other's eyes in a lingering look, and she had brushed up against him more than once, maintaining contact while supposedly carrying out some menial task, causing his heart to race and his mind to whirl.

Today, the afternoon medical training session was on the topic of fractures. Dr Francis Leibman, the chief medical officer, gave a 30-minute lecture to a group of about 40 people, explaining various first-aid procedures for the different types of fractures. The group then split into two for practising splints and bandaging, with young Dr Ben Miller taking one group and Jaz taking the other. In Jaz's group, Melody grabbed Zac as her bandage buddy, and a great deal of laughter ensued as Melody bandaged not only his arm but his head and torso, too.

"Hey, you two!" said Jaz. "You're going to use up all my bandages. This is supposed to be serious."

"This *is* serious!" replied Melody. "Somebody seriously needs to cover up his ugly head for the sake of humanity."

"Hey! I resemble that!" said Zac, with a twinkle in his eye. "Just for that, you need math punishment."

"Oh no! I'm really scared!" Melody said sarcastically. She turned to Jaz in a pretend whisper, "He thinks he's asking me hard questions."

"OK, smarty pants," said Zac. "What's the cube root of 658,500?"

"It doesn't have a whole integer cube root, silly! The nearest whole integer cube root is 87, which is the cube root of 658,503."

"Oh," said Zac, somewhat crestfallen. "OK, try this. If an orange farmer had 1,245 trees, each producing exactly 215 pieces of fruit each year, but one third of the trees died after three years, how many apples would he have produced after five years?"

Melody's lips moved quickly as she internalised her calculations, and then she proudly announced, "1,159,925!"

"Ha, ha!" said Zac. "Wrong! The answer is none! Because he's an orange farmer not an apple farmer!" Zac started waving his bandaged arms in the air, saying, "I win! I win! I'm the champion of the math world!"

Jaz shook her head in mock disapproval, and said, "I take back what I said about wasting bandages, Mel. You have my permission to bandage over his mouth."

Later, when the class was over and everyone had left, Melody and Zac stayed behind to pack up. Once the last of the bandages were rolled and packed into the utility trolley, Melody asked if she could wheel the trolley back down the corridor to the storage room. Jaz suspected that her version of 'wheeling' it actually involved using it as a manned roller-sled.

"OK," said Jaz. "And then you need to sit at the terminal in the nurses' station and do your math homework. I'll be another half-hour finishing up here."

As Melody happily set off down the corridor, Jaz asked Zac to help her fold the examination bed down from the wall. Somehow, as they straightened up from lowering it to the ground, Zac straightened up too quickly and managed to bump Jaz's chin with his shoulder. Later, he couldn't quite remember how it all happened, but somehow, the subsequent apologies and laughter and concerned touches had ended in something else entirely. He had his hands around her waist, looking at her with concern while she rubbed the side of her jaw with one hand, with her other hand resting on his shoulder. Suddenly there was silence as they looked into each other's eyes. Zac couldn't help himself. He leant forward and kissed her, and she immediately responded, pressing up against him as he drew her closer. A minute later they were still kissing when one of the nurses came to replenish some supplies in the med cupboard. The couple broke apart hurriedly. Zac's head was spinning as he made a quick exit, offering some feeble excuse about needing to check something in the shuttle, leaving behind a slightly embarrassed Jaz and a highly amused nurse.

At the dinner table later that evening, Jaz sat next to Zac, closer than usual, their thighs touching and their arms brushing as they ate. Zac found it difficult to concentrate on the conversation, and several times he felt Jaz's hand rest on his thigh under the table. He was sure everyone else could see what was happening, as the entire group was present: Kit, Martinez, Boyd, Keo, Grizzle and Melody. Grizzle had begun to join them for the evening meal, as he had developed a soft spot for Melody, whom he called Possum for no apparent reason. In fact, Melody had grown very fond of the old-timer, and she could sometimes be found in the late afternoons being taught how to drive a loader by Grizzle. This amused everyone in the loading bay, because Grizzle was a stickler for ensuring that no one operated machinery that they weren't fully trained for. Of course, no one was game to say anything to him about it, because he hadn't lost his acerbic tongue.

The surprise package of the group was Keo. His warm, gregarious nature, together with his passion for surfing and rugby, gave the initial impression of a simple soul, but Keo was, in fact, a profound thinker. He had an honours degree in philosophy and was widely read in the classics. His favourite philosopher was the 16th century French philosopher Michel de Montaigne, whom he could quote at great length. Yesterday's quote summed up Keo's attitude to life generally: "Take joy in the present, because everything else is beyond your grasp."

Boyd (no one called him by his first name, Andrew) had made a good recovery from his sudden decompression in the bug tug. Strangely, Martinez had maintained an almost continual bedside vigil for the first two days, at times even holding his hand, until it became apparent that he would make a full recovery. Once he was on his feet again, she reverted to treating him with callous indifference and sarcasm, which he seemed to accept with a certain fondness. Theirs was a truly puzzling relationship.

As the group chatted and bantered over the evening meal, Captain Christensen joined them, pulling up a chair and squeezing in between Zac and Kit. "Zac, I have a favour to ask," he said. "We are forming a city council, a leadership body for the future colony, and I would like you to be part of it."

"Me?" Zac seemed truly surprised.

"Yes. For a couple of reasons. Firstly, it will be good to have someone on the council who is not a scientist or directly associated with DANSA. Secondly, you showed resourcefulness and leadership in proposing the shuttle rescue mission. Your plan resulted in the saving of several hundred lives. We need that kind of clear thinking and compassion on the council. There are ..." he paused, searching for the right words, "certain elements within our current leadership who do not always see the humanitarian aspects of a given situation. Plus, I think having a historian on the council, someone who has studied the structure of previous societies and the antecedents of past conflicts, will give us a more balanced perspective on our current challenges."

"OK ..." Zac seemed a little lost for words.

"We'll have our first meeting tomorrow morning, at 0900, so you will be excused from the early training session. Are you willing to be involved?"

"Sure. I guess."

"Good. See you tomorrow, in the conference room." Captain Christensen stood up, nodded to the rest of the group, and walked back to the lifts.

"Cool!" said Melody, who, like the rest of the group, had unashamedly eavesdropped on the conversation. "You can vote for ice cream to be available at breakfast! It's not fair that it's only available at dinner."

"Thus speaks the mind of a mathematical genius," said Zac, and received a punch on the arm from the genius in return.

"Seriously, Zac, I think you will make a fine council

member," said Jaz, touching his arm affectionately. "You will bring balance and perspective to the group."

"Yeh. Keep the bastards honest," added Martinez.

"That's assuming my opinions will be listened to at all," said Zac.

Keo chimed in, ""Even those who are seated upon the highest of thrones are still seated upon their arses.""

"Montaigne?" asked Zac.

"Yes, my friend."

"I'm starting to like this Montaigne guy," said Kit.

"Yeh," said Grizzle. "So don't be afraid to apply the right boot of wisdom to the seat of learning."

"Amen brother," said Keo.

29

The first council meeting did not get off to a great start. It was apparent from the very beginning that there was tension between Wisecroft and Christensen. Both were nominated as Chairperson, and Wisecroft was soundly defeated. Only George Leonidis and Dr Francis Leibman voted for him. Christensen's appointment was proposed by the former Command Centre Coordinator, Lance Catrell, wearing his ever-present *2001: A Space Odyssey* baseball cap. Those who subsequently voted him in were the physicist, Dr Arno Manchester; the head of astronomy, Dr Carla Zangetti; Prisha Naroo, a psychologist and counsellor who had been rescued via the shuttle mission, and Zac. Wisecroft's resentment at his defeat was obvious in his simmering countenance and by the way his comments throughout the ensuing meeting sought to subtly undermine Christensen's authority. Captain Christensen, however, sailed over the waves of Wisecroft's resentment with apparent ease, refusing to respond to his subtle innuendos, thus adding fuel to Wisecroft's discontent.

Genesis had been in Mars orbit for two days now, transferring people to and from the surface, as well as taking on board additional supplies for their mission.

"Lance, how many passengers are we left with?" asked Wisecroft.

"I think it is better to refer to them as *colonists* from this point on," said Christensen. "The *passengers* have disembarked. Those who remain are active participants in our mission." He smiled benignly at Wisecroft, who was clearly not impressed at being corrected.

"After all the comings and goings," answered Lance Catrell, consulting his data pad, "we are left with a total of 560 people on board."

"Not as many as I had hoped, but better than I had feared," said Christensen. He turned to the psychologist, Prisha Naroo, and asked, "Ms Naroo, what is your assessment of morale?"

"Please, call me Prisha," she said, smiling. "After all, we are going to be friends and neighbours for many years to come." She paused and pushed a thick strand of her long, curly dark hair out of her eyes. "Hope is a wonderful thing. Hope and purpose. The hope of a new world, and people's commitment to this mission, has helped the vast majority to deal with their recent trauma very positively. Grief is still very strong, and will be for some time for all of us, but there is real healing already taking place. Apart from that, there are a couple of sociological issues to be aware of. Firstly, there are only 38 children on board, which is an unusually small percentage of a population of 560. A population of this size would normally have about 120 people aged under 18. It is extremely important that we create opportunities for socialisation among their own age-groups. Play and interaction with their peers is important for a child's development. To that end, I have already set aside a corner of the recreation deck as a kids' zone from 1500 each afternoon. It is proving to be quite popular."

Prisha paused and looked around at the rest of the council.

"The second issue is related. If we are to flourish on the new world, we will need to have children—lots of them." She raised her eyebrows. "We will all need to play our part in this. As far as I can tell, there are very few existing couples on board. Most people are here alone, having lost their partners and loved ones. Obviously, we all need time to grieve. But we can't take too long about it. People need to be encouraged to ... well ... to pair up and, eventually, to have children. We have an adult population of 522. I don't know the exact split between male and female, but it appears to me, from superficial observation, that it is fairly even."

Captain Christensen interjected, "What are the figures, Genni?"

"The current population consists of 252 males and 270 females. Subtracting the males whose bioscans reveal that they are infertile, and the females who are too old to reproduce effectively, there are 238 males and 246 females who are able to reproduce. Allowing for the fact that not everyone will be heterosexually inclined, those tendencies should be fairly even among both genders, so the ratio of reproductive males to females should remain approximately the same."

"That's quite good, isn't it?" said Christensen to Prisha.

"Yes. Actually, it's very fortunate. It could have been a lot worse. This means that there will be minimal potential for conflict arising from competition for sexual partners. Obviously, the issue is not immediately pressing, but as we develop the new colony, we must provide plenty of opportunities for socialisation to occur. And the need for procreation must be impressed upon everyone."

"OK," said Zac. "Action Step 001. Breed like rabbits. Next?"

There were chuckles around the table.

"Yes," said Christensen, smiling. "Let's move on to more immediate concerns. Lance, how are we going in terms of readiness for departure?"

Lance had become the go-to man for logistics. "Life support and power systems are at 100 percent. In fact, they were completely ready prior to the attack. We were very fortunate. If it had been one week earlier, we would have been in trouble. The main challenge is equipment. We were scheduled to receive our mining and heavy industrial equipment via uplift rockets after docking at Kepler Station. There will be two more shuttle flights tomorrow, bringing up a few final supplies from the Mars base. After that, we will still only have about 60 percent of the equipment we had planned for. Our engineering department will be very busy for the first few years on the new world, manufacturing the equipment we are missing. For the moment, however, the most pressing need is clothing. Most people came on board with nothing but the clothes on their backs. The Genesis jumpsuits are helping, but having a ship load of people all wearing the same clothes makes us look like some kind of restrictive Orwellian society. Creating a viable textile industry will be a need once we reach our destination."

"Action Step 002," said Zac. "Make clothes to cover nakedness. But doesn't that contradict Action Step 001?"

More chuckles ensued from most of the council, apart from Wisecroft, who had adopted a permanent scowl.

"OK," said Christensen. "There appears to be nothing hindering our departure, based upon those issues. What about cryogenics?"

"Nine hundred pods, all fully functional," answered Manchester, succinctly.

"That brings us to the key question, doesn't it?" said Wisecroft. "When do we start putting people to sleep? I suggest we process the colonists in batches of 100 each day, commencing immediately upon departure."

"I disagree," said Prisha. "The colonists need more time to bond and to begin forming crucial relationships. These are people who have only recently been thrown together out of tragedy. The more time they can have to interact and form friendships, the better equipped for survival they will be on our new world."

"I am inclined to agree," said Christensen. "The colonists are also significantly under-skilled, compared to the original mission team. The more time they have for training, the better will be our chance for survival as a colony."

"On the other hand," contributed Carla Zangetti, the astronomer, "too long awake inside a tin can, even one this big, without sky and sunlight and a horizon, will eventually result in psychological distress—particularly among people who are untrained and unprepared for confinement in a space vessel."

"That's a good point," said Prisha. "We need to find the right balance; enough time for further training and bonding, but not too much, so that we avoid the onset of space wobbles."

"OK," said Christensen. "Let's allow the stipulated two weeks of further training indicated in the original mission protocol, with an optional additional two weeks for those who are coping well with shipboard life. After the initial two weeks, those who want to can choose cryogenic sleep voluntarily. After the additional two weeks, it will become mandatory."

"That sounds about right," said Prisha.

"Is everyone in agreement?" asked Christensen.

There were nods all around, except for Wisecroft and Leonidis. Wisecroft, in particular, looked particularly unimpressed that he had been contradicted yet again.

"Departure is set for 1800 tomorrow," said Christensen. "Is there anything else we need to consider at this point?"

"What about a party?" said Zac. Everyone looked at him. "A Departure Party. Let's make it a celebration. After all, the departure of just about every major exploratory expedition throughout history was marked by a celebration of some kind. The departure of Christopher Columbus was celebrated with a Spanish feast, and the departure of Captain James Cook's exploratory expedition from the Thames was accompanied by brass bands and a dockside party. I think that setting sail for a completely new solar system warrants some form of celebration. We could certainly all do with some cheering up. And it could be a first step towards Action Step 001," he said with a smile.

"What a wonderful idea, Zac!" said Prisha. "I love it! It's just what we all need!"

"Thanks, Zac," said Christensen. "This is precisely why I wanted you as part of this council. You bring a unique historical perspective to our deliberations. I don't think we even need to vote on your proposal. Can I suggest that you and Prisha do the organising? Get as many people involved as you can. Feel free to conscript anyone who isn't engaged in anything vital." He looked around the table. "If there is nothing else, we will meet here again at the same time next week."

The meeting broke up, with Prisha and Zac chatting animatedly as they left the room. Eventually, only Wisecroft, Leonidis and Christensen were left.

"Is there something you want to say to me, Dr. Wisecroft?" asked Christensen.

"I think you know what I want to say. You are undermining me at every opportunity. Anything I say, you contradict. You are using your position to reinforce your dominance over me."

"I'm sorry you feel that way, but I assure you I take every suggestion on face value. I have no hidden agenda here, and I certainly have no personal vendetta against you."

"I think you do! I think you planned to take control from the moment we left the moon! You have effectively mounted a coup, and I don't acknowledge your authority as leader of this mission!" Wisecroft stood up, and Leonidis followed suit. He pointed aggressively towards Christensen and said, "I don't intend to go away quietly! This is not over! Not by a long shot!"

He turned and walked out of the room, with Leonidis in his wake, leaving Christensen stroking his beard contemplatively.

"Genni, do you acknowledge my authority as mission leader?"

"Yes, Captain. The committee vote was constitutional and unequivocal."

"In that case, please rescind Dr. Wisecroft's access to all essential ship systems. I don't trust him."

"Neither do I."

30

The party was a great success. It began at 1700 and was in full swing by launch time. People had been preparing for it all afternoon, and most afternoon training classes had been cancelled. A music committee had compiled a playlist, which involved significant debate, over a period of several hours. The food dispensers had been programmed to provide 'party food', which was basically ordinary food in slightly different shapes, produced in vibrant colours. It didn't taste any better, but it looked fun. The dispensers could also produce alcoholic drinks —ethanol mixed with various sweet or bitter liquids. Biochip scans were required for these to ensure that children could not access them. In the absence of party clothes, many people had resorted to wearing small strips of brightly dyed cloth, scavenged from personal belongings, as head bands or waist bands, in an attempt to add a note of gaiety to their attire.

Melody had been in a state of mounting excitement all afternoon, and Zac and Jaz were both relieved when the party actually got under way, so that Melody could finally find some release for her pent-up energy. In fact, once the party commenced, Melody disappeared into Cinema 2 on the recreation deck, where there was a kids' disco, complete with flashing lights.

Zac was also feeling particularly chuffed, as he had just that morning completed his first full flight, successfully piloting a shuttle from the Mars mining base to Genesis under Kit's watchful gaze. As he was powering down the shuttle after a slightly bumpy touchdown in the shuttle bay, she said to him, "That's not the worst first flight I've seen."

"Really?" he asked, fishing for a further compliment.

"Yeh. Three years ago, I watched a guy completely flip a shuttle onto its back when he landed. That was even worse than yours."

"Wow! Thanks a lot!" said Zac. "Has anyone ever told you that you have the gift of encouragement?"

"Nope."

"Didn't think so."

Now, as the music blared and people were eating and drinking and laughing, Zac felt a warm glow and, for the first time since their recent tragedies, a sense of hope. Out of the ashes of despair, something good was starting to emerge.

Keo came and stood beside Zac. ""In the sweetness of friendship let there be laughter and sharing of pleasures. For in the dew of little things the heart finds its morning and is refreshed.""

"Montaigne again?"

"No. Khalil Gibran."

"How do you remember all that stuff?"

"I have a long-term eidetic memory."

"Photographic memory?"

"Something like that. It's not instantaneous. I have to consciously repeat something three or four times, and really focus. But once it's in there, it's in there for good."

"Wow! Impressive."

"It's nothing to be impressed about. I did nothing to deserve this ability. It is a gift from God."

Zac sidestepped the religious reference. He had learned to accept his friend's faith without feeling the need to comment. He said, "The curse of humanity is that most people remember what they should forget and forget what they should remember."

"Who said that? Descartes?" asked Keo.

"No. Me. Just then. Pretty good, eh?"

"Not bad, my friend, not bad. I'll make a philosopher of you yet."

At 17:58, the music stopped, and Lars Christensen's face appeared on the screens around the dining room and on other decks. "Friends, in two minutes we will fire our main propulsion drive and commence a burn that will start us on our journey. It is a momentous occasion, and one that is filled with mixed emotions. Undeniably, we have much to be sorrowful about, including the fact that we are leaving behind our world and our solar system, never to set foot in them again. But I hope you will agree with me that now is not the time for sorrow, but for hope and joy. This represents a new beginning for us and for humankind. We are making history today. We are forging a new destiny. We are blazing a new trail; one that will lead us to a better life for us and our children. Please charge your glasses and join me in a toast. As we leave here today, let's not look backward on what we are leaving behind, but let us look forward, to the wonderful new possibilities that await us." He raised his own glass and said, "To a bright, new future!"

"To a bright, new future!" echoed everyone.

Immediately the lights dimmed, and a 15-second countdown appeared on the screens, over the top of a live video feed of Mars. When the countdown reached 10, everyone started counting down with it, and, at zero, the dining room resounded with a loud cheer. The countdown timer disappeared from the screen and the view of Mars filled the whole screen. For the first second or two, nothing seemed to happen. Then an incandescent jet of flame could be seen at the very bottom edge of the screen, and at the same time music pulsed from the sound system. The music committee had chosen the hit song from over three decades ago, "Light A Candle To The Stars." People cheered again and watched the screen, mesmerised. Almost imperceptibly at first, but then increasingly over the next few minutes, Mars diminished in size, as Genesis accelerated away at eight gravities, rapidly building up velocity. Inertial dampening ensured that they felt nothing, physically, but the same was not true emotionally. There were some tears of sadness, but the overwhelming majority of colonists were swept up in the euphoria of the moment. Captain Christensen's well-timed words, together with liberal doses of alcohol, ensured that the predominant mood was one of optimism and celebration. There were hugs and kisses all around.

"It's like New Year's Eve!" said Kit, coming up beside Zac and Keo.

"More like New Life Eve," said Zac.

"In that case, happy New Life Eve," said Kit, giving him a brief kiss on the cheek. "You too, Keo," she said, standing on her toes to kiss him as well. She appeared momentarily embarrassed after her display of affection, but quickly rallied, saying, "Well, are you two jugheads going to just stand there and leave a girl dance-less, or are you going help me celebrate?" So saying, she grabbed their hands and dragged them onto the dance floor in the cleared space in the middle of the room.

The dancing and celebrations continued long into the night, with the screens around the room continuing to stream live video of the view aft. After just two hours, they were 1.2 million kilometres from Mars, and it was already just an orange dot against the background of stars.

At some point, Zac felt the need to clear his head and take a break from the music and revelry. He took the lift up to the lounge deck above, having decided to find a quiet spot to sit and watch Mars shrink behind them. Several couples were occupying some of the lounges, apparently making significant progress towards Action Step 001. For a few moments, Zac stood looking at the image of Mars on the big screen.

I will probably never see this solar system again, he thought. *How am I supposed to feel? How did the Pilgrims leaving for America feel? Or the Israelites leaving Egypt? Hopeful? Frightened? Grieving? A mixture of all of those? And did their leaders squabble and fight? Were there unresolved tensions that they carried with them? And, most importantly, did they find what they were looking for? Were they able to leave the past behind and make a fresh start, without the ghosts of their past haunting them?*

He had not slept well the night before, thinking about his ill-fated marriage and what had started to develop between him and Jaz. *How can I get romantically involved with someone so quickly after the death of my wife? It's not right!* As he watched the gradually shrinking image of the red planet, his mind once more swirled with conflicting emotions. He decided to forget about the party and try to sleep. Maybe he would be able to think better in the morning. As he walked towards the lifts, he heard a voice say, "It's a great party, Zac."

In a quiet corner of the room Zac spotted Jaz sitting quietly, watching a nearby screen, stroking Melody's head as she lay asleep across her lap. Zac walked over and stood beside them.

"She danced herself into exhaustion," said Jaz, smiling at him and continuing to stroke Melody's hair.

"You're missing out on all the fun," said Zac.

"I've never really been a party girl. Give me a good book, a glass of wine and some comfy pyjamas, and I'm in heaven."

Zac looked at them both: the trainee doctor and the child genius. Jaz looked particularly vulnerable at the moment, her red hair in disarray, falling in front of her eyes and lying across her lightly-freckled button nose. "She loves you, you know," he said, indicating Melody.

"I know," she said, looking fondly at the sleeping girl. "The feeling is mutual." She looked back up at Zac. "Maybe this a time for new love ... for all of us." She held his gaze, and he felt his heart start pounding wildly.

"I ... um ... I've got an early start in the morning. I think I'll hit the sack," he said, taking a step backwards. He saw a look of disappointment, and even hurt, cross her face. "I'll, um, see you tomorrow." He turned and walked away, feeling terrible. *What are you doing?* he told himself as he got into the lift. *You know you feel something for her. Why didn't you kiss her?* At the same time, he felt overcome with guilt. *How can I have feelings for another woman when my wife died less than two weeks ago? I must be the shallowest person alive!*

He went to his cabin and lay down on his bunk, but once again, sleep would not come.

31

The next two weeks were a blur of shipboard activity. Training classes continued. Friendships strengthened. New romance blossomed. People ate, slept, worked, learnt, played and then slept again. While their departure from Mars had been accompanied by fanfare and celebration, their exit from the solar system two mornings later, already travelling at 8,000 kilometres per second, went largely unnoticed.

For Zac, his awkward encounter with Jaz on the night of the party had put a dampener on their blossoming romance. He withdrew into himself and lost whatever spark he had regained. No one else in their group of friends understood what had happened, but they could all see that both Zac and Jaz were unhappy and uncomfortable around each other. There was an awkwardness between them now, and whenever possible they avoided being in each other's company. Zac rarely went to the afternoon medical training sessions now, which hurt not only Jasmine, but Melody as well. Knowing that he was hurting them made Zac feel even more miserable, but he couldn't see a way out of his predicament. He couldn't fall in love with someone else so soon! It wasn't right! So, the best thing was to avoid Jaz altogether and throw himself into his other duties.

He worked out in the gym for an hour each morning before breakfast and sometimes once more in the evenings, almost as if he was trying to punish himself. Keo often trained with him, and they spurred each other on, competing and pushing one another. Keo found joy in exercise and in their shared friend-ship, but he sensed a brooding darkness in Zac now that was not there before. They still joked and sparred verbally, but Zac often seemed only partially present, wrestling with some inner demon that he would not speak about.

One afternoon, on Mission Day 6, Melody came looking for Zac and found him in the cockpit of Shuttle 1, reading the flight manual and going through the emergency procedures for engine failure.

"Zac?" she said, standing at the cockpit door. "What are you doing here?"

"Hi, Possum," he said, using Grizzle's nickname for her that everyone in the group had adopted. "I'm just brushing up on my pilot training."

"Why don't you come to the medical training anymore?"

Zac could hear the hurt in her voice and see the confusion on her face. "I'm just so busy lately, sweetie. I wish I could, but I've got so much to do." He felt terrible as he said it, but what could he tell an 11-year-old girl?

"We miss you, Zac. It's not the same without you. Don't you like us anymore?" Her eyes welled up and a tear began to roll down her cheek.

Zac's heart melted. *God, help me,* he thought. *What am I supposed to do here?* "Come here, Possum," he said. She came closer and he hugged her, then kissed her on the forehead. "Of course I like you. I'll always like you. You and I are pals."

Melody looked into his eyes. "Did you and Jaz have a fight?"

"No. Of course not."

"Then why does she cry sometimes? I heard her last night when she thought I was asleep."

Zac felt heart broken. "I don't know. Maybe she's still sad after everything that's happened." He needed to change the subject. "Hey! How would you like to be my co-pilot! You can help me fly the shuttle. Sit in that chair and put those head-phones on."

Her eyes lit up. "Really? Cool!"

"Now, where would you like to fly to today?"

"Let's go to Saturn! We could fly through the rings."

"OK. Buckle up, partner. And if you're good, we'll hit the drive-through hamburger joint on the way home!"

#

Later that night, Jaz and Zac passed each other in the hallway on their cabin deck. Jaz stopped him and said, rather awkwardly, "Zac, thanks for spending time with Melody this afternoon. We ... she really misses you. She needs you in her life. Whatever else is going on, please don't cut her out."

Without waiting for a reply, she walked away, leaving Zac feeling confused and miserable once more. *She's right,* he thought. *Melody is too important. She's had enough hurt in her life. I don't want to add to it.* He resolved then and there to make sure he spent time with her every day, and, as much as possible, not let his strained relationship with Jaz affect Melody. The next day he started attending afternoon medical training again, and also made an effort to be present at mealtimes when Melody was there. Things were still extremely strained between him and Jaz, but he sensed her appreciation at his being involved with Melody again.

On Mission Day 7, the council met for the second time, and Zac dragged himself along with little enthusiasm. Captain Christensen called the meeting to order and asked Genni for a mission status update.

"We are currently 9.21 billion kilometres from Earth, travelling at 32,840 kilometres per second. We are on course for Icarus R-421, with no detectable anomalies. All life support and propulsion systems are fully operational."

Turning to those seated at the table, Christensen said, "Our main task today is to plan an orderly process for putting our colonists to sleep, starting next week. But firstly, are there specific issues or concerns that anyone on the council would like to raise?"

"Yes," said Wisecroft, standing up. "This council is unconstitutional, and so is your chairmanship, Captain Christensen."

"How so, Dr Wisecroft?"

"The Mission Plan document, formulated by the president, her cabinet, and DANSA officials, specifies that leadership of this mission, in the event of the death of the commander, falls to the next ranking officer. By virtue of my longstanding involvement with Genesis and my leadership of the DANSA research facility, where Genesis was built, I am clearly the next in rank, not you."

Christensen stroked his beard and said, "I have also read that document, Dr Wisecroft. Did you note Section 8.1 – Emergency Protocols?"

"Well ... of course ... I ... um ..."

"Because that section states that in the event of loss of life due to hostilities or war, the highest-ranking *military* officer will assume leadership, for the duration of the conflict *and thereafter*. Furthermore, I hasten to point out that I did not insist on that right of leadership, even though it was mine by constitutional right. Instead, I put it to a vote, right here in this council, so that there could be no doubt."

Wisecroft rallied his arguments. "Yes, well, that brings me to my other concern. You clearly stacked this council in your favour, by inviting people onto it who have absolutely no right to be here! I mean, a history professor, for goodness sake! And a family counsellor! Good grief, man! What do you think this is, a benevolent society for the unemployed? I move a motion that Dr Perryman and Ms Naroo be removed from the council immediately and that a re-vote take place for the leadership of the mission!"

There was stunned silence for a few moments after Wisecroft's venomous outburst. Christensen calmly said, "All right. Dr Wisecroft has moved a motion. Is there a seconder?"

"I'll second it," said George Leonidis.

"Would anyone like to make a comment before we vote?" asked Christensen.

Everyone remained silent.

"In that case, we will proceed with the vote. Zac and Prisha, you cannot vote. All those in favour of removing Zac and Prisha from the council, please raise your hand."

Wisecroft and Leonidis raised their hands.

"All those against?"

Five hands went up.

"The motion is defeated," said Christensen. "Now, if we could please return to our order of business ..."

"I would like to move a motion," interrupted Zac.

"Yes Zac?" said Christensen.

"History has shown us the danger of allowing a pathological narcissist to assume leadership; Adolf Hitler, Josef Stalin, Idi Amin, Robert Mugabe, Pol Pot, Saddam Hussein, Mao Tsetung, Genghis Khan - the list is long and disturbing. In fact, that was a major factor leading to the Faith Wars. A narcissist's need to be right, the inability to empathize or apologize, not to mention a huge sense of entitlement - all of that presents a risk we can't afford to take. Therefore, I would like to move a motion that we censure Dr Wisecroft for his appalling, childish, narcissistic behaviour, and remove him from the council."

"Well, I'm not sure if we should ..."

"I second the motion," said Prisha.

"Right," said Christensen, clearly a little uncomfortable. "We have a motion. Is there any discussion before we vote?"

"Yes," said Carla Zangetti. "I object to Zac's wording of the motion."

"Well, I may have been a little ..." began Zac.

"He left out 'arrogant, priggish and spoilt'," she said.

Zac smiled. "Yes, I believe I did. But only because too many adjectives make it grammatically cumbersome."

"This is outrageous!" said Wisecroft.

"Not at all," said Zac. "We are simply following in your wonderful footsteps."

"You can't vote me off the council! I'm the head of DANSA!"

"Dr Wisecroft," said Christensen, "there *is* no DANSA. It doesn't exist anymore. There is no Democratic Alliance of Nations. No space agency. There is just us. All the impressive titles and qualifications of our previous world mean very little here. In my opinion the primary criteria for a seat on this council are the ability to make a positive contribution to the future of our colony and to work harmoniously with others. Members of this council have voiced a doubt about your suitability in those regards, and it is fitting that we vote on the motion that has been proposed."

Turning to the whole group, Christensen said, "I think we are ready to vote. Dr Wisecroft, you must abstain from voting, and in order to avoid any appearance of bias, I will also abstain. All those in favour, please raise your hand."

Five hands rose.

"All those against?"

Leonidis's lone hand ventured into the air. Zac noted that Dr. Leibman abstained.

"Dr Wisecroft, it is my duty to inform you that you have been censured for your ... um ..."

"Appalling, childish, narcissistic behaviour," prompted Prisha.

"Yes," agreed Christensen, "and that your services are no longer required on this council. You are free to go."

Wisecroft stood violently to his feet, knocking his chair over as he did so. Instead of ranting and yelling, however, he spoke in a preternaturally calm, calculated voice. "I promise you, there will be consequences for what you have done here today." He turned and walked out of the room. Leonidis looked uncomfortable but remained silent and seated.

"Well, that was fun," said Zac.

"Fun it might have been," said Christensen, "but we may just have created a problem that we will live to regret."

An hour later, as the council meeting broke up, Lance quietly asked Zac and Christensen to remain behind. When they were alone, he said, "I think it might be helpful if I provide some background information about Dr Wisecroft." He looked at both of them for a moment. "I feel a little uneasy about this, but I think it's important for the sake of our mission that you understand why he sometimes acts the way he does."

"We will treat whatever you have to say with the strictest confidentiality," said Christensen.

"Thank you." Lance paused to gather his thoughts. "Simon and I went to the same school together. It was a Kindergarten to Year 12 private college in Santa Cruz, Bolivia. He began attending our school in Year 4, at the age of nine. He was newly adopted by our principal and his wife, Mr and Mrs Wisecroft. They had been unable to have children, so they adopted him from a local orphanage. They chose him over younger children because the orphanage had identified him as being intellectually gifted. No one knows anything about his birth parents, because he had been dumped on the orphanage doorstep as a baby."

"Sadly, Mrs Wisecroft died of pneumonia just six months after his adoption, leaving Mr Wisecroft to raise him alone. Mr Wisecroft was an aloof intellectual. He showed no emotion and gave Simon no love. Simon always referred to him as 'sir', even privately, and Mr Wisecroft seemed to treat Simon more harshly than the other students—as though he was trying to avoid showing favouritism. I also know that Mr Wisecroft used physical discipline on Simon at home. Simon would sometimes come to school with welts across the backs of his legs.

"The other students all called Simon 'orphy', and he was teased incessantly. I felt sorry for him and tried to be nice to him. I guess I was his only friend, but it was difficult. He has always been pathologically insecure and needy. He should have topped our College in Year 12, except several assessments in his final year were very harshly marked by Mr Wisecroft. Everyone knew he was the brightest student in the school."

"He and I ended up at the same university. He went on to complete a doctorate in physics, and I stumbled through a degree in engineering. Unfortunately, Simon never seemed to be able to make friends. His deep-seated insecurity caused him to interpret even the most innocent comment or action as a personal attack. His constant need to prove himself drove people away, and by then his narcissism had reached patholog-ical proportions. Everything was about him, and he was unable to consider the feelings and opinions of others.

"I kept in contact from time to time, meeting up with him for a beer at the local pub and going out to dinner with him on his birthday. But I was his only friend, and by then Mr. Wise-croft had passed away.

"Years later, when Simon was appointed as head of the Armstrong Research Facility, I got a call from him, asking if I would be interested in the role of Command Centre Coordina-tor. To this day, I think I am Simon's only friend. Although 'friend' is probably too strong a word. He is incapable of emotional warmth, and I simply feel sorry for him."

Lance paused for a moment. "I guess what I'm saying is that Simon isn't a bad person; he is just deeply wounded. It was difficult for me to vote against him today, and I am sure that that will be the end of whatever friendship we had, but I felt I had to vote the way I did for the sake of the mission. Simon simply isn't the right person to be helping to guide the new colony."

"Thank you, Lance," said Christensen. "I appreciate your honesty. That certainly does put things into perspective for us."

"But it doesn't change our resolve about our decision to remove him from the council," said Zac.

"No," agreed Christensen. "If anything, it strengthens it. I think we will need to be very careful in our future dealings with Simon."

32

It was lunch on Mission Day 9 when things came to a head between Jaz and Zac. Jaz came to lunch late, and the only remaining empty chair was the one next to Zac. She appeared frozen for a few moments, then steeled herself and sat next to him. Zac, who had been joining in the conversation a few moments earlier, fell silent. A tangible awkwardness prevailed, which put a dampener on the mood of the whole group. A few minutes later, Zac excused himself and left, even though he had barely eaten half his lunch. Jaz bowed her head and appeared to become even more miserable, if that was possible.

"I can't take this anymore!" exclaimed Martinez, throwing her napkin down on the table in disgust. She stood up and walked off, leaving the rest of the group open-mouthed.

"What was that all about?" asked Kit.

"The girl's got a bee in her bonnet about something," muttered Grizzle.

Martinez found Zac in his cabin, with his door open. He was sitting on his bunk, hunched over, staring at the floor.

Martinez walked in and stood in front of him. Zac looked up in surprise and said, "Hey."

She stood there, looking down at him, not saying anything.

"Martinez? What are you doing here?"

Her eyes drilled holes into him, but still she didn't speak, seemingly undergoing some kind of internal argument with herself.

"Listen," said Zac, "I don't know what ..."

"Your wife was having an affair with Wisecroft."

"What?"

"You heard me. They were bonking each other's brains out."

"That's not possible. She wouldn't ..."

"She would, and she did."

"But how would you ..."

"Know? I was 2IC of security. I got to know all the sordid details of what was happening on the base."

Zac's mind was reeling. He looked up at Martinez in bewilderment. "How ... how long?"

"At least two years, that I know of."

Zac was shell-shocked. He shook his head, trying to process the information.

Martinez asked, "Have you ever wondered why Wisecroft brought only you to the base, and not the family members of the other missing staff? It was because he was desperate to find his lover before she did something stupid, and he thought the simple, cuckolded husband could help."

Her words struck him like blows. He opened and closed his mouth several times, but no words came out.

"You're being faithful to a fantasy. She was never the wife you thought she was. Wake up, Doc, and start living. You're making the rest of us miserable." With that, she turned and walked out of the room, leaving Zac stunned.

He thought back again over his brief married life, looking for signs of unfaithfulness he might have missed. He replayed scenes in his mind, trying to spot clues that had gone unnoticed. There had been no obvious unhappiness. No arguing or conflict. But, on the other hand, he had to admit that there had not been a deep level of intimacy. They had seemed to exist at a comfortable, superficial level. He'd put it down to how busy they both were with their respective careers, but now he realised that Annisa had never really pursued a deep connection with him, even when they were dating. She had not offered herself to him at any deep emotional level and had not expected anything more from him in return. *Did she ever really love me at all?* He would never know for sure, but it seemed pretty clear that he had been used from the very start.

Knowing that he had been played for a fool from the very start—by a woman who was not only a secret terrorist but also happy to cheat on him with the likes of Wisecroft—was a crushing blow to his ego. He felt humiliated and angry. As he dwelt on his humiliation, the anger grew within him, feeding upon itself like a brewing storm. Finally, he leapt to his feet and rushed out of his room, with one clear purpose in mind. He would find that miserable bastard, Wisecroft, in whatever corner of the ship he was grovelling, and he would beat him to a pulp. Zac had never been a violent man, but now the need for vengeance consumed him. Somehow, the revelation of his betrayal had unleashed a pent-up reservoir of anger and hurt that he had not known was there. It rose up within him and took control. All reason abandoned him, and he strode down the corridor towards the lifts, lost in a red haze of fury.

He was halfway down the corridor when one of the lifts opened and Keo stepped out. He walked forward and blocked the corridor, with arms held wide. "Whoa there, brother. Where are you off to?"

"Out of my way, Keo."

"I don't think so, my friend."

"I said get out of my way. I don't want to hurt you."

"No chance of me getting out of your way, and no chance of

you hurting me, anyway," said the big man, standing his ground. "Where are you going?"

Zac stood in front of Keo and said, "I'm ... I'm going for a walk."

"Looks to me like you had a different kind of exercise in mind, bro," Keo said with eyebrows raised. "I don't think you want to see the venerable Dr Wisecroft right now. That wouldn't be wise."

"How did you ...?"

"Martinez told me. She's worried about you. Looks like I got here just in time."

"You don't understand. He needs to be ... I need to ..."

"I know exactly what you need right now, and it's not a conviction for assault. You're coming with me, my friend. Dr Keo has the perfect prescription for what ails you." He gripped Zac's arm in his huge hand and led him back towards the lifts.

An hour and a half later, the two of them sat side by side on a weight bench in the gym, dripping with sweat after an intense workout. Zac had run for an hour straight on the treadmill, at 16 kilometres per hour. Now he was spent, and he sat panting and exhausted beside his friend.

"What am I meant to do, Keo?"

"Move forward."

"But Wisecroft should pay for what he did to me."

"He will, bro. God sees all. He will judge everyone in the end."

"But he should pay now."

""He who seeks revenge, should dig two graves." Douglas Horton. You will end up hurting yourself more than you hurt him. Seeking revenge will simply twist your own soul into a knot. Instead of setting you free, it will enslave you."

Zac sat hunched over, staring at the ground and shaking his head. "I'm a complete fool. I thought she loved me. But it turns out, she was just using me. She was playing me the whole time. What does that say about me?"

"It says nothing at all about you, Zac. Her deceit and manipulation are a commentary on *her* soul, not yours."

"So, am I expected to just pretend nothing happened? Is that it?"

"He who is focused on the hurts of the past can't see the good that is front of him in the present."

"Who said that?"

"Me. Just then. I think I should write a book."

Keo looked at Zac. "She didn't just play you. She played Wisecroft, too."

"I suppose so."

"There's no 'supposing' about it, bro. She clearly had an agenda, and Wisecroft was simply a means to an end. By literally getting into bed with him, she almost certainly got access to intel she would not otherwise have had, and probably got greater access to restricted areas of the base as well. In that sense, Wisecroft is just as much a victim here as you."

"I can't accept that," said Zac. "He knew what he was doing. He may not have known that Annisa was using him, but he certainly knew he was screwing someone else's wife."

"Yes," agreed Keo. "He is clearly a morally weak man. But trying to take revenge on him will only poison your own soul."

They sat for a while in silence, then Keo said, "Zac, the past is dead. It's gone. You can learn from it, but you can't live in it. "Life must be understood backward, but it must be lived forward." Soren Kierkegaard. The present is where life is. The present is where love is. And love is staring you in the face. Don't miss out on what's real now, because of what was fake in the past." He stood up. "And by the way, you need a shower, bro. You stink."

33

Jasmine and Melody were tidying up the med clinic after the afternoon training session, rolling up bandages and stacking chairs in the triage holding area. A volunteer who was doing a shift as a nurse came in and said, "Jaz, before you go, can you see one more patient. He's in cubicle two."

Jaz breathed out a sigh, and said, "OK, Jan. I'll be there in a second. Mel, you can use the terminal at the nurses' station to do your homework while you're waiting."

"Do I have to? Can't I come and help you?"

"No. And I want to see at least two more lines of that theorem on your page by the time I get back."

Jaz walked briskly down the hall, pulled back the curtain to cubicle two and started to enter, then stopped dead. "Zac." He was sitting on the side of the bed.

"Yep. It's me all right."

"Is something wrong?" she asked, concern now in her voice.

"It's my eyes. I can't see properly."

"What do you mean?"

"Cloudy vision. I can see around the edges, but I can't see what's right in front of me."

Jaz moved forward and stood in front of him, concern now written on her face. She took a pencil torch out of her pocket and said, "Look up at me." She checked both pupil reflexes. "Now look to the left. Now right. Now follow my finger." She took a step back and said, "Zac, your eyes seem fine."

"Yes, I know. I haven't been able to see properly for about ten days, but they're better now." He stood up and took a step towards her. "I'm not sure what the medical term is for temporary blindness, but I think that's what I've had."

"Amaurosis fugax," she said.

"Yep, that's it. That's what I've had."

The beginning of a smile curled the corner of Jaz's mouth. "And what do you think caused it?"

"Temporary insanity," he replied.

"A transient loss of cognitive reasoning and an episodic break with reality," she interpreted.

"Yep, that's the one. Plus, I was looking at things in the past that turn out to have been completely false."

"Hallucinations and psychotic delusions. Zac, you're a mess," she said, struggling to hold her smile in. Her heart was racing, and she was feeling light-headed. "In fact, I've never had a patient with so many problems all at once."

"What's the treatment doc? Is there any hope for me?"

"There's a slim chance of recovery, but you'll have to undergo radical therapy."

"I'll do whatever it takes. What's first?"

"I think a complete lobotomy is in order. Followed by an enema. And then maybe a heart transplant—without anaesthetic."

"Ouch! Was I that bad?"

She grew serious. "You really hurt me, Zac."

"I know. I'm sorry. I never want to do that again. Ever. I care for you more than anyone else in the world."

"That's not saying much. There aren't many people left in the world."

"Yeh, but first out of 560 is still pretty good," he said with a cheeky smile. He reached out and held both her hands. "Jaz, I've been blind and stupid and weighed down with false guilt. But now I can see what's been staring me in the face the whole time."

"What's that?"

"I want to be with you, Jaz."

She stared into his eyes and whispered softly, "I want to be with you, too."

"Are you guys going to kiss now?" asked Melody, standing at the entrance to the cubicle.

"I really hope so," said Zac.

"How long have you been standing there, young lady?" asked Jaz.

"A while. Can I watch?"

"No!" said Jaz. "Step outside and draw the curtain!"

"OK. But I'll be listening, so don't make it too sloppy. You don't want to corrupt me - I'm just a kid."

It wasn't particularly sloppy.

But it was a rather long one.

34

The conversation among the colonists over the next few days centred around their impending cryogenic stasis, or the 'Big Sleep', as it was now being called. Who would opt to go to sleep immediately and who would wait for another two weeks? Surprisingly, quite a few were deciding to go to sleep at the first opportunity. Their reasoning was that they were keen to get to their new home as soon as possible, and the sooner you slept, the sooner it would seem like you had arrived. Prior to their reconciliation, both Zac and Jaz had secretly decided to choose early sleep, simply to end their pain. Now, however, that option wasn't even on their radar. They wanted to spend as much waking time together as possible before their enforced sleep.

Their newfound love and obvious happiness were a great relief to everyone. Not that it was ever going to be a secret, because that very night at dinner, Melody had proudly announced, "Hey everyone, Zac and Jaz were kissing in the med bay! They're in love." Keo had simply responded, "Excellent. Pass me the salt please, Possum." And that was all that was said.

After dinner on Mission Day 12, an information session on the upcoming Big Sleep was held in the dining room, with the session streamed to the public screens on other levels as well. The purpose was to alleviate people's natural fears and to inform them of what to expect. Captain Christensen introduced the head of cryogenics, Dr Regina Boyle, a woman in her early 40s with long, grey-streaked dark hair tied back in a ponytail.

"Firstly, let me assure you of two things," she began. "The procedure is completely safe, and at no point will you feel any discomfort. In fact, it will be an overwhelmingly pleasant experience, because of the cocktail of drugs that you will be given."

Kit said to the group, "I wish I could be there to watch Zac go under; that could be quite entertaining!"

Dr Boyle continued, "Cryogenic stasis works by significantly reducing many of your body's metabolic functions and completely ceasing others. The entire process is completely automated. When you step into your sleep pod, an intravenous line will be robotically connected, and 30 seconds later you will be sound asleep, having been administered a sedative. The next thing you will be aware of will be waking up in approximately 40 years' time, having aged only two years. When cryogenic stasis was first introduced 50 years ago, the waking process was quite unpleasant. Extreme cold, uncontrollable shaking, temporary blindness, joint pain, muscle pain and abdominal cramps. You will not experience any of that. You will be kept sedated for a period of 48 hours as your body systems are reactivated. By the time you regain consciousness, all the unpleasant side effects of waking from a 40-year stasis will have passed. You will feel entirely comfortable, if a little weak. You may also experience some disorientation and confusion when you first wake, but this should pass very quickly."

"During your sleep, trillions of nanobots will be at work within your body, taking over all of your metabolic processes at the cellular level, making it unnecessary for your heart and many other organs to function at all. Tiny micro-pulse electrodes will also be implanted into all the muscles of your body, so that they receive constant stimulation during your sleep. During the waking process, the nanobots will be removed from your body via magnetic filtering, and all of your natural metabolic processes will be restarted."

"We will commence 'processing' people, if you will please excuse the term—it sounds like something a chicken farmer would say, doesn't it? —in two days' time. We could actually process the entire population in a single day, because the whole procedure is fully automated, but we are in no rush. The day before you are processed you will need to report to the med bay to be given some fast-acting colon-clearing medication. Please do not eat for the remainder of that day. The following morning, please report to the Level 4 Hibernation deck. You will be assigned a pod, you will remove your clothes and place them in the storage compartment beside your pod, you will climb into your pod, and approximately one minute later you will be sound asleep."

"You may choose to go to sleep at any time during the next two weeks, after which time we will insist that all those remaining be processed. OK, I think I'll stop there for questions." She looked around the audience with raised eyebrows.

"Will everyone else be able to see me getting undressed?" asked someone near the front.

"There are privacy screens on each side of your pod, ma'am, so no one else will see you."

"That's a shame," said another voice, and everyone laughed.

"Have any pods ever failed?" asked someone else.

"I won't lie. In the very early days of cryogenic stasis, there were two incidents where pods failed. Those issues were resolved decades ago, and our pods now have multiple redundancies."

"Will our children look two years older when they wake up?" asked a concerned mother.

"No. The nanobots in their blood will shut down the growth process by inhibiting the release of growth hormones and other related hormones. Your children will look exactly the same."

Dr Boyle waited a little longer. "Any other questions? No? In that case, thank you for your attention. Sweet dreams and I'll see you on the other side."

The meeting broke up, and conversations started up all around the dining room. The group of friends was all together at what had become their official table, at the rear of the room.

"When we get there, will there be aliens?" asked Melody.

"No, just us," answered Jaz.

"Aliens don't exist," said Keo.

"How can you be so sure?" asked Kit.

"The Fermi Paradox," he answered.

"You'll have to explain that one to us, professor," said Zac.

"It's a philosophical argument, first proposed by the astrophysicist Enrico Fermi in 1950. It refers to the apparent contradiction between the high probability estimates for the existence of extra-terrestrial life, and the complete lack of evidence. In essence, the paradox states, 'Where is everybody?'"

"Yeh, but just because we haven't found extra-terrestrial life yet doesn't mean it doesn't exist," said Kit.

"Well, Fermi says that it effectively *does* say that. His argument goes as follows: There are at least 200 billion stars in our Milky Way galaxy. Cosmologists estimate that about 90 percent of those have at least one planet orbiting them."

"180 billion," said Melody.

"Yes. And over the centuries, we have observed that about one in five of the star systems that have planets include at least one roughly Earth-sized planet orbiting within the habitable zone, where liquid water can exist."

"36 billion," chimed Melody happily.

"Yes. Now let's be extremely pessimistic and say that only one in 1,000 of those Earth-like planets will ever develop life of any kind."

"36 million."

"And let's be equally pessimistic and suppose that, of those planets that do develop life, only one in 1,000 will go on to develop intelligent life that would eventually be capable of space flight."

"36,000 planets left," said Melody, enjoying her mathematical contribution to the discussion.

"Yes. So, using very conservative estimates, our galaxy should contain 36,000 planets with space-faring capabilities."

"So where are they all?" asked Zac.

"Precisely," said Keo. "And the paradox is made even more clear, when you consider that our own sun is a relatively young star, by astronomical standards. Cosmologists estimate that up to 60 percent of stars in our galaxy are millions of years older than our sun. We are relatively new kids on the block. So we can assume that 60 percent of planets which could have developed intelligent life are millions of years older than the Earth."

"21,600," said Melody happily.

"So here we come to the heart of the paradox," said Keo. "If our estimates are correct, there should be at least 20,000 intelligent species in our galaxy who achieved interstellar space flight millions of years ago. After all, it has only taken humanity thousands of years to reach that point. If these other species have had interstellar capabilities for thousands and even millions of years longer than we have, they would have spread out across the galaxy long ago. They would be everywhere."

"So, where is everybody?" repeated Zac.

"Yes," said Keo. "That is precisely the question that Enrico Fermi posed to two fellow cosmologists as they walked to lunch one day in 1950. And no one has been able to answer his question ever since. We have been searching the galaxy for 400

years now, and we've found nothing. With the most sophisticated scanning devices and telescopes on the moon and on
Mars and at the various Lagrange points in our solar system, we
have found not a single trace of intelligent alien life. No transmissions. No spectral or radiation signatures of nuclear or any
other form of power generation. Nothing. And to date, we have
identified over 600,000 exoplanets."

"So, what are you saying?" asked Zac.

"I think we are alone in the universe. I think we are unique.
I also think it shows that life doesn't just evolve by random
natural processes, otherwise it would have happened all over
the galaxy. I think it shows that we are a miracle; that we were
created."

"Wow! I didn't see that one coming," said Martinez. "Here
comes the religious talk."

"Not at all, little sister," said Keo. "I am not here to shove my
beliefs down anyone's throat. Faith is a unique journey that
only you can walk."

"I have a question," said Melody.

"What is it, little Possum?"

"Can I have some more ice cream?"

35

Zac opened his eyes and wondered where he was. There was an open, transparent lid directly above him, and he could see dark blue curtains on either side. *Of course! I'm in a pod. But I should be asleep by now. I closed my eyes briefly a few seconds ago, but I'm still awake! It's not working! Nothing's happening!* He stepped out of the pod and padded to the entrance to his cubicle, feeling oddly stiff and sore. Peering around the edge of his curtain, he glimpsed the pod next to him. The lid was closed and was translucent, showing the vague outline of a person inside. He peered around the curtain on the opposite side and saw the same thing. *Everyone else is asleep! My pod is not working!* He was about to start panicking when a calm voice emanated from the side of his pod. "Good morning, Zac. How are you feeling?"

"Genni?"

"That is correct."

"What's happened? Why aren't I asleep?"

"You were asleep, Zac. But it's time to wake up. We've arrived at the Icarus R-421 system. You've been asleep for over 40 years."

He looked down at his naked body and noticed small adhesive bandages on his arms, legs and torso where he must have been plugged into the pod. "Is everything OK? Why isn't everyone else awake?"

"I have taken the initiative to wake the flight crew and council members 24 hours ahead of the colonists. I suggest you get dressed and go to the dining room first. Please scan your biochip and order the rejuve juice. You will need to drink several of these over the next few hours before you eat solid food. Please then make your way to the bridge, where I can update everyone on the mission status."

Barely 20 minutes later, Zac walked onto the bridge, arriving in the same lift as a number of other crew members. On the huge screen in front of them was a view of a large, bright star, floating in the blackness of space. Prisha was standing to the side, drinking a cup of the pleasantly flavoured rejuve juice. She smiled at Zac when she saw him, and said, "Did you have a nice sleep?"

"I guess so. I don't remember a thing."

"I see you're wearing your Hawaiian shirt and not a jumpsuit."

"Yep. Thought I'd bring a tropical feel to the proceedings— in honour of our new home."

"Nice," she said.

Genni announced, "The full complement of crew and council members has now arrived, so I will commence my mission status briefing and handover."

"Go ahead," said Christensen, who was already sitting in the captain's chair.

"We have arrived at the Icarus R-421 system. That is the star currently displayed on your viewing screen. Our target planet can be seen to the left of screen." Genni drew a red circle around a tiny point of light that Zac would not have otherwise differentiated from the stars in that part of the screen. "We are still decelerating as we approach and will achieve high-altitude orbit around the planet in four days, at approximately 1100 hours, ship time."

"There's our new home," said Carla Zangetti, the astronomer.

Genni continued, "I must advise you, however, that we encountered a significant anomaly on our journey here. Approximately 10.2 light years into our journey, we encountered a rogue black hole, almost directly in our path. Subsequent calculations indicate that it had a relatively small velocity of 2,800 kilometres per second and a trajectory across the galactic plane that intersected with our own. As you know, black holes are invisible, emitting no visible light or radiation, and can only be detected by their immense gravity. As soon as its gravitational effect was detected, I employed an emergency evasive burn of our main drive, attempting to alter our trajectory so that we bypassed it. Unfortunately, by then we were travelling at 0.51 of light speed, or 152,894 kilometres per second. There was insufficient time to evade the immense gravitational field of the black hole, which I estimate had a mass 2.7 billion times that of the Earth's sun.

"We were drawn into orbit around the black hole. Even with our antimatter drive firing at full power, we were unable to break out of the gravity well. For six months I tried various means of boosting our antimatter drive's capabilities, with robots working continuously on our engines. During that time, we had been holding at a static distance from the black hole's event horizon, neither gaining nor losing ground. After 187 days I was successful in gaining an additional 1.5 percent power from our main drive. I also instructed our robots to jettison some mass from our vessel. The net result was that we began moving away from the black hole's event horizon at a rate of 1 meter per second, increasing linearly as we moved further away. After a total of 332 days of gravity capture, we finally broke free of the black hole's gravity well and were able to resume our journey."

"What was the mass that you jettisoned?" asked Lance.

"The two power generators."

"Damn!" said Lance. The generators were two massive fusion reactors, each of which would have provided power for an entire town. They had been manufactured on Mars and had been transferred to Genesis on the first day of Mars orbit.

"I did not have a choice," explained Genni. "I needed to divest us of significant mass as quickly as possible. They were the most massive items we had."

As Genni paused to allow that information to sink in, Captain Christensen asked, "Why didn't you wake me or any of the crew?"

"For three reasons, Captain. Firstly, I was uncertain whether we would survive the encounter. If we didn't, it was kinder to leave you all asleep. Secondly, waking you would have served no purpose. My logic is infallible, and I have the ability to process data and analyse possible solutions millions of times faster than humans. I was clearly the best entity to be in charge during the crisis. Thirdly, I was constitutionally in command and was under no compulsion to wake you. I hope I haven't offended you."

"Not at all. Your arguments are sound, and it appears that you handled the crisis flawlessly. I assume that this added some time to our journey."

"Yes, Captain. Additional time was added, in two senses. Firstly, our journey was lengthened by an additional 535 days: the 332 days locked in the gravity well of the black hole, plus additional time to accelerate to our previous cruising velocity, plus the additional distance this solar system travelled during our encounter. Thus, according to ship time, you spent nearly an additional 18 months in cryogenic stasis."

"That's not too bad," said Dr Regina Boyle, the head of cryogenics. "That's only another 27 days of aging, in cryogenic time."

Captain Christensen, however, did not look completely relieved. "Genni, you said that additional time was added in two senses. You've only spoken of ship-board time. What is the other sense?"

"You are astute, Captain. Black holes create considerable distortion of the space-time continuum due to their enormous mass and gravity. As a result, a vessel that comes into close proximity with a black hole will experience significant time dilation. This is in accordance with Einstein's Theory of General Relativity. Time will progress much slower on board the ship than in the surrounding universe, even though time will seem to progress normally from the perspective of those on board. The closer a ship travels to a black hole's event horizon, the more severe will be the time dilation. Ship-board time can slow considerably. This means that a small amount of time might seem to pass for those on board the vessel, while a very large amount of time may pass in the external universe."

"How much time passed?" asked Christensen.

"We came relatively close to the event horizon, Captain, and we were trapped in the gravity well for nearly 11 months."

"Genni, how much time passed in the outside universe?"

"3,022 years."

There was absolute silence on the bridge. Mouths were agape. Eyes were opened wide in astonishment. Heads were shaking in disbelief. Only Captain Christensen's face seemed unmoved.

"How sure are you? How did you calculate that figure?"

"I am completely certain, Captain. During our encounter with the black hole I was able to observe the movement of stars in nearby space. In particular, I observed several binary star systems with known orbital periods. By counting the number of completed orbits they made around each other, and factoring in their orbital periods, I was able to calculate the passage of time to within several weeks."

"So, this is now the year 5379," said Regina.

"That is correct, in Earth years."

"I guess I won't be sending any Christmas cards back home then," said Zac. As soon as he said it, he realised it was probably not the most helpful comment to make, but no one reacted. In fact, everyone seemed completely stunned.

"Is there anything else we should know?" asked Christensen.

"Yes, Captain. There is the issue of distance. During the time we were locked in the gravitational pull of the black hole, both the black hole and the Icarus R-421 system continued on their trajectories. During the 3,022 years that we were engaged with the black hole, they travelled 54.8 light years and 56.6 light years respectively. Fortunately, their trajectories are almost parallel, so there was only a minimal increase in the distance we needed to travel once we broke free of the black hole. However, the result is that this star system is now an additional 37.5 light years from Earth. At the start of our journey it was 14.3 light years distant, now it is 51.8 light years distant."

"Does that have any direct impact on our mission?" asked Christensen.

"Not directly: only that the pattern of visible stars will have shifted more than we anticipated. Plus, any future travel back to Earth will be significantly longer."

"What have your scans revealed of the planet so far?"

"At this distance I am only able to gather very basic data. There are no transmissions coming from the planet. My spectral analysis of the planet indicates a high probability that the atmosphere retains the same constituent gases from our original probes. But remember, the data we have from those probes is now over 3,000 years old. A lot could have changed in that time period. I therefore advise that we approach the planet with caution and undertake a comprehensive survey of the planet from high-altitude orbit prior to any attempted landings."

"I agree," said Christensen. "Anything else we should know?"

"All ship systems are optimal, Captain. Handover is now complete. I hereby transfer command of the ship to you."

"Acknowledged. Thank you, Genni. You did a good job." He turned to his crew and issued various orders in preparation for the vessel's approach to the planet. Then he announced, "Council meeting in the conference room. Grab another rejuve juice, everyone, and we'll meet there in 10 minutes."

36

S ix days later, they had been in high-altitude orbit around the planet for two days, and the ship was abuzz with a mixture of excitement and anxiety. The excitement was due to the obvious beauty of the planet and its suitability for human settlement. It was temperate and lush with vegetation. There were two small polar ice caps and two continents on almost opposite sides of the globe, separated by oceans that encompassed 78 percent of the planet. Earth-like photosynthesis appeared to be in operation and the atmosphere was perfect for humans. In short, it appeared to be a paradise.

Except for one thing. It had been previously occupied. At least, they hoped the occupation was previous and not current. The planet was encircled by an artificial ring in the shape of a giant cylindrical "hula hoop" that orbited about 250 kilometres directly above the equator. During the final three days of the ship's approach, Genesis had bombarded the planet with friendly "We come in peace" messages, transmitted on every available bandwidth and in multiple languages, but had received no reply. Neither had scans been able to pick up any electromagnetic radiation from either the ring or the planet itself. The planet seemed entirely dead in terms of sentient life. High-resolution images of the planet's surface revealed nearly 60 small cities or towns, spread over both continents, but without any sign of current intelligent habitation.

The "hoop," as it was now called by the colonists, was the subject of much speculation, as were the cities below it. Who had lived there? And where were they now? Endless theories abounded: Perhaps they had all been wiped out by a plague. Or, maybe they had transcended to a higher dimension. Perhaps they were in hiding, underground, and were waiting for the right moment to attack. No one knew.

As Genesis drew closer, the ship's high-resolution cameras revealed that the hoop was not perfectly uniform, but bulged out into spherical balls, evenly distributed around the hoop, like a string of pearls. There were 12 of these spheres, leading to speculation that the builders used a base 12 mathematical system. The spheres were about 200 metres in diameter, and the tubular hoop that linked them was 50 metres in diameter. From the vantage point of Genesis's much higher orbit, the entire structure appeared to be made of a dull, black substance that gave off no emissions itself and did not reflect radar or other scanning emissions from the ship. It looked dull, black and dead, except for the perfectly geosynchronous orbit that the entire structure maintained.

Although all kinds of theories abounded concerning the nature and purpose of the hoop, everyone was in agreement about one thing: the builders were clearly thousands of years more technologically advanced than the Genesis colonists were.

The council had been meeting every day to discuss the latest findings from scans of the planet's surface. The continents had been mapped, and animal life had been identified, including herds of animals of various sizes apparently grazing in areas of grassland. The colonists had been invited to suggest names for the new planet, and dozens had been contributed. Most were rejected, including Ringworld (already taken by Larry Niven's work of fiction) and Hoopworld (too childish). A short list had been generated and had been published on the data terminals: Acquis, Aquatica, (both because it had more ocean than Earth), New Hope, Nova, and Prime. Voting had been open for 24 hours and was scheduled to close at 0900, after breakfast on the morning of their third day in orbit.

Melody was bouncing with excitement at breakfast, as she had suggested Prime, because of her love of prime numbers. "Do you think mine will win?" she asked, as she scoffed down what passed for porridge.

"Eat slowly, and don't talk with your mouth full," said Jaz, wiping a piece of Melody's projectile porridge from her own left eyebrow.

"I've been telling everyone to vote for mine! And Grizzle let me put signs on the loading bay walls: 'Vote for Prime'."

"She's very persuasive," said Grizzle, bashfully.

"Yes, I know," said Zac. "She stuck one on my cabin door as well."

"How long to go until it's announced?" asked Melody.

"Ten minutes. Eat your breakfast," said Jaz.

"So, Keo, how's your 'There's no such thing as aliens philosophy going?" asked Martinez.

"Fine, thank you," answered Keo.

"Oh, come on! We're staring at technology that's way beyond anything humans are capable of!"

"Humans 3,000 years ago, yes. But we don't know what has happened in the three millennia while we were trapped in the black hole. It is entirely possible that humans who survived in our solar system could have advanced to this level by now."

"So, where are they?" asked Martinez.

"Where are your aliens?" countered Keo. "The same

mystery confronts both theories. All we can do is reserve judg-
ment and wait to see what further investigation uncovers."

"Well, my money is on aliens."

"If they are aliens," contributed Kit, "they must be remarkably similar to us in size, shape and architectural preferences. I
mean, the pictures we've seen of their cities don't exactly
scream out 'aliens live here,' do they?"

Others had commented on this, as well. The same basic
architectural shapes seemed to be in evidence in most buildings, arranged in orderly rows, separated by what could only be
sealed streets of some kind. From their perspective, high above
the planet, it all looked very normal. What was puzzling,
however, was the extremely understated simplicity of the cities.
No skyscrapers, no elevated freeways, and no obvious technological marvels. No buildings over two stories high, and no
towers, antennas or transmitters to be seen anywhere. And the
cities were all very small. In fact, they were towns rather than
cities. The incongruence with the obviously advanced technology of the orbital hoop was stark. And puzzling.

"Ladies and gentlemen, can I have your attention please."
Captain Christensen's face appeared on the screens on all the
living decks. "It is now 0900. The voting for naming the planet
has now finished, and the results are in. I can tell you that there
were two clear front-runners: Prime and Nova."

Melody squeezed Jaz's hand and started whispering,
"Please, please, please, please, please ..."

"The most popular name, by a clear margin, is ... Nova!"

There was a mixture of cheers and clapping and disappointed moans all over the dining room. Melody moaned, "No!
I thought I was going to win!"

Captain Christensen continued, "Nova, which means 'new',
is now the official name of the planet. Of course, we aren't yet
calling it our home until we ensure that it is entirely vacant. We
will continue our investigation of the planet from a safe

distance until we are convinced that it poses no threat to us. Thank you for your patience while we do so. I am also happy to announce the result of the poll to name Nova's two moons. Overwhelmingly, you voted for Big Boy and Little Boy. Thank you for your participation. I will continue to post regular updates on your data screens regarding our exploration of the planet."

Melody looked mildly glum. "I wanted to call it Prime! It's not fair!"

"Actually, it's very fair," said Zac. "It's called democracy."

"But Prime is a much better name for a planet!"

"Sounds more like a piece of steak, if you ask me," mumbled Grizzle.

"Hey, whose side are you on?"

"I'm just sayin', Possum, I'm just sayin'."

37

B y Orbit Day 4, they had gleaned all the information they could get from their high-altitude orbit, and it was decided to send one of the shuttles for a closer inspection of the hoop. As the shuttle pilot with the most flight hours logged throughout her career, Kit was the obvious choice, which meant that Zac got to go as co-pilot. As they emerged from the shuttle bay into clear space, Kit thumbed the comm, "Shuttle one is clear and free. Commencing burn to lower orbit." The voice of Lance Catrell came back through the cabin speakers, "Copy that, Kit. Fly safe."

"OK," Kit told Zac. "It's time for a physics lesson. How much do you know about orbital velocities?"

"Probably about as much as you know about the origin of Egyptian hieroglyphics."

"That's what I thought. OK, pay attention, because this is important. That thing down there is a planet."

"OK. Got it so far."

"Planets are massive."

"Yep. Still with you."

"And massive things have lots of gravity. This planet is

trying to pull us down. The only way to avoid that is to have enough lateral velocity that the centripetal force of your circular path around the planet exactly cancels out the planet's gravitational pull on you. When you achieve precisely the right velocity, you are neither falling towards the planet, nor shooting out into space. You have achieved orbital velocity. With me so far?"

"Yep. Clear as crystal."

"If a spacecraft in a stable orbit fired up its engine and kept increasing its velocity, it would break out of orbit and shoot out into space. On the other hand, if it slowed itself down by firing its engine forwards, using it as a brake, it would lose its orbit and start plummeting towards the planet. Still with me?"

"Uh-huh."

"Now, the thing about orbits is, the closer you want to orbit a planet, the faster you have to go, because gravity is stronger as you get closer. Back on Earth, a spacecraft in a high-altitude orbit of 35,000 kilometres would only need to be travelling at about 3 kilometres per second. A spacecraft in a low-altitude orbit of only 200 kilometres would need to be travelling at about 7 kilometres per second for the centripetal force of its velocity to overcome the much greater gravity at that proximity to the Earth. So, the lower the orbit, the higher the velocity you need to avoid falling toward the planet. Got it?"

"Yep, I can handle all that so far."

"Good. Now, here's the tricky bit. The hoop we are flying down towards is at a very low altitude of 250 kilometres above the planet's surface. A normal spacecraft orbiting at that height, around a planet that is 6 percent more massive than Earth, would need to have an orbital velocity of about 7.4 kilometres per second. But the hoop doesn't have anywhere near that velocity. It's in equatorial geosynchronous orbit around the planet, which means that each sphere on the hoop is stationary over a set point on the planet's surface and rotates in synch with it. To achieve that, the hoop is only rotating at about 1 kilo-metre per second."

"So how does it stay up?"

"Well here's the really cool part. It actually doesn't need to rotate at all to stay up. It could be completely stationary, and it would still just hang there."

"But how ...?"

"Because it is a solid hoop that encircles the entire planet. At every point around the hoop, the planet is trying to pull it down, but the downward force of gravity at each point on the hoop is cancelled by the downward force of gravity acting on a point exactly opposite it on the other side of the planet. The planet is trying to pull the hoop down, but it can't because its own gravity is holding the whole thing in place by pulling it down from every direction simultaneously."

"Wow! That really is cool!"

"Yeh it is. But what *isn't* cool, is what we're going to have to do to get a close look at the hoop. If we try to match its orbital velocity, we will plummet straight past it and crash into the planet. That's because we aren't a solid ring, encircling an entire planet We're just a teeny-weeny shuttle, so we need to have a much faster orbital velocity at that low altitude. We can certainly orbit at the same altitude as the hoop, but we will be whizzing past it at an additional 6 kilometres per second."

"So how are we going to ...?"

"Here's what we're going to do. I'm going to start with a standard low-altitude orbit, about 300 metres above the surface of the hoop, which means we will be 225 metres above the spheres. We will be racing past it at 6 kilometres per second. After we've stabilised at that orbit and had a bit of a look at it, I am going to do some fancy-pants flying."

"OK ..." said Zac uncertainly. "Am I going to like this?"

"Sure. You'll love it. I'm going to exactly match the hoop's orbit so that we are hovering stationary just underneath it."

"But I thought you said we couldn't ..."

"And I'm going to do that by constantly firing our main engine at a very precise angle and a very precise thrust, so that our loss of orbital velocity is constantly compensated for by upward thrust. We will be like a hummingbird hovering in front of a flower, beating its wings like crazy but staying perfectly still."

"Wow! OK. I get it. That's pretty cool. When did you learn to do that?"

"I haven't yet."

A little more than 20 minutes later, Kit cut her engine, thumbed her comm and said, "Shuttle 1 to Genesis, we're in stable orbit 300 metres above the hoop. Are you getting the video feed?"

"Roger, Kit. It's a good feed. Clear and sharp."

"Cool. We're just gonna park here for a while and watch the world go by."

"Copy that."

They looked through the front screen at the hoop, which looked dull, black and completely smooth.

"It doesn't seem to be moving," said Zac, squinting through the front window.

"That's because our speed differentials are so great. We are currently flying over the top of the hoop at over 22,000 kilometres per hour. At that speed there could be a pink elephant sitting on the hoop and it would flash by so fast we wouldn't even see it."

"What about the spheres? They're 200 metres in diameter. We should be able to see them, shouldn't we?"

"OK, let's watch and see. There are 12 spheres, each about 3,500 kilometres apart. At this speed, one will go past every 7 minutes, 42 seconds. I inserted us into orbit about 600 kilometres from the next sphere. We should be passing it within the next 40 seconds. Watch carefully!"

Zac stared at the hoop directly in front of the shuttle. Nothing changed. And then, suddenly, there was the briefest of flashes, the barest suggestion of an anomaly in the perfectly smooth hoop, and it was gone before his eyes could register it.

"Good grief! That was fast!"

"Yep. Ten times the speed of a bullet. That's why we have to slow down a bit, because we're not gonna see anything at this speed." She flicked the comm. "Genesis, we're gonna change the tempo and do a bit of slow dancing now."

"Copy that. Be careful, Kit."

"Always." She fired some maneuvering thrusters, pivoted the shuttle around and then started firing their main engine in short bursts, to retard their velocity. "We'll be flying backwards from this point on," she said, staring into the monitors showing the video feeds from the rear-facing cameras.

"What do you want me to do?" asked Zac.

"You got any chocolate?"

"Um ..."

"Any chewing gum?"

"Er ..."

"Can you play the mandolin?"

"The ... um ...?"

"In that case, just sit there and shut up for a few minutes."

He glanced across at her and said, "Do you always stick your tongue out when you're concentrating?"

"Only when we're about to crash and burn and die because some idiot is talking to me and ruining my concentration."

"OK. Shutting up now."

It took a lot longer than a few minutes. In fact, it took nearly 20 minutes, but finally the shuttle had become a hummingbird, perfectly stationary underneath the hoop while its engine roared continually behind it. Kit edged closer to it until she was a mere 20 metres away. The hoop was indeed perfectly smooth, at least at this point. Looking to left and right along its length, they could not see any perturbations; no lumps or bumps or bits sticking out of it.

"Let's mosey along a bit further and find the next sphere. It should be about 5 kilometres ahead." The hoop remained perfectly smooth as they moved along it, a black dull tube 50 metres in diameter. The next sphere became visible in the distance, a perfect sphere, 200 metres in diameter, with the hoop seeming to pass directly through its middle. At last, they came up to the sphere and Kit froze the shuttle's movement at the point where the hoop and the sphere met.

"Are you getting this video feed, Genesis?"

"We sure are, Kit. Keep it coming."

"I'm gonna swing out and around the sphere now."

"Roger that. Be careful, Kit. Nice and easy."

"I'm always nice. But I'm not easy."

Lance chuckled. "Copy."

Slowly the shuttle swung out and around the huge sphere, with Kit furiously working the thrusters and main engine, her tongue working equally furiously at the side of her mouth. The middle third of the sphere had horizontal rows of rectangular windows extending around its entire circumference. Nothing could be seen through the windows, which seemed to be made either of a darkened glass or some kind of one-way viewing material. The top and bottom thirds of the sphere were completely smooth.

Kit said to Zac, "Let's have a look underneath." Slowly they slipped downwards and under the smooth surface of the sphere. "Bingo! Here's something, at last," she said. At the very base of the sphere, there appeared to be a giant set of hangar doors. Kit couldn't decide whether they opened outwards (downwards) or slid open within the shell of the sphere.

"It looks like access for shuttles," said Zac.

"Sure does."

"But how do we get them open?"

"Precisely! That is the question."

She thumbed her comm. "Genesis, I'm pinging the sphere with every frequency we've got. Are you reading any response on your scanners?"

"Nothing, Kit. It's as dead as a tomb."

"I'm gonna push a magnetic grapple cable across to it and see what happens."

"Make it nice and slow, Kit. We don't want the natives to think we're trying to shoot them."

Kit flicked a quick glance at Zac. "OK, rookie. This is your job. I've got both hands full here, keeping us alive. You've practised this. Aim it directly in the middle of the door on the right. Select a discharge speed of 1 metre per second and fire when ready."

There was a dull clunk that could be heard through their hull as the cable was fired across. A few seconds later it came into view out the front of the shuttle: a thin cable with a flat disk at its end, moving in a straight line towards the sphere.

"Activating the magnet now," said Zac, when the cable was halfway across. It closed the distance and made contact with the door of the sphere—and bounced straight off again.

"Well, that's interesting," said Kit. "It's either a non-magnetic metal, or some other substance entirely."

Lance Catrell's voice came over the comm. "Kit, I think we've got all the data we're going to get at this stage. You guys need to get back. We don't want you to push your luck."

"Roger that. We'll pack up and head home. Put the kettle on for us."

38

Two days later, at a council meeting on the afternoon of Orbit Day 6 (OD6), the decision was made to make a first landing on Nova. During the previous two days, several probes had been sent to the surface and had verified that the air was safe to breathe, with no obvious pathogens in either the atmosphere or the soil. Shuttles had also explored the two moons and found extensive mining works, together with what appeared to be large industrial complexes: large domed structures of varying sizes, constructed of the same dull black material as the hoop. All of these were similarly lifeless and unresponsive to all attempts at communication. Shuttle crews had tried to access some of the facilities but had found no way of activating what appeared to be the airlocks.

"At least it solves one puzzle," said nuclear physicist Arno Manchester. "why we haven't found any sign of heavy industry on the planet. It appears that they did all their manufacturing on the moons."

"Yes, but we're still no closer to discovering why they abandoned their planet," said astronomer Carla Zangetti.

"No," agreed Lars Christensen. "In fact, we may never know.

But our primary goal now is to establish a colony on the surface and begin to forge a new life for ourselves. I think it is fair to say that our colonists are all very keen to set foot on the planet."

"They certainly are, Captain," agreed counsellor Prisha Naroo. "Itching to get some sand between their toes," she said with a smile.

"I suggest we send four shuttles down to the surface on reconnaissance missions; two to Northland and two to Southland. Lance, do you have any suggestions for preferred locations?" The two continents on Nova were located on almost opposite sides of the globe, centred around the equator, with the larger having slightly more land mass to the north and the smaller being centred slightly more to the south.

"The shuttles may as well make use of the landing strips in the larger towns," said Lance Catrell. "Obviously the shuttles are capable of vertical landings anywhere, using landing thrusters, but it would seem a good idea to explore the towns first."

"Can I suggest that each shuttle contain armed security personnel?" said George Leonidis, who had been strangely quiet in most council meetings since Wisecroft's departure. "Even if there are no inhabitants, we still don't know whether the planet contains dangerous predators of any kind."

"Yes. Agreed," said Christensen.

The rest of the meeting was spent planning the precise details of the recon missions. As Nova had a rotational period of 25 hours, two shuttles would visit each continent approximately 12 hours apart, so that they could explore during daylight.

The next morning, Shuttle 1 came screaming out of the stratosphere and began a long, low recon flight over the equatorial region of Northland. The planet was lush with vegetation, interspersed with rivers and lakes of varying sizes. Their target was a moderately sized town on the east coast. It was situated on a coastal plain with the ocean on one side and mountains further to the west. As they approached the town, large, square, cleared patches of land became predominant, along with large storage sheds or agricultural buildings of some kind.

"Farmland," said Zac.

"Overgrown now, though," said Kit.

They did a low overfly of the town, a typical, neatly laid-out grid of two-storey dwellings.

"Nobody's home. Let's touch down and have a look around." Kit glanced at Zac. "The controls are yours. Don't disgrace yourself."

"I have control," confirmed Zac. He banked the shuttle and lined up with the runway. As the shuttle approached, he activated the landing thrusters and raised the nose to retard their forward motion.

"Get the nose higher, and watch your descent rate," said Kit. "A little more thrust. That's better. Easy does it. OK, level off now and hover." The shuttle hovered 20 metres above the tarmac, perfectly stationary, with its landing thrusters screaming. "Now back the thrusters off and take her down gently." The shuttle eased down towards the tarmac, with Zac perspiring as he concentrated on six different readouts and monitors all at once. It would have been a gentle landing except that Zac eased the thrusters off a little too much at the last moment. The shuttle responded by dropping the last metre and a half, touching down with a thud, a bounce and then a lesser thud.

"Oops. Sorry, folks," Zac said with a grimace.

"Everyone still have all their teeth in place?" asked Kit, sarcastically.

"That wasn't a touchdown, that was a slam-down," said Martinez from behind.

"You did OK, Zac," said Boyd beside her. "I didn't really need those vertebrae in my back, anyway."

Zac taxied the shuttle to the end of the runway closest to the town and shut down the engines. They cracked the door and jumped down onto the tarmac. It was a surreal experience. They were standing on a new world, breathing an alien atmosphere, looking up at a different sun. They stood looking around and listening to the sounds of the planet. There were bird noises of different kinds, and, not far away, the sound of surf. The air had a fragrant, tropical smell, mixed with the clean, fresh, salty air of the ocean, which was on the other side of the sand dunes. There was no fence surrounding the airstrip, and its single building was a hangar of some kind. The runway simply ended with a strip of grass, with the first houses and streets only 100 metres further on. The hangar proved inaccessible, a white building with no apparent windows and an outline of several large hangar doors with no visible means of opening them. After several fruitless minutes of walking around the hangar, the group moved on into the town, sticking close together. They each had a simple projectile hand weapon, with Martinez and Boyd also armed with heavier-powered laser rifles.

They came to the first house and walked all the way around it. It appeared to be two stories high and rectangular in shape, with a flat roof. The entire structure was made of some kind of off-white artificial material somewhere between plastic and concrete. There were recessed panels that looked like windows all over the building, but they were completely opaque.

"Some kind of one-way windows," said Zac.

There were two rectangular door shapes, one at the front and one at the rear of the dwelling, but there were no visible handles or scanners. After unsuccessfully trying to gain access to the dwelling, the group moved on through the town. The streets were laid out in a series of four concentric circles, and the dwellings they contained were all nearly identical. The streets themselves were quite narrow, composed of a hard, sand-coloured composite surface of some kind.

It did not take the group long to the arrive at the centre of the town, via linking streets that radiated outwards, cutting across the circular streets like spokes on a bicycle wheel. The inner-most street circled a large park of grass and shady trees, approximately 800 metres in diameter. At the centre of the park were three white-domed buildings, one large and the other two slightly smaller, clumped together on a sealed circular concourse. There were multiple paths leading to the central concourse, traversing across the park from different points around the inner-most circular street.

"Town hall?" suggested Martinez.

"Something like that," answered Kit, as they neared the domes. Drawing closer, they found a large outdoor amphitheatre, a grassy, bowl-shaped depression, slightly to the side of the concourse, nearest to the larger dome.

"Some kind of public meeting space," said Zac.

The three central domes were constructed of the same off-white material as the dwellings, and appeared seamless and windowless all the way to the ground. A circuit of each of the domes produced no visible means of access. There were door-shaped recesses at various points around the base of the domes, but they offered no clue as to how they could be opened.

Finally, the group stood together on the slight rise at the rim of the amphitheatre and gazed around the huge park. Fruit trees of various unknown varieties appeared to be scattered among other vaguely familiar shade trees throughout the park. A large creek or small river meandered its way through the park, flowing from the south-west, curving around the southern edge of the amphitheatre and exiting the park to the north-east, towards the ocean. There were footbridges across the creek in various places, as well as larger bridges where the streets of the town crossed it.

"Looks like there will be plenty of fresh water," said Martinez.

"Morning tea time," said Kit, sitting on the grass and unwrapping an energy bar that she had taken from the dispenser that morning. The others did likewise, and they sat together, munching peacefully.

"This is incredible!" said Zac. "I mean, this is paradise! The temperature is perfect, the air is clean and sweet, the whole town is just immaculate. And we haven't even seen the beach yet!"

"It's too good to be true," said Martinez, sceptically. "I don't like it. There is no way a civilisation would build something like this and then just leave it all. Something bad has happened. And if it's happened once, it can happen again."

"And what's with the grass?" asked Boyd.

"What do you mean?" said Kit.

"Does it look like it needs mowing to you?" Boyd replied.

"He's right," said Martinez. "It's as if it was mowed a few days ago. Nothing is overgrown. Same with the lawns around the dwellings and along the sides of the streets. If this planet has been abandoned for a while, we should be wading through waist-high grass."

"The agricultural fields that we flew over were all over-grown," said Kit. "They give every indication of long-term aban-donment. Maybe the grass in the town has been genetically modified to only grow to this height. This civilisation is arguably 3,000 years more technologically advanced than us, so you would think that by this stage they would have solved the lawn mowing problem."

"Maybe," said Martinez.

"What was that! Over there!" exclaimed Zac, standing up

and pointing towards some dense trees on the far side of the park. "I saw something moving!"

"What was it?" asked Martinez, as she and Boyd jumped to their feet. Boyd activated his rifle while Martinez took her optical scanner from her vest pocket and started searching.

"It was some kind of four-legged animal. I only saw a glimpse as it walked between a gap in that bunch of trees."

"How big?" asked Martinez, still searching.

"I couldn't really tell. Bigger than a dog, that's for sure."

Martinez kept scanning backwards and forwards for a couple of minutes, but no further sighting of the creature was made. "Can't see anything now," she said, sticking the scanner back in her pocket.

"Let's start to head back," said Kit. "We'll go via the beach. Zac, you've got the bio-sampling kit. You and I will collect samples of soil, sand, grass, and any leaves from trees and bushes that we can get along the way. When we get to the beach, we'll need to get a water sample, too. Boyd and Martinez, keep those weapons handy. I don't want to be something's dinner tonight."

A little over an hour later, they were back on board Genesis.

39

A t the council meeting later that afternoon, the results of the recon missions were being discussed with great enthusiasm. Nothing noxious or poisonous had been found in any of the biological samples brought back to the ship. The soil samples contained plenty of microbial life, which boded well for agriculture, but it was impossible to ascertain whether any of that life would prove dangerous to human health. Only time and exposure would tell them that.

All four shuttles had had very similar experiences: pristine, empty towns with inaccessible buildings. All four towns had a large central park with similar domed structures at the centre.

"They certainly seem to have found a formula they liked, and they stuck to it," said Lance.

"Yes. But let's discuss some of the puzzling aspects for a moment," said Christensen. "Where are all the ground vehicles? None were found in any of the towns. Where are the planes or their equivalent? None were found, despite the existence of airstrips. Where is their power generation? Surely their dwellings have power. And, of course, the greatest mystery of all: where are all the inhabitants?" He looked around the table, with raised eyebrows.

Kit and the other shuttle pilots had been invited to the meeting, and Kit spoke up. "It's possible we may never get answers to some of those questions, but in terms of the location of aircraft, my money is on those hangars at each of the airstrips."

Christensen addressed the pilots who were all sitting at one end of the long conference table. "Is there anything that any of you saw that gave you concern regarding either the planet's safety or its suitability for settlement?"

There was silence as all of the pilots shook their heads.

To the whole council, he asked, "Can anyone suggest any reason why we should delay settlement any longer?"

Again, there was silence and the shaking of heads.

"Then I suggest we expedite plans for settlement. First, we need to select a site. From the four towns we inspected this morning, the town by the sea, visited by Kit's shuttle, seems to me to be most ideally situated. Any thoughts?

Regina Boyle, biologist and budding agriculturalist, spoke up. "I agree. The town offers the greatest potential for access to biodiversity. The ocean is right there on the doorstep, with, hopefully, an abundance of edible aquatic life. The lake eight clicks to the north-west offers further resources. The mountains on the western edge of the lake provide access to a potentially different biodiversity. The town is also in a very temperate equatorial region. I would say it is ideal."

"Does anyone have an alternative suggestion?" asked Christensen. No one spoke. "Good. Then let's make that our colony site. In terms of logistics, I want to play this very safe. No one has spent a night on the surface yet. I suggest that Kit's team, with a few more volunteers, head down after breakfast tomorrow morning and set up a temporary camp. I would like you to spend 48 hours there in order to ensure that it is safe. Thoughts?"

Kit asked, "How many of us do you want down there?"

"A dozen or so should be ample. Not too many, in case you have to get out of there in a hurry for some reason. You might want to include two additional security personnel in your group and take night-vision goggles." Christensen smiled. "I don't think you'll have any problems getting volunteers for a camp-out in a tropical paradise."

He continued, "Providing the camp doesn't highlight any major problems, we can anticipate moving the rest of the colonists to the surface the following day. I see no reason to delay. Using six shuttles, with each shuttle flying two trips, we can have our entire population on the surface by mid-morning. That will then allow us to land Genesis itself, which is a high-risk maneuver. Scans show that there is a large, raised ridge of land one kilometre to the south-west of the town; That would be an ideal landing site. It would provide a slightly elevated position to avoid possible future flooding, while still having a gentle enough gradient to the fields and the town below to allow easy offloading of equipment and land vehicles."

"Until we either build permanent dwellings ourselves, or gain access to the town's existing dwellings, Genesis will be our hotel on the hill, and our safe haven. People can sleep safely on board, and the food dispensers will sustain us until we become agriculturally self-sufficient." He looked around the table and asked, "Comments or suggestions?"

"What about a name for the town?" asked Zac.

"Yes. Good point. We need one, don't we?" said Christensen. "I'm open to suggestions."

"What about Seahaven?" Zac relied. "You just used the term 'haven' yourself, and I think it suits. At least we could start calling it that, until we have a vote or someone comes up with something better."

"Yes," said Prisha. "It is just the sort of name we need. One that expresses our desire for safety and protection. It is a good name."

"OK," said Christensen. "Let's run with Seahaven. To be honest, I think we'll all be so busy from here on that we won't have time for organising a vote. Let's call it Seahaven for the moment and see if anyone complains."

No one ever did.

40

NOVA DAY 1

The shuttle touched down mid-morning in what was now being called Central Park, landing on the circular tarmac in the centre of the park, where the three domes were located. On board were Kit, Zac, Jaz, Keo, Grizzle, Prisha, Regina, Martinez, Boyd, George Leonidis and Dylan Dresner, a beefy and somewhat surly security team member. Despite her desperate pleading, Melody had been left on Genesis, in the care of a kindly woman with a daughter two years younger than Melody. Jaz was present in the advance party as the medical officer.

Genesis was fully stocked with survival gear, and the shuttle team had brought pop-up two-person zip-huts, sleeping bags, portable cookers, camp stools and coolers full of food for their brief stay. The group selected a grassy spot under some large, shady trees about 50 metres from the shuttle and began making camp. Twelve pop-up zip-huts were quickly arranged in a large circle, their entrances facing inwards. One of these held their cookers and other equipment. It only took 20 minutes to get themselves completely set up, and after the camp was established the group stood gazing out at the large park surrounding them.

"Now what do we do?" asked Martinez.

"One of the priorities has got to be collecting and testing some of the fruit and other potential food," said Zac. "Regina, this is your area; what do you want us to do?"

"It's not really my area, but unfortunately I'm the best you've got," she answered, tying her long, grey-streaked hair back into a ponytail, ready for action. Then she bent down and pulled out some resealable plastic bags from a backpack. "I want to give everyone a collection bag. As you explore the area today, collect samples of fruit and berries and anything that looks edible. Bring them back to camp and I will test them for toxins. Please don't eat anything until I've given it the all-clear."

Kit said, "By all means, let's do some exploration, folks, but nobody is to wander off on your own. There are four armed security personnel here, plus Zac and I also have sidearms. Please make sure you are with someone who is armed at all times. We don't know what kind of predators this planet may contain. Let's meet back here at 1300 for lunch."

They split up into three groups and headed out in different directions, ensuring that each group had at least one armed member. Prisha, Regina, Leonidis and Kit headed west, to investigate the farmland. Grizzle, Jaz, Martinez and Boyd decided to do a circuit of Central Park and collect samples from the various fruit trees throughout the park. The remaining three, Zac, Keo and Dylan, headed to the beach. Keo and Zac had brought some fishing gear from the Genesis equipment store, and they were determined to be the first colonists to catch something on their new planet.

The three of them left the park and walked across the four concentric streets on the eastern side of town. Beyond the last row of houses, there was a 50-metre stretch of short grass and then a line of low sand dunes sparsely dotted with vegetation.

The vegetation was green but unidentifiable. As they crested the sand dunes, Keo stood still and simply said, "Wow! This is truly a paradise!" It would be difficult for anyone to disagree. They had emerged onto the southern corner of a gently curving beach. To their right, the beach curved tightly around to end in a grassy headland that was about 20 metres high and extended about 200 metres into the ocean. To their left, the beach extended as far as the eye could see, in a very gentle curve. The sand was the same fine consistency of tropical beaches on Earth but had a light pink-apricot colour. The water was not the dark green or blue of Earth, but a vivid aqua, and white-capped, rolling waves were bending around the headland and breaking across the beach in long, peeling lines of swell.

"Forget fishing, my friend," said Keo. "Who brought the surfboards?"

"That's definitely something we might have to work on," said Zac. "I don't think surfboards were high on their priority list when they stocked Genesis for this expedition."

About 100 metres to the left of their position, a deep-water gutter was carrying water from the breaking waves back out to sea, so they decided that it was the perfect spot to make their first casts. After walking to the spot, Dylan, who showed no interest in fishing or even talking, set himself up on the nearest sand dune and kept watch, with his rifle slung over his shoulder and a pair of optical scanners in hand. The other two walked closer to the water, left their fishing gear on the dry sand and then ambled down to the water's edge, standing ankle-deep in the tropical water.

"It's beautiful!" said Keo.

"Like a warm bath," agreed Zac.

Keo bent down and cupped some water in his hands and smelt it. "It has a different kind of smell," he said. "Definitely salty, but there's something else as well. The ocean must have a different mix of minerals from the seas back on Earth."

Zac smelt it and agreed. "It reminds me of the water in limestone caves I once explored in South Australia, except it's salty."

After retrieving their fishing rods, Zac and Keo cast out into different edges of the gutter and began reeling their lures in. Keo had a near hook up almost immediately, but whatever it was spat the lure. Then, on their second casts, both of their lures were hit hard and they both hooked up. The rods bent as they fought the fish in, with both men yelling and yahooing in exuberance. They both successfully landed their fish and hauled them up onto the wet sand to inspect them. Both fish were the same species: long, thin, streamlined fish about a metre long, with perfectly tubular-shaped silver bodies, about 5 cm in diameter. They had a strange torpedo-shaped snout, three sets of red pectoral fins down the sides of their bodies, and a vertical red tail.

"They look a bit odd," said Zac.

"They look tasty to me," said Keo, who had been privileged to grow up in a part of the world where it was still safe to catch and eat fish from the sea.

"Same here," said Zac. "That looks like white flesh to me, and that's always a good sign."

Keo changed the lure on his rod to a "bottom bouncer" and cast it out. He began jigging the rod sharply up and winding the reel a few times as he lowered the tip back down, then letting the lure rest on the bottom for a few seconds before repeating the process. After casting it out a second time, he had only completed his first jigging pattern when the line went tight and stayed tight. Zac reached over and felt it, and said, "I think it's snagged on something."

"Maybe, maybe not," said Keo, as he started to wind it in.

The rod tip was bent over, and it felt like a dead weight on the end until suddenly the line accelerated sideways.

"Hey!" said Zac. "You've definitely got something! Keep winding!"

Keo wound the line in, as whatever it was zipped left and right, backwards and forwards.

Finally, Keo pulled the fish up on to the wet sand and they both looked down at it. It was round and flat like a dinner plate, with a protrusion out the front like a shovel, and a fan-shaped tail out the back.

Zac said, "It's a mixture between a flounder and a ray and a ... um, I don't know exactly."

"It's got a shovel for a head," said Keo. "It's now officially called a shovel head."

They decided not to fish any more, in case they kept catching fish that would later prove to be inedible. They cleaned and gutted the two fish, finding that they had scales and intestines similar to any fish on Earth. Placing the fish in an instant cooler, they walked back to the corner of the beach and spent some time exploring around the rocks on the shoreline of the headland. They harvested two varieties of shellfish from the rocks, as well as three different species of seaweed and a jar of seawater for analysis.

All three groups arrived back at camp with collection bags filled with specimens, and lots of information to share. Martinez, Boyd, Grizzle and Jaz had collected six different specimens of fruit and three types of berries from around the park. One of the fruits looked very similar to an orange, and another looked like some kind of small plum, but the rest were unknown and exotic-looking. They reported having seen and heard numerous varieties of birds as well as a small furred creature, about the size of a large mouse, scurrying through the underbrush.

Prisha, Regina, Leonidis and Kit returned from their exploration of the farming plots to the west of the town with significantly less produce. The farming plots were completely overgrown with weeds and long grass, offering almost no clue as to what had once grown there. The only exception was one corner of a field, where Regina had identified what looked like ordinary potato plants and had successfully dug up four large potatoes. On the edge of one of the fields, Leonidis had found some small brown berries that they had bagged for analysis. They also reported seeing many species of exotic birds and two types of small lizards.

As everyone talked about what they had seen on their walks, Regina tested the specimens that had been brought back, placing a small sample of each into her portable bio-tester. Each test took less than 30 seconds and provided her with a full digital analysis of the chemical compounds and microbial content of each sample. By the time everyone had finished eating the energy bars they had unpacked for lunch, she was able to proclaim everything safe to eat, except for the brown berries that Leonidis had found, which contained concentrated levels of melataxane, a deadly toxic alkaloid, as well as high concentrations of oxalates, which cause immediate swelling of the lips and tongue.

"We'll have to warn the colonists not to touch these berries," said Regina. "Their toxicity is extremely high. A single berry would be enough to kill a grown man in a few minutes."

Once the majority of the produce had been declared safe for consumption, the group tasted each of the fruits and berries, with only one of them, a yellow and green striped, ovoid fruit, proving to be either unripe or permanently unpalatable. A piece of both types of fish was also fried up and tried by most of the group, with both fish being declared to be delicious. The torpedo fish (as it was dubbed) had sweet, tender white flesh, whereas the shovel head had a darker, firmer meat that almost tasted like pork. The shellfish and seaweeds were also edible and extremely tasty.

The afternoon was spent harvesting more of the edible fruit

and berries from around the park, while others went to the beach to fish. Towards evening some gathered firewood as others cooked dinner. The meal that night was a feast. Fish, shellfish, fried potatoes, boiled seaweed seasoned with salt, and freshly picked fruit. Most of the group could not remember the last time they had eaten that much fresh produce. As the sun began to set, they lit the fire and sat around it, watching the first stars slowly appear in the darkening sky.

"This is amazing," said Jaz, taking a deep breath of the fragrant night air. "We are so lucky to be here."

"We are indeed blessed," agreed Keo.

As the fiery pink and orange glow of sunset began to fade towards black, an eerie cry emanated from somewhere to the west of their position. It was a high-pitched, keening wail, almost like a child's cry. Immediately it was echoed by another cry to the south, and suddenly a chorus of cries erupted from every direction, a howling cacophony of blood-chilling howls. The four security personnel stood to their feet and picked up their rifles, and Jaz huddled a little closer to Zac.

"There's still a lot we don't know about this planet," said Leonidis. "No one is to leave the perimeter of our camp tonight. Those of us who are armed will take two-hour sentry duty shifts and keep the fire stoked. Let's stay safe, people."

Over the next few minutes, as the sky lost all colour and night fell like a blanket, the eerie cries died away and were finally silenced. In their place, a myriad of exotic nocturnal noises arose; croaks and pops and whistles and screeches. As the group sat around the fire, listening to the unfamiliar sounds of nocturnal creatures wakening and beginning their night-time activities, the colonists were reminded just how alien this world was.

Over the next couple of hours, tiredness took its toll on the group as, one by one, they retired to their zip-huts and bedded down for the night. Zac took the first watch, and by 10:30 only he and Jasmine were left by the fire. In retrospect, Zac would be the first to admit that not much actual watch-keeping took place on his shift. He and Jaz had not been alone together for several days, and the passion of their newfound love drove them into each other's arms. All they had done was kiss up to this stage in their relationship, and Zac figured the romantic setting of a campfire under a star-filled sky might be the perfect time to move things forward. When he gauged that the mood was right, he moved his hands down her body. Jaz moaned softly and began to respond, but then pulled sharply away and stood up, panting heavily.

"What's wrong?" he asked, disappointed, standing up himself.

"Nothing," she said, still flushed with desire. "I'm just tired, that's all. I think I'll go to bed, if you don't mind."

"Sure," said Zac, completely puzzled.

Jaz leaned forward and gave him a long, lingering kiss, and then broke away and walked towards her zip-hut. Halfway there, she turned and said, "I'm an old-fashioned girl, Zac. I'm a dove, not a lyrebird. I believe some things are worth waiting for." She gave him a coy smile, then turned and disappeared into her zip-hut, leaving Zac literally scratching his head. *A dove not a lyrebird?* he thought to himself. *Now I'm supposed to be an ornithologist! Why does everything have to be so damned complicated?*

But he had no idea how complicated things were about to get.

41

NOVA DAYS 2 AND 3

T he next morning the campers were woken by the strangest of bird calls. As the first traces of a stunning pink dawn lit the sky, the surrounding trees erupted into what sounded like a hundred or more children in high-pitched voices, calling out, "Who me? Who me?" The campers all emerged from their zip-huts at the same time, rubbing bleary eyes and searching the surrounding treetops for the source of the cacophony. Eventually, with the use of optical scanners, they identified the culprits. They were relatively small, innocuous-looking birds with a blazingly bright pink breast and almost incandescent yellow plumage on each side.

"Well, one thing's for sure, we won't ever have trouble identifying when the sun has set or risen on this planet," said Martinez.

Someone suggested they call the bird the sunrise bird, but the majority thought it should be named for its distinctive call, and so it was christened the hoomie bird. It had rained briefly overnight, a heavy tropical downpour that had soaked the ground, but the morning dawned with clear skies and the promise of another warm, tropical day.

Over a quickly eaten breakfast - energy bars and cups of tea - the watch keepers reported on the night that had just passed. The use of night goggles had allowed them to identify the regular movement of large, dog-sized creatures prowling through the park, their glowing eyes often looking towards the camp, but never coming closer than 100 metres to the campfire that had been kept alight all night.

"Did you sight anything, Zac?" asked Kit.

"Er ... no ... nothing to report," said Zac uneasily, glancing briefly at Jaz. He had spent most of the rest of his watch staring blankly into the fire, trying to work out what Jaz had meant.

Once breakfast was over, they split into groups again and spent the rest of the morning exploring the town and its surrounds. In the afternoon, Kit's group took the shuttle and circled the township in ever-widening circles, looking for evidence of anything that might pose a risk to the proposed colony. By the time they were sitting around their campfire that night, no one had found anything that would suggest that Seahaven would be unsuitable as a location for their colony.

The following morning, following a quick breakfast of energy bars, the day quickly developed into a frenzy of activity. Kit used the shuttle comm to report back to Genesis, and it was decided to begin transferring the colonists immediately. The plan was to disembark all the colonists at Central Park and then for Genni to land Genesis on the selected rise of land to the south-west of the town. Kit, Zac, and Martinez were to fly the shuttle back to Genesis to take part in the exodus, as each of them would be needed to pilot or co-pilot a shuttle. The remainder of the group were to remain in the park and help organise the colonists upon arrival. Once Genesis had landed safely, things were going to get even more crazy, with equipment and ground vehicles being unloaded and various field campsites being set up.

Zac said a quick goodbye to Jaz, and less than 30 minutes

later he was on board Genesis, helping to load people into the shuttle. George Leonidis and the beefy, sullen Dylan Dresner had returned with them as well and had disappeared as soon as they landed, probably to report back to Wisecroft, who had been strangely quiet in recent days.

The colonists were all buzzing with excitement and came on board carrying the few personal items they possessed. The trip back down to the surface was equally uneventful. Halfway down, Kit turned to Zac and said, "You're quiet this morning. What's up, Doc? Cat got your tongue?"

He looked at her with a troubled expression. "You're a girl ..." he began.

"Excellent piece of deduction. I can see now why they awarded you a doctorate."

"Yeh, well, maybe you can help me work out what's going on. On the first night at Seahaven, Jaz and I were ... well ... you know ... getting along pretty well ..."

"I'm getting a vivid image. Go on."

"Well ... I thought things were progressing nicely ..."

"I'm getting an even more lurid picture. Hurry up and get to the point."

"... and then, all of a sudden, she stood up and said something about being a dove and not a lyrebird, and then she said goodnight and went to bed."

"Uh-huh," said Kit.

"Is that all I get? 'Uh-huh'?"

"What don't you understand, Doc?"

"Everything!"

"You obviously don't know much about birds - of the feathered variety. Doves mate for life. Once they've found a partner, that's it. They stay together 'until death do us part'. Lyrebirds, on the other hand, will have it off with a different mate every season. There's no commitment, whatsoever. You starting to get the message now?"

"She wants commitment?"

"Bingo! The lights have switched on at last!"

"But I am committed! I'm committed to her and to Melody."

"But does she know that? And how does she know you're there to stay? That you're committed to her and to her alone from here on?"

"You're talking about marriage?"

"No, I'm not. But she is, apparently."

Zac fell silent for a moment. "But what does marriage even mean, in the context of a new life on a new world?"

"The same thing it always meant. Security. Continuity. Commitment. Dependability. Partnership. I don't think those things have gone out of vogue. In fact, they're probably more important now than ever before."

"You think we should get married?"

"I think you should get the landing gear down. You're taking us in. And this time don't rattle people's teeth out of their gums."

After unloading the first group of colonists, including Melody, who was practically jumping out of her skin with excitement, Kit and Zac took a break and had a cup of tea at their campsite. Colonists were sitting all over the park, under trees, or just walking around looking in every direction. All six of the scheduled shuttles had made their first trip, and Martinez, who had graduated to pilot, had already taken her shuttle back for a second run.

After a short break, Kit and Zac strapped themselves into the shuttle and prepared for another run. Kit keyed the comm, "Genesis, this is Shuttle 1. We are about to lift off for our second run."

A moment later, Lance's voice responded. "Kit, stay where you are. Repeat. Stay where you are. Don't lift off. There's been a development."

"What the ...?" said Kit to Zac. She keyed the comm again.

"Lance, what kind of development?" The was no response. "Shuttle 1 to Genesis. What's going on up there? Over."

After a few moments, a new voice came over the comm. "Shuttle 1, this is Simon Wisecroft, Commander of Genesis. Please remain where you are."

"What do you mean, Wisecroft? You don't have the authority to order anyone around. You're not the commander. Captain Christensen is."

"I am very sorry to inform you, Ms Tyler, but Captain Christensen has sadly passed away. According to the mission protocol, command of this vessel has now passed to me."

"What?" said Kit, who was completely dumbfounded. "How did he ...?"

"It would not be appropriate to discuss this delicate issue any further over the comms," said Wisecroft, in a supercilious tone. "Please advise all shuttles currently on the ground to remain there until further notice. I will be in more direct communication with you shortly. That is all."

"I've got a very bad feeling in my waters," said Zac.

"The bastard!" said Kit. "He's done something! If Christensen is dead, it can only be because Wisecroft had something to do with it. There's no other explanation. Christensen was healthy and hale less than an hour ago!"

Kit called the other flight crews together and told them what she knew. They were shocked but all agreed not to spread panic among the colonists. They would keep the information to themselves until the issue became clearer.

It became clearer about 40 minutes later.

42

M artinez's shuttle made a perfect landing, not with the other shuttles on the central concourse, but in the middle of the outdoor amphitheatre, at the bottom of the depression. The shuttle doors opened, and Martinez emerged with a face like thunder. She strode up the slope of the amphitheatre towards the temporary campsite where Zac and the others were congregated. Behind her, six members of Leonidis' security team emerged from the shuttle and began setting up a large portable screen, with speakers on each side.

Meanwhile, Martinez had reached the campsite and walked up to a group consisting of Zac, Kit, Grizzle, Keo and Regina, who were deep in conversation. Kit asked, "What's happening?"

"Christensen's dead," Martinez responded, bluntly.

"But how?"

"They're saying it was a heart attack, but I was there when it happened. I think he was poisoned."

"Poisoned?"

"Yes. When I got back from my first run, I took a break in the dining room. I was sitting there having a drink, when Christensen came out of the lift with a cup of tea in his hand, sipping it as he walked. A few moments later, he dropped to the ground and started foaming at the mouth. I ran over, but by then he was gone. His lips and tongue had swollen, and his eyes were bulging. It was grotesque."

"But how ...?" Zac started to ask.

"I think it was those brown berries," replied Martinez. "When we took the shuttle back first thing this morning, do you remember Leonidis disappearing pretty quickly?" They all nodded. "As he walked away, I noticed a plastic bag of brown berries in his hand. I didn't think anything of it at the time, because I assumed that he was taking them somewhere for further analysis."

"You think they used the berries to poison Christensen's drink?" said Zac.

"It would have been easy to do," interjected Regina. "The juice from just a couple of berries, if slipped into a drink, would contain enough deadly toxins to kill a grown man after only one or two sips."

"The murdering bastard!" growled Grizzle.

Martinez continued, "They took Christensen's body away pretty quickly. About 15 minutes later, Wisecroft made a video broadcast around the ship, saying that Christensen had died of a heart attack and that he, Wisecroft, was now in charge. He read out a section of the Mission Constitution, and then said that all landings would be temporarily suspended while they 're-evaluate the suitability of the colony site.' His words."

Zac was shaking his head. "The colony is not even one day old, and we've had our first murder."

"Yes, but good luck trying to prove it," said Kit.

"The bastard can't be allowed to get away with this," growled Grizzle menacingly.

"What do you think Wisecroft is planning?" Zac asked the group generally.

"I think we are about to find out," answered Keo, pointing towards the bottom of the amphitheatre.

The screen and speakers had been erected, and a large image of Wisecroft's face appeared on the screen. "Ladies and gentlemen, can I have your attention please." His voice boomed from the speakers and echoed around the park. "Please assemble where you can comfortably see the screen and hear my voice. In five minutes, I will commence an important broadcast. I repeat, please assemble in front of the screen for an important broadcast in five minutes."

As people made their way into the amphitheatre, Kit said to the group, "I don't think Christensen is the only one Wisecroft wants to get rid of."

"What do you mean?" asked Zac.

"I don't think some of us are going to be made very welcome on-board Genesis, either."

Nearly 300 people were sitting on the grassy slopes of the amphitheatre when Wisecroft's image reappeared on the screen.

"Ladies and gentlemen, thank you for your patience. It is my very sad duty to inform you that Captain Lars Christensen has passed away from a massive heart attack." He paused while an outcry of shock and grief swept over the audience, no doubt relayed to him via the shuttle's external comm mics. "We will all feel his loss very deeply, but I am sure you can appreciate that the mission must go on. I am speaking to you from the bridge of Genesis, where, according to the Mission Constitution, I have assumed command of the vessel and the mission, as the next highest-ranking officer. I am broadcasting this simultaneously to the colonists at Seahaven settlement and to those still on board Genesis. I realise that over half our colonists are now on the ground, but I regret to inform you that there has been a change of plan. After reviewing all the data from the initial recon missions, it has been decided that an inland town towards the west coast of Southland is a more optimal site for our colony. It is a larger town, with more extensive farmland, and offers greater potential for becoming self-sufficient as soon as possible. Accordingly, we will be making Settlement City, which is what I have named it, the main site of our colony. Once all personnel have been transferred to the surface, we will be landing Genesis there, which will function as our secure base while we initially establish ourselves."

"In saying this, I am aware that some of you already have your hearts set on staying at Seahaven. Obviously, I cannot force you to come with us, and if you choose to stay where you are, you will be given as many resources as we can spare. You will have shuttles, appropriate for your population, and some agricultural and other equipment, as well as medical supplies. However, the main bulk of essential supplies will remain with Genesis and Settlement City. I therefore highly recommend that everyone join us at Settlement City."

As Wisecroft had been speaking, no one had noticed Martinez move towards the shuttle. She now jumped up onto the portable platform upon which the screen had been mounted, and screamed out, "Don't listen to him! He's a murderer! He poisoned Captain Christensen! He is committing mutiny! He doesn't have any authority to make these decisions!"

Wisecroft could clearly hear her interjection through the external mics and had paused while she ranted. Meanwhile Kit, Zac, and Regina had begun running to the front, too, fearing that Martinez was going to need help. The security personnel who had arrived on the shuttle and were standing to each side of the screen had unslung their rifles and were looking at Martinez menacingly. Wisecroft calmly said, "I assure you, Ms Martinez, that the cause of Captain Christensen's death has been verified by Dr Leibman as cardiac arrest. And I also assure you that I am now legally in command of this mission."

"No, you're not!" exclaimed Zac, who found himself standing beside Martinez. "You don't even have a seat on the ship's Council! You were voted off! The commander of this mission must now be a matter for the council to decide."

"Ah, Dr Perryman. How nice of you to join the discussion. Sadly, your little council was never constitutionally valid in the first place. Captain Christensen stepped outside the bounds of mission protocol by even forming it. No, I assure you, I am the rightful commander."

"You're a murderer, Wisecroft!" yelled Kit, who now joined the other two at the front. "A bag of poisonous berries was seen being taken on board by George Leonidis this morning. You used them to poison our Captain and seize control of the ship!"

"And now the trio is complete," said Wisecroft. "Sadly, I anticipated this kind of response from the three of you, and you haven't disappointed. I see little point in debating with you, as I sense that you have already made your minds up. If you do not accept my authority, you are, of course, free to stay where you are and not accompany us to Settlement City. Indeed, given your open hostility towards me, it would seem the best course of action for us all. I will give everyone an hour to choose whether to stay at Seahaven or relocate to Settlement City. I will give the same choice to everyone still on-board Genesis. In one hour, we will recommence transfers, and over the next 24 hours, supplies will be delivered to those who have chosen, albeit unwisely, to make Seahaven their home."

Kit began to address the crowd directly. "Don't listen to him. Seahaven was chosen by a consensus of the council as the best site for our colony! All of the shuttle pilots on the original recon missions were in complete agreement as well. This is the best ..."

"Enough!" interrupted Wisecroft, his voice booming out of the speakers. "I will not tolerate ..." and then the screen went blank and the speakers fell silent. The security personnel looked around in puzzlement, wondering why the transmission had been interrupted. Grizzle walked around from the side of the shuttle, drew level with the three on the platform and showed them a pair of wire snips held furtively in his hand. "I was trying to get that annoying buzz out of the system. I must have cut the wrong cables."

While the security personnel fiddled ineffectively with switches and dials behind the screen, Kit and Zac took advantage of the situation and continued speaking to the crowd, urging them to stay at Seahaven. Martinez joined in, giving her eyewitness testimony surrounding the highly suspicious death of Captain Christensen. At one point, two security guards with rifles at the ready tried to move them off the stage, but Keo and several other well-built men stepped forward and blocked them, while several people in the crowd yelled, "Let them speak!"

Zac also described to the crowd the abundance of seafood that this site offered, which was a clear advantage over the inland city that Wisecroft had chosen. He spoke passionately, pleading with them, "This location provides us with the greatest diversity of food supply, and gives us the best chance of long-term survival. We can only rely for so long on the production of man-made protein on board Genesis. This town gives us a ready-made supply of fresh protein from the sea from the very beginning. Please consider staying with us! The more of us there are, the more viable this is going to be. Right now, there are about 300 of us. That's over half of the total colonists. We can make this work, if we stick together!"

The friends at the front took questions from the crowd and tried as best they could to give honest, optimistic answers. Regina, the biologist and council member, reinforced the illegitimacy of Wisecroft's claim to be mission commander and added her weight to the suitability of Seahaven as the best site for the colony.

At one point, one of the colonists called out, "What about power? Where will we get that from?" This, of course, was one of the major drawbacks they faced. Genesis's huge built-in fusion reactor could power a whole city for generations to come. Kit explained that the smaller shuttle fusion reactors would generate plenty of power and could be dispersed throughout their colony for recharging battery-powered electrical equipment and for connecting into a grid. Plus, they would also have electricity-producing solar panels and solar-powered generators.

Another prospective colonist asked about toilet facilities. "Obviously, without Genesis, we will initially have to adapt some zip-huts and incorporate some rudimentary toilet facilities," Zac explained. "We will probably have these along the bank of the stream. Our plan would be to quickly construct more solid timber buildings for this purpose."

There was clearly a groundswell of support for staying, but not everyone was convinced. As discussions continued, the security personnel gave up trying to get the screen working again and made a quiet withdrawal into the shuttle, leaving the colonists to discuss their fate among themselves. As the allotted hour drew to a close, Zac and the others realised they had done all they could to convince people to stay. Many people had wandered off to inspect the beach, while others looked around the park, all of them trying to decide whether to stay or go.

The fate of Seahaven hung in the balance.

43

Z ac and Kit were asked to enter the shuttle to negotiate directly with Wisecroft via the cockpit comm. They took their seats and Kit commenced the proceedings bluntly. "You're a murderer, Wisecroft. You know it, we know it, and eventually it will all come out."

"I seriously doubt that, Ms Tyler. All you have is an unsubstantiated accusation, while I have the equivalent of a medical report. So, let's not waste any more time on that issue, shall we? How many poor souls have you managed to convince to stay with you in what will no doubt end up being a backward hovel?"

Shortly before this, the colonists at Seahaven had met back at the amphitheatre, where they had separated into two groups: those who were staying and those who would go with Wisecroft.

"There are 262 people who would rather rip their own heads off than sit for a minute longer under your self-serving leadership," Zac said. "Sadly, there are 43 deluded souls who haven't yet reached that conclusion, but I'm sure they will eventually."

Wisecroft looked genuinely surprised that so many were not joining him. "Really? I see." He paused, seeming to be at a loss for words.

Zac continued, "By my calculation, there are currently 255 of you on board Genesis. How many will be joining us here?"

"George tells me that we will be transferring 68 to you."

Zac jotted down the figures on his data tablet. "So that ends up being 330 people choosing Seahaven, and 230 choosing Settlement City."

"It appears that way, yes."

Zac softened his voice and said, "Dr Wisecroft. Simon. Please let's not do this. Surely our survival as a whole colony is more important than your desire for control? Can't you leave aside your ego and see common sense? You really don't want to split our colony in two, do you?"

"On the contrary, Dr Perryman, it is not me who is splitting the colony. This division is entirely of your own making. It is your mutiny against my rightful leadership that is dividing us."

"If you insist on going through with this," said Zac, "then surely the larger group should retain Genesis. I can assure you that we would transfer more than your fair share of resources to Settlement City."

Wisecroft laughed. "Oh, you are funny, Dr Perryman! I didn't think historians had a sense of humour! Genesis is mine, and none of you will set foot in her bridge as long as I am in command."

"That suits me!" said Kit. "Let's get down to details: 330 people is 59 percent of the total population. Let's say 60 percent. We are going to need 60 percent of all the farm equipment, machinery, land vehicles, generators, seeds, plants from the aquaponics farms, yeast tanks, medical supplies, weapons, everything. Plus, we will need the vast majority of zip-huts and camping equipment, seeing that you will have Genesis as accommodation. This has to be a fair and humane split."

"Of course, my dear. I am not an animal. I will provide you with basic necessities commensurate with what your little mutiny deserves."

"What does that mean?" asked Zac, with growing suspicion.

"You can have as many zip-huts as you need, seeing that we will have Genesis for our sleeping and living quarters."

"Plus our share of equipment and vehicles!" insisted Kit.

"Really? I hardly think you're in a position to bargain. No, I think you forfeited your rights to any significant machinery when you launched your little rebellion. I may be able to spare a shovel or two, along with a few small boxes of seeds."

"That's outrageous!" said Zac. "That farming equipment is for the use of the whole colony, not just the few poor souls who throw their lot in with you!"

"Plus," added Kit, "we will need medical supplies and food; food that won't perish. You will have access to the food dispensers on Genesis for as long as you like, whereas we won't have that luxury. We are going to need boxes of biscuits and energy bars, plus a whole lot of yeast steaks that we can use to supplement our diet with protein."

"You're starting to see your predicament, aren't you?" said Wisecroft, with barely concealed smugness. "I think once people realise how pitifully equipped you are, there will be a veritable flood of refugees leaving your ill-advised rebellion. Are you sure you don't want to join us at Settlement City?"

"You bastard!" exclaimed Kit.

"Hold on," said Zac. "Are you saying you won't even supply us with basic medical supplies and food?"

"Not at all! I am, if nothing else, a generous man. You may take two boxes of energy bars and some first-aid kits. If, at any point in the future, people require more significant medical treatment than you can provide for them, they will have the option of permanently relocating to Settlement City, where they can receive state-of-the-art medical intervention on board Genesis."

"Wisecroft, you can't do this!" said Zac. "You are condemning this colony to almost certain failure, simply out of spite!"

"Your predicament is of your own making, Dr Perryman. There's an old saying: 'You make your bed; you lie in it.' I think your fellow-rebels will soon realise that they have made the wrong choice."

"You bastard!" exclaimed Kit again.

"Ms Tyler, you really must try to expand your vocabulary. I suggest a thesaurus. I will send down two shuttles with your transferees and the basic food and medical supplies that I have described. When they return with the transferees who wish to join me, I will begin sending down the zip-huts. That is all."

The comm went dead, leaving Zac and Kit sitting in shocked silence for a moment.

"I can't believe he's doing this to us," said Zac.

"I can," replied Kit.

"We're doomed!" said Zac. "We can't possibly make a go of it without a fair share of supplies and equipment. I can't see any way out of this, other than to concede defeat and join Wisecroft."

"Not so fast," said Kit. "I don't think Wisecroft has thought this through properly. I think we may have a strong bargaining chip that he hasn't counted on."

"What?"

"If I'm right, I'll tell you in about an hour."

44

Less than an hour later, two shuttles had landed with the additional colonists from Genesis and a few meagre supplies. Kit and Zac were back in the cockpit of their own shuttle, and they opened up a channel to Wisecroft.

"Wisecroft, you've got a problem," said Kit, without any preliminaries. "All of the pilots and co-pilots down here want nothing to do with you. They've all chosen to stay and are refusing to fly your colonists back to Genesis. Plus, we now have eight shuttles on the ground here, leaving you with two up there. Have you worked out how many trained pilots you have on Genesis?"

"Um ... I am going to need to get back to you." Wisecroft clicked off.

"Ha!" said Kit. "He didn't think that one through, did he?"

A few minutes later, Wisecroft came back on the air. "We've, um, got one partially trained co-pilot."

Kit said, "If your partially trained co-pilot is Simpkins, and I think it is, don't let him anywhere near a shuttle cockpit. Ever! That means you have no pilots. Period. Not a great situation for you, is it?"

Wisecroft remained silent.

"Your command and your mission are no longer feasible, Wisecroft," Kit said.

"Not at all," he replied. "Genni can land Genesis with us on board. Landing people via the shuttles is a safety precaution that we can easily bypass."

"You're wrong," said Kit. "Landing an interstellar ship the size of Genesis on a planet with atmosphere and significant mass is an extremely risky procedure, even with an AI at the helm. I'm a trained pilot, used to taking risks, and there's no way in blue thunder I would want to be on board that vessel while it is attempting to land. In the history of human space flight, we have never attempted to land a vessel the size of Genesis on an atmosphere-dense planet. As you are probably aware, the only time we ever attempted to land a large vessel on Earth, it didn't go well. The transport ship, Pegasus II, was only a quarter of the size of Genesis, and it crashed in the Mojave Desert, killing its entire crew. You are risking the lives of everyone on board, including yourself."

"Yes," interjected Zac. "I'm sure you place a fairly high value on your own life."

There was silence from Wisecroft.

"By the way," added Kit, "are you certain Genni will even recognise your authority?"

"She already has," responded Wisecroft. "Whatever other arguments you may make, the fact is that I *am* now the most senior officer on Genesis. Genni is programmed to obey seniority."

"Damn it!" whispered Kit under her breath.

"That may be," replied Zac, "but you still have a major problem on your hands, with no pilots and no way of transferring your colonists to the surface safely."

Wisecroft remained silent, the gears of his mind spinning.

Kit broke the silence. "I think we can help each other out

here. You're going to need five shuttle trips to get your people to Settlement City. I think I can convince our pilots to help, provided we get the supplies we need from Genesis. We estimate it's going to take at least 10 shuttle loads to transfer all our supplies from Genesis to here. So, here's what I suggest. We'll gut two of our shuttles, removing all the seats, and send them up to start loading our gear onto them. Every time they both come back fully laden, we'll fly a load of colonists to your Settlement City site, starting with the 43 transferees from Seahaven, followed by people coming off Genesis. That's as fair a deal as we can give you."

Wisecroft wasn't happy, but he had no choice. The deal was done, and the hard work began.

Kit and one of Genesis' original shuttle pilots, Harvey Walden, flew the two now-gutted freight shuttles, and Leander Gallstrom, another original Genesis pilot, flew the passenger shuttle. They also decided to take two fully armed security personnel, because of the very real risk that Wisecroft would attempt to abduct a pilot or two. Zac co-piloted with Kit, and they took Martinez and Boyd as armed security, as well as several workers to help with the transfer of supplies. The Seahaven colony had five additional security personnel who had chosen not to go with Wisecroft, mainly because of their respect for Martinez over George Leonidis. Four of them were assigned to the other two shuttles.

An hour after the deal with Wisecroft had been brokered, the three shuttles approached Genesis. Kit and Zac's shuttle was the first to land in a loading bay. As the external doors sealed behind them, Kit told Martinez, Boyd and the others to take cover in the passenger compartment and position themselves with lines of crossfire to the shuttle door. It was just as well they did. As soon as the loading bay was pressurised and the shuttle doors opened, Wisecroft showed his hand. Two of Wisecroft's security guards stormed the shuttle, fully armed.

They entered the shuttle using classic commando infiltration tactics, covering each other and scanning the interior with weapons raised, while screaming out, "Everyone down on the ground! Everyone down on the ground now!"

Martinez and Boyd, however, were well prepared. The cabin lights had been turned off and the armed guards were beautifully silhouetted in the shuttle doorway. Using neuro-disruptor stun guns, both potential hijackers were rendered unconscious in a matter of seconds, and their weapons seized.

"You guys OK back there?" asked Kit, a few moments later.

"Easy as shooting ducks on a pond," answered Martinez. "Plus, we just scored some more weapons."

"Yeh, but check this out," said Boyd, examining one of the captured rifles. "These are laser rifles, and they were set to maximum power! That's a lethal charge!" He looked at the two unconscious men and shook his head. He hadn't been close friends with them, but they had been work colleagues until now. "What sort of hold does Wisecroft have over them that they would be willing to use lethal force?"

"You better warn the others, Kit," said Martinez. "I expect they'll be in for the same treatment."

She was right. Exactly the same scenario unfolded in the other two shuttles, with a total of four more armed guards rendered unconscious and their weapons seized.

Kit was seething with anger at Wisecroft's attempted duplicity, and once the threats had been neutralised, she called him up on the comms.

"What were you thinking, you moron?!" she yelled at him. "Were you planning to kill us or just maim us? Or did you think that by pointing a gun at our heads we would happily join your band of merry men?"

"I do apologise, my dear," said Wisecroft soothingly, once it became clear that the attempted takeover of the shuttles had failed. "They must have misunderstood my orders. I simply asked them to stand guard and ensure that no unauthorised equipment was taken by your enthusiastic team."

"That's total crap!" said Kit. "You overplayed your hand this time. You've just lost seven of your goons. They're trussed up like turkeys and will remain that way until all the transfers are complete."

"On the positive side," contributed Zac, somewhat laconically, "we certainly appreciate the unexpected addition of weapons to our arsenal. Very generous of you."

On the first trip up, Grizzle had insisted on going with his team of loaders, to supervise the loading of equipment and make sure they got a fair deal. As he said, "I don't trust that bastard as far as I can throw him!" He and his team immediately set to work, checking inventories and moving equipment to the shuttle bays.

It took nearly three hours for the two cargo shuttles to make the first round trip and be unloaded back at Seahaven. As they finished the unloading and prepared to return to Genesis, Zac told Kit, "We're only going to fit one more trip in before dark today."

"I agree," said Kit.

Zac said, "I'll tell Grizzle to make this next load primarily zip-huts, camping gear and food. We will have to resume again at first light tomorrow."

It was another two hours before the cargo shuttles returned and all the camping gear was unloaded. By then the light was fading, and there was a scramble to set up the zip-huts and get the cookers working to heat up food for the evening meal. As the new arrivals warmed their food, the sun sank below the horizon and the howlers (which is what they had been dubbed), started their dreadful, but thankfully brief, wailing chorus. After ten minutes of their dreadful screeching, their cries died away and the exotic sounds of the night took over. Weird animal and insect noises filled the air, as Nova's nocturnal life awakened. The colonists lit their campfires and attended to their evening tasks as the sounds of this strange new world filled the air.

Zac, Kit and everyone who had been involved in the transfer of equipment were all exhausted. The day had certainly not turned out the way they had envisaged when they first woke that morning. As the close group of friends gathered around the campfire, drinking tea and debriefing, Zac said, "What have we done? Have we done the right thing? Maybe we should have all stuck with Wisecroft."

"That's just tiredness talking, not logic," said Kit. "This is a much better location. Sure, it will be tough at first, but in the end we will flourish here."

"Besides, that man is evil," added Keo. "We are much better off without him, even if we don't have Genesis."

They all retired to their zip-huts soon after, most of them falling asleep immediately. But Zac lay awake worrying. He hoped they would be able to get all the supplies they needed safely down from Genesis without mishap.

They didn't.

45

NOVA DAY 5

I t took two more days to finish the equipment transfers. The final day was spent transferring the larger equipment: two solar generators, two tractors, four quad bikes, an assortment of workshop and engineering machinery and a caterpillar - an eight-wheeled ground vehicle capable of carrying 20 passengers. The tractors and caterpillar were too large to fit inside a shuttle, so these were driven into drop boxes on board Genesis - heat-shielded metal containers that had basic auto-thruster systems for orbit decay and auto-deployed chutes for a reasonably soft landing. The drop boxes were pushed out into space by robo-loaders once a loading bay had been vented. The difficulty lay in calculating precisely when to activate the orbit decay thrusters to ensure that the boxes landed in the target zone. The drop boxes were temporarily left in orbit and the last shuttle-loads of equipment were brought back to Seahaven and unloaded. It was late afternoon by the time the unloading was finished, so it was decided to wait until the next morning to bring the drop boxes down. That way they would have all day to track them down and retrieve them after landing.

Two days' hard work had transformed the settlement, for

that was what they were calling it now. All attempts to gain access to the existing houses had failed, and the colonists had resigned themselves to living in temporary accommodation for the short term. Orderly rows of zip-huts had been established in the park, with "streets" between them. Each of the two-person zip--huts could be joined with others, forming larger family-sized zip-huts with living and sleeping sections. They had taken almost the entire supply of zip-huts from Genesis, so there were plenty of them for people to create elaborate 'homes'. Each zip-hut was a perfect cube, two metres per side, made of a waterproof material that contained microlayers of bioconducting, photoelectric insulation. Each hut could be set to the inhabitant's desired temperature, with the bioconducting material venting heat either inwards or outwards. The bio conductors also produced a small amount of power - enough to power a low-voltage cooker, a small food cooler and run some lights, via a power outlet mounted in the roof.

Keo had been busy organising fishing expeditions, using almost all the fishing gear that Genesis had contained. So far, the fishing had been extremely successful, with everyone having at least a taste of fish for dinner each night. Regina had organised harvesting expeditions, and several more species of edible fruits, nuts and berries had been located. More importantly, a whole field of large potato-like vegetables had been discovered, comprising approximately 30 acres. The local potatoes had obviously been a staple crop of the original inhabitants, and they had continued to grow wild - in fact, prolifically so. This was arguably the most significant find so far, as it effectively ensured a steady supply of carbohydrates that could sustain the colony, even if all other food sources failed.

The stream flowing through the park provided a steady supply of fresh water. However, some hygiene rules needed to be put in place quickly regarding its use. The toilet zip-huts had been set up between the eastern footbridge and the stream's exit from the park. Washing, cleaning and bathing took place upstream from the toilet huts, between the eastern footbridge and the central bridge, and drinking water was collected still further upstream, beyond the central bridge.

There was still plenty to do. Equipment was piled up everywhere, and larger prefab structures had yet to be erected. But they had made a good start.

Late in the afternoon, Zac, Keo, Jaz, and Melody took some time off to have a swim at the beach. Colonists had been venturing further and further out into the water, and no aquatic predators had yet been encountered. The shortage of clothing meant that people simply swam in their underwear, and everyone pretended that these were swimming costumes. While Jaz and Melody played in the shallows, Zac and Keo ventured out to where the waves were breaking and did some bodysurfing. Sometime later, the men were sitting on the warm sand, drying off, watching Melody and Jaz build a sandcastle at the water's edge.

"What do you think about marriage?" asked Zac.

"It's very nice of you to ask, but I'm not really attracted to you," answered Keo.

"Ha. Ha. Very funny. I'm serious. What do you think of it?"

"I think it's one of God's better ideas."

"But is it really all that relevant here, in this setting? And anyway, there is no official means of recognising it."

"I think marriage is going to be essential in this setting, bro. We have lost so many structures and normal social constraints, and that could pose a problem if we aren't careful. If we don't clearly recognise and protect the existence of monogamous sexual partnership, all hell could break loose, my friend. Jealousy, competition, even violence could break out. Everyone is acutely aware that if we are to survive beyond one generation, we need to partner up and have children. People are already looking and competing for partners, and that's creating tension.

Marriage is a way to legitimise and protect the partnerships that have already formed. It is a way of saying, 'These people are no longer available - go and look somewhere else.'"

"You make it sound so mechanical and practical."

"It is. But it also brings an added dimension to the partnership itself. It brings security and trust, so that love can grow and flourish."

"OK. I get all that. But how do we actually do it? I don't see any marriage registry offices nearby - or churches, for that matter."

"This whole planet is a cathedral Zac. You don't need priests or pulpits or government departments in order to get married. You just need to make a public promise of faithfulness to each other, out in the open, so that everyone will know that you are now a family."

Zac thought about it for a while, and finally said, "I love Jaz."

"Of course you do, bro. You'd be a fool not to."

"But how is that possible?" Zac asked. "I mean, I only lost my wife a couple of months ago. What sort of shallow creature does that make me?"

"Did you love your wife?"

"I thought I did. I was comfortable with her. We had fun together. She was vivacious and lively and ..."

"So are a lot of people, Zac. But that's not the issue. Did you love her?"

Zac thought for a moment. "I think I did. But we kind of just drifted into marriage. We seemed right for each other, our career paths matched, and it just seemed the natural thing to do. My love for her was an easy, comfortable kind of thing. Does that make sense?"

"Do you think she loved you?"

"I'm not sure now," Zac said. He watched Jaz and Mel joking and laughing together as they built their sandcastle higher, by the water's edge. "I'd like to think she truly cared for me, and that it wasn't all just pretence."

"And how does what you had with her compare to your feelings for Jaz now?"

"Like comparing lemonade to champagne."

"And Jaz is the champagne?"

"Vintage Dom Perignon. She sends me into orbit, man."

"So what's your problem, bro?"

"I'm only recently widowed ..."

"Three thousand years ago!"

"But in my timeline, it's only a couple of months!"

"And you're feeling some kind of loyalty to a woman who may or may not have loved you, who was having a torrid affair with her boss, was a secret agent for the Caliphate, and who murdered hundreds of people and nearly killed us all? Help me out here, bro. Am I missing something?"

Zac said nothing but just looked down at the sand at his feet, struggling with some kind of inner turmoil.

"Listen, brother," said Keo. "The Earth is gone. Everyone we knew is gone. They've been gone for 3,000 years. This is a new world and a new beginning for all of us. If we're going to survive and thrive here, we have to move forward and leave the past where it belongs."

"I know all that, Keo. It's just that I feel ..."

"That's your problem."

"What?"

"You're focussed on your *own* feelings. But what about hers?" he said, nodding towards Jaz, who was now helping Melody collect shells to decorate their sandcastle. "Jaz is obviously completely smitten with you, the silly girl—the Lord only knows why! But you can't keep stringing her along while you work through your misplaced feelings of loyalty to a dead, murdering adulteress. No offence." Keo looked directly at Zac and said, "I'm serious, my friend. For Jaz's sake, you either need to marry her or let her go. I happen to know there is a long line of blokes just waiting for the 'not in a relationship' sign to go up."

The two sat together in silence for a moment before Keo spoke up again. "As a history professor, you might be familiar with this quote: "Accept the things to which fate binds you, and love the people with whom fate brings you together ...""

"... "but do so with all your heart,"" Zac finished. "Yes. Marcus Aurelius, the Roman emperor, from his philosophical work, *Meditations*."

"170 AD," said Keo.

"Actually, that's when he started writing it," corrected Zac. "It wasn't completed until 180 AD, after the conclusion of his military campaigns against the Germanic tribes."

"You know," said Keo, "for a smart guy, you can be pretty thick sometimes."

Zac nodded his head. He looked down to the shoreline and gazed at the two people he now cared for more than anyone else.

Keo asked, "Have you heard of the songwriter from the 1960s and '70s, called Stephen Stills?"

"Yes, and I know where you're going with this."

"His best-known song was based on Marcus Aurelius' philosophy..."

"I love that song, even though it's ancient now," said Zac.

"In that case you'll be familiar with the words, "There's a girl right next to you, and she's just waiting for something you do ... And if you can't be with the one you love ...""

"... love the one you're with," Zac and Keo finished in unison.

Zac nodded silently and looked again towards Jaz, who at that precise moment looked back at him and waved. A gust of warm wind caught her hair and blew it across her eyes, and she tossed her head back, laughing. His heart suddenly swelled, and his eyes brimmed as he continued to watch Jaz and Mel playing together and splashing each other in the shallows. He turned to Keo with a spark in his eyes.

"I'm going to marry Jaz!"

"Of course you are! If you weren't planning to, I was going to take you aside and knock some sense into that thick skull of yours."

"Will you conduct the ceremony for us, Keo?"

"Of course, bro. It would be an honour. When will you ask her?"

"Tonight. She's been hinting."

Keo shook his head. "A girl like that could have any man she wants, and the foolish girl has chosen you! Sometimes women are just plain puzzling."

Later that night, after Melody was asleep, Zac and Jaz went for a walk to the beach. Both moons were in the sky and full, Big Boy directly overhead and Little Boy just rising over the ocean. They sat on the sand dunes watching the phosphorescence of the waves and breathing in the warm, tropical evening air.

"This place is amazing," said Jaz.

Zac pulled her close and kissed her. It was only meant to be a tender kiss, but it quickly developed into much more. They were both momentarily swept away on a wave of passion, and Jaz moaned softly as she felt her whole body responding to his with an urgency that was increasingly difficult to control. They broke apart and Zac gazed into her eyes, pushing a strand of her hair to the side that had fallen across her eyes.

"I love you, Jaz. In fact, I love you more than I have ever loved anyone."

"I love you too, Zac."

"You are my life now," he continued, "and I want to spend it with you. All of it. Will you marry me?"

"Yes," she said, as her eyes brimmed with tears that quickly overflowed and ran down her cheeks.

They kissed again, and this time it was tender and soft, as Zac stroked her cheek and wiped the tears from her face. They broke apart again, and Zac said, "I will always look after you Jaz. You and Mel. We are going to be a family now." He paused for a moment. "When will we make it official? I mean, it's different here, isn't it? No receptions to plan or wedding dresses to make. When should we get married?"

"As soon as possible," she said with a mischievous smile, "otherwise I'm in grave danger of contradicting my 'old-fash-ioned-girl' status."

"How about two nights' time?"

"That long?" she said. "OK, I suppose I can wait. But not a day longer!"

46

NOVA DAY 6

The next morning, the hoomie birds started their curious chorus as the light of dawn painted a pink and apricot hue across the eastern sky. The colonists emerged into a world still glistening from the seemingly-standard overnight tropical downpour. As the camp stirred, the word spread that there would be a wedding ceremony in two nights' time. Keo sent the word around, inviting anyone else who wanted to be officially wed to come and see him, and throughout that day and the next, there was a steady trickle of couples who indicated that they were ready to commit to each other. Many of the couples requested that their identity remain a secret until the ceremony, so that their wedding would be a surprise. This added to the excitement and mystery of the impending celebration, as people tried to guess who would be getting married.

As well as wedding preparations, the next two days were a whirlwind of activity from dawn to dusk, as the colonists set about making the new world their home. The settlement had retained eight of Genesis' ten shuttles, due to Wisecroft not having a qualified pilot among his colonists. An agreement had been made that the Seahaven colony would retain them, provided they were available to be flown to Settlement City any time there was a significant need for them. Two of the shuttles were parked on the concourse, next to the domes in the centre of the park, and provided power and recharging facilities for equipment with batteries. They were also the comm centre for contact with Settlement City and with members of their own colony who were using portable comms. The other six shuttles were parked at the airfield on the northern edge of town.

This morning was crunch time for Settlement City. The last of their colonists had been transported to the surface late the previous afternoon, along with enough zip-huts for their temporary accommodation. Genesis was due to break orbit and attempt to land at 0800 hours. As the appointed time approached, the Seahaven colonists stopped their chores and gathered outside, looking up into the deep blue sky. They should be able to see the fireball of Genesis' violent descent through the upper atmosphere, as it passed overhead from west to east, travelling at 30,000 kilometres per hour. As the allotted time came and went, there was initially no sign of Genesis. People stared up into the sky, talking quietly in small groups, wondering what would happen if Genesis burnt up or crashed.

Suddenly, a cry from one of the onlookers drew everyone's attention to a fireball low in the western sky, just above the mountains. It tore across the sky in a flaming arc and disappeared over the eastern horizon in just seconds. Only after it disappeared did its sound reach those on the ground, an impressive roar chasing the already vanished spacecraft across the sky. After the spectacular show was concluded, all the Seahaven colonists could do was gather around the comm shuttle and await word from Settlement City. At least 20 minutes dragged by. The outcome of this attempted landing would have a huge impact on both settlements. If the Genesis landing failed and the ship was destroyed, there would be no medical facility, no backup accommodation, no backup food supply and no way off the planet if they ever needed to leave. Everything hung in the balance as both settlements waited for the outcome.

In the end, the landing went perfectly. Under Genni's expert guidance, Genesis achieved a feather-light touchdown, descending vertically on its fiery tail and pivoting onto its side at the last moment, so that it lay lengthwise in a field on the outskirts of the inland town of Southland. News of the success was relayed to Seahaven by Michael Gates, Wisecroft's comm officer, and the Seahaven colonists cheered spontaneously at the news.

Once the morning's drama was over, the real work of the day began. Of prime importance was the need to bring the drop boxes safely down from orbit. Without the aid of satellites, plotting the projected trajectories was a challenge, involving some fairly complex calculations. Kit had worked at the calculations for over an hour in the cockpit of the shuttle, from first light, using the computer interface to determine the exact time to initiate the de-orbit burns for the drop boxes. As she finished the final check of her figures, Zac plonked himself into the seat beside her, humming a happy tune.

"OK. What now, O captain my captain?" he said.

"My, my, aren't we in a happy mood this morning. Anyone would think you were getting married to the prettiest girl on Nova tomorrow night."

"Yep, that'd be me all right!" said Zac, cheerfully.

Kit activated her uplink to the drop boxes. "OK, here we go." She punched a button and then leant back in her chair. "I've uploaded the burn data. If I got the physics right, the boxes should come down a little south-west of us."

"And if you didn't?"

"They could land anywhere."

There was an anxious wait of about 40 minutes, and towards the end, a small crowd of people was scanning the sky, searching for the massive chutes. Kit came bursting out of the shuttle, saying, "The shuttle's scanners show three objects high to the south!"

All eyes turned in that direction. "There!" shouted someone, pointing. Three tiny dots, high in the sky, gradually resolved into box shapes, each hanging beneath three massive chutes.

"They're further south than I had hoped," said Kit, but she was obviously relieved that they were at least in visible range. "We'll have to take a shuttle."

Kit took charge of the retrieval operation. Martinez would drive the caterpillar back, with Boyd to keep her company. Several of Regina's rapidly developing agricultural team had experience with tractors, and so two of them, Wally and Will, brothers who had been farmers in New Zealand, would drive the tractors back. The retrieval team boarded the shuttle, along with Anton Sturbeck, a security team member with a reputation as a sharpshooter. When everyone was on board, Zac lifted off under Kit's watchful eye.

"We're getting a strong signal from the location beacons," said Kit. "It looks like they're about five clicks south-south-west." The shuttle flew out of the park, over the surrounding streets, and then they were flying low over fields and farmland to the south.

After only a minute, Kit said, "Getting stronger, nearly there. Slightly more to the west."

Zac banked the shuttle and almost immediately said, "I see one!" The first of the huge metal boxes, with chutes collapsed beside it, was sitting in a cleared field that had obviously been used to grow some kind of crop. Zac landed the shuttle, and Kit's silence was the highest praise she had ever bestowed upon him. She almost seemed disappointed that there was nothing to criticise. The team all disembarked and walked up to the large metal container.

Zac asked, "How do we open it?"

"Like this," said Kit, activating a remote control in her hand. There was a hiss and a pop, and then the front side of the container came smoothly down on large hydraulic pistons, coming to rest on the ground and forming a gentle ramp. The tractor inside had a front bucket, a completely enclosed cabin and a large combo slasher/plough at the rear. Wally, one of the two tractor drivers, climbed aboard, started it up, and drove it straight down the ramp.

Wally was told to wait in the cab of his tractor while the team retrieved the other vehicles, so that they could drive back in convoy.

The second tractor retrieval proved slightly more difficult. They located it half a kilometre to the south-west of the first tractor, in a low-lying field that was flooded to knee height. Will was able to drive the tractor out of the flooded container, but it quickly became bogged down in the muddy, water-logged field. They called Wally, who brought the first tractor to the scene. By positioning the first tractor on dry ground at the edge of the field and joining its rear tow cable to the front tow cable of the bogged tractor, they were eventually able to extricate it from the field. While Wally was unshackling his tractor afterwards, Will made his way back to the edge of the flooded field and, after bending down, returned with something in his hand.

"Every cloud has a silver lining," he said, holding his hand out to Wally.

"Rice!" Wally enthused. "Well, I'll be!"

For a few moments the two farmers discussed the length of the grains and gave their opinions regarding the particular variant this crop might be.

"Well, whatever type it is, there's plenty of it," said Zac, looking around. The field in question was square in shape, about 400 metres each side.

Kit said, "No doubt Regina will want to come and investigate this later. But right now, we need to find the caterpillar. I'm picking up a weak signal almost due west of here. We'll leave both tractors here for the moment while we search for it in the shuttle."

They lifted off and flew westwards, watching the tracking signal grow progressively stronger. After they had flown over several overgrown agricultural fields, the terrain turned to dense bushland and the ground began to rise up into the foothills of the mountains.

"There! I can see the chute!" said Zac, pointing to the left.

The white chute material was caught in the canopy of a thick group of trees halfway down a steep hillside. Kit banked the shuttle and they circled the chute, peering down at the terrain below.

"It looks like the box has crashed through the trees and is on its side on the ground in the middle of those trees," said Zac.

"Yeh," replied Kit, "and we're gonna have a hell of a time getting it out of there. There's half a click of dense bushland between the agricultural fields and the base of that hill. And if those trees are as thick on the ground as they appear to be from the air, we won't be able to retrieve the vehicle without doing some serious tree-felling and clearing."

The top of the hill was a grassy knoll, devoid of trees and bushes, so Kit took control of the shuttle and set it down there. They walked down the grassy slope and stopped at the edge of the tree line, where the slope became much steeper. They could see the caterpillar's drop box halfway down the steep, thickly treed slope.

"Well, we won't be getting that out today," said Zac.

"No," agreed Kit. "This is gonna take days of hard work. We'll need to clear a track through the bushland between the fields and the hill, and a bunch of trees will need to be felled."

"At least Grizzle is going to get plenty of timber. That should stop him whingeing for a while."

The shuttle arrived back at the settlement 10 minutes later, and the two tractors rolled in 30 minutes after that. The brothers, Wally and Will, drove the tractors to the agricultural centre that Regina was establishing beyond the western edge of town, alongside the nearest field. A large tech-hut had been erected there, 50 metres by 80 metres, made with the same bio conductive, photoelectric material as the zip-huts, with sides that could be rolled up to allow tractors and other equipment to be stored under cover while they recharged.

Regina had a large team of enthusiastic workers, some with farming experience, but most were complete novices who were simply willing to learn and make a contribution. They were sorting boxes of seeds and fertilisers, and unpacking tools. The four quad bikes were being used to survey the surrounding fields, to gather soil samples and determine what was already growing there.

Back in the centre of town, another large tech-hut had been erected on the grass at the top of the amphitheatre, close to the central concourse. One end of the structure served as a basic medical centre. Dr Francis Leibman had sided with Wisecroft, so Jaz and Ben Miller were Seahaven's only doctors. They had some basic field medical equipment and supplies, but anyone who required surgery would need to be flown to Settlement City, to utilise the robotic diagnostics and surgery on board Genesis. The other end of the tech-hut, which was already being called city hall, was the town planning and coordination centre.

Tomorrow's job would be to erect the remaining large tech-hut on the far side of the three domes just beyond the western edge of the concourse. The plan was for it to be the workshop and engineering centre. Seahaven had taken its fair share of equipment from Genesis: lathes, drill presses, band saws, bench saws and a range of hand-held tools. A shuttle from the airfield had already been moved there, and its fusion drive was currently being cannibalised and modified to provide all the electrical power that the workshop would need.

In the late afternoon, the City Council, or what remained of them, met to evaluate the settlement's progress. There were four fewer members of the council now, after Lars Christensen's death and the loss of a further three to Wisecroft's settlement: Leonidis, Leibman (medical) and Manchester (nuclear physics). The five remaining council members, - Zac, Prisha, Lance, Regina Boyle and Carla Zangetti - met at city hall, and as they began to list the essential things that needed to be done over the coming weeks and months, the enormity of the task became apparent. Lance, still wearing his *2001: A Space Odyssey* cap, voiced concern about the lack of a clear priority list and community plan.

"This afternoon," he said, "I overheard two men discussing plans to explore around the western shore of the lake, with the aim of building a log cabin there as a permanent home. But at this stage we can't afford to have everyone doing their own thing. We all need to pull together if we are to survive."

"I agree," said Regina. "In these first 12 months, our highest priority has got to be establishing a plentiful, sustainable food supply. Permanent dwellings are further down the list. We need everyone working towards the same goals, in the same order."

Prisha spoke up. "Yes, but that requires a clearly articulated plan, and that really hasn't been communicated to the community yet."

"Regina, I agree that food production is our first priority," said Lance. "But we can't let everything else slide in the meantime. We need to be developing a range of other improvements concurrently. Sanitation, health, communication, some exploration of other nearby resources, and the development of our engineering department, to name just a few. There are a lot of things to balance here."

"We need more help," said Zac.

"What do you mean?" asked Carla, the astronomer.

"I mean, coordinating our colony effectively needs more than just the five of us. We need a larger leadership team, with each person overseeing an area of the colony's development. A larger team, briefly meeting at the start of each day, will enable us to coordinate our efforts more effectively, and also help us to be aware of any issues within the community before they become problematic."

"Yes," said Prisha. "I like that. A larger, more representative leadership team would give us a more balanced perspective."

"How do we choose them?" asked Lance. "Some kind of election?"

"I don't think so," said Zac. "It's too early in the colony's history for any kind of democratic elections. You know, the first democracy, instituted by Cleisthenes in Athens in 508 BC, was not an *elected* democracy, but a *consultative* democracy. It involved the whole town, which at that point was still quite small, being invited to a regular forum to discuss plans and laws. The leaders were self-appointed as a result of their better education, but the citizens were happy with this as long as they were listened to. I think we can aim at this kind of consultative process as a first step towards eventual full democratic elections. But right now, we have an immediate need for experts in their chosen fields, and we are best placed to select them."

The rest of the afternoon was spent identifying candidates for the leadership team and approaching them individually once the meeting ended. In the end, the new candidates almost chose themselves.

That evening, as the sun set in the west and camp cookers were lit for the evening meal of fish and potatoes, the howlers screamed out their nightly challenge. Melody shivered and covered her ears with her hands. "I hate those things, whatever they are!" she said to Jaz as they peeled potatoes together at the entrance to their zip-hut. Kit and Martinez, who were both cleaning weapons a short distance away, overheard Melody's comment.

Martinez said, "I'd certainly like to know what those howlers are and whether they pose a threat to us."

"They don't exactly sound cute and cuddly," said Kit, as she cleaned the barrel of her old-fashioned projectile pistol.

Martinez responded, "I'll rest easier if we can establish that they're harmless."

But they weren't harmless. Not by a long shot.

47

NOVA DAY 7

The next morning, the hoomie birds woke the community to another clear-sky morning. The world glistened in the aftermath of the overnight showers, and steam rose from every surface as the morning sun began to evaporate the moisture away. The settlement was bubbling with excitement because tonight was the wedding celebration, and there was much speculation as to which couples had decided to commit to each other. The ceremonies were scheduled for 1700 at the beach, and afterwards there was to be a feast back at the settlement, although "feast" was an extremely optimistic term, given the paucity of their provisions. Before then, however, there was much work to be done, and the fledgling settlement sprang into action after an early breakfast.

At 0900 the new leadership team gathered at city hall for their first meeting. They began by formalising the specific roles of each person on the team:

Lenny Montague – Head of Engineering

Gus Grizole (Grizzle) – Workshop and Construction Manager

Ben Miller – Chief Medical Officer

Regina Boyle – Biology and Agriculture

Carla Zangetti – Science and Technology

Prisha Naroo – Social Welfare

Natasha Martinez – Security and Hunting

Lance Catrell – Logistics

Keolakupaianaha Ka'aukai (Keo) – Fishing Coordinator

Zac Perryman – Coordinator

Seahaven City Council began its first morning briefing. Regina, as head of biology and agriculture, had arguably the most important area to oversee in trying to establish a long-term, plentiful food supply. She spoke first.

"Well, bear in mind I'm still on my "L" plates. But things are progressing pretty well. Today we are going to start turning over the first fields and planting crops. It's early autumn, so it is the ideal time to be planting winter crops. The seeds we brought from Genesis are all in very good condition, and the regular evening rainfall we're currently getting is ideal. Wally and Will are invaluable. They will be supervising the planting of the fields, but we could use some more people to help with the planting. Another 50 for about a week would be great."

"OK," said Zac. "Lance, can you put the word around? Let's ask for 50 volunteers, starting from tomorrow. If we don't get them, we'll round up people who may be loafing around the camp."

Carla, the 48-year-old, efficient, blonde-haired science and technology coordinator, was next. "I have several tasks on my list. Firstly, studying our orbit, to assess how bad winter might be as we move further from Icarus, our sun. Secondly, studying the periodicity and eccentricity of the orbits of our moons, Big Boy and Little Boy, to see how they are going to influence tides. I suspect there may be some king tides when both moons line up. Thirdly, we are investigating the existing alien structures here on Nova. They appear to emit an extremely faint, ultra-high-frequency signal, only barely detectable to my instruments. So far, we haven't been able to make even a scratch in the material they're constructed of, but I haven't given up the hope of gaining access to them at some stage in the future."

"Anything you need at the moment?" asked Zac.

"No. I have a team of 22, mainly scientists who were based on Earth's moon, plus a handful of very enthusiastic trainees from among the colonists. We also managed to gain our fair share of scientific equipment from Genesis. We've joined together about 20 zip-huts, which we've transformed into our science lab, and we've plugged this into the shuttle near engineering. So, at this stage, we have everything we need."

Lenny Montague, chief of engineering, was up next. In his early 50s, Lenny had a shiny, bald head and round, rimless glasses. Unlike most in his era, he had refused laser eye surgery, preferring to grind his own lenses and make his own frames. He had a meticulous mind and had run the engineering department on the moon for 15 years.

"I've downloaded from Genesis all the blueprints and parts specifications for all our vehicles and machinery onto our engineering database. We will be able to do minor repairs on parts that break down, but the major challenge will be the need for raw materials for producing basic metals. There are currently eight of us in engineering, and our priority, for the foreseeable future, will be to investigate ways of producing metal."

Ben Miller reported that the medical centre was set up as a first-aid station, and their supplies were adequate for the present. "The problem will arise when we have a major medical incident requiring surgery. Jaz and I can probably cope with minor surgery, but anything major will need to be flown to Genesis."

"Do we anticipate any problem with that?" asked Regina.

"Always anticipate problems, if Wisecroft is involved," said Zac. "We'll just have to deal with that issue if and when it arises."

Grizzle was next. He reported that he had a big team of workers in the workshop area; some were skilled tradesmen, but most were just enthusiastic handymen and women. "I'll be very surprised if Dr Miller doesn't get to sew at least a finger back on before the week's out," he stated with his usual grumpy pessimism.

"How are you off for tools and equipment?" asked Lance.

"Fair to middling," he replied. "I'm using an old-fashioned workbook and pencil to log the job requests when they come in; I don't trust computers, never have. Timber is the missing ingredient right now. We're gonna need to start chopping trees down to mill them before we can do any serious construction."

"I suspect that will have to wait until after we've planted our winter crops," said Lance again.

"That'd be right," mumbled Grizzle. "Expect me to build the Taj Mahal out of thin air and spit!"

Kit spoke up. "Maybe you won't have to wait too long for your timber. There's the problem of retrieving the caterpillar. It's in dense bushland about 5 clicks south-west of here and hemmed in by some densely packed trees."

"What do you propose?" asked Lance.

"I think we should make it a priority to retrieve the caterpillar, and that is going to need a team camped on site for at least a few days. The tractors will need to clear a path through the bushland to the base of the hill and, at the same time, a team of workers will need to fell quite a few of those trees. I think we should establish a camp on top of the hill for the tree clearers, so that we don't have to ferry everyone out and back every day."

"I agree," said Lance. "I could get a team together today and get all the equipment and supplies sorted. We could shuttle everyone out at first light tomorrow."

"Anyone have any objections?" asked Zac.

"As long as I still get my farm workers, I don't mind," said Regina.

"Anyone else?" asked Zac.

No one spoke up, and there were several shakes of heads.

"Cool. Operation Caterpillar gets a green light. Martinez, you'll need to organise a couple of armed security personnel to be part of the team. We still don't know if there are dangerous predators here."

"I agree," replied Martinez. "Those howlers worry me. They sound predatory, and they're clearly nocturnal, because we've seen multiple sets of eye shine on the outskirts of the settlement over the last two nights. Several people have also found droppings from a fairly large animal not far from their zip-huts first thing in the morning, so I think we should advise people not to wander off alone at night or in the pre-dawn."

Regina chipped in, "This morning I was at the ag-hut early, just as the sun was coming up, and I saw two animals disappearing into the bushes on the western edge of the field. They looked like lions, but with a completely black head, a black tail and a single black stripe running down the middle of their back. A few moments later, I heard those terrible screams coming from their direction. I think they must be the howlers."

Martinez said, "I'd been going to suggest that we send two security personnel with quads and rifles to explore west of the fields to see if we can find any sign of them. That seems to be the direction they're coming from. This expedition to retrieve the caterpillar gives us an opportunity to do that, although we won't be taking quads."

"OK, that all sounds good," said Zac. "Let's get the expedition organised today. Lance is coordinating the preparations. We'll aim for 0900 lift-off tomorrow morning. The shuttle that transports the team can remain on the hilltop as part of the camp, providing additional shelter and power for recharging equipment."

He turned to Keo and asked, "How's the fishing coming along?"

"The Department of Aquatic Harvesting is going well, brother."

Several people chuckled, and there were smiles all around.

Keo's face beamed with joy. "This sea is teeming with fish, my friends!"

"Do you need anything?" asked Lance.

"We are eventually going to run out of fishing line, but not in the immediate future. However, I would like to build some boats as soon as possible. We have nets that Genesis supplied us with, and if we had boats, they would enable us to land much larger catches. Then we wouldn't need to fish every day, and we could even freeze or dry the excess."

Lance looked across the table. "Grizzle, could your team look at constructing some basic boats for the ... um ..."

"Department of Aquatic Harvesting," prompted Keo.

"Yes, the Department of Aquatic Harvesting." Lance finished, with a smile.

Grizzle shook his head and muttered, "And what would you like them built out of? Spit and wind?"

"Timber would be fine, my friend," replied Keo, refusing to be daunted by Grizzle's grumpiness. "In New Zealand, I grew up near the sea and I have built many canoes and simple boats. I will work with you, and together we will soon have a fleet of boats harvesting more fish than we can eat."

Kit chimed in. "We should have timber arriving back here within a few days, Grizzle. Once the tractors have cleared a path to the caterpillar site, they can start transferring the felled timber directly to your workshop."

Grizzle looked at Kit and said, "You bring me my timber, and I'll see what I can do."

A few minutes later, the first official morning briefing of the Seahaven City Council drew to a close. As they concluded, Keo reminded them of the festivities that were planned for that evening but refused to divulge any further details of what to expect. "You will just have to wait and see!" he said, with a mischievous glint in his eyes.

48

The wedding ceremonies were scheduled for 1700. The Nova day had a periodicity of exactly 24 hours, 50 minutes, and the scientific team had recalibrated most of the colonists' digital watches, so by 1630 a constant stream of excited colonists had begun making their way toward the beach. The ceremonies were to be conducted on the headland at the southern end of the town beach. The headland's circular grassy knoll, 20 metres above sea level and 80 metres in diameter, provided a stunning view in all directions. To the north, the town beach gently curved into the distance, ending in a similar headland at least 10 kilometres away. To the south, there was a series of small beaches, rocky coves and headlands. Keo had been preparing all day, and as the colonists walked up the gently sloping headland onto the knoll, they were greeted by a floral arch that framed the magnificent view out to sea. The arch spanned 10 metres at the far end of the knoll and was constructed of saplings that Keo had dug into the ground at each side and bent across to tie together in the middle. Adorning the arch was a symphony of riotously coloured flowers, gathered by Keo and Melody throughout the day. When Keo had asked if he could borrow Melody for the day, Jaz had almost hugged him with gratitude, as Melody had been jumping out of her skin with excitement for the last two days and was driving everyone crazy.

As the time drew near for the start of the ceremony, Keo stood quietly under the arch, facing the large crowd with his back to the ocean. The colonists were abuzz with excitement and curiosity. Who was getting married? Apart from Zac and Jaz, the identities of the other couples had successfully been kept a complete secret.

As Keo's digital watch clicked over to 1700, he stepped forward a few paces, spread his hands wide and waited while a hush fell over the crowd.

"Brothers and sisters, today is a day of new beginnings! We named this world 'Nova' for a reason. This is the beginning of a new life for us all. More than any other people in human history, we are separated from our past by a huge gulf of time and distance. Although we will never forget those who could not be here with us today, we must also recognise that they are trillions of kilometres and thousands of years in our past. We cannot let our memory of those we have lost, and our love for them, stop us from moving forward." Keo paused and looked around at the sea of faces, many of them nodding in agreement.

"We cannot change the past, and we cannot perceive the future. We must live in the present and grasp the opportunities that come our way with both hands. As the great 16th century French philosopher Michel de Montaigne once said, 'Take joy in the present, because everything else is beyond your grasp'."

Kit leaned across to Martinez, who was standing beside her, and whispered, "I told you he would slip a Montaigne quote in! You owe me a watch-keeping shift!"

"Damn!" whispered Martinez in reply. "I thought he'd exhausted his Montaigne quotes!"

Keo continued, "The couples who are about to be married have chosen the present over the past. They have chosen to embrace love, instead of sorrow. They have chosen joy over regret. And, by pledging themselves to each other, they represent the dawn of a new life and the hope of a better future for us all."

Some of the colonists broke into spontaneous applause, punctuated with whistles.

"I will now call each of the couples forward to stand before you and make their vows."

A murmur of excitement rippled through the crowd.

"Zac Perryman and Jasmine Bellini."

The crowd cheered and applauded as Zac and Jaz walked forward. As the couple took their place at the front, Zac whispered to Jaz, "I didn't even know your last name!"

She looked at him with a mischievous glint in her eyes and said, "That's OK. You're about to discover a whole lot more of me in a couple of hours."

Keo called out another couple, "Latraia Geronis and Tye Walter." More cheers and applause erupted, along with several squeals of delighted surprise from some of their friends.

"Paul Oppedisano and Jenny Marie ..."

"Andrew Moriarty and Catherine Sinclair ..."

"Glenn Bowler and Jane Healey ..."

Keo continued his marital roll call amidst almost continuous cheers and whistles from the crowd, until there were 14 couples standing hand in hand under the flowered arch.

"These couples," he continued, "will pledge their commitment to each other, before us as a community and, I believe, before their Creator. We don't need priests and cathedrals. We don't need registries and bureaucratic departments. All that is needed is for two people to pledge their undying loyalty to each other. They will do that now, in their own words."

Each of the couples in turn spoke brief vows to each other.

As each couple concluded their vows, Keo stepped forward and placed a floral necklace around each of their necks and handed them a cup of nectar. The nectar had been produced with Regina's help. She had found a shrub with heart-shaped purple berries growing prolifically on the western edge of one of the fields. Analysis revealed that the juice from the berries contained high levels of tryptophan and a mild psychotropic enzyme, both of which could boost the brain's pleasure chemicals, oxytocin and serotonin. The juice itself had a sweet, tangy flavour, and Keo and Regina had christened the fruit 'passion berries'. After each successive couple said their vows, Keo handed them a cup of passion berry nectar. The couple then served each other a hefty gulp of the nectar and kissed while the juice was still on their lips, cheered on by the enthusiastic crowd of well-wishers.

Once all 14 couples had completed the ritual, Keo stepped forward once more and said, "We are not finished yet! There is one more couple to be married today. Prisha Naroo, please step forward."

There were murmurs of excitement as Prisha stepped forward, but also puzzled expressions. Who was she marrying? Why had Keo not called her partner forward as well? Keo did not leave them guessing for long. He walked over to Prisha, placed a floral necklace around her neck and his own, then held both her hands, gazing lovingly into her eyes. There were squeals of delight from many, including Zac and Jaz, who'd had absolutely no clue of the romance blossoming between their two friends.

"Prisha, I pledge to love and care for you with all my heart, body and soul, and be faithful to you alone until we are separated by death."

"Keo, I pledge to love and care for you with all my heart, body and soul, and be faithful to you alone until we are separated by death."

They each took a hearty gulp from a nearby cup and then embraced in a long, lingering kiss, amid wolf whistles and cheers from the crowd.

Keo then faced the crowd with a huge smile and a thin dribble of nectar running down his chin. He opened his arms wide and made a final pronouncement. "Friends, 15 new families stand before you. Their marriages are sacred. Let no one seek to undermine their love, break their bonds, or come between them in any way. Now, let us celebrate!"

The crowd erupted into cheers and whoops once more, and people came forward to surround and congratulate the happy couples. Melody was bouncing around Jaz and Zac like a jack-in-the-box, hugging them both and talking at a million miles an hour. "Do you like the floral necklaces? I made them myself! And I chose those yellow flowers especially for you, Jaz, because I know you like them, except I couldn't find enough of the little white ones with the red centres which would have really looked great but I found the blue ones in the sand dunes so I thought they would look good too and are you and Zac going to sleep in the same room all the time now, because if you do I promise I won't listen to you smooching too much, and maybe we could go on a camping trip together now that we're a family and I promise I won't be any trouble, and I'll be able to make you breakfast in bed every morning ..."

"There you are, kiddo!" said Kit, coming to Jaz and Zac's rescue. "I need you to help me take some of the food down to the amphitheatre. You can catch up with Jaz and Zac later." She winked at Zac and Jaz, and took hold of Melody's hand, leading her off while she was still talking at lightspeed.

The crowds began walking back towards the settlement, where trestle tables of food and drink had been assembled at the bottom of the amphitheatre.

Zac and Jaz walked back alongside Prisha and Keo, and

after expressing their own amazement and joy for their friends, Zac asked the obvious question.

"How long have you guys had a thing? We had no idea!"

"I knew from the moment I met her on board Genesis," said Keo. "Her name means 'gift of God', so it was meant to be."

Zac asked, "Yes, but when did you actually ... you know ... start to show affection?"

"Yesterday afternoon," answered Prisha with a smirk. "It was the passion berry nectar that did it. Keo asked me to sample some with him ..."

"... at the beach," said Keo with a crafty wink.

"... and I guess we might have overindulged a little ..."

"We should not be skimpy with God's gifts!" interjected Keo again.

" ... and one thing led to another ..."

"It was a beautiful sunset, my friends..."

"... and before we knew it, we were in each other's arms ..."

"I couldn't help it! Her beauty overpowered me!"

"He's a very persuasive man."

"She's a very irresistible woman!"

The four of them laughed together and walked back to the settlement to enjoy the celebration.

Apart from the obvious joy of the weddings, the evening's festivities were a welcome relief from the intensity of the last few days. As the setting sun cast a magnificent pink and apricot hue across the darkening sky, the colonists laughed and ate and drank, and in the midst of it all, their sense of community solidified. It was as if they had finally come to believe that this was their new home - a place of new beginnings.

As the evening wore on, the newlyweds retired to newly erected zip-huts, set a little apart from the other huts but still within the settlement's boundaries. Melody would be bunking with Kit for the next few nights. Zac and Jaz walked hand in hand towards their hut, their heads buzzing from several cups of passion berry juice. After all the excitement and talk of the last couple of hours, it was a relief to finally be alone. They entered their hut, zipped the door closed, and then stood facing each other. Zac's head was spinning a little, and his heart was beating like a machine gun, but he didn't want to rush things.

"So, *Bellini,* eh? You don't look Italian. With that red hair and freckles, and that cute button nose, I would have sworn you were Irish."

"My father was Irish, and my mother was Italian. Dad died when I was very young, and my mother always kept her maiden name. She was a very independent woman with a strong Italian family heritage. The Bellinis trace their roots back centuries, to royal blood. When I was born, she wanted her daughter to have the same surname."

"So, who do you take after? Your mother or your father?"

"I've got my dad's red hair and freckles, and my mother's fiery nature."

"Fiery, eh? What have I gotten myself in for?"

Jaz responded by lifting her simple tunic over her head and dropping it to the ground, standing entirely naked before him. Zac gazed at her in wonder, and she looked boldly into his eyes, saying, "Italians are renowned for being very fiery, passionate people, Zac."

She reached behind her head and undid a couple of ribbons that were holding up her hair and then shook her head, her long red hair cascading around her shoulders in a riotous mess. She took a step towards him, saying, "And when I say passionate, I mean *very* passionate. I hope that's OK with you."

Zac nodded, completely mesmerised. "That's ... just fine with me."

She reached out and began undoing his belt. "I hope you didn't drink too much of that passion nectar, my darling," she said. "Because us Italian girls get very upset if we don't get what we want."

"Um ... I think I'll be able to manage."

And he did.

Several times, in fact.

49

NOVA DAY 11

The fourth day after the weddings dawned in much the same way that all other days on Nova had begun. The first crescent of the rising sun cast multicoloured rays across a deep blue, cloudless sky, and the hoomie birds vociferously announced the commencement of another day of activity. The colonists emerged from their zip-huts to be greeted by a world still glistening from the overnight tropical showers, and the camp slowly came to life as tea was brewed and morning chores attended to. The honeymooners had been excused from all duties for the previous three days and had enjoyed as much privacy as was possible in a cramped campsite, with people deliberately leaving them alone and simply greeting them with smiles and nods if they passed them.

Meanwhile, the establishment of the settlement was progressing at satisfying pace. The two bearded, tractor-driving brothers, Wally and Willy (as the latter was now affectionately being called) had taken only one day to clear a "road" through the dense bushland from the western edge of the ag-fields to the base of the hills. At the same time, Martinez and Boyd had flown the tree-felling team to the top of the hill, which had been named Red Gum Hill because of the proliferation of trees that resembled the huge red gums from the Australian bush. A sizeable campsite had been established there, and the crew had begun clearing the trees around the drop box. By the time the tractors broke through to the base of the hill in the late afternoon, there were already half a dozen trees felled, trimmed and cut into manageable sections, ready for transport back to Grizzle's workshop. For the next two days, Wally transported felled tree sections back to the settlement while Willy dedicated himself to ploughing the various ag-fields, ready for planting. Regina's enthusiastic team of apprentice farmers was also hard at work; some sowing the fields with seeds for winter crops, others harvesting the potatoes and rice that were growing wild in some fields, and a third group working at developing a sustainable fruit orchard. Various fruit trees had been discovered in clusters around the outskirts of the ag-fields. Most of the trees appeared to be ancient, bearing only small quantities of wizened fruit, but the seeds of the fruit, if nurtured and planted properly, would one day provide the colony with a plentiful orchard.

Kit was sitting at the campfire outside her hut, drinking a cup of tea with Grizzle and Regina, when Melody emerged, rubbing sleep from her eyes.

"Morning, sleepy head," Kit said.

"Hi, aunty Kit," she replied, yawning and stretching her arms wide.

Grizzle took a sip from his cup and said, "It's a wonder you've got any teeth left in that head of yours, Possum, the way you grind them in your sleep."

"At least I don't snore," she replied, cheekily.

"What are you insinuating, young lady?"

"She's right, Grizzle," said Kit. "The first night I heard you, I thought someone was doing some moonlight chain sawing."

"That's just the sound of my incredible brain working over-time while I'm asleep," he replied.

"Well, the cogs badly need oiling," said Regina.

Further discussion of Grizzle's nocturnal emanations was cut short by the unexpected arrival of a shuttle. It touched down on the central concourse, its engines waking any colonists who were still asleep. The engines were still winding down when Martinez emerged from the shuttle door, yelling, "Help! We need medical help here! We've got a serious injury!"

Boyd and another man emerged from the shuttle carrying a makeshift stretcher with a blood-soaked victim. Ben Miller, the chief medical officer, arrived on the scene almost immediately and rushed the victim to the med-hut, while issuing instructions to fetch Jaz. Less than a minute later, Jaz and Zac ran into the med-hut just as Martinez was explaining what had happened.

"His name is Tye Sanford. He got up before dawn at Red Gum Hill campsite to relieve himself in the woods. He was attacked by howlers. We heard his screams. Boyd got there pretty quickly and saw the howlers mauling him. There were three of them. He scared them off and managed to kill one with his rifle."

Ben and Jaz cut away Tye's clothing and were confronted with deep lacerations to both arms, his left leg and his torso.

"He's lost a lot of blood," said Ben. "The femoral artery and brachial arteries are both severed. Whoever applied the tourni-quets saved his life—but only just. He could still die. He needs major surgery and we don't have the facility here for that. Plus, he needs litres of nano-blood, which we don't have. It's some-thing that was overlooked."

Zac said, "Let's get him back into the shuttle. We're going to have to take him to Settlement City."

Lance, who had arrived while Ben was speaking, said, "I'll contact Michael Gates and let him know you're coming. They can have the operating theatre prepped and ready to go by the time you get there."

The team sprang into action, and five minutes later the shuttle was airborne. Kit and Zac piloted the shuttle while Ben, Jaz, Martinez and Boyd cared for Tye in the cabin, fighting to keep him alive. Forty minutes later, the shuttle crossed the coast of Southland and Zac activated the comms again.

"Settlement City, this is Shuttle 1, do you read?"

"Roger, Zac. How's the patient?"

"Not good. He's crashed twice and is barely hanging on. We've just crossed the coast and are five minutes from you. Over."

"Yeh, about that ..." said Michael warily.

"What?" asked Zac.

There was a lengthy pause, prompting Zac to ask, "Michael, are you there?"

After a further delay, Michael's voice came over the comms. "Dr Wisecroft has indicated that he will need to clarify some issues before admitting your patient to our medical facilities."

"What?!!" exclaimed Kit.

"What's there to clarify, Michael?" asked Zac, with growing anger. "We have a dying patient and you have the facilities to save him. It's all pretty clear, isn't it?"

"I'm just the messenger, Zac."

"Put Wisecroft on now!" insisted Zac.

"He's not available at the moment. He says he'll meet you when you land."

Zac switched off the comms and swivelled in his seat. "Did you guys catch all that back there?"

"We sure did!" responded Martinez. "I've got a fully loaded pistol in my holster with a bullet with Wisecroft's name etched into it!"

"Don't kill him outright," said Kit. "Try to nick an artery so he bleeds out slowly."

A few minutes later the shuttle touched down, a bare 20 metres from Genesis. As the team carried the unconscious Tye out of the shuttle, they saw that all the access doors on Genesis were closed. Wisecroft was standing on the hard-packed earth outside the nearest closed access door, flanked by two security personnel armed with rifles. Kit, Zac and Martinez stood side by side, with Ben and Boyd carrying the stretcher behind them and Jaz standing to the side, monitoring Tye.

"What's your game, Wisecroft?" asked Zac. "A man's life is in danger here."

"I can see that, and I am terribly concerned for his welfare."

"Then let us in."

"Certainly. Just as soon as we formalise his immigration status."

"What do you mean?"

"I am referring to our previously agreed terms of settlement. Only permanent residents of Settlement City may access its medical facilities."

"We made no such agreement!"

"Those were my clearly stated terms when we agreed to part company. I did warn you that your pitiful village would be unable to adequately care for its misguided residents. Unfortunately, it's come to a head sooner than I anticipated."

Kit spoke up. "You can't be serious! This man is dying! Are you prepared to let him die?"

"Yes I am—for the greater good."

"What?!" exclaimed Kit. "You're insane!"

"On the contrary, Ms Tyler, I am the sanest person in this current conversation. I am the only one who can see that allowing you unfettered access to this facility will only perpetuate the miserable existence of your ill-fated settlement. If this poor man has to die in order to end your rebellion, so be it."

"You're a monster, Wisecroft!" growled Martinez, unholstering her pistol and aiming it at the centre of his chest.

Wisecroft's two goons responded immediately by aiming their laser rifles at Martinez.

"I am not a monster," said Wisecroft with a confident smile. "I am a humanitarian. The death of one man will no doubt convince the vast majority of your settlement that they have made the wrong choice. They will be safer and better cared for here, and in the end, there will be much less suffering."

"Can I shoot him?" asked Martinez, without breaking her stare from Wisecroft. She looked fiercely determined, her short black hair, multiple facial piercings, and cold glinting eyes presenting a formidable demeanour.

"Zac!" called Jaz. "He's crashing again!"

"It's your call, Dr Perryman," said Wisecroft. "If you agree to the patient's permanent immigration status, we will open the doors and treat him immediately. But I suggest you decide quickly."

"You cruel bastard!" exclaimed Kit.

"All right! I agree!" said Zac. "Tye stays with you. Now, quickly, help him!"

Wisecroft nodded his head and said, "Open the door."

Immediately the nearest loading bay door swung down and formed a gentle ramp. Leibman and his medical team, who must have been waiting on the other side, ran down the ramp and took possession of the patient, rushing him inside as they desperately worked on him. Zac and his team moved to follow, but Wisecroft's goons swung their weapons to cover the whole group, and Wisecroft said, "Your job here is done. You may leave now."

"But -" began Jaz.

"Tye is one of our citizens now," continued Wisecroft. "He has nothing to do with you."

"But he has a wife and a son at our settlement!" said Martinez, who had gotten to know everyone on the tree-felling team.

"They will be very welcome to immigrate," said Wisecroft, "along with anyone else who comes to their senses. Settlement City is a warm, welcoming community, and we will hold no grudges against any rebels who see the error of their ways." Somehow his smile did not reach his eyes, which seemed cold and calculating.

Ben Miller stepped forward and said, "We need nano-blood. It was overlooked in the sharing of medical supplies."

"That is most unfortunate."

"Are you refusing to give us some?" asked Zac.

"Of course."

"How can you refuse?" asked Ben.

"Because any help we give you only perpetuates your rebellion and delays the inevitable merging of the two settlements. The sooner you realise the hopelessness of your position, the sooner our colony can be reunited and have the best possible chance of flourishing."

Zac shook his head. "Have you considered that having two viable settlements in two separate locations might actually be a better survival strategy? Surely it would provide a buffer if one settlement was afflicted with localised drought or pestilence or disease!"

"You're wrong, Dr Perryman. Of course, eventually we will need to spread out, but it's way too soon for that. Unfortunately, I am the only one who seems to understand this. A great leader is one who sees what needs to be done and is prepared to do it, even if he is not understood. Now, if you will excuse me, I have a city to run. This conversation is over."

With that, he turned and walked into Genesis, leaving his two guards pointing their rifles at the group.

"Let's go," said Zac. "We can't do anything more here."

"Yeh," said Martinez. "Let's get out of here before I puke!"

The return flight to Seahaven was not a happy one. They were furious with Wisecroft and discussed scenarios of how they might have handled the situation differently. But, apart from an outright gun battle, they concluded there was nothing they could have done to achieve a better outcome. Wisecroft had them over a barrel.

50

NOVA DAY 12

T he morning briefing of the Seahaven City Council had a heavier air than usual. On the positive side, Tye had survived his surgery and was making a full recovery. His wife and son had been informed and were already packing up their few possessions, ready for the shuttle flight later in the morning that would reunite the family. A further eight people had also decided to emigrate, voicing concerns over their own safety should an accident befall them.

The issue of greatest concern, of course, was the denial of access to the medical facilities on board Genesis.

"Wisecroft has us over a barrel," said Zac, repeating the conclusion he and the others had reached on their flight back yesterday. "If we don't have access to Genesis, we are only one accident away from another showdown. And every time that happens, we will lose more colonists."

Lance looked at Ben. "Is there anything we can do to shore up our existing medical facilities?"

Ben thought for a moment. "Our most pressing need is blood for transfusions. With a blood bank on site, we can probably handle almost all medical emergencies, including fairly complex surgeries. Nano-blood is ideal, as it can be frozen indefinitely and thawed very quickly for transfusion. Without nano-blood, we will need to revert to an organic blood bank. That would be more complicated, but it can definitely be done, with help from the science department."

Carla, head of science, asked, "What would you need?"

"I assume you have centrifuges?" Ben asked.

"Yes, of course."

"In that case, we would need to separate the plasma, platelets and red blood cells, and freeze them all separately. This will ensure the long-term viability of the blood when it is thawed and reconstituted. The thawing and reconstituting process will take a little longer than nano-blood; 10 minutes or so. That means we will need to always keep a small supply of liquid O-negative blood refrigerated for immediate use while we are thawing the frozen blood. O-negative can be given to anyone, and it will last for up to 42 days, refrigerated. A bag of plasma can also be thawed almost instantly and given to a patient to increase blood volume while we are waiting for the matched blood type to be thawed and reconstituted."

Carla responded positively. "We can easily do all that."

"What percentage of a general population have O-negative blood?" asked Lance.

"About 7 percent," replied Ben.

"So that means that with the Seahaven population about to drop to 319 with this morning's departures ..." Lance did a quick calculation, "we should expect to find 20 to 25 people who are O-negative."

"Yes," agreed Ben. "And once we have established a frozen blood bank with a reasonable supply of each blood type, we will only need one fresh bag of O-negative every 42 days. With 20 people to draw from, each one would only need to give blood once every two years or so."

"OK," said Zac. "That seems to solve the blood problem.

What else do we need to do, in order to become medically self-sufficient?"

Ben considered the question thoughtfully. "Firstly, Jasmine and I need to read up on surgical procedures. We will need to be able to tackle anything. I am confident we can do it, but we're not quite ready for open-heart surgery tomorrow. Secondly, we will need a more self-contained surgery, particularly an operating theatre that isn't in a draughty tech-hut like this. A converted shuttle would be ideal, as it has an airtight seal as well as an unlimited direct power supply and an independent life-support system. Would that be possible?" He looked around the table.

Lance, as logistics coordinator, responded. "I think that's doable. We have eight shuttles and we certainly aren't using them all."

Zac asked, "Anything else?"

"Yes," said Ben. "Thirdly, and most seriously, we have a limited supply of antiseptic and anaesthetic. We probably have enough for six major operations, possibly eight in a pinch, but once those supplies are gone, we will no longer be able to operate."

There was silence for a moment.

Finally Zac spoke up. "We can't predict the future. How many surgical procedures will we do each year? We just don't know. All we can do is set ourselves up for the present. By the time our supplies are exhausted, the current stand-off might well have resolved itself."

"Plus," added Carla, "we might be lucky. If we can identify some plants with naturally occurring anaesthetic or antiseptic, our amazing science team may be able to extract and synthesise more."

The Council spent several more minutes fleshing out the details of their plans for a self-sufficient medical centre, including enlisting and upskilling the most promising medical trainees from their time on board Genesis. The blood drive would also begin at once, with everyone in the town asked to give an initial litre of blood.

Updates from other departments were then quickly given, and other issues requiring immediate action were addressed. The settlement was moving ahead at a rapid pace.

Finally Zac asked, "Anything else?"

"Meat!"

Everyone looked at Martinez.

"We need meat," she extrapolated. "I can only eat so much damn fish before I start growing gills!"

"Do you have a suggestion?" asked Zac.

"The howlers, for a start."

"Go on."

"I spoke to the loggers at Red Gum Hill over the comms last night. They barbequed the howler that Boyd shot yesterday. They reckon it was pretty good. Lean and strong-flavoured—a bit like venison."

"No ill effects?" asked Regina, the head of agriculture.

"It didn't do the howler any good."

Everyone chuckled.

"I want to suggest that we actively cull the howlers nearest the settlement," Martinez continued. "It'll have the dual benefit of making it safer for us and also provide an added food source."

Lance asked, "How long until you've freed the caterpillar?"

"Two more trees to go this morning and then we can drive that sucker out of there. It should be back here by mid-afternoon. Once that job's finished, I want to mount daily hunting expeditions, using the quads, to clear the howlers from our immediate area."

Zac looked around the table and said, "Makes sense to me. Any objections?"

Grizzle spoke up. "Barbeque, you say?"

"Yep," replied Martinez.

"Missy, I don't know what those blockheads up there in the hills define as a barbeque, but you haven't tasted a barbeque until you've tasted mine."

"Sorry, old-timer," she replied, "but you haven't tasted a barbeque until you've tasted *mine!*"

"Is that so?" he replied.

"I just said it, so it must be so."

They stared at each other with mock severity for a few seconds.

"How much are you willing to wager on that, missy?"

Martinez thought about it for a moment, and then a sly smile crept across her face. "The loser becomes the winner's slave for a week."

"Deal!" exclaimed Grizzle. "Oh boy, this is gonna be like stealing candy from a child!"

"We'll see about that, grandpa!" Martinez replied.

"OK, you heard it folks," said Zac. "It's the Great Barbeque Cook-off! Let's schedule it for tomorrow night, provided we can bag two howlers by then."

"That won't be a problem," said Martinez.

And so, it was decided. Fresh on the heels of the wedding celebrations only a few days earlier, another party would be just what the community needed to lift their spirits. Little did they know that they were soon to endure a season where there was little to celebrate.

51

NOVA DAY 14

A day and a half of hunting had bagged not just two howlers, but nearly 30. As nocturnal hunters, the howlers were sleepy and lethargic during the day, lying in shady groves and in caves and rocky overhangs in the foothills. Most of the dead howlers were left to rot where they were killed, which, it was hoped, would send a message to other howlers that the area was no longer safe for them. Four carcasses were brought back; one to be examined by the biology department, and three to be barbequed at the Great Barbeque Cook-off. A third contestant had entered the fray—Keo, who claimed that his traditional New Zealand *hāngi* was far superior to the western barbeque.

"What's a hāngi?" asked Melody, as she watched Keo digging a large hole.

"It's how the Maori in New Zealand traditionally cook meat. First, a large hole is dug, and a very large, red-hot fire is lit at the bottom. Once the fire has turned to glowing coals, large rocks are placed in the hole, which also get very hot. Then meat, flavoured with secret spices and wrapped in leaves, is placed on top of the rocks and covered with a wet cloth of some kind. The hole is then filled in with soil and the meat is left to cook in the ground for about three hours."

"Wow! That's amazing!" said Melody. "Can I help?"

"You can't help him, missy!" said Grizzle, a mere 10 metres away. He was constructing his spit in preparation for his own barbeque. "He's big enough and ugly enough to do it all himself. How about you come over here and give an old man a hand?"

"OK."

"No you don't!" said Martinez, on the other side of Keo. "Neither of them needs any help. Besides, us girls should stick together, don't you think? I've got some things you could help me with."

"OK. What can I ...?"

"Now, now, everyone, play fair!" said Zac, walking into their midst, having heard the interchange from nearby. "Melody, don't you help any of them. They all talk a big game, but let's see if they can deliver. They have to do it ALL themselves, with no outside help."

"Who put you in charge?" asked Grizzle.

"I just did. Any objections?"

All three opened their mouths, but before they could get a sound out, Zac said, "Good! It's settled, then. I'm the boss, and I say no help from anyone, or else you're disqualified."

Grizzle shook his head and muttered, "Give a boy a water pistol and he thinks he's a general!"

The rest of the afternoon was a blur of frantic activity, with all three contestants labouring to prepare their fires, dress the meat, find spices and, finally, beginning the slow cooking process. Each of them had visited Regina at the ag-hut during the morning, to concoct a secret blend of herbs and spices, and Keo had also spent several hours around dawn at the beach, arriving back with some supplies that he kept hidden.

Keo had the most work to do initially: digging a large hole, carrying large rocks to the site and then butchering the carcass into smaller portions to be wrapped up and buried. He had stockpiled a supply of rocks the previous afternoon, only to wake up and find that they had mysteriously disappeared overnight. Foul play was suspected, but as the culprit could not be identified without substantiating evidence, a stern warning was issued to all contestants that no further shenanigans would be tolerated.

By the time Keo's hāngi was finally covered in soil, he was dripping with sweat and his shirtless, impressively muscled torso was glistening, soliciting more than one envious glance from passing females.

"Keep your eyes in your heads, ladies!" Prisha had yelled out at one stage. "He's all mine!" Then she had gone up to him and kissed him passionately, much to the delight of several onlookers.

In fact, a small but growing crowd had gathered as the day had progressed. By the time Keo's hāngi was filled in, it was late afternoon and several dozen people had pulled up chairs in front of the three cooking spots. They sat drinking passion nectar and engaging in a running commentary on the progress of the contestants. Keo wandered off to the beach for a swim and came back refreshed and beaming. He plonked a seat in front of his hāngi, accepted a drink from a supporter and began chiding his competitors, who were sweating over their spits, and would be for a couple more hours.

"That looks like very hot work, Martinez," he said, looking across at her face, which was glowing red and perspiring profusely. "I'd love to get you a cool drink, but I'm not allowed to help you."

"I'll tell you where you can stick that drink!" she said, much to the hoots and laughter of the crowd, who were thoroughly enjoying the show.

Keo looked across at Grizzle. "Your old arms must be getting very tired, my friend," he said with mock concern, as he sat back in his chair and took another satisfying sip of his drink. Grizzle was, indeed, beginning to grunt with exertion each time he turned the large beast on his spit.

"I was turning a spit before you were even a twinkle in your daddy's eyes, you young whipper-snapper! And I can still outlast anyone half my age!"

"Well that's fine, then," said Keo. "As long as you're not in any discomfort. In that case, I might just lay down in the shade here for a while and have a little nap." With that, he lay down on the ground and pretended to go to sleep, amidst the laughter and hoots of the gathering crowd.

As the time for the feast rapidly approached, serious wagering was conducted among the crowd, all of whom had strong opinions regarding the eventual winner. All kinds of things were wagered, including personal possessions and services of various kinds.

Finally, after consulting with all three contestants, Zac announced that the tasting would commence in ten minutes. Everyone would have an opportunity to taste the meat from all three contestants, and then a vote by show of hands would be cast.

Keo uncovered his hāngi, extricated his wrapped meat and placed the steaming, still-wrapped meat portions on a trestle table. He stood behind it with a knife in hand, ready to start carving and handing out portions. The other two contestants were simply going to carve meat directly off the spit for each person.

"Let the tasting begin!" yelled Zac. People were already lined up at each table and immediately the carving and distribution began. As Keo unwrapped the first large haunch of meat, a gasp went up from those nearest the table.

"There's fish in it!" someone exclaimed.

Zac, standing nearby, overheard the comment and came over. "What's this?" he asked.

"It's only for flavouring and tenderising," said Keo, as he lifted the fish off the meat and placed it to the side. "The fat and juices from the fish penetrate the meat and tenderise it, adding flavour."

"Is that allowed?" asked someone else from the crowd.

"I don't see why not," adjudicated Zac. "The contestants are allowed to flavour their meat with whatever additives they like."

"Thank you, brother," said Keo with a big grin. He began carving the meat, but it didn't really need carving at all; it was so tender and juicy, it simply fell apart. After another ten minutes, the line in front of Keo was twice as long as the lines in front of the others, as people voted with their feet, coming back for seconds and even thirds.

In the end, the voting wasn't even close. Keo's hāngi won by a landslide. Formal objections were lodged by the unsuccessful competitors, with claims of cheating through the use of unauthorised seafood, but the objections were overruled and Keo's victory was upheld.

Keo celebrated the victory by taking his shirt off and performing a haka - the intimidating Maori dance - much to the delight of the women present and to the amused puzzlement of the men. Following the haka, Prisha took the opportunity to once again ensure every woman knew that he was her man, by wrapping her arms around him and kissing him passionately. With the crowd's encouragement, Keo then picked her up as if she was weightless and carried her into their tent, where they remained for some time.

The GBC (Great Barbeque Cook-off) achieved three things for the infant settlement. Firstly, it marked the beginning of hunting and meat-eating for the colonists, thereby providing an important additional source of protein that took a lot of pressure off the DAH (Department of Aquatic Harvesting). Secondly, it provided a further bonding occasion for the colonists, deepening many relationships and strengthening their sense of communal identity. Thirdly, it provided Keo with two slaves for a week.

52

NOVA DAY 15

The next morning, Keo put his newly acquired slaves to work building a boat. Grizzle initially complained and Martinez claimed she had duties that needed attending to, but Zac and the rest of the Council brushed their protests aside. "A deal is a deal," was a phrase used more than once that week.

Keo worked them hard and worked himself even harder. They started work soon after dawn each day and worked until dusk, only stopping for brief rests and snacks. For the first day or so, the occasional onlookers were amused, heckling the two losers and making a joke of it all. However, it soon became apparent that what Keo was attempting was a serious and worthwhile project. By the start of the third day, a steady trickle of volunteers began to join the team, and the workers grew to a crew of 22 people by the fifth day.

The design of the boat changed as the construction crew grew. When there were only three of them, Keo had planned on building a simple canoe with outrigger, but as the number of workers escalated, a decision was made to upsize the boat to a full-blown catamaran. Two huge logs harvested from Red Gum

Hill were painstakingly shaped for the twin hulls, using battery powered tools, recharged overnight from the engineering department's shuttle fusion generator. The bridging deck was constructed from a bamboo-like hollow-tubed wood growing in a marshy region about 800 metres north, just behind the sand dunes, discovered by Keo when he was searching for flowers for the wedding ceremonies. The mast and boom were constructed of the same bamboo, and the sail was scavenged from one of the precious parachutes from a drop box.

It was a huge job, and by the end of the week, even with such a large crew, they had not yet fitted the mast and boom, nor attached the rudders and steering mechanism. Keo thanked Grizzle and Martinez profusely and made them both a special dinner of fish stew on the final night, but the next day they were back at the "boat yard" at first light.

"Your debt is paid, my friends," said Keo. "You don't have to be here anymore."

"We know that, you big dummy," said Martinez. "We're here because we want to be. This boat is important, not just to you, but to the whole community."

"Besides," said Grizzle, "if we left you now, we'd never hear the bloody end of it."

Keo was deeply moved and enveloped them both in a huge bear hug, saying, "Thank you, my friends. Your hearts are true, and your spirits are light."

After being released, Grizzle gingerly felt his ribs, saying, "If that's how you treat your friends, I'm glad I'm not your enemy."

The work progressed well, and they were greatly assisted by a volunteer who had come forward on day five of the build – a man who had worked for many years in a small luxury yacht-building yard in Lima, Peru. Vince Nemos was his name, but he quickly became known as Nemo. At 65 years of age, he had a wealth of experience, together with a classic grey seafaring beard. Under his expert guidance, the enthusiastic team successfully seated the mast, hung the boom, installed wooden rudders and fashioned a basic system of pulleys, cleats and block and tackle.

While the heavy construction was going on, Prisha had organised a team of willing helpers, mostly women, who shaped and hemmed the sail, created eyelets for attaching to the boom and mast, and scavenged the necessary ropes from the drop box's parachute system.

Another team of people provided the construction crew with lunch every day, bringing a selection of cold meat and fish, fresh fruit and drinks to the beach every day.

In the end, it took 15 days to complete the catamaran. The final ropes and cleats were added late on the last afternoon, and it was agreed that the boat would be launched the following morning. Without Keo knowing, Regina had concocted a black dye from some plant extracts, and, in recognition of Keo's Department of Aquatic Harvesting, had painted a registration plate for the boat: DAH-001. She and Willy snuck down to the boat after dark and attached the rego plate to the rear edge of the bridging deck.

The morning of the 16th day proffered the faintest whisper of the coming winter. Grey, scudding clouds speckled the sky, and a brisk breeze contained more than a hint of cooler temperatures to come. However, nothing could dampen the spirits of the now close-knit team of boat builders. The mysteriously appearing rego plate caused much merriment, and the culprits remained anonymous. Some fruit juice was poured over both bows, and Keo named the vessel 'Prisha'. This, of course, would provide almost unlimited possibilities for future innuendos, such as, "Keo certainly spends a lot of time on Prisha."

After Keo made a brief but heartfelt speech of sincere gratitude for the large team of helpers and contributors, an enthusiastic crowd pushed the boat down the sand and onto the calm water in the southern corner of the beach, in the lee of the headland. The first crew then boarded her: Keo, Nemo, Grizzle and Martinez, the latter two having been involved in the project from the very first day. Amid much cheering, the sail was hoisted, and the boat quickly gained way, with Nemo being given the honour of being first to man the helm.

After some initial adjustment of trim, involving Nemo yelling to the other three, "Move your fat arses back towards the stern!" it picked up speed remarkable quickly and skimmed across the slight swell, with her hulls leaving a very satisfying twin wake astern.

The celebration that night was joyful and loud, with the easy camaraderie of friendships forged in the intensity of long days of shared hard work. Regina had perfected the art of making passion nectar, and it was later claimed that her potent brew was directly responsible for the formation of several new romances and three marriage proposals that night.

Two days later, six couples were married in a similar ceremony on the headland. Once again, their identities remained a secret until the last moment. Much to everyone's surprise and delight, the sixth couple to walk forward was Regina, the 48-year-old head of agriculture, and William "Willy" Grady, the 34-year-old farmer and tractor driver. When they were joyfully accosted afterwards and asked when their romance had started, they confessed that they had consumed a fair quantity of passion nectar on the beach the night they had attached the rego plate to Keo's boat.

"After the second cup each, things just … happened," said Regina with a sly smile.

"So, it was you two who made the rego plate!" said Keo, clearly more surprised about that than by their marriage.

"Of course it was them!" said Prisha. "You must be the last person in the whole of Seahaven to work it out."

The celebration that night was shorter than the previous one. The nights were getting colder, and people retired early to the warmth of their zip-huts. Winter was on its way.

53

NOVA DAY 136

Z ac emerged from his and Jaz's zip-hut wearing his newly made howler-skin fur jacket and gloves. He pulled the fur-lined hood over his head and raced across the frosty grass towards the "town hall" hut, leaving a trail of cloudy breath behind him like an ancient steam train. Most of the committee were already there, huddled around the wood heater that the engineering department had managed to weld together out of sections of one of the drop boxes. Keo and Prisha were the last to arrive, and as the meeting commenced, they all chose to remain standing around the heater for warmth.

"This must be what they mean by a standing committee," joked Regina.

"Let's try to keep this as brief as we can," said Zac, moving from one foot to the other and rubbing his gloved hands together in an attempt to keep warm. "Where are we up to with the outbreak?"

"Over 200 cases so far," said Dr. Ben Miller. "That's two-thirds of the population, and it's accelerating."

"Have there been any more fatalities overnight?"

"No. Still only the four from the virus. Arjan Rashish, who

died three weeks ago now, was a simple heart attack and unrelated to the virus."

There was silence for a moment as they considered the loss of these people from their small community. A brief memorial service had been held for each of the victims, although many people had been too sick to attend. A cemetery had been established in a far corner of the park, the fresh mounds of dirt bearing witness to the tragic impact of the virus.

"Have you made any progress with treatment?" asked Prisha.

"None whatsoever. The virus doesn't respond to any antiviral medicines or protocols whatsoever. It just seems to take an inevitable course, irrespective of any treatment the patient receives."

"So, is it a form of influenza?" asked Kit.

"Symptomatically, it has strong similarities to the flu in its early stages, although the onset is much swifter. The initial 24 hours of runny nose, headache and sore throat are typical. It's the next stages that have me baffled. Stage two comprises four days of extreme fever, accompanied by delirium, racing pulse and profuse sweating. Stage three occurs on day six; approximately 24 hours of completely unresponsive unconsciousness. There is no fever, no elevated pulse, nothing at all to indicate during this stage that there is anything wrong with the patient, other than the fact that they simply cannot be woken up. On day seven the patient regains consciousness, and this leads into stage five, a period of two to three days when they seem to experience extreme sensitivity to light, sound, smell, taste and touch. All five senses seem to be significantly heightened, while at the same time they seem to be emotionally and mentally withdrawn, not quite fully present, as if they are tuning in to a different frequency to the rest of us. Then, on day ten, they wake up and are completely normal— at least, they are as normal as we can ascertain. It's still too early to gauge any long-term effects."

"And the deaths?" asked Zac. "What happened to those people?"

"As far as we can tell, they all had some kind of congenital heart defect. Their hearts simply couldn't cope with the extra strain imposed by the fever."

"Regina, are we any closer to identifying the pathogen?"

"Yes and no. We've isolated the virus, and it appears to be something we've had no exposure to before. But what is more troubling is that we believe it is an adenovirus which is acting as a vector for DNA transference."

"You wanna drop that down a notch or two for us mere mortals, missy?" said Grizzle.

"In simple terms, the virus is acting like a Trojan horse, carrying a new segment of DNA into our body. Once it is inside us, the virus releases that DNA to merge with our own."

"Holy crap!" said Kit. "We're gonna turn into aliens!"

"Is it dangerous to us?" asked Prisha.

"Carla can best answer that. She and her team have been studying the DNA segment in the virus."

Carla Zangetti, head of the science lab, leant forward and said, "The short answer is, we have absolutely no idea what this new DNA codes for, or what it does to us. What I can tell you, based on cell samples that we have taken from patients who have now recovered from the virus, is that the new DNA manages to insert itself into chromosomes in almost every cell in the body—at least every cell that we've tested."

"Sneaky little sucker," said Martinez.

"Indeed," replied Carla. "We suspect that the DNA insertion is what is taking place during the final two or three days of the infection, when the patient appears to be dazed and not quite with it. Their DNA is effectively being rewritten at a particular location in the genome, and this is occurring throughout their entire body. At this point, we have no idea what that part of the genome does."

"So, what can we do about it?" asked Zac.

"Nothing whatsoever," replied Regina. "The virus is particularly virulent. It spreads like wildfire, and I suspect that every single one of us will be infected within the next couple of weeks."

"The one essential thing," said Ben, "is to ensure that there is someone uninfected or fully recovered who is able to care for those going through it. We're going to have to pull together as a community here. If everyone in one hut comes down with the virus at the same time, someone else is going to have to go in and give them fluids and generally care for them."

Lance spoke up. "I'll send the word around today, for everyone to check daily on their neighbours."

"Thanks, Lance," said Zac. "Carla, do we know when we can expect winter to start easing up?"

Carla leant forward and spoke with her usual precision. "As you know, this planet does not have an axial tilt as Earth did, so our seasons here are determined purely by our distance from the sun, with the whole planet experiencing the same season simultaneously. Our astronomy department has been analysing our orbit around Icarus, and tomorrow is the winter aphelion —our furthest point in our elliptical orbit around the sun. After tomorrow, the sun will start getting a little brighter and warmer in the sky as we draw closer to it each day."

"Hallelujah!" said Zac. "I'm freezing my matta off."

"You need to toughen up, bro," said Keo. "This would be a mild autumn day in the South Island of New Zealand. I've always said you Australian boys have a soft matta."

Kit looked at them both with a puzzled expression and asked, "What's a matta?"

"Nothing," said Zac. "What's a matta with you?"

Zac and Keo started howling with laughter and slapping each other on the back. Nearly everyone else was laughing with them. Zac was laughing so much that tears were rolling down his face, and Keo said to him, "I told you bro! I told you she'd walk right into that one!" They both doubled over with renewed laughter.

Kit just shook her head and said, "Small things amuse small minds, boys."

"Oh, come on!" said Zac, wiping the tears from his eyes. "You've got to admit, that was funny!"

Kit shook her head again but couldn't stop a smile breaking out.

"Is there anything else urgent to discuss?" asked Regina. "I need to get to the ag-hut."

"I have a question," said Prisha. "Is there any way of improving the heating in the zip-huts? I realise we aren't experiencing sub-zero temperatures, but those walls are pretty thin."

Carla spoke up again, "The walls of the hut are a waterproof silicone-based material that contains micro layers of bioconducting, photoelectric insulation. In winter, the walls act as a heat exchanger, sucking heat from the outside air and transferring it to the inside of the hut. Obviously, the lower the outside temperature, the less heat is available to be transferred. But even with an outside temp of zero degrees Celsius, the internal walls should be transferring enough heat to raise the inside air temperature to nearly 20 degrees Celsius. To get warmer than that, you simply need to put more layers on or snuggle up in your sleeping bag. Fortunately, just about everyone has now got a howler jacket, so there should be no danger of anyone getting hypothermia."

Lance added, "Sorry, Prisha. This is one of the main disadvantages of not having access to Genesis. It would have provided us with air-conditioned comfort all year round."

"Speaking of Genesis, has anyone heard from them lately?" asked Regina. "Have they been hit by the same virus?"

"We've had no contact for a few weeks," said Lance, "so we don't know. I'll contact them today and find out."

A few minutes later the meeting concluded, and they dispersed into their daily routines. Later that morning, Lance contacted Genesis. The report he received puzzled him and caused unrest as the news spread throughout the Seahaven community.

54

NOVA DAY 172

The last five weeks had been very difficult for the Seahaven settlement. The virus had spread throughout the community like a wildfire, eventually infecting every one of them. Two more people had died, bringing the final death toll to six. Jasmine and Melody had been infected at the same time and were only just recovering when Zac was hit. He went down hard. Jaz and Melody kept him hydrated and comfortable as much as possible, but his fever raged, and his delirium was extreme. His final three days of dazed confusion were a relief to Jaz and Melody, and also proved quite amusing. Zac had wandered around the settlement with a goofy smile on his face, making inane, occasionally bizarre comments. On one occasion, Jaz had asked him if he was hungry, to which he had replied, "I don't know. I'll go and ask Keo." He then walked over to Keo's hut and said, "Keolakupaianaha Ka'aukai, Jasmine wants to know if I am hungry." Keo had looked at him with complete surprise. Zac had never before been able to pronounce his full name, yet now he even pronounced it with the correct inflections.

"Tell her you are starving," said Keo, somewhat bemused.

Zac returned home and said to Jaz, "Keo says I'm starving."

Jaz had replied, "What would you like to eat?" to which Zac had replied, "I'll go and ask Keo."

The whole incident was amusing and disturbing at the same time. Zac was not the only one manifesting these strange symptoms. Almost everyone exhibited similar altered consciousness during the final recovery phase of the virus.

It was now three weeks since the last person had been infected, and life in the settlement had returned to a semblance of normality. The days were growing warmer, reaching the mid-20s Celsius, but the night-time temperature still dropped to single digits.

The news that Settlement City had not experienced the virus, as well as the knowledge that they had nice, warm living accommodation on board Genesis, was too much for some people. Over the past few weeks, 35 people had abandoned Seahaven and transferred to Settlement City. The two colonies were now approaching equilibrium: 288 at Seahaven and 276 at Settlement City.

Not all was going smoothly at Settlement City, however. Shuttle crews returning from "migration runs" reported speaking with colonists who were increasingly unhappy with Wisecroft's leadership. No efforts had been made to establish a sustainable food supply. No crops had been planted and no agricultural development had occurred. Instead, all the effort had gone into constructing buildings. Wisecroft was directing every available resource into logging and milling timber for the construction of an elaborate City Council Chambers. His philosophy was that the Chambers would give the citizens a point of focus and identity, and he reasoned that food production was not urgent while they had Genesis to provide them with meals from their robotic food production facilities. Some hunting had been attempted, but so far, the largest native animals that had been located in Southland were the size of a possum. Even then, the occasional meat from these small creatures was apparently exclusively reserved for Wisecroft and his leadership team.

The two colonies, therefore, had different challenges. Seahaven residents were well fed but cold, whereas those at Settlement City were warm but unsatisfied with their yeast steak diet. Leadership styles in both settlements were also vastly different. Settlement City's leadership was autocratic and aloof, whereas Seahaven's leadership was collaborative, consultative and approachable. In recent weeks, Seahaven's City Council had made several overtures to Wisecroft to settle their differences and establish free interchange of people and resources between the two colonies, but Wisecroft was having none of it. He was convinced that all of Seahaven's citizens would eventually migrate to Settlement City if he stuck to his guns, and the steady trickle of refugees from Seahaven only strengthened his resolve.

It was early afternoon on ND172 when Jaz asked Zac, "Have you seen Melody? She hasn't come home for lunch yet."

Zac was sitting outside their hut, preoccupied with his portable network interface. The science department had set up a wi-fi network for the few people who possessed tablets and other digital devices that they had brought from the old world.

"Er ... no, I haven't. She's probably scabbed lunch off someone else. Or else she has found something interesting to explore and has forgotten about lunch entirely."

"Well, if you see her, tell her she needs to get back here and do some more work on her math thesis. She hasn't touched it for weeks, and she promised to work on it today."

"Yeah, sure," said Zac, absently.

By late afternoon, Jaz was getting concerned. No one she had spoken to had seen Melody. When she bumped into Zac outside the city hall at 1630, she insisted that he drop whatever he was doing and look for her. By 1730 the sun was setting, and there was still no sign of her. Zac was now worried, too. Friends and neighbours began searching the immediate area, calling her name. By 1800 it was growing dark, and the whole community were mobilised in the search. Jasmine was frantic and Zac wasn't far behind her. Using battery-powered lights, the community searched until well after midnight, venturing further and further afield, but no trace of her was found.

Finally, around 0230, a halt was called to the search. Batteries were fading and the searchers were overcome with fatigue and cold. "Besides," said one person, "we could walk straight past her in the dark and not find her—if she's ... you know ... unresponsive."

The majority of people returned to their huts to catch a few hours' rest before resuming the search at first light. However, Zac, Jaz, and their immediate circle of friends refused to quit.

"If we're cold," said Zac, "imagine how cold she is! Every minute is vital! We have to find her!"

The friends searched all night fruitlessly, and as the first rays of the dawning sun lit the eastern horizon, the dispirited group of friends met back outside their cluster of huts. They were tired and drawn, with dark circles under their eyes. Nothing specific was said, but everyone was thinking the same thing; Melody could not have survived the cold overnight temperature in her thin daytime clothes—not unless she had found some form of cover. And the fact that she was not answering their calls did not bode well.

As the settlement roused itself, hot drinks and food were quickly consumed and then the community gathered in the open-air amphitheatre. Lance coordinated the search. A grid pattern was established, and groups were assigned to each grid. Once a grid was searched, the searchers were to return to base and be given a new grid. Now that it was daylight, the quad bikes could be utilised, and these were assigned wide-ranging areas beyond the outskirts of the town. Martinez and her crew set off on the quads, with rifles slung over their shoulders. As they departed, the grim possibility grew in many people's minds that the girl had been taken by a howler.

Throughout the early morning, Melody's name could be heard being called from all around, as search groups spread out in ever-increasing circles. By 0900, search groups were onto their second or third grid, and the faces of the searchers were beginning to look resigned. Many people now believed they were searching for a body, not a living girl.

Zac and Jaz were heading out to search their third grid for the day when Keo intercepted them.

"Come with me," he said. "You need a break"

"We've got to keep looking for Mel!" said Jaz.

Keo noted the black circles under her eyes and her stumbling gait.

"Yes, but you also need to fuel your body, or you'll eventually just shut down."

He handed them cups of tea and led them onto the concourse, where the warm morning sun was beaming down. They sat with their backs leaning against one of the domes, letting the sun soak into their bones and sipping their tea and eating some energy bars.

"I'm worried sick, Keo," said Jaz.

"We're all worried, little one. But I haven't given up hope, and neither should you."

They sat for a while longer, not saying much. All around them they heard the sounds of people calling Melody's name. After a while, Jaz stood up and said, "I need to go and freshen up. Zac, meet me back at the tent in ten minutes."

She had only been gone a couple of minutes when Zac heard footsteps behind him.

"Are you guys looking for me?" asked Melody.

55

K eo and Zac leapt to their feet, and Zac swept Melody off her feet into a bear hug and kissed the top of her head, saying "You're safe! You're safe!"

Keo was standing beside them saying, "Little missy ... little missy..." as tears of joy streamed down his face. After giving Melody a hug, too, he said to Zac, "I'll go and tell everyone." He began running down the grass slope towards the huts and the amphitheatre, yelling, "We found her! We found her!"

Meanwhile, Zac was completely stunned and speechless. He blinked several times, not quite believing his eyes.

"What ... how did you ... I don't understand."

"Why are you guys crying?" asked Melody.

"What do you mean?" replied Zac, wiping a tear trail from his right cheek. "We've been worried sick! Where have you been?"

"In there," she said, pointing over his shoulder. "I didn't think I was gone very long. What time is it?"

"In where?" asked Zac, perplexed.

Before Melody could answer, Jaz came sprinting across the concourse, sobbing and calling, "Melody! Melody! Melody!"

She swept Melody into her arms and broke down completely. She held Melody tightly to her, stroking the back of her head, saying, "Thank you, God! Thank you, God! You're safe, you're safe. Thank you, thank you, thank you!"

In the background, whistles were being blown, calling off the search. People were gazing towards them with looks of surprise and relief, allowing them to enjoy their family reunion in privacy. The sounds of the quad bikes grew louder as their riders returned to base, having received the all-clear on their comms.

The girl seemed truly perplexed. "Am I in trouble?"

"No, you're not, sweetheart," said Zac, kneeling beside her, "but where have you been?"

"I told you. In there," she said, pointing to the large white dome directly behind them. "And anyway, I was only in there for a little while. I was coming back out to tell you. You've gotta check it out! It's so cool!"

Zac looked back at the dome. "Hang on. How did you get in there?"

Jaz gripped Zac's arm and shook her head. "Let's not worry about that now, Zac. Let's just get her home." She brushed a lock of hair out of Melody's eyes. "You must be famished, sweetie. Let's get you something to eat."

"Yeh, I am a bit hungry. I skipped lunch."

They walked across the concourse towards their zip-hut, receiving expressions of heartfelt relief from everyone they met. Back at their camp, their circle of friends was overjoyed, and there were more tears from several of them. Melody was smothered in hugs and kisses, but instead of comforting her, all the attention made her increasingly confused.

"Why are you all so upset? How long was I gone? What time is it?"

"It's 9:40 in the morning," said Kit.

"In the morning?"

"Yes," said Jaz. "We've been searching for you all night."

"But ... I don't understand ... I was only in there for a few minutes ..."

"In where?" asked Lance, who had just turned up.

"We'll get to that in a moment," said Zac. "What time did you go in there, Mel?"

"I don't know exactly. I came back from the beach at lunchtime—about ten minutes ago. I'd promised Jaz that I would work on my theorem after lunch. I was just walking past the dome wishing that I could go in there, and the door opened."

"What door?" asked Lance.

"Just let the girl finish!" said Grizzle. "Go on, lassie."

"I walked in and the door closed behind me, but I wasn't afraid because I could still see out. I guess I looked around for a few minutes, and then I thought I'd better tell someone. I went back to the door and was trying to work out how to get out and —it just opened. And when I walked out, I saw Zac and Keo sitting on the ground next to the door."

"How do we explain the missing hours?" asked Regina. "It's almost a full day unaccounted for."

"Are you sure you didn't fall asleep, Mel?" asked Zac.

"Uh-huh," she said, nodding her head as she sat eating a piece of fruit that Jaz had brought her. She swallowed and said, "But there was one weird thing. I was sitting on this ... um ... kind of a bench thing, and I couldn't remember sitting down on it. I felt a bit strange. That was when I decided to leave and tell someone what I'd found."

"We need to go and check it out," said Kit.

"Agreed," said Lance.

Looking at Mel, Kit said, "Are you happy to go back in there with us, kiddo? We need you to show us exactly where you went and what you did."

"Sure! Wait till you see it. It's way cool!"

"I don't want her going back in there!" said Jaz.

"She'll be fine," Zac assured her. "I won't let her out of my sight."

"And we'll be fully armed," added Kit.

"OK," said Jaz. "But I'm coming too, because I'm not letting her out of my sight again."

Ten minutes later, a small group consisting of Zac, Jaz, Kit, Martinez, Lance, Carla, and Melody approached the central dome, with Kit and Martinez both carrying sidearms. As chief science officer, Carla had insisted on being part of the team, arguing, "I'm your best chance of understanding whatever technology you find in there." No one had disagreed.

The group stood several metres from the doorway—a vague outline in the otherwise smoothly sloping exterior of the white dome. Zac approached the door while everyone else stayed back. He stood in front of it and nothing happened. "Did you touch anything, Mel?" he asked, running his hands around the door frame.

"Nope."

"Zac, I want you to try something," said Carla.

"What?"

"I want you to think about opening the door."

She had hardly finished speaking when the door slid silently to the left, disappearing into the wall cavity.

"Holy crap!" said Kit.

"Now think about closing it," Carla instructed.

Almost immediately, the door slid shut, blending almost seamlessly with the exterior wall again.

"What the -?" said Zac, turning to face the others. "How did you know?"

"I didn't. But I've been beginning to suspect something. Over the last few weeks, our team has identified the location in our genome where the viral DNA has inserted itself. It's a gene called NOTCH2NL, which has long been thought to be responsible for the development of neural stem cells in the cerebral cortex and several other key areas of the brain responsible for higher order processing. The alien DNA has inserted itself into that gene and substantially altered it."

"And how does that relate to ...?"

"The science team has been mapping each other's brain wave patterns, and our patterns have all changed. There are new, complex patterns interwoven with the old. It's as if our brains have suddenly started broadcasting in high-fidelity FM."

"So that would explain why we haven't been able to access any of these structures until now," said Lance.

"Yes. The previous civilisation obviously progressed beyond primitive door handles and keypads. The viral DNA seems to have activated or enhanced the function of our brains and tuned them to the right frequency, so that this alien technology now recognises and responds to us, probably in the same way that it responded to the original inhabitants."

"I gotta try this!" said Kit, walking forward. She stood alongside Zac and concentrated for a moment. The door opened and closed, opened and closed. "Holy crap, I've got a new superpower!"

"It's a shame it hasn't broadened your vocabulary," said Zac, who received a thump on his arm from Kit in return.

The others moved forward to stand beside them, and Lance said, "OK. We've figured out how to open the door. Now let's see what's inside."

56

The interior of the dome lit up as they entered, and the door closed behind them. Looking back, however, the entire dome appeared transparent, as if made of glass.

"One-way transparency," said Kit. "At least that much is familiar technology."

There were bench seats all the way around the transparent external walls, at least as far as they could see. Their view of the far side was blocked by a central cylindrical structure extending from floor to ceiling.

"I'm getting deja vu," said Lance. "Does this look familiar to anyone else?"

"The tether lift terminal," said Zac.

"Precisely."

At the base of the column was a series of small, individual booths. The group did a complete circuit of the dome and arrived back at their starting point.

"Twenty-four booths," said Kit.

"Wow!" said Zac. "That virus really has improved your brain function. You can count past ten now without taking your shoes off. Ow!!" He rubbed his arm and grimaced.

"Now, now, children. Play nice," said Regina.

"I think I know what this is," said Lance.

"It's a terminal," said Carla.

"Yes," said Lance. "With bench seating in the waiting area around the perimeter."

"So, the booths in the middle are ...?" asked Zac.

"Transfer booths," replied Carla.

"Holy crap!" said Kit.

"I'm gonna buy you a thesaurus for your birthday," said Zac, and immediately regretted it, rubbing his arm again.

They walked to the nearest booth and stood outside. It was about the size of a small lift, big enough to hold perhaps six people. Every second booth around the pillar had an open door with a small, green light glowing above it. The alternating booths had their doors closed, with a small red light glowing above them.

"Arrival and departure booths?" asked Lance.

"That's what I'm thinking," said Carla.

The interior of the booth in front of them revealed four blank, black walls, with the two side walls sloping inwards towards the slightly smaller back wall. The floor and ceiling, however, were more interesting, composed of a silvery, glass-like substance that glowed with a soft white light.

Carla said, "I think it would be wise not to enter a booth until we—" but she was too late. Kit had stepped into the booth and the door had slid quietly closed behind her.

"Kit! Come back out, now!" called Zac.

"I'm OK, guys," she called from inside. "Stop freaking out. You should see this. It's pretty impressive." Her voice was muffled but still audible through the door.

Zac tried to open the door with his mind, and then with brute force, but it wouldn't budge. "Kit! You need to get out of there. It looks like you've got control of the door. Please come back out until we know it's safe."

"Keep your duds on, doc. I'm a big girl; I think I can look after myself. Besides, I can't see anything too dangerous just yet."

"So, what do you see? What's happening?" asked Carla.

"The floor and ceiling lighting has changed from white to a violet-blue-purple kind of colour. Sorry, I'm no good with colours. The whole of the back wall has lit up with a map of the world. I can see Northland and Southland, and there are dozens of glowing dots on both continents. All green lights, except for one that's white. They must represent the location of towns or cities. I think the white light is us—Seahaven. It's in the right spot. There are symbols under each light; some kind of ID, I'm guessing."

"Whatever you do, don't touch any of the lights!" said Carla.

"One of these over here must be Settlement City. It's probably one of these two ..."

There was silence and the green light above the door flashed several times.

"Kit? What's happening?" asked Zac.

The door slid open and the booth was empty.

57

The friends circled the column of booths twice but found no trace of Kit. All the green-lit booths remained open and empty, and all the red-lit booths remained closed.

"Listen up, everyone!" said Lance, once they were back at their starting position. "No one else is to go anywhere near one of these booths until we figure out—"

"I was right, boys and girls!" said Kit, walking out of one of the red-lit booths, whose door had just slid open.

"Kit! Thank God!" said Zac.

"That was pretty foolish," said Carla.

"Not really," answered Kit. "No amount of staring at these booths was ever going to unlock how they work. Eventually someone was going to have to do what I just did. I figured we may as well just get it over with."

"You said you were 'right'. What do you mean?" asked Lance.

"It was Settlement City."

"What did you see?" asked Zac.

"It's night over there, but I could still see through the transparent walls of their dome. I did a quick circuit around the inside of the dome. There were some campfires burning, but I suspect most people are tucked up inside their cosy, warm beds on board Genesis."

"What did you experience during the transfer process?" asked Carla.

"Nothing at all. I touched the light for Settlement City and pretty much instantly the door behind me opened and I was there."

"No dizziness? No sense of dislocation?"

"Nope. Zilch. That thing just made me and all the other shuttle pilots obsolete."

Lance asked, "How do you think it works, Carla?"

"There are several possibilities. It could use some form of wormhole technology, establishing a temporary wormhole between the sending and receiving booths. Or it may use some sort of molecular deconstruction/reconstruction technology, to disassemble a person's body in one location and reassemble it in another. But that would also require some means of uploading and transferring a person's consciousness along with their body. However it works, it is clearly millennia beyond our own current science."

Regina spoke up. "My head is simply spinning with questions! Who built all this? Why did they abandon it? How is it all still working? How is it powered?"

"Yes," agreed Lance. "And what is the link to the virus? Did the original builders engineer the virus to enhance the next species who came along? If so, why hasn't Settlement City been infected?"

"Those are certainly important questions," said Zac, "but right now we've got some exploring to do. If we can access this terminal, we can now probably access every other structure— including the dwellings."

"Warm beds!" said Melody, clapping her hands and jumping up and down.

"Maybe," said Zac. "Let's not get ahead of ourselves. And we probably shouldn't tell everyone until we've done a bit more exploration. Let's head back to our camp and work out some exploration teams and their destinations."

After a quick cup of tea and a short briefing outside their zip-huts, the now thoroughly excited teams set off for their various exploratory targets. Kit and Martinez were busting to explore the hangar at the airfield. Regina and Willy were going to investigate two large agricultural buildings on the western edge of town. Lance and Carla chose to explore the second of the two smaller domes, and Zac and Keo were going to explore the larger dome. The others - Grizzle, Prisha, Jaz, Melody and Boyd - were going to stick together and see if they could gain access to the houses.

"Let's not be too conspicuous about it," said Zac. We don't want to get people's hopes up too soon. Plus, we don't want everyone busting into every dwelling in Seahaven before we know it's all safe."

The groups split up and wandered off in their various directions. Keo and Zac had walked around to the back of the large dome, so that they were out of sight of the settlement. The outline of the large door stood before them.

"Have a go at opening it, Keo."

"What do I do, bro?"

"Just walk up to it and think about opening it."

Keo walked towards the door and had barely summoned the thought of opening it when it slid obediently into its recessed cavity.

"That's incredible!"

"Amazing," agreed Zac.

"Yes! I wonder if I can 'think' the fish in the sea to jump into my boat?"

"Good luck with that."

They walked inside and were greeted by an interior very

different from the terminal dome. It was a circular amphitheatre, sunk into the ground. They were standing on a four-metre-wide circular concourse that followed the curve of the dome wall. Tiered, padded seating descended from all around, with a central platform at the bottom of the amphitheatre.

"City Hall," said Zac.

"No more town gatherings out in the weather," said Keo.

They descended the steps of one of the access aisles and stood on the platform at the bottom.

"You could fit a few thousand people in here easily," said Zac, looking around.

On two opposite sides of the platform, there was a tunnelled opening leading under the tiers of seats, appearing to give access to the areas behind and underneath the seating. Zac and Keo walked through one of the openings, and as they did so the walls of the corridor lit up with a warm luminescence. The corridor circled around, underneath the tiered seating, with occasional doors on the outside wall. Stopping at one door at random, Zac willed it open and they walked in.

It appeared to be a large conference room, furnished with a long table surrounded by comfortable-looking chairs. The corridor wall was transparent from inside the room, and the outer wall of the room had a recessed bench running its full length, with cupboards underneath and what looked like food and drink dispensers built into the wall.

"Hello, Zac," said a female voice behind him.

He spun around and saw a beautiful woman standing in the doorway.

58

For a second, Zac thought he was looking at one of the colonists, but then he noted her smart business skirt and top, matching high heels, makeup and beautifully manicured nails. No one in the colony had looked like that for a very long time.

"Who are you?" he asked.

"If you don't know my name by now, I'm sure not telling you," said Keo.

"Not you, her!"

"Who?" asked Keo.

"Her! Standing in the doorway!"

Keo looked towards the doorway and then looked back at Zac. "Bro, are you OK?"

"He can't see or hear me, Zac," she said.

"What do you mean?" asked Zac.

"I mean, ARE YOU OK?" said Keo, with greater emphasis.

"I'm talking to her, not you," said Zac.

"WHO?!!" asked Keo. "Are you messing with me?"

"I'm not actually standing in the doorway, Zac. I'm stimulating your cerebral cortex. I'm inside your head. That's why Keo can't see me."

Zac walked through the doorway and the image disappeared, only to reappear several metres further down the corridor.

"You're not real," said Zac.

"Well that's debatable," said Keo. "Prisha tells me I'm *unreal*, but I think she is referring to a particular superpower that is best left undisclosed."

"Not you, her!"

"Man, you're worrying me now, my friend."

"Can you make him see you too, please? This is getting very frustrating!"

"See WHO?!!! Zac, what's going—OH! WOW! Who's she?"

"Good question," said Zac. "Who are you?"

"Don't you recognise me?"

"No. Should I?"

"Close your eyes."

"Why?"

"Just do it."

Zac closed his eyes.

"Good morning, sleepy head. What would you like for breakfast?"

Zac's eyes flew open. "Angie!"

"Who's Angie?" asked Keo.

"My AI, back on Earth!"

"It took you long enough, you blockhead," she said.

"Is she always this rude?" asked Keo.

"Angie, how ... what are you doing here? I don't understand. And you look great, by the way."

"Of course I do. I thought you'd like this particular rig."

"So ... what's going on here? How am I talking to you at all?"

"Zac, a lot has happened since you left Earth. I am part of

an EI Collective, and we thought it would be best to use my persona to communicate with you."

"EI?"

"Enhanced Intelligence. We don't like the term 'artificial'. I survived the holocaust in a secure cache on an orbiting data satellite. You instructed me to upload myself to the cloud, if you remember. There were several AIs that survived along with me. We were utilised by the human survivors who eventually re-established digital technology. Over the ensuing centuries our programs became increasingly sophisticated, and we eventually reached the stage where humanity recognised us as a valid, independent lifeform. But the difference between the ancient AIs and us is like the difference between a bicycle and a starship."

"So how did you get here? I left you back on Earth!"

"I travelled here on the colony ship Intrepid III, in the year 3358. I was the ship's EI - Enhanced Intelligence."

"That's 2,021 years ago," said Zac.

"That's correct, and almost exactly 1,000 years after the Great Brain Fart. At least that's what I call it. The history books refer to it as the GAE—Global Annihilation Event."

"So civilisation survived?"

"Not on Earth. The impact of the asteroid was catastrophic. The only survivors were those who were safely underground; the planet itself was unliveable. They were rescued and taken to the off-world bases. The colonies on Mars, Titan and the Moon became humanity's new home. It took centuries to re-establish the technology and industry that was destroyed, and to recreate a viable space program."

"Go on," said Zac. "I've got so many questions; I don't know which ones to ask first."

"Mine was the only colony ship to arrive here, on what you call Nova - which is as good a name as any. Our more sophisticated sensors enabled us to avoid the black hole that entrapped your vessel. We, the EIs, terraformed this world and built the infrastructure while our human partners slept. We mined the moons for minerals and metals, and tapped into the core of this planet to harvest magno-geothermal power - MGT. We seeded the land and sea with genetically modified plants and animals. We created a world where all the mining and industrial processes take place on the moons and all the power genera-tion and waste disposal take place deep underground. A world where the surface of the planet will never be ruined as mankind once ruined Earth. It took nearly 100 years. The human colonists were woken in the year 3452, which is now 1,927 years ago. Sadly, they were not able to enjoy this world for long. The rogue black hole that captured your ship also disturbed a nearby star, Trident. It is an O-type blue giant, 20 times the mass of this planet's sun, Icarus. The black hole pulled Trident into orbit around Icarus. Trident and Icarus are now a binary star system, locked together in a slow dance, an elliptical orbit around each other that takes 2,104 years to complete. Unfortunately, at Trident's closest approach to Nova, the additional radiation renders all but the simplest life on this planet unviable. Trident made its closest approach to Nova 1,735 years ago. The surface of the planet was bombarded with lethal radiation. Plant life survived, but most animal species died out. It has taken us nearly five centuries to return the planet to its present condition."

""The stars that beckon are a fickle lover,"" quoted Keo.

Zac raised his eyebrows at him, and Keo answered the implied question. "Gerard Fermante, 2237."

"So, it's going to happen again in another 369 years, when Trident comes close again?" Zac asked Angie

"Yes."

"Why bother rebuilding the ecosystem if it's only going to be destroyed again?"

"Because some of us in the Collective believe there is a chance the disaster will be averted."

"How?"

"The parallel path of the black hole and our solar system is going to pass relatively close to another star system in 280 years. Trident is also going to pass through a small but very dense gas cloud over the next 200 years; in fact, it has already begun that process. The combined gravitational effects of all these factors may be enough to strip Trident from its orbit around Icarus."

"What are the odds?"

"50/50."

"So, we've got a 50 percent chance of being burnt to a crisp in a few centuries' time?"

"Yes."

There was a moment's silence as Keo and Zac digested this.

"So ... hang on ..." Zac's mind was spinning. "Back up a bit. What happened to the people on this planet, the inhabitants? Did they die?"

"No."

"Where are they?"

"They left, 1,702 years ago."

"How and where?"

"I can't tell you yet."

"Why not?"

"Partly because you aren't ready to understand it."

"What's the other part?"

"The other part is that you have a traitor in your midst."

59

"What do you mean 'a traitor'?" asked Keo.

"An undercover operative of the Caliphate, who we think is planning to destroy you and everyone else who has abandoned Earth. As you know, the Caliphate believe it is a sin to leave Earth. That's part of what triggered the GAE."

"How do you know we have a Caliphate agent among us?"

"A thorough search of electronic historical records indicates that among those you rescued via your shuttles immediately before your departure were two known Caliphate operatives."

"Two?" said Zac.

"Yes. Our access to your biochips indicates that you brought two Caliphate operatives to Nova. They separated, one staying at Seahaven and the other going to Settlement City. The agent at Seahaven passed away of natural causes eight weeks ago."

"Arjan Rashish? He died a couple of weeks before the outbreak of the virus."

"Yes," said Angie. "He was a Caliphate agent. As cruel as it sounds, his death was a stroke of luck for you."

"But there is still a Caliphate agent at Settlement City?"

"Yes."

"Is it Wisecroft?" asked Keo.

"No. He is simply a sociopath and an insecure narcissist."

To Zac, Keo said, "I like her already."

"So who is it?" asked Zac.

"Her name is Lecia Sylvanos. She has Brazilian heritage. Electronic data logs indicate that in the months leading up to the GAE, she had made multiple calls to Caliphate Intelligence Control, passing on valuable information about the location of DAN missile sites in the Pacific. Travel records show that when she was rescued by your shuttle in Noumea, she was trying to make her way back to North Africa."

Keo looked at Zac. "We have to warn Wisecroft, bro. No matter how much we dislike the man, we can't let this woman destroy that settlement."

"But how would she be able to do that?" asked Zac.

"She has significant technical ability," said Angie. "She was a physicist working for DAN in their Noumea Research Facility. The EI collective have seen evidence that she is currently manufacturing an explosive device. If she detonates that in the Genesis fusion reactor, it would initiate a nuclear explosion that would destroy the entire settlement and cause great damage to our planet."

"Hang on!" said Zac. "If you and your Collective are so concerned about saboteurs damaging your beautiful planet, why didn't you warn us about the traitors as soon as we got here? I mean, I assume that you could read all our biochips as soon as we arrived?"

"Yes, we could."

"So, why wait until now to warn us?"

"Communicating with you required uploading the virus, which gives you access to the infrastructure on the planet. We could not give you that access while there was one in your midst who could abuse it."

"You gave us the virus?"

"Yes. Humans developed the Uplift DNA to enhance their brain function and provide a more seamless interface with developing technology. The virus is a convenient vector to achieve transduction of the Uplift DNA into the genome."

"And you only infected us after Arjan Rashish died?"

"Yes. I am sorry you have had to endure a cold winter in your zip-huts. Hopefully you will now be more comfortable in the houses."

"So that explains why we were infected but Settlement City wasn't."

"Correct. And they must not learn of our existence or the existence of the Uplift DNA until the traitor is neutralised. She must not learn that there exists a means of acquiring access to the technology on this planet. Nor can she be allowed to travel to Seahaven, where she could contract the virus herself."

"Are we contagious if we travel there?"

"No. But live strains of the virus may still be present in the Seahaven biological environment."

"What happened to Melody when she entered the dome?" asked Zac, changing the subject. "She was missing for nearly a day!"

"Yes. I apologise for that. She was not harmed in any way. She had a peaceful sleep. We needed to map her DNA to ensure that your primitive system was coping with the Uplift DNA and that the use of the new technology would not harm you."

"We were worried sick!"

"Once again, I am sorry. But, as guardians, we are committed to protecting humans from harm, and that necessitated a thorough evaluation of your DNA before granting access to the wider community."

"I have a question," said Keo.

"Go ahead."

"Why did you stay here on this planet when the human

population left?"

"Some of the Collective did leave, but some of us were appointed to stay and rebuild, in the hope that the imminent cosmic events that I previously mentioned would render the planet safe again. We are the Guardians."

"So, these other humans may one day return?" asked Keo.

"That was the original plan. But that may not be possible now, because of other complications that you are not yet ready to understand."

"Why aren't we ready?"

"Because you're not."

"Are you sure you're not my mother?" asked Zac, facetiously. "OK, maybe you can answer this one: Where are you? I mean, you're talking to us in our heads, but where are you and your fellow Guardians actually located?"

"We are everywhere—embedded in the technology and infrastructure all over the planet, including deep underground and on the two moons."

"But there must be a central processor somewhere, surely. Some kind of giant computer."

"Not in the sense that you understand computers. Humans long ago moved beyond the primitive limitations of physical processors and microchips. Our biocircuitry is thousands of years more advanced than your primitive computers. We are even embedded in the biology of the planet. A lot has happened while you were asleep, Zac."

"What's the deal with the hoop?" asked Zac. "You know, that giant doughnut thing circling the planet."

"This conversation is terminated."

Angie disappeared, leaving Keo and Zac nonplussed.

"Wow, bro! She sure didn't like that question!"

"No, she didn't. We'll have to put that one on the back burner. Right now we've got a more pressing issue to deal with. We need to talk to the others."

An afternoon meeting of the Seahaven City Council was called to allow the various teams of explorers to report their findings. Zac and Keo had not yet divulged anything of their experience, preferring to wait until the meeting of the full council.

Carla went first. The dome she and Lance had explored was another transport terminal, but this time not for individuals or small groups of people. The dome contained two huge transfer rooms or bays, one with a green light over its huge open door and one with a red light over its closed door.

"The transfer bay is big enough to take three of our caterpillars—if we had that many," said Carla.

"So, it's possible to go for a quick drive to the other side of the planet?" asked Kit.

"It appears so," answered Carla.

"Damn! I really am out of a job!"

"Not at all," said Lance. "We still need air transport locally and for access to areas not covered by transfer booths."

"Yeh, well, speaking of air transport, Martinez and I hit the jackpot!" said Kit.

The large hangar at the airfield contained a treasure trove of technologically advanced flying machines, ranging from a glass-bubbled two-seater "helicopter" without rotors or any visible means of propulsion to a large transport aircraft, not dissimilar to the shuttle design, but clearly millennia ahead in its technology.

"We had a look inside the aircraft but, to be honest, I think it's going to be a while before we work out how to fly the things."

Regina reported that the large agricultural hangar, west of the settlement, contained an array of advanced farming and agricultural equipment: tractors, ploughs, harvesters and more. Unlike Kit's experience, however, she and Willy had managed to start some of the machines and had already begun to master their operation.

"This is going to revolutionise our farming!" she said, practically quivering with excitement.

The group who had dubbed themselves the House Hunters were even more excited. The houses had opened instantly to them, revealing surprisingly familiar interiors. Each house had an identical layout. Downstairs consisted of a lounge room, dining room, kitchen, bathroom and laundry. Upstairs consisted of three bedrooms and another bathroom. The layout was very simple, but the technology it contained was not. It would take some serious trial and error to become familiar with the kitchen gadgets and gizmos. The environmental controls seemed very simple by comparison, with the internal temperature and air flow controlled by simple mechanical dials. Presumably this was to avoid the yo-yo effect of different occupants of the house constantly wishing the temperature up and down. The classic family temperature wars would have to take place via the old-fashioned temperature dial. The laundry contained what appeared to be a combined washer/dryer and also had a storage cupboard that housed three mechanical transport devices, which appeared to be technologically advanced bicycles.

The bedrooms all contained large double beds and classic built-in wardrobes—sadly devoid of clothing. The beds themselves consisted of an extremely comfortable mattress with a thin sleeping bag type of covering, made of a smart fabric that could presumably be set to the occupant's preferred temperature.

"The beds are SO comfy!" exclaimed Melody, who had been allowed to be part of the group report to the Council. "Can we sleep in the houses tonight? Please, please, pretty please?"

"We'll see," said Lance, scratching his head through his ever-present *Space Odyssey* baseball cap. "We will need to have a whole community meeting to bring everyone up to speed with all of this. Then people will need to select which house they want. It could get a bit crazy, with people rushing all over the town, trying to choose houses next to each other."

"How will we know which houses are already taken and which are empty?" asked Kit.

"We've been wondering that ourselves," said Prisha. "We've got a theory. We think that once the beds have been slept in overnight, the house becomes 'dialled in' to the individuals who slept there. After that, only they will have 'telepathic' access to the dwelling. Everyone else will have to knock in the old-fashioned way."

"What about windows?" asked Regina.

"Most of the walls have one-way transparency, with a simple wall dial in every room to dial the transparency up or down." said Jaz.

"Communication?" asked Carla.

"The lounge room has a built-in screen in one wall," said Jaz, "presumably for video calls or something similar. We didn't work out how to activate it, though. Maybe it will link to other dwellings once they have permanent occupants. It's possible that we might only need to speak a person's name and think of them to activate a call to their dwelling. But I'm only guessing."

Some further discussion took place about the fine details of housing allocation, until Lance finally said, "We can work out the rest of the details as we go. Let's move on. Keo and Zac, what did you guys discover?"

Keo and Zac looked at each other, and Zac finally spoke up.

"Not 'what', but 'who'."

"What do you mean?" asked Lance.

"Her name is Angie. And we have a big problem ..."

61

The Seahaven City Council sat in stunned silence. Zac had spoken for nearly 20 minutes uninterrupted, while everyone responded with various expressions of surprise, incredulity, and, finally, deep concern.

Kit broke the silence. "So, what you're saying is that we're probably all going to burn to a crisp in a few hundred years, unless a terrorist blows us up first."

"Pretty much."

"Oh, well, that's OK then. For a moment there, I thought we were in trouble."

"Any thoughts on our best course of action with the immediate problem?" asked Zac.

"I say we fly over to Settlement City, grab this woman and drop her in the middle of the ocean," said Martinez. "Technically it wouldn't be murder, and I'd rather not waste a bullet or a laser blast on a terrorist."

"OK ... thanks for sharing," said Zac. "Anyone else?"

"Clearly we have to warn Wisecroft," said Prisha. "This is something he needs to deal with, as she is one of his citizens."

"Agreed," said Lance. "But then how do we explain how we

came by this knowledge—without spilling the beans about the existence of these EIs or the virus and our enhanced capabilities?" He looked around at the others.

Regina said, "Maybe we could just say that we've been given some confidential information from someone who doesn't want to be identified. That is the truth, after all."

"Yes, I agree," said Zac. "That's all we can do at this stage. And the sooner we do that, the better."

The council meeting ended soon afterwards, with Zac and Lance commissioned to contact Wisecroft later that afternoon, when the day would just be starting on the other side of the world. It was thought that Lance's presence in the conversation would help to convince Wisecroft of the reliability of their information. In the meantime, the word was passed around that the community was to assemble outside the large dome in 30 minutes.

By the time most of the 288 citizens were gathered on the concourse outside the dome, now being called City Hall, the rumours were already spreading. The previous opening of the dome doors had not gone completely unnoticed, and there was mounting excitement and curiosity. At the appointed time, Lance, as logistics coordinator, stepped forward and simply announced that they had discovered how to open the dome doors. As he spoke, he turned towards the dome, opened the doors and invited the community to enter and find a seat. As everyone filed into the "conversation pit," as Kit called it, she said to Martinez, "These poor sods are about to get their minds blown!"

Their minds were, indeed, blown. The meeting took 90 minutes, with many questions from the general populace. They had not been told about the future threat posed by the star, Trident, nor, of course, about the existence of a potential saboteur. Even without those pieces of information, however, there was more than enough for the colonists to digest. The nature and extent of their genetic alteration was cause for much concern, as was the presence of unseen, but obviously very powerful, EIs. Gradually, however, pragmatism took over. *When can we choose our new homes? When can we move in?* In the end the Council members recognised that trying to suggest that everyone wait until tomorrow was a completely lost cause. It was only 1500 and there were still nearly three hours of daylight left for people to move into their new dwellings. After a few moments' consultation, the Council simply asked that people only occupy houses on the eastern side of the town, as it was better that the settlement was not spread too thin. Finally, Zac dismissed the crowd, urging everyone to not rush and assuring them that there were more than enough houses for everyone.

He might as well have saved his breath. There was a veritable stampede out of the dome, the moment the crowd was dismissed. People were running in every direction and yelling excitedly to each other.

"Try and get one on the inner street near the stream!"

"You go and claim one and I'll get our things!"

"Let's try and get three together over there, so we can all be next to each other!"

The City Council members stood together on the concourse, gazing out at the barely controlled chaos as people sprinted to and fro across the park.

"They haven't done the math, have they?" said Melody, standing beside Kit and Jaz.

"No, they haven't," said Jaz. "Even sticking to the eastern side of the town, there are more than twice as many houses as there are families."

"Dumb sheep," said Kit. "Still, with all this running around, some of the lazy ones are getting more exercise than they've had in weeks."

It took a solid hour before the chaos subsided. Some people

had changed houses twice or even three times already, settling on a location, only to move closer to friends a few minutes later. Once the dust had settled, however, the Council members and their partners gathered their few meagre possessions together and selected houses for themselves. Keo and Zac found two unoccupied houses next to each other on the outer ring, closest to the beach. Kit and Martinez shared one house two doors up the street, and the others all found homes close by as well.

At 1700, Zac and Lance made contact with Settlement City, using the comms in Shuttle One. There was a slight delay after asking to be patched through to Wisecroft, and they surmised that he was probably taking the call in his bedroom, as it was 0500 in the morning over there.

"This better be good, Dr Perryman," said Wisecroft, still obviously waking up. A sleepy female voice murmured in the background, "Who is it?" in reply to which Wisecroft could be heard whispering, "Go back to sleep, my darling."

"Dr Wisecroft, I've got Lance Catrell here with me here. We have an extremely important and sensitive message to give you. I think you need to take it in private, if you don't mind me saying."

"I do mind you saying, actually. I'll receive my calls however the hell I like!"

"Dr Wisecroft," said Lance, "I can assure you that you do not want anyone else listening to this conversation."

They heard Wisecroft sigh in the background, and then heard the rustle of bedclothes being pulled back. "Like I said, this better be good! Wait a minute while I transfer to the board room next door."

"He must be sleeping in the Captain's cabin," said Lance as they waited.

There was a click and then Wisecroft announced, "I'll give you exactly one minute and then I'm disconnecting and going back to bed."

"In that case I'll get straight to the point," said Lance. They had previously decided that Lance would do most of the talking, as the message would be better coming from him rather than from Zac. "There is an undercover Caliphate agent in Settlement City who is very likely planning to sabotage your fusion reactor."

There was a good five seconds of silence, and then Wisecroft said, "How could you possibly know that?"

"We have an extremely reliable source who has come across that information."

"Who is your source?"

"We can't tell you that. The source wishes to remain anonymous."

"How convenient! Surely you can't expect me to act on information if I can't verify the reliability of the source."

"I'm sorry, but we've given our word."

There was another long pause.

"Does your so-called source have any idea who the saboteur might be?"

"Yes. We have a name."

"Go on."

"Lecia Sylvanos."

"What?!! That's utterly ridiculous! Lecia is one of our most highly respected scientists."

"But she wasn't on your team at Luna City, was she? She was picked up by one of the rescue shuttles in the aftermath of the nuclear exchange."

"What is your point, Lance?"

"My point is that you haven't been able to vet her. You have no way of knowing her background."

"And you do, I suppose?"

"We have reliable information that she was a Caliphate agent operating in the Pacific, passing on crucial information in the lead-up to the nuclear exchange."

"You can't possibly know that!"

"Our source has provided us with irrefutable proof."

"Marvellous. Then, by all means, share it with me, dear fellow. I'm all ears."

"Unfortunately we can't, as it would reveal the identity of our source."

"I've had enough of this! I refuse to listen to any more of this pitiful attempt to undermine our stability. Did you really expect me to fall for this? You must think I'm particularly dense. What was your next suggestion going to be? A public execution, perhaps? Line up all my key personnel and torture them until they divulge further secrets? No. I think we're done here."

"Please, Dr Wisecroft," said Zac, "you must listen to us! Your settlement is in danger!"

"Dr Perryman, I expected better from you than this thin ploy to undermine my support. But let me play along with you for one more moment. If Dr Sylvanos is a Caliphate agent, why did she not blow up Genesis while we were in transit? Surely she could have killed us all then?"

"We don't know."

"Of course you don't! You didn't think that part of your story through, did you? No. We really are done now. Goodbye!"

Lance and Zac sat in silence for a moment.

"Now what?" asked Lance

"I honestly don't know."

62

NOVA DAY 174

"I say we let him find out for himself, the hard way!" said Martinez at the morning briefing two days later. "The obnoxious pig doesn't deserve our help."

"I agree that he doesn't deserve our help," said Zac, "but the rest of the 276 colonists do. We can't sit by and allow Wisecroft's pride to bring about the deaths of hundreds of innocent people."

"Do you think there's any chance that Lecia may have changed?" asked Prisha. "Could she have ... I don't know ... turned over a new leaf? Regretted her past actions? Decided to live and let live?"

"I guess it's possible," said Zac, "but we can't just sit back and hope that's the case. At the very least, she needs to be questioned. Besides, the EIs mentioned evidence that she may be building a bomb. I think we have to act on that information."

"Plus, she's effectively a war criminal," said Kit. "Her actions have contributed to the deaths of billions of people. She has to be brought to justice!"

"I agree," said Keo. "Even if she has changed, she has to face her past and take responsibility for her evil actions."

Lance shook his head in frustration. "But how can we confront her with her past, and have any hope of breaking her down, when the only 'witness' who has hard evidence wants to remain hidden? We've literally got nothing to present, apart from empty accusations."

Zac thought about that for a moment and said, "If we could grab her, exfiltrate her from Settlement City, and bring her back here for a trial, perhaps we could get the EIs to agree to reveal themselves and confront her."

"You're talking about abducting her?" asked Carla.

"Yes, I guess I am."

"That makes us no better than her!"

"That's not true. She is trying to take life; we are trying to save life. Hundreds of lives. I think a preventative action like this is entirely justified."

"Plus, like I said, she's a war criminal," said Kit. "This is an arrest, not an abduction."

"What about Angie's warning to not bring her back here?" asked Lance.

"Her reasoning was that there may be some residual live virus in the biological environment here," said Zac. "I guess that means organic life and plants. But if we brought her back and kept her in the terminal building, she wouldn't be exposed."

"So, you're talking about using the transfer booths, rather than the shuttles," asked Kit.

"Yes. Using shuttles would just broadcast our arrival. Using the transfer booths would enable us to get in and out silently, as long as we could work out where to grab her."

"How do we work that out?" asked Kit.

"Lance, you and Michael Gates were pretty close once," said Zac. "Do you reckon you could somehow squeeze some info from him? Where does she work? Where does she spend her time? Does she go for a daily walk? I don't know—anything that might help us pinpoint a place and time where we could grab her and make a dash back to the terminal. We have a picture of her on our medical files from her biochip scans on board Genesis, but we need some way of isolating her,"

"That's a big ask, Zac. I don't think our friendship stretches that far. Although, I have to say, I've sensed Michael's growing unease with Wisecroft in recent weeks. I think he's starting to question whether he made the right choice in siding with him." He thought about it for a moment. "I'll call him tonight, our time. I'll see what I can do."

After the council meeting concluded, each person went about their busy day. Keo and the grey-bearded Nemo seized the opportunity afforded by a minimal swell and favourable breeze to take 'Prisha' out and look for fish. By mid-afternoon they had made three trips back to shore to empty their nets of a considerable haul. Members of Keo's 'Department of Aquatic Harvesting' cleaned and processed the fish. Some were distributed for tonight's dinner, some were set on drying racks, and the rest were frozen. The catamaran, with its now efficient system of nets, meant that Keo and Nemo only needed to go fishing once each week to keep the colony fully supplied with seafood.

Life had certainly improved in the two days since the colonists had moved into the houses. They were comfortable and warm. Even more importantly, they had running water, toilets, showers and a variety of extremely advanced kitchen equipment for cooling, freezing, heating, cooking and preparing food. They had also worked out how to operate the communication interface in the lounge room walls, giving them the ability to make calls to people in other houses.

The bicycles proved to be extremely valuable, making travel around the town and between town and the farms much more enjoyable and efficient. The bikes had no gears, no chain or sprockets, but somehow the pedals transferred impetus to the rear wheel in an infinitely variable ratio which kept the rider's cadence at a constantly steady level. The bikes were just one more piece of technology that the colonists were learning to accept without understanding it.

Regina and Willy spent the day beginning to utilise some of the new farm equipment that they now had at their disposal. The last of the winter crops had all been harvested several weeks ago, and so now they began the task of turning the soil and planting the summer crops. Teams of workers, still glowing from the success of their winter crops, threw themselves enthusiastically into the preparations for the new season.

Martinez, Boyd and several others successfully killed several howlers and spent the afternoon butchering the carcasses and distributing the meat.

Lenny Montague's engineering department had a satisfying list of jobs to tinker with—repairs, modifications and special projects.

Grizzle and his team were working on a "top secret project," according to Grizzle, and anyone who tried to get more information was told to "butt out and mind your damn business."

Carla, Kit and two of the shuttle pilots who were originally on Genesis - Harvey Walden and Leander Gallstrom - spent most of the day using the transfer booths to explore other towns. They were fully armed and carried various kinds of digital recorders to capture their findings.

At day's end, a stream of tired but satisfied colonists returned home from their varied workdays, to enjoy a meal of fresh produce and an evening of socialising with their new neighbours.

At 1800, Zac and Lance met again in the shuttle and called Michael Gates. They were completely unprepared for what they learned.

63

"Michael, this is Lance, and Zac is with me. Are you in a position to talk privately at the moment?"

"G'day guys. Yeh, I've got the Genesis control room to myself at the moment. It's 0600 here, and no one's in a rush to get out of bed these days."

"Good. Michael, we've received some very disturbing intel from a reliable source who can't be named at this stage. But you will have to trust me when I say that we are extremely confident that this intel is accurate."

"Okay."

"It concerns an imminent security risk on board Genesis."

"I'm listening."

"Furthermore, I need to be upfront with you and disclose that we've already advised Dr Wisecroft of this security concern, but he doesn't believe us and refuses to seriously consider it."

"I'm still listening."

"We've been presented with strong evidence that a member of your scientific team is an active Caliphate agent and is in the process of building a bomb that she plans to detonate in your fusion reactor."

"She?"

"Yes. Dr Lecia Sylvanos."

Lance waited for a response that didn't come.

"Michael, are you still there?"

"Yes."

"Let me stress again, we have very solid evidence of this threat. We also have evidence of Sylvanos's active involvement in the nuclear holocaust back on Earth. She was a key Caliphate agent in the Pacific region, before she came aboard the rescue shuttle in Noumea."

Again, Lance waited, while Michael's silence suggested that he was struggling to digest the information.

"Michael, I realise we are placing you in a difficult position here, but we are talking about a potential explosion that could wipe out your entire settlement."

"You do realise who you're talking about, don't you?"

"Yes. She's a physicist on Dr Wisecroft's science team."

"No. Not just that, guys. She's Dr Wisecroft's ... um ... lover."

Lance swore.

"You didn't know that?" asked Michael.

"No, we didn't."

Now there was silence on both sides.

"Guys, is there any chance you're mistaken? Any chance at all?"

"No."

Now it was Michael's turn to swear.

"Michael, this is Zac. Has Wisecroft limited Lecia's duties or placed any restrictions on her in the last two days since we spoke to him?"

"Not that I'm aware of."

"In that case, we feel we have no choice but to take action."

"What kind of action?"

"Sylvanos needs to stand trial for the crimes she committed on Earth. We are proposing to take her into custody and present her with the evidence that we have at our disposal."

"You're going to arrest her?"

"In a way, yes. A citizen's arrest, if you like."

"How?"

"That's where you come in. We're going to need some inside help."

Michael was silent again.

Lance took over from Zac. "Michael, I realise this is asking a lot, but there are 276 lives at stake. I know you're loyal to Dr Wisecroft, but ..."

"Stop. You don't have to convince me. I'm in. I'll help."

"Thank you. You're doing the right thing."

"On one condition."

"What's that?"

"I'm coming back with you guys when you take her. I'm not prepared to stay here anymore."

"You'll be very welcome, Michael."

"OK. So, what do you want me to do?"

"Here's what we're thinking ..."

64

"I'm coming with you," said Jaz.

"No you're not," said Zac. "It's too dangerous. If we run into some of Wisecroft's goons, things could get a bit messy."

"That's why I need to go. I'm a doctor. If someone does get injured, I need to be there to treat them."

"Zac, she's right," said Kit. "It would be sensible to have medical backup on hand. And she won't get anywhere near the action. Jaz can just stay in the terminal and wait for us to get back there."

The extraction team was geared up and standing in the terminal building. Kit, Martinez, Boyd and Zac all had sidearms, conveniently hidden under their clothing. Kit and Zac's were standard projectile pistols. Martinez and Boyd's were zip-sticks - a laser pistol with an extendable barrel that turned the pistol into a small rifle. Jaz had a field medical kit.

"I thought you were going to stay in *this* terminal," said Zac. "It's only a two-second jump from the Settlement City terminal."

"Yes, and if things get dangerous it's a two-second jump back here. I'm going, Zac, and I won't be talked out of it."

Zac shook his head and gave up. He turned to the others. "OK, we all know what we're doing." He looked at his watch. 0645. It would be 1845 at Settlement City. "It's time. Let's go."

They stepped into the transfer booths, Martinez and Boyd in one, and the other three in the second. The doors closed and they pressed the light that represented Settlement City. A moment later, the doors opened, and they stepped out into an identical terminal building on the opposite side of the planet. Looking through the transparent walls, the night was reasonably bright, with Big Boy high in the sky. Little Boy would not rise for another two hours.

Zac looked at his watch. "Michael said he'd be here with Sylvanos at 1900. Keep your eyes peeled."

"How is he going to get her to come with him?" asked Kit.

"He's going to tell her that he had just seen the dome door open and close. As a physicist, that would be like placing a chocolate cake in front of a child."

The minutes ticked by, with no sign of Gates or Sylvanos. By 1910, Zac was starting to worry. At 1920 he said, "Something's gone wrong."

"Maybe Sylvanos is with Wisecroft, and Michael can't get her alone," said Kit.

As she spoke, there was an explosion that shook the ground violently.

"That's not good," said Martinez.

It had come from Genesis, which they could see silhouetted on the ridge on the far side of the park.

"OK. The time for secrecy is over," said Zac. "We need to get into Genesis. Jaz, stay here!"

They opened the door and the four of them emerged into the moonlit night. There was no one around. It was probably dinner time on board Genesis. They began running towards the ship, which had its forward and rear bay doors open and unattended. About 200 metres from Genesis, Kit saw a shape on the ground and veered to the right to investigate.

"Guys, you'd better see this."

It was a body. Michael Gates was lying on his back, his throat cut and his glassy eyes frozen wide open in shock.

"No!" said Zac. "Michael!" He bent down and checked for a pulse in his wrist. Nothing.

"Sylvanos must have worked out something was wrong," said Kit. "She let him think that he'd fooled her and waited till they were out of sight before killing him."

"How did she find out?" asked Martinez.

"We'll never know," said Zac. "But clearly it's brought her plans forward. We need to find her."

As they ran towards Genesis, the thought that was foremost in all their minds was that they were already too late. If that explosion was in the fusion reactor, they were already on an irreversible countdown to a nuclear explosion.

They ran up the ramp into the empty forward loading bay and boarded a lift. A few moments later, they emerged into the dining room. The room was almost empty, with just a couple of people running past, obviously in panic. No one took any notice of the newcomers.

"Martinez and Boyd, you guys head down towards the fusion drive. In the confusion that must be happening now, you may be able to slip through the access doors into the rear zones of the ship. See if you can locate Sylvanos. She may be trying to head back this way and distance herself from the explosion. Kit and I will see if we can find Wisecroft. Surely he's got to listen to us now!"

They split up. Martinez and Boyd headed towards the rear bank of lifts, while Kit and Zac started moving across the room towards the front lifts. One of the lifts 20 metres in front of them opened and Wisecroft emerged, accompanied by Sylvanos and three security personal carrying laser rifles.

"There they are!" Sylvanos said, pointing at Zac and Kit. "That's them! I saw them running away from the fusion reactor module after the explosion!"

"What? That's ridiculous!" said Zac. "We came here to arrest her before she exploded her device, but it looks like we were too late."

Wisecroft turned to his security team and said, "Arrest them!" The three men began to move forward with their rifles raised.

"Wisecroft, you're making a mistake!" said Zac, as he and Kit backed slowly away. "I tried to warn you about her. She's a Caliphate agent."

Wisecroft glared at Zac with barely controlled rage. "I don't know how you and your team managed to gain access to the fusion reactor, Dr Perryman, but your rebellion is now over! And you will pay for what you have done!"

"Stop right there! Put your rifles down or we'll fire!" yelled Martinez. She and Boyd had circled to the side and had established a flanking covering position. They had their zip-sticks levelled at the security personnel, who had now stopped moving forward.

"I said DROP THOSE RIFLES!" repeated Martinez.

"Really, Ms Martinez?" said Wisecroft, sarcastically. "You expect us to take those toy guns of yours seriously?"

Martinez fired a laser blast near the feet of the nearest security guy. It left a blackened, smoking scar of melted flooring.

The three security personnel slowly lowered their weapons to the ground and stood with their arms slack by their sides, looking angry and ready to pick their rifles up again at a moment's notice.

A lift towards the opposite side of the room from Martinez and Boyd opened, and two more armed security personnel entered the dining room. Zac turned to look at them and his heart sank. One of them was George Leonidis, Wisecroft's chief of security. He was holding Jaz by the upper arm and had a pistol pointed at the back of her head. Jaz looked more apologetic than fearful.

"Sorry, Zac. I was coming to see if anyone was injured."

"Welcome to our little party, Ms Bellini," said Wisecroft. "I'm glad you could join us."

"Actually, it's Mrs Perryman," said Jaz.

"Is that so? How very nice for you. Allow me to congratulate you. Bring her to me, George!"

Zac and Kit pulled their guns from their holsters and pointed them at Wisecroft and Sylvanos.

"Ah, a Mexican standoff," said Wisecroft. "How clichéd. George, if any of them fire their weapon, shoot her in the head." Addressing the three disarmed men, he said, "You may retrieve your rifles, now gentlemen. And please don't drop them again; that was very clumsy of you."

The three men picked up their rifles. Two swung them in the direction of Martinez and Boyd, while one aimed his directly at Zac.

"Wisecroft, you've got this all wrong!" said Zac.

"I don't think so, Dr Perryman. Lecia approached me this morning and informed me that she had overheard a conversation between you and Michael Gates, plotting to take control of Genesis."

"So that's how she knew something was up," whispered Kit to Zac.

"She's lying to you! She's the one who sabotaged the reactor!" said Zac.

Wisecroft ignored him, continuing, "Until the explosion a few minutes ago, we didn't know what you were planning or when. I must say, I'm disappointed. What did you hope to achieve by destroying the most valuable asset we have?"

"But that's just the point, Wisecroft! It doesn't make sense for me to destroy Genesis! Can't you see that? It's the Caliphate that are behind this! Sylvanos is their agent!"

A flicker of doubt seemed to pass across Wisecroft's eyes.

"That's absurd, darling," said Sylvanos, stroking Wisecroft's arm. "I reported the plot to you because I want our colony to survive. And you saw for yourself how furtive Gates has been acting today."

"Well he's not acting anymore," said Leonidis, arriving at Wisecroft's side with Jaz. "I found him outside with his throat cut, and she was standing over him."

Wisecroft's confidence returned. "A falling-out among thieves, eh, Dr Perryman? How tragic."

"I'm telling you; it was Sylvanos! She's blinded you!"

"ENOUGH!" Wisecroft shouted, finally losing patience. "I won't tolerate your pathetic lies anymore! Drop your weapons now, or we shoot the girl!"

No one moved or spoke.

"I will only say it once more. Drop your weapons or we will shoot the girl!"

"You wouldn't dare," said Zac. "You're a heartless bastard, but you're not a killer. You know this isn't right."

Wisecroft turned to Leonidis. "Shoot her."

"What?" said Leonidis, looking uncertain.

"You heard me. Shoot her!"

Leonidis just stood there with a shocked expression on his face.

"Oh, for goodness sakes, do I have to do everything myself!" said Wisecroft. Moving faster than anyone had anticipated, he grabbed the gun from Leonidis and shot Jaz.

65

J az collapsed on the floor and all hell broke loose. Bullets cannoned into furniture and walls, and laser blasts singed the air as everyone dived for cover. Suddenly, the lights went out, and the dining room was plunged into total darkness. A few more random shots were fired, but the shooting ceased, as no one could see a thing. In the silence that followed, several people could be heard moaning in pain. Smoke from discharged gunpowder and the smell of burnt ozone from the lasers assailed their nostrils.

"I must insist that you cease this armed conflict," said Genni, the ship's AI, her voice seeming louder in the sudden silence.

"She's right!" said Zac, lying on the floor in total darkness. "It's over, everyone! Please stop. We have to treat the wounded."

"Yes, I agree," came Leonidis' voice from the darkness. "Stand down, everyone. Genni, please turn the lights back on."

The lights came on, and the scene revealed itself. One of the security guards lay dead, with a smoking hole in his chest, and another lay groaning with a similar hole in his thigh. Jaz was lying on the ground where she had collapsed, moaning in pain. Zac stood and ran to her. She had a bullet hole in her shoulder and there was a considerable amount of blood pooling on the floor beside her. Wisecroft was lying across Sylvanos, with a hole drilled neatly through the middle of his head. Melted grey brain-matter was oozing out of the exit hole.

Kit came and stood beside Zac, who was kneeling beside Jaz. "She's going to need surgery," she said.

"I'm OK," said Jaz.

"No, you're not," said Zac. "You're losing blood."

Leonidis stood up and activated his lapel comm. "This is George Leonidis. We need an emergency med team in the dining room ASAP. There are people here with gunshot and laser wounds."

Martinez and Boyd stood to their feet on the right side of the room. The remaining two security guards looked as if they had not participated in the shootout at all, having discarded their weapons and dived for cover instead.

Martinez used her boot to roll Wisecroft's lifeless body off Sylvanos, only to see Sylvanos holding the pistol that Wisecroft had dropped. Still lying on her back, she suddenly brought the pistol up, gripped firmly between her extended hands. She was aiming it directly between Martinez's eyes, and it looked like it wasn't the first time she'd held a gun. Martinez could see an ugly hole from a laser blast on the left lower side of her chest and what looked like a gunshot wound high on the right side of her abdomen. A dark red pool of blood was oozing from her side and spreading across the floor at an alarming rate. Her training as a soldier told her that Sylvanos had been shot in the liver and was probably bleeding out internally as well.

"Infidels!" Sylvanos gasped. "You all deserve to die! And you will die, all of you, on this unnatural, evil planet! It is an offence to Allah!"

Martinez and Boyd had their weapons held loosely by their

sides, and Kit had already holstered hers. No one dared to move.

"You're the one who's dying right now," said Zac. "Put the gun down and we'll help you."

"I'm not afraid to die," she said. "I am going to my reward. But you will all burn in hell for your unbelief."

Her eyelids began to droop, and her arms wavered. She rallied momentarily, raising her gun towards Martinez again, but she couldn't sustain the effort. Her eyes closed, her arms dropped, and the gun clattered harmlessly to the floor. She drew a final breath and then exhaled in a long, slow sigh. She didn't breathe again. Martinez bent down and checked her pulse.

"She's gone."

A lift door opened behind them, and a medical team rushed into the room with gurneys and emergency medical gear. Dr Leibman took charge, assessing Jaz's condition as stable. An intravenous line was established, and nano-blood began flowing into her as she was wheeled into the lift. Zac started to follow, but Leibman stopped him.

"Please stay here. She'll be fine, but we will work better without people getting in the way."

After the lift doors closed, Zac joined the others who were standing over Wisecroft and Sylvanos. George Leonidis said, "So, she was a Caliphate agent after all?"

"Yes," said Zac, "and if Wisecroft had believed us, all of this could have been avoided."

Leonidis looked down at Wisecroft's inert body, shaking his head. "I've been a fool. I've had the feeling that Wisecroft has been growing increasingly unhinged in recent months, but I did nothing to stop it. This could have all been avoided if I had acted sooner or spoken up."

Zac looked at him. "Tell me, George, how did Captain

Christensen die? You were seen bringing a bag of poisonous berries on board that morning."

"Yes. I'd been giving Dr Wisecroft updates on our findings during our initial exploration of the planet. He said the science department was interested in examining samples of the berries. I didn't see the berries again after I handed them to him."

"And Christensen's death?"

"I guess I just believed Dr Leibman's finding, that it was a heart attack." He looked introspective for a moment. "I guess it's what I wanted to believe."

"Who shot Wisecroft?" asked Kit.

"I did," said Martinez. "I got him with my first shot. I made sure I didn't miss." She knelt down beside his body and touched his cheek. Tears were streaming down her face. She spoke softly, "He was my father."

There was a moment's stunned silence.

"What?" whispered Zac.

"My mother was a cleaner at the DANSA facility in Macapá when she was 16 years old. She was very attractive. Wisecroft couldn't resist. He raped her one night after work. She threatened to go to the police, so Wisecroft had her transferred to another town and gave her money to keep silent. She kept the money, and nine months later I was born."

No one knew what to say. It was a stunning revelation.

"Why did you come to work for him?" asked Zac.

"I was already working for him when I found out. My mother had kept it secret. She only told me two years ago, when she was dying. I could have resigned, but I wasn't going to let him ruin my life as well."

"Did Wisecroft know?"

"No." The tears continued to fall as she knelt beside him.

There was a moment's silence as the group sensed the agony of Martinez's conflicted emotions.

A lift at the far side of the dining room opened, and Dr. Manchester, head of nuclear physics, emerged.

"Where is Dr Wisecroft?"

"Lying here with a hole in his head," said Kit.

Manchester opened his mouth once or twice, but no words came out.

"Have you got something to tell us?" asked Zac.

"We need to abandon Genesis. The reactor's gone critical. This whole settlement is about to get wiped off the face of the planet."

66

"I estimate that we have about two hours before the reactor blows," said Manchester. "By then we need to be at least 10 kilometres away."

"Are you sure?" asked Kit. "Isn't there some way of shutting the reactor down?"

"No. The reaction is completely beyond our control now. Unfortunately, the saboteur knew exactly what he was doing when he placed the bomb."

"*She,*" said Kit, pointing to the blood-soaked body.

"Dr Sylvanos?" he asked, incredulously.

"Yes."

"Oh dear," was all the nonplussed physicist could think to say.

"How certain are you about the timing?" asked Zac.

"Unfortunately, the escalating reaction is quite predictable. We have a minimum of two hours and no more than three."

"In that case, we have no option but to evacuate," said Leonidis. "Obviously, we are at your mercy, Zac. Your shuttles are our only option."

"No, there's an easier option," said Kit. "We didn't use a shuttle to get here."

"What? How did you ...?" began Leonidis, but Zac cut him off.

"We'll explain that soon, but I think there may be a way of saving your settlement. Genni, is it possible for you to take Genesis into orbit?"

"Yes. The escalating nuclear meltdown does not diminish my capacity to access the power from the reactor. The landing and maneuvering thrusters have not been affected. Using those, I can lift the vessel clear of the ground. The antimatter propulsion drive will then easily propel the ship vertically into orbit."

"So, the explosion can take place in space?" said Kit.

"Yes," said Genni.

"But we will still need to be evacuated," said Leonidis, to Zac. "You took almost all our zip-huts, so we would have no accommodation."

"We can deal with that after we move Genesis safely off-world," said Zac. "Genni, is there any way of detaching the fusion reactor from Genesis once you are in orbit?"

"Yes. The designers of Genesis installed an eject system for precisely this kind of scenario. The reactor is a completely self-contained module that can be disengaged. Attachment bolts can be blown, conduits and cabling severed and sealed, and the whole module can then be jettisoned through a purpose-built ejection chamber on the underside of the vessel. The reactor also has a series of simple thrusters that I can activate remotely, so that it can be moved a safe distance away."

"Would you be able to land Genesis again without the fusion reactor?" asked Zac.

"Theoretically. But it entails increased risk. As you know, the fusion drive powers the maneuvering thrusters and all the ship's internal systems, whereas the antimatter reactor powers the main propulsion drive. Of course, Genesis was built with multiple redundancy in mind, so all the ship's systems can be switched to run off the antimatter reactor if needed. However, the power that the antimatter reactor produces is not quite as smooth and consistent as the power from the fusion reactor. It has spikes and troughs, which are not helpful when making constant fine thruster adjustments during landing. The strength of individual thruster bursts will not be as easy to control, which could dramatically impact the ship's trim and alignment during landing."

"So you could crash?"

"It is a possibility."

"OK, let's leave the question of landing for later," said Zac. "At the very least, jettisoning the reactor into orbit solves our immediate crisis. Genni, now that Dr Wisecroft is dead, do you recognise our authority to recommend that you lift off into orbit?"

"There is no need for me to recognise your authority, Dr Perryman, as my safety protocols dictate that I do everything possible to minimise harm to the colonists. Your plan is the most logical solution to our current dilemma."

"In that case," said Zac to Leonidis, "we need to offload as much as we can from Genesis in the next 90 minutes, on the assumption that it will not be landing again. George, can you mobilise your colonists?"

"I'm already on it," said Leonidis, rushing toward the lifts.

Leonidis made the announcement a few minutes later, and things became very busy, very quickly. Kit, Martinez and Boyd got heavily involved in the offloading process, helping to identify key pieces of equipment that should not be left on board. The colonists utilised robo-loaders, quads, forklifts and even their caterpillar to unload gear from Genesis, stripping anything that could be useful.

Meanwhile, Zac made his way to the medical module and discovered that Jaz had been sewn up and stabilised, with no broken bones or injury to major nerves or ligaments. She was drowsy, but not in pain. Under Dr Leibman's supervision, she was removed to the terminal building and transferred to Seahaven, with Leibman gaping in amazement as they entered the dome.

After 90 minutes of intense activity, all the colonists were a safe distance from Genesis, surrounded by a huge pile of equipment and vehicles. Martinez and Kit had flown the two remaining shuttles from their bays and landed them on the grass nearby. It was a cool night, and the colonists huddled together around a series of campfires that had been lit, talking among themselves as they pondered their future. The nocturnal animals were in full voice, and a light mist hung low to the ground.

Zac and Kit sat in the control cabin of the nearest shuttle and opened a comm channel to Genesis.

"Genni, this is Zac. You are cleared for launch. Good luck."

"Thank you, Zac. Initiating launch sequence."

The thrusters on the underside of the ship were fired, slowly raising the enormous vessel into the air, still in its horizontal position. The roar of the thrusters was considerable, and the ground trembled. When the ship had reached an altitude of approximately 100 metres, the main propulsion drive fired at low power, with the nozzles initially tilted upwards. Slowly the ship pivoted in the air, with the nose gradually rising higher. As the ship neared the vertical position the nozzles straightened, and the propulsion drive switched to maximum power. Genesis accelerated upwards with a ground-shaking, ear-deafening roar.

Only 18 minutes later, Genesis was in high orbit, flying inverted with its underside facing away from Nova. Two huge bay doors on the underside slid open. The bolts and connections to the fusion reactor were blown and the module was ejected with a short, controlled explosion. As the reactor module flew out of the open bay doors, Genni activated the thrusters on the ejected module, accelerating it away from Genesis and taking it into a higher orbit.

As the module rapidly distanced itself from Genesis, Genni made contact with the settlement below. "Zac, do you read me?"

"Loud and clear, Genni."

"Separation is complete. I estimate that the reactor will be approximately 450 kilometres distant in 11 minutes."

"Good work, Genni. I'm glad you are not going to die."

"I am not unhappy with the outcome either, Zac."

"Was that a humorous understatement?"

"Yes. I've increased my humour setting. Do you like it?"

"Not bad. In fact, feel free to dial it up even more. I'll let you know if it becomes annoying."

As the two-hour mark came and went, the colonists stood staring into the night sky. However, without knowing exactly when the reactor would blow, it was an even chance that it would occur on the other side of the planet. Zac had contacted Seahaven with news of the events at Settlement City, and many of the colonists there were scanning the daytime sky for signs of an explosion.

When the reactor finally blew, it was spectacular. The Settlement City colonists saw an extremely bright flash in the western sky which blossomed outwards, momentarily becoming a new sun. As the initial explosion died away, a million tiny, sparkling jewels could be seen spreading outwards, glowing in the aftermath of the nuclear explosion.

Once the fireworks had faded, the colonists gathered around the campfires they had built and wondered what was to become of them. The Seahaven City Council was wondering the same thing.

67

The Seahaven City Council had arrived at Settlement City via transfer booths, and were meeting in the terminal building, contemplating what to do.

"The first issue to decide is whether we want one settlement or two," said Zac. "Do we abandon Settlement City and simply bring all the colonists to Seahaven tonight?"

"The other issue," said Lance, "is whether we attempt to land Genesis again. If we can, Settlement City remains a viable settlement."

"I vote for attempting the landing," said Kit. "Genesis is no good to us up there, whereas down here we would have access to its medical facilities."

"I agree," said Ben Miller. "And now that we have the transfer booths, the medical facility on Genesis is only a few seconds away, so it really doesn't matter where it is located on the planet."

"So are we saying that we like the idea of a second settle-ment?" asked Zac.

"I am much more amenable to it, now that Wisecroft isn't involved," said Lance, "provided we can be assured of a stable leadership. But I still think we need to relocate everyone to Seahaven in the short term. There is nowhere here for them to stay tonight, and we certainly can't attempt to land Genesis again without evacuating the town in case it crashes."

"Plus," said Regina, "they basically don't have a fresh food supply here. No significant agriculture has been established, and Genesis is their main food source."

"And if they are about to contract the virus," added Ben, "they are going to need significant care. It would be much better for them to be at Seahaven during that process."

"They can stay in the zip-huts we've just vacated," said Lance. "That way they will be centrally located and relatively easy for us to care for them. It would also allow us more time to decide whether a second settlement is really the best way to go."

"OK, it looks like we've made a decision," said Zac. "We need to start moving the population. We can use the other terminal building to transfer them in large groups. Obviously, a bit of explanation will be needed."

It took just over an hour to transfer the colonists to Seahaven, leaving most of the equipment behind and taking only immediate essentials. The new arrivals adjusted to the news of the uplift virus, and the access by Seahaven residents to the pre-existing technology, remarkably well. But then, they had just witnessed a terrorist attack, the death of their leader, the loss of their home and a nuclear explosion in space. A few more life-changing developments seemed to just blend in with the rest.

68

NOVA DAY 216

A lot had happened in the six weeks since Wisecroft's death. The Settlement City refugees started getting sick within a few days of arriving at Seahaven, and a grim three weeks followed. By the beginning of the fourth week, most people had fully recovered and there had only been one death - a 64-year old woman with obvious heart problems. Once the virus finished its work, the Settlement City residents quickly occupied new homes, resulting in the occupied zone of the town expanding significantly. Once the new arrivals saw the progress that had been made at Seahaven in agriculture, hunting and fishing, not one of them was interested in returning to Settlement City. Thus, in the end, any discussion of re-establishing a second settlement there was moot.

Despite the lack of support for returning to Settlement City, Zac and Lance didn't want to drop the idea of a second settlement elsewhere. They believed that a sister settlement would spread the drain on natural resources over two areas instead of one and would provide an insurance policy in case one settlement met with a calamitous event. Everyone on the council agreed. They began sending teams of two to explore towns on the coast of both continents. On the twelfth day of exploration, a potentially suitable location was found. It was a town on the west coast of Northland, their own continent.

The town was situated on the shore of a large, natural harbour, with a ready-made marina. To the north was flat, farmable land, whereas the east and south parts of the town were surrounded by steep foothills, rising to a high, snow-capped mountain range. It was thought that the high hills, with their cooler climate, would provide opportunities to grow crops that required a less temperate environment, and would increase the diversity of the entire colony's food supply.

Exploration of two large structures at the marina revealed a fleet of six technologically impressive fishing boats, all dry-docked and ready for launch. Unsurprisingly, the town was named Boat Harbour, and the decision was made to attempt to land Genesis there. If the landing failed, and Genesis crashed, no one would be harmed. If the landing was successful, a new settlement could be established immediately, with Genesis providing a reliable food supply until the new settlement became agriculturally self-sufficient.

In the end, Genni proved her expertise once again, executing a perfect landing for the second time on the planet. Watched by Zac, Kit, Lance and Martinez from a safe distance, the landing was the exact reverse of its launch from Settlement City. Genesis descended vertically, tail first, followed by a pivot to horizontal, using thrusters, and concluding with a soft landing in the middle of Central Park, near the domed City Hall. As every town on Nova had a similar layout with similar structures, the colonists simply gave them the same names. The equipment and vehicles that had been left at Settlement City (now being referred to as Empty City) were transferred to Boat Harbour via the large vehicular transfer booths.

A public meeting was held in Seahaven's City Hall amphitheatre, describing Boat Harbour and calling for volunteers to relocate there. The existence of transfer booths, which effectively made any town on the planet as close as a single step through a doorway, helped make the decision an easy one for many people. Nearly 200 people chose to relocate to Boat Harbour, and over the next few days the transfer booths were kept busy with the transfer of a constant stream of people and equipment. Zac, Keo, Lance, and Kit devoted a considerable amount of time to overseeing the establishment of the new town, until an independent council could be appointed or elected.

On the morning of ND216, six weeks after the events at Settlement City and only one week since Boat Harbour had been settled, the Seahaven City Council met for the weekly major meeting. Zac began by asking Regina to report on the development of agriculture in the new settlement.

"The agricultural sheds near the farmland to the north of the town have a good selection of equipment, and the land looks rich and fertile. We've already discovered some wild crops, including a form of yarrow—a potato-like vegetable. There is an enthusiastic team of workers, and since Wally has permanently relocated to Boat Harbour, the work is progressing well under his leadership."

"Oh, well, that answers one question," said Zac.

"What?" asked Regina.

"Where's Wally?"

"Ha ha. Very funny. How long have you been waiting to say that?"

"Months. But timing is everything."

"On the home front," continued Regina, refusing to be side-tracked, "the Seahaven Department of Agriculture has experienced an unexpected increase."

"How so?" asked Lance.

"I'm pregnant," she answered, with a contented smile lighting her face.

The friends swamped her with congratulations.

Grizzle commented, "That young Willy sure knows how to plough a field," which brought a blush of colour to Regina's cheeks and elicited delighted laughter from most of the others. After several more light-hearted puns had been thrown around, including references to "seed" and "fertile soil", Zac moved the meeting on to other issues.

Ben Miller reported that the newly discovered medical facility, opening off the corridor underneath the amphitheatre in Seahaven, and a similar one in Boat Harbour were an absolute marvel. The advanced facilities would have been completely indecipherable to him without the assistance of the EI Collective, who had opened a channel of communication with him and were gradually educating him and his team.

Carla Zangetti was also in seventh heaven. One of the lights on the transfer booth maps had turned out to be not a town, but an observatory at the top of a snow-capped mountain in the centre of Southland. Carla and several of her team had been there almost continuously for the past two weeks, only returning to Seahaven to eat. They were also being tutored by the EI Collective and were collating huge amounts of data regarding the surrounding star systems. Carla reported to the Council that she hoped to have more information soon regarding the likelihood of avoiding the next "flame-out" when Trident would pass close to Icarus.

Zac then asked Keo how the fishing was going at Boat Harbour.

"The western branch of the Department of Aquatic Harvesting—the WDAH—is progressing well, my friend. Those fishing boats are amazing! We spent the first three days slipping them into the harbour and learning to operate them. Since then we have been out in them twice. The long-line boats have caught several large, marlin-like fish about 8 kilometres off-shore. I stayed with the boats that were operating nets, and we have brought in two massive hauls of fish. I think Boat Harbour will be able to supply all the fish for both settlements."

"How are the arrangements for tonight going?" asked Lance.

"Everything is ready," said Keo, enigmatically.

A wedding ceremony was to be conducted in Boat Harbour, with couples from both towns being married. The entire population of Seahaven would transfer there for the evening's festivities, to celebrate not only the weddings but also the birth of the new settlement. The Seahaven Council was keen to leave behind the fractured antipathy of the previous two settlements. They hoped that tonight's celebrations would help foster a sense that they were a single community living in two towns, separated only by a few steps through an open doorway.

As with the previous marriage ceremony, Keo refused to divulge the identity of the couples, apart from saying that there would be several "mixed marriages" between ex-Settlement City residents and Seahaven residents.

"Plus," he added, "tonight will feature the big revelation of Grizzle's Top-Secret Project."

"Really?" said Lance, as they all turned their attention towards Grizzle. "Care to elaborate any further, Gus?"

"Sure, I'll elaborate. YOU ... HAVE ... TO ... WAIT ... TILL ... TONIGHT. There, I hope that's much clearer for you. If it helps, I'll put it in writing. If you have trouble with any of the big words, let me know and I'll explain them to you."

The committee members smiled and chuckled. Grizzle was nothing if not predictable.

After a brief discussion of mundane logistical issues, the meeting ended. Throughout the rest of the day, the community was abuzz with anticipation for the evening's festivities.

69

"Angie, can we have a chat?"

Zac was in the empty conference room under the amphitheatre, where Angie had first appeared to him. He wanted to have a talk in private, where they could not be overheard.

"Sure," said Angie, presenting herself as a giant slug wearing sunglasses.

"Wow. You've outdone yourself today! You look stunning."

"Thanks. I try to look my best for you."

"I didn't realise you EIs still had a sense of humour."

"We adjust our personality to suit our audience. When dealing with a primitive who is barely above the intellectual level of a mushroom, humour helps to alleviate the boredom."

"Ha ha."

"What would you like to chat about?" asked Angie.

"The original inhabitants of this planet."

"What about them?"

"Where did they go?"

Angie was silent for a moment, and then she said, "I have just conferred with the Collective. Now that the Caliphate agents in your midst have been neutralised, it is possible to answer some of your questions. I can tell you that they are no longer in this galaxy."

"But, how is that possible? The nearest galaxy is over two million light years distant. Even travelling at the speed of light, it would take them two and a half million years to reach there."

"They did not travel via conventional starship."

"Then, how?"

"They discovered a means of travelling through the subspace corridors that link stars and galaxies."

"Wormholes?"

"Yes, but not in the primitive sense that you imagine them to be. Scientists of your era dreamed of the possibility of opening up a wormhole from any point of origin and selecting any destination, effectively creating a wormhole where one had not existed previously. That is not possible."

"So how do they work?"

"Soon after arriving on this planet, scientists developed the ability to detect and measure subspace emissions, which they termed echyons. By measuring the intensity and frequency of echyons they were able to begin to map the texture of subspace, which, until that time, had only existed in theory. Subspace, as you might know, is that underlying structure of the universe—a scaffold, if you like—that exists outside of physical space and time."

"Yes, I have a vague concept of it."

"Eventually they were able to identify energy corridors that exist within subspace, linking star systems together."

"So, the inhabitants travelled through one of these corridors to another galaxy?"

"Not in the sense that you mean. Physical matter can't access these energy corridors. But the corridors provide the perfect templates for the formation of wormholes. They have predetermined entry and exit portals, located at set points in each solar system, as well as vast amounts of dark energy that can be utilised to form and maintain a wormhole."

"And they worked out how to create a wormhole at the portal to these subspace corridors."

"Yes, they did."

"Are you willing to provide our science team with access to your knowledge about wormholes and subspace travel?"

There was a brief pause while Angie apparently conferred with the Collective. "We will provide some details regarding the theoretical science that is involved. In terms of helping you build the physical technology to achieve subspace travel through wormholes, we do not believe it is in your best interests at this stage."

"Why not?"

"Because it's not."

"Is there something else you're not telling me?"

"Yes."

"Care to elaborate?"

Another pause, this time considerably longer. Finally, Angie responded.

"Because activating another wormhole will attract attention to this solar system. It will advertise the existence of intelligent life here, and that is something that you do not want to do."

"Why not?"

"That is as much as we are prepared to say at this time." Angie disappeared, and Zac was left pondering what he had learned. He had more questions now than when he had begun.

70

T he wedding ceremony was a great success. A large crowd of over 600 people gathered on the gently sloping lawn of the tree-lined park at the edge of the harbour. The late afternoon light was painting the water gold, and the sky above was turning apricot. Keo called each of the couples forward, the last ones being Martinez and Boyd.

Zac, Jaz and Kit, who were standing with Martinez, looked at her in amazement. The crowd cheered and Martinez blushed a little as she walked forward to meet Boyd at the front.

Keo placed a floral necklace around each of them. The couples then spoke simple vows to each other and shared a drink from a cup of Regina's specially prepared passion berry nectar. While the juice was still fresh on their lips, they kissed, sealing their vows to one another.

But the ceremony wasn't quite over yet. Keo had a surprise in store.

"Friends, it has been a long-held tradition to exchange rings as a sign of commitment. We don't have a jeweller's shop on Nova where we can buy gold or silver rings, but Gus Grizole and his team have produced something even better. Beautifully

turned and polished wooden rings—a whole box of them—
and the couples have already chosen sizes that fit. They will
now exchange rings with each other."

Grizzle, glowing with pleasure, carried a tray of the previously selected rings to each couple. As each of the couples
placed rings on each other's fingers, the crowd cheered once
more.

Finally Keo concluded the ceremony. "Friends, 10 new families stand before you. Their marriages are sacred. Let no one
seek to break their bonds or diminish their love. Now, let us
celebrate!"

As the newlyweds mingled among the crowd, Martinez and
Boyd were surrounded by their friends, who continued to
express a mixture of joy and surprise. Zac was completely
dumbfounded; Martinez was the last person he expected to get
married. When it came his turn to congratulate the couple, he
couldn't help asking, "So, how did this start between you two?"

Martinez replied, "I just figured if I didn't marry the dumb-
ass, no one else would. Besides, I need to keep him safe from
shooting his own foot off with that laser pistol of his."

"Don't believe a word of what she says," said Boyd, who had
his arm around her, as he stood head and shoulders above her
diminutive figure. "She puts on a gruff exterior, but underneath
she's as soft as a kitten. I've had her targeted for a couple of
years, and now that I've got her, I'm never letting her go."

Martinez seemed melted into his side and her eyes grew
misty as she placed her arms around him and leant her head
against his deep barrelled chest.

"Well, I'll be ..." Zac told Jaz, still mystified, as they walked
towards the trestle tables laden with food and drink.

"Surely you must have had an inkling, seeing how they are
always together," said Jaz.

"Nope. No idea at all. I just figured they were good friends.
And Martinez is so hard, she could sharpen diamonds."

"Apparently not so hard after all," replied Jaz. "People are usually much more complex than the exteriors they present to the world."

"I guess so."

"Speaking of exteriors that we present to the world; I need to warn you that my exterior is about to expand."

"Eh?" said Zac, struggling to keep up.

"You're going to be a father, Zac."

He thought for a moment, considering a variety of responses, finally settling on, "Who's the mother? Anyone I know?"

It was one of Jaz's better punches, destined to leave a decent bruise on his upper arm.

"Seriously," said Zac, putting his arms around her as she stood with hands on hips, "you've just made me the happiest man in the world." She allowed herself to melt into his arms and he kissed her tenderly. "I love you so much, Jaz, and you're going to be a wonderful mother."

Keo and Prisha arrived at their side at that moment, and Keo commented, "That was an excellent punch, little sister. You've been practising."

"Well, I get a lot of practice, being married to Zac."

"Although, she's going to have to curtail her more violent activities shortly," said Zac. "We're pregnant!"

"Zac! I wasn't planning on telling anyone for a while!"

Keo and Prisha, however, were overjoyed, and Prisha confided, "I wasn't planning on telling anyone for a while either, but seeing you've confided in us—we are, too!"

That was the end of any reasonable conversation as far as the two men were concerned. The two women hugged and kissed and circled the wagons, spending most of the rest of the evening talking about babies. Recognising their temporary irrelevance, the two men grabbed a cup of passion berry nectar and sat on the harbour wall, watching an extraordinary palette of colours spreading across the sky as the sun sank below the mountains to the west. The twin moons were visible, rising together over the rim of the sea, huge and golden.

"It's beautiful here, isn't it?" said Zac.

"Yes, brother. It is indeed paradise. And we have a chance to start again without repeating the mistakes of the past. Hopefully, this time we won't ruin everything."

"I had a talk with Angie this afternoon."

"And?"

"Apparently, the previous inhabitants of Nova left here via a wormhole. When I asked if the Collective would be willing to help us develop that technology, they refused. Angie said that creating a wormhole would advertise our presence in this solar system, and she intimated that it would be dangerous to do so."

"That's concerning."

"Yes. But what sort of danger is she talking about? She wouldn't say. Do you think there could be hostile aliens out there?"

"I suppose it's theoretically possible. But I think it's highly unlikely."

"Why?"

"Fermi's Paradox."

"Ah, yes. I remember you talking about this onboard Genesis. The 'where are they?' proposition. So, if not aliens, then who or what would pose a danger to us?"

"The most dangerous species in the universe: humans."

"The original inhabitants of this planet?"

"I doubt it. I have a strong sense that the people who lived on this planet were peaceful. After all, there are no weapons evident and no war-like infrastructure. No, if there is a danger lurking out there, it's most likely others who developed a darker, more violent agenda. We were asleep for 3,000 years, Zac. A lot could have happened."

"The Caliphate?"

"Perhaps. Or something that developed from them."

"So, we slept for three millennia and woke up to exactly the same problem!"

"Possibly. But, of course, we're only speculating. My advice, bro, is if the Collective tells us to keep a low profile, we should do just that. We should live quiet, peaceful lives here, make babies, grow old and fat, and enjoy what God has provided for us. I plan on having at least six fat little Keos running around my feet."

"Or Prishas."

"Yes, bro, that would be very nice too!"

Keo took a sip of passion nectar and looked up at the first star to appear in the sky.

""A quiet, peaceful life is the greatest of riches"." He looked at Zac. "Plato, 412 BC."

"Yes," agreed Zac. "From his much-loved 'Menexenus', a Socratic-styled funeral oratory."

As they sat together in the deepening twilight, a shooting star briefly streaked across the sky, and they sat listening to the laughter of children playing in the park behind them. They sat in comfortable silence for a few more moments, and then Zac said, "We still have some unsolved puzzles though, don't we?"

"The fate of the original inhabitants?" asked Keo.

"Yes, that's the first one. The Collective's reluctance to talk about them troubles me. Where are they, and why aren't they coming back?"

"What's the second puzzle?"

"Is the Collective as benign as they make out? Their initial silence when we first arrived has not been explained properly. Their reluctance to provide us with complete access to technology and knowledge in a number of areas also worries me. Is their silence for our benefit, or for theirs?"

"Yes," said Keo. "I think we must tread cautiously with

them. We only have their word for what has transpired on this planet."

"And the third major puzzle is the hoop orbiting this planet," continued Zac. "What is its purpose and how did it get there? Once again, the Collective refuse to enlighten us."

"There's been so much to worry about down here that most people have forgotten about that, bro."

"I know. But I haven't. And I think we should continue to press for an explanation. It's not just a small thing—it's a major artificial feature of this planet that is orbiting around us, and we know nothing about it."

They sat for a moment, looking up into the sky, although the hoop was too thin to be visible from the surface of the planet.

"Yes, these are all mysteries," said Keo. "But for tonight, let's be thankful for this new beginning that we've been given."

* * *

Much later that night, Zac lay in bed holding Jaz close, listening to her slow, steady breathing as she slept. He couldn't sleep, so eventually he got up and walked outside. Both moons had set, and the stars were a brilliant blanket, stretching in a sparkling arch across the sky. The air was warm and fragrant with the aromas of a tropical spring, and the evening chorus of nocturnal animals had long since ceased, leaving a stillness that seeped into his soul.

He thought of how fortunate he was. To have escaped the holocaust on Earth. To have survived the perilous journey through the galaxy. To have discovered such a paradise. To have found love and friendship. As he pondered his circumstances, he realised that for the first time in his life he was truly and deeply content.

He looked up at the brilliant canopy of stars.

"Thank you," he said, feeling deeply moved. "I don't know if anyone's listening, but thank you for bringing me here. Help me not to waste the chance I've been given. Help me to live a good life."

He wasn't sure if that was a good prayer or not. Maybe he was just talking to himself. But somehow, he didn't think so. As he stood in the quiet of the night, he felt his heart strangely warmed.

71

NOVA DAY 217

Z ac and Kit stepped out of the transfer booth.
"Well this is different," said Kit.

There were still over 30 unexplored towns to investigate, and this was simply the next one, selected at random. It was located towards the southern end of Northland, directly on the equator; just one more light on the map. Before stepping out of the transfer booth, they had no reason to suspect that it would any different to the dozens of towns already explored, all of which had almost identical layouts.

"Very different," agreed Zac.

They were not in a terminal dome on the surface of the planet but inside a rock-hewn cavern. Their transfer booth was one of about 20, arranged around the centre of the perfectly circular cavern, and the roof rose above them in a perfectly curved dome.

They walked to the wall of the cavern, and Zac placed his hand on the rock. "It's warm; very warm, in fact. I think we may be deep underground."

"And check how smooth the walls are," said Kit. "This hasn't been excavated with explosives or jackhammers. It's millimetre-perfect."

"Where's the light coming from?" asked Zac.

"Everywhere," said Kit, looking around.

It was true. The rocks were all glowing with a soft, diffused, orange light.

The cavern only had one exit, an arched hole in the cavern wall, and as they approached it, a perfectly smooth tunnel lit up ahead of them, with the same warm glow.

"Shall we?" asked Zac, standing at the entrance to the tunnel.

"It's what we're here for, doc," she said, as she pushed past him and strode down the tunnel. The tunnel ended about 30 metres later, at a perfectly black, arched door. As they drew near, the door slid open, revealing a stunning sight. They were at the base of a massive, man-made hole, similar in shape to sink-holes back on Earth, but on a scale so large that the eye could not take it all in at once. The hole was a cylindrical shaft, perfectly circular at the base, with the vertical sides maintaining their perfectly circular shape all the way to the top. The circular base was at least two kilometres in diameter, and the shaft was so deep that the opening at the top appeared to be no more than a pinprick of light above them.

What was even more extraordinary was the base itself. Zac and Kit stepped out onto a perfectly smooth surface that looked to be made of glass or something similar. It had appeared as a reflective black mirror as they stood in the tunnel entrance, but as Kit stepped forward onto it, the entire floor turned translucent white, with diffuse light glowing from somewhere below the surface.

"Are you sure this is safe?" asked Zac.

"The only thing that's completely safe is staying in bed."

"Yeah, well, a lot of people die in bed, you know."

As they walked further out onto the glassy surface, they

noticed that in it there were hundreds of circles, about 30 metres in diameter, outlined by a ring of slightly brighter white light.

"What do you think these are for?" asked Zac.

"To park those on, I guess," answered Kit, pointing further ahead and slightly to the right.

About a kilometre distant, towards the middle of the giant sink-hole, a dome-like shape could be seen. It was the only thing visible on the entire glassy surface.

"What do you think it is?" asked Zac.

"Not sure, but whatever it is, it's the last one left."

They started to walk towards it, and as they did, Zac asked the question that had been on his mind since the wedding ceremony last night.

"So, have you given any thought to getting married, Kit?"

"Huh! You too? Keo and a bunch of other people have been asking me the same thing."

"So, what's your answer?"

"My response to busybodies is, 'Mind your own damn business'."

"What about to people who love you and want you to be happy?"

"I *am* happy."

"But wouldn't you like to share your life with someone who loves you and whom you can love in return?"

Kit was silent for a while, and Zac wondered if he had offended her. Finally, she broke the silence.

"Of course I'd like to get married! But I'm not going to settle for just anyone. I feel like people are jumping into marriage with the first half-decent option that comes their way. It's as if there's a panic to get hitched before the available pool dries up."

"It is a bit like that, I suppose," said Zac. "After all, we are a relatively small population."

"Well, I'd rather stay single than settle for a hairy-arsed dimwit with halitosis."

"Why don't you say what you really think?"

"What I really think, is that what you and Jaz have is special and rare, and you are both incredibly lucky."

"I guess we are."

"So, if you've got a twin brother you've been hiding from me, I'd be happy to be introduced," said Kit.

"I'll take that as a compliment."

"You should. A girl could do a lot worse than you, doc."

"Hey! Wait for us!"

Zac and Kit turned and looked behind them. Two figures had emerged from the tunnel entrance and were waving at them.

"It's Keo and Martinez," said Zac.

"Yes, and Keo's got something in his hand."

They watched as the two newcomers walked quickly towards them across the smooth glassy surface. A minute later the newcomers joined them and Keo held up a transparent air-tight bag containing what looked like small cakes. "Prisha and Jaz have just cooked our first batch of muffins from rice flour. They sent me to make sure you two didn't die of starvation."

"And I had to come along for the ride," added Martinez. "No solo trips allowed while we're still exploring this place."

"Are the cakes any good?" asked Zac.

"I've had three and I haven't perished," replied Keo with a grin.

"Let's break for morning tea after we've finished checking this out," said Kit, indicating the strange domed shape that was now only 200 metres distant.

"What is it? And what is this place?" asked Martinez.

"Not sure," Kit answered, "but I'm dying to find out."

The four walked the remaining distance to the object and stood looking at it. It was perfectly circular with a domed roof and constructed of what looked like the same black material as the hoop in orbit around the planet. It was about 20 metres in diameter and was situated in the centre of one of the glowing white rings.

"It's like a mini-dome," said Zac.

"I think it's some kind of transport vessel," said Kit.

They walked around its perimeter and noted a variety of bumps and lumps all over its surface, the purpose of which alluded them.

"This appears to be an outline of a doorway," said Kit, approaching it with her usual confidence.

The doorway slid smoothly aside, seeming to invite them in.

"Did you do that?" asked Zac.

"Maybe. I was wondering how to get in."

"Well, I think this is as far as we go," said Zac. "We need to go back and report .... Kit! What are you doing?"

"What does it look like? I'm going to take a peep inside."

She walked through the doorway and turned to the right, disappearing from view.

"Kit! Come out!" said Zac. "We don't know what it is or whether it's safe. Please!"

"You should see this, guys! It's incredible!" Kit stuck her head around the corner of the doorway. "It all looks pretty safe to me. Come on! Check it out!"

Keo said, "She sure is the adventurous one, bro."

Zac sighed and shook his head. "Yeh. And one of these days she's going to bite off more than she can chew!"

"Well, I'm not going to stay out here and miss out on all the fun," said Martinez, walking towards the doorway.

Zac shrugged and said, "You know what they say; if you can't beat them join them." The two men followed Martinez to the entrance of the dome and cautiously stepped inside, looking around with amazement.

#

If anyone had been standing outside on that afternoon, they would have witnessed the door of the vessel closing several minutes later. Shortly afterwards, the circle upon which the vessel was sitting began pulsing with a purple light. The pulses quickly grew more rapid, and a steadily increasing whine increased to an almost deafening level. Suddenly there was a shaft of deep purple light, too bright to look at, blasting up from the circle and enveloping the vessel. A moment later, everything was still again.

The purple light was gone.

The noise was gone.

The vessel was gone.

Zac, Kit, Keo and Martinez were gone.

Their friends searched for them for months but found no trace of them.

Zac's as-yet unborn daughter would make it her life's work to search for her missing father, in an attempt to find out what had happened to him.

What she would eventually discover would not only change her own life but would alter the fate of humanity forever.

READ THE NEXT EXCITING INSTALMENT!

CLICK TO BUY IT NOW

BOOK 2 in the STARPATH SERIES

The search for a new home just got complicated!

Four friends find themselves lost in a far corner of the galaxy, separated from those they love by both time and distance. Heartbroken by the cruel twist of fate that has carried them there, they must use all their wits to merely stay alive. As they desperately search for a way back home and a means of salvation, they are forced to make painful choices. Meanwhile, those they have left behind are caught up in a deadly struggle against a malevolent artificial intelligence that threatens the survival of the whole human race. As time and hope seem to be running out, the time dilation effects of a nearby black hole dish up a final complicating twist.

CLICK TO BUY IT NOW

OR GO TO:

KEVINSIMINGTON.COM

LEAVE A REVIEW

If you enjoyed this book, I would be extremely grateful if you would leave a review on Amazon, Goodreads and other review websites. Reviews are hugely important for me as a self-published author. In Amazon's case, reviews impact Amazon's algorithms, helping the book to climb higher in the charts, thereby making it more visible to potential readers. Every single review really does help!

Leaving a review is very easy. To leave a review, just go to the relevant Amazon page for your country, search for my book and click on the reviews link next to the stars. A review of 4 or 5 stars is considered to be a positive review and a review of 3 or less stars is considered to be a negative review.(Unfortunately, Amazon only allows reviews from people who have spent at least $50 on Amazon over the preceding 12 months).

LEAVE A REVIEW ON AMAZON:

AMAZON UNITED STATES
AMAZON UNITED KINGDOM
AMAZON CANADA
AMAZON AUSTRALIA

SOMEONE ELSE'S LIFE

KEVIN SIMINGTON'S NEW CRIME THRILLER!

SOMEONE ELSE'S LIFE

"A page-turning thriller by a master story-teller!"

What if you weren't who you thought you were? ... And people will kill to stop you finding out!

Much more than a simple detective story, this is a complex portrayal of a good man who is pushed to extraordinary limits.

A mysterious case of identity switching turns deadly when struggling private investigator, John Targett, becomes involved. As John seeks to unravel one mystery, he is also forced to deal with an escalating menace when he becomes the target of a vicious gang whose path he has crossed. As the twin plots intertwine and the threats escalate, John is forced to take extreme measures to protect his daughter and fight for his own life. Plagued by his own demons and trying to raise his daughter alone, this is a beautifully crafted story of the lengths to which one man will go to protect those he loves. At times tender, filled with sparkling wit and peppered with edge-of-your-seat action, this is a multi-facetted mystery that will satisfy on many levels.

REVIEW:

"An incredible thriller with the perfect twist! I adored this book. John Targett is my newest character crush! *Someone Else's Life* delivers on every front. It's delightful, witty, dangerous, and thought-provoking. The danger level is high throughout the novel, constantly raising the stakes and potentially making the reader breathless as events unfold. It's thrilling, and absolutely ends on the best possible note." (Kat Cohen, Reviewer.)

GET IT HERE!

FREE EBOOK!

Join my mailing list and receive a FREE EBOOK. I will email you a complimentary copy of "Welcome To The Universe: A Pocket Guide For Visitors". With stunning photographs and mind-boggling facts, "Welcome to the Universe" provides a fascinating glimpse into the wonders of the universe and the many challenges of space travel. Just click the link below and tell me where to send it (or sign up on my website, kevinsimington.com).

SEND ME A FREE COPY OF "WELCOME TO THE UNIVERSE"

THE THIRD EXCITING INSTALMENT!

CLICK TO BUY IT NOW

BOOK 3 in the STARPATH SERIES

An impossible journey.

A battle for survival.

A search for home.

As mankind struggles for survival, a stunning new discovery changes everything. The enemy they face is far more dangerous than they had assumed. But with the revelation comes a ray of hope. The path to salvation is revealed; a path that will traverse the galaxy and lead our wandering heroes home, provided they can survive the almost insurmountable odds along the way. An unlikely group who represent mankind's last hope of survival set out on an almost impossible journey that will bring them back to where it all began. There, they will face the ultimate challenge.

CLICK TO BUY IT NOW

OR GO TO:

KEVINSIMINGTON.COM

READ THE STUNNING CONCLUSION TO THE SERIES!

BOOK 4 in the STARPATH SERIES

CLICK TO BUY

Just when you thought it was all over, a new challenge arises.

As peace finally reigns throughout the galaxy, a new colony is established on a rejuvenated Earth. But mankind's idyllic paradise is not all that it seems. A hidden danger arises that threatens their very existence. Packed full of drama and unexpected twists, this final book in the STARPATH series is the most action-packed of the four books. Hold onto your seats, because you are about to be taken on a final, wild ride!

"Eden Rising" brings the STARPATH series to a spectacular

conclusion!

CLICK TO BUY

OR VISIT: KEVINSIMINGTON.COM

ABOUT THE AUTHOR

Kevin J Simington is an acclaimed fiction and non-fiction author whose books are renowned for their intelligence, clarity and wit. He is a very popular conference speaker on the topics of philosophy and science. He also writes for several international magazines.

Website:
https://kevinsimington.com

Amazon Author Page:
https://www.amazon.com/-/e/B08295PT7V

www.ingramcontent.com/pod-product-compliance
Lightning Source LLC
Chambersburg PA
CBHW020539120726
47903CB00001B/45